REYR THE GOLD

BOOK 2 OF THE DRAGONWALL SERIES

MELISSA MITCHELL

DRAGONWALL
Dragonfire Sea
Shadowkeep
Belne
Eagle Lake
Mistport
Redport
Squall's End
Scattered Islands
Kastall Dyn
Bay of Bandu

Northedge
The Gable
Forest
Kaljah
Castle
South Sea

PROLOGUE

Kastali Dun

Irelia gasped, rubbing her temples, trying to massage away the headache, but it was no use. She stood in the largest chamber of a vast cavern system. It smelled of seawater and earth. The scent should have calmed her, but nothing could anymore.

Nothing could deaden the voices in her mind. They'd plagued her for months, since the turn of her thirteenth year, since the day she'd discovered her magic. She should have loved the idea of carrying magic. Her mother did. Isabella spoke of magic as one spoke of the wonders of the forest, with awe and reverence; she treated magic as if it were religion. But magic had turned sour in Irelia's mouth with each pulsing voice in her mind, and she wondered how much longer she could stand it before she went insane.

She placed her palm upon her flushed face, holding a torch aloft in her other hand. Then she plotted a path forward. Her slippered feet began to move across the uneven floor of the cave.

This was her chance to escape her insanity. There might not be another opportunity, especially under the watchful eyes of her kenna. Her heart thudded and she paused to listen, glancing about. Nothing but the trickle of water. After several deep breaths, she continued.

Two pillars loomed before her, their mirrored black surfaces dancing beneath the illumination of her torch. The symbols upon them flickered and transformed in the firelight. She reached forward, tracing her fingers along them. The old way of writing. The *Aldinn Malasarlaí* was a dying language, though its magic would remain intact long after it did. These symbols were imbued with the forces necessary to transport her away from this place.

One could simply step through the portal and vanish. That alone made it dangerous. It's why her parents had kept it hidden all these years.

A tumbling rock echoed through the cave. She froze, then pulled back her hand, lifting her torch aloft for an unseen pursuer. Her kenna, perhaps? No. Only stillness.

Sighing, she shook her head, attempting to push her mother's warning from her mind. Isabella had made her promise never to come here alone, never to come near these pillars. They were buried deep beneath the city, and much older. Dangerous, even, because stepping through this gate would transport her to another world.

A world without magic.

Her mother looked at the gate and saw condemnation, but Irelia looked at it and saw possibility. The possibility for a fresh start. For happiness.

Something tugged at her middle. An unknown force even greater than that of hope. A deep urge. A *need*.

Resolved, she inhaled, knowing that her destiny stood before her. She gave the cave one final glance before stifling her fear. Then she stepped forward. Her feet carried her, one at a time, until she was swallowed up by darkness.

The cold left her gasping. It struck new terror into her heart. The world was void. She cried out in alarm, reaching forward into the darkness before dropping the torch. She stumbled. She despaired. Soundless screams poured from her lips. Then a warm glow flared into existence, surrounding her. A sigh of relief escaped her lips.

She opened her eyes to find dancing firelight. The snare of fear loosened its hold upon her heart as she studied her new surroundings. Torches and great pyres rested atop an elegant marble floor. Everywhere there were large columns of white limestone supporting a vast ceiling. Statues and sculptures sat upon plinths much larger than any person. She looked upon her surroundings in awe. It was a large temple for the gods.

When she looked behind her, she saw no sign of the portal that had ferried her through. In that moment, she knew there would be no returning home. Courage and hope were her only companions now.

She stood still, waiting, hoping beyond all measure that her plan had worked. As time passed, she was met with silence. Not a single voice. Ever so slowly, the ache in her head dissipated into a dull throb. Then it disappeared entirely. Relieved, she smiled.

Her mind was her own.

Joy took hold of her, lifting her heart. This new feeling was magical, even if there was no magic in such a world. Turning full circle, she stopped to face the goddess before her and gasped. Towering over her was Asjaa, for who else could it be? She blessed the Mother of Protection.

She had only just gotten to her knees to pray when a shout echoed behind her. More shouts followed, disturbing the peace of the sanctuary. She froze in place. She was not afraid, for Asjaa guarded her in this world when she had failed to do so in the last.

Footsteps sounded behind her. A tight grip encircled her forearm, pulling her to her feet. Still, she remained calm. She did not protest. Instead she squared her shoulders and lifted her chin. She was Princess Irelia. She confronted her captor's accusing brown eyes knowing it was her destiny to come to this place, this new world. Her new life awaited her, and she welcomed it. The daughter of King Eymar and Queen Isabella was finally free of her suffering.

CHAPTER 1

THE DRESS SHOP

Kastali Dun

Claire had grown up dreaming of magical worlds, wishing she might escape and leave her mundane life behind. She'd buried her nose in book after book, collecting a veritable library in her childhood bedroom. She'd never dreamed that one day, she would be here in Dragonwall, living out her wildest imaginings. That she would be strolling through the city of Kastali Dun, with Reyr by her side.

It was a warm, late summer day. The sun was out in full force, windows thrown wide to catch the sea breeze. She and Reyr made their way through the merchant district. It was her first venture beyond the keep. She'd been confined behind its walls ever since her arrival into the vast city, first as a prisoner, and then as a servant. Now, she'd become the king's ward, which, apparently, made her royal.

Hence, today's outing.

Spying her destination, she stopped in front of a tall building. Large windows offered passersby a glimpse from within, of elegantly dressed mannequins flaunting Kastali Dun's latest fashions. Her lips parted, taking it all in.

The gowns were extravagant, with layers of lace and silk and tulle, delicate embroidery, and embellished beading. She stared at a simple beige colored dress. The skirts and sleeves were silk brocade. The sleeves were trimmed in lace, which opened at the elbow, a popular trend in the capital. The front panel of the bodice was fashioned with different color fabric, a dusty blue with white lace and a blunt, square neckline. It was subtle, but beautiful.

She stepped back a pace, looking up. A wooden sign hung above the entrance with *Rosanne's Finery* written in gold lettering. Beneath that, *Finest Clothes in Dragonwall.*

"Is this the place?" she asked, spinning on her heel to find Reyr.

"It is," he said, grinning. "You'll find no better place in Dragonwall."

A shiver of excitement raced over her. She glanced down at the dress she had on, eager to be rid of it. She'd worn little more than serving uniforms for weeks.

Reyr opened the door and together, they stepped over the threshold. A chime tinkled from within. She blinked several times, allowing her eyes to adjust.

"Be with you in a moment," a throaty voice called. Rosanne. She was a squat, older woman with red hair pinned back into a bun. Currently, she was occupied with the hem of a patron's tunic. He stood on a pedestal and gave them respectful nods.

Turning away, Claire wandered into the shop. It was a single, spacious room with tall ceilings, and filled with more than enough to keep her occupied. Colorful bolts of fabric lined the walls in columns, stretching floor to ceiling. They were assembled in an orderly manner—like a library of colorful books. There were two mirror arrangements with platforms for tailoring. The rest of the room was cluttered with well-dressed mannequins, shelves of fashionable items like bows, buckles, and hats, and tables laden with leather-bound sketchbooks.

On a nearby table, one of the sketchbooks lay open. She went to it, lifting it into her hands. A model had been sketched wearing a stately light blue gown. A closer look revealed seemingly impossible details, like beading, lace, and even sequins. Claire's eyebrows drew together in wonder.

She reached to flip the page and gasped, nearly flinging the book back on the table. Reyr chuckled, coming to stand at her elbow. She ignored him and reached forward to touch the page again, this time keeping her hand upon it. The model in the blue dress came to life, twirling and moving to show off her gown.

"It's magic!" she breathed, caressing the sketch with her fingertips. The model gracefully stepped from beneath her fingers to continue her movements. She began turning one page after another, delighted. Each sketch displayed an impressive gown that magically came alive.

"Rosanne is known for her enchantments," Reyr said. "She weaves magic into everything she makes. Her reputation is a prominent one. You will find no better clothing in the kingdom." He reached over, turning the pages back to the first, noticing the life he breathed into the drawing.

"So, it isn't simply *my* touch that does it?"

"No. The touch of anyone is enough to fuel their movements."

"And...she did all of these herself?"

"You bet I did!" Claire whirled around. Rosanne wore a warm, dimpled smile, brown eyes glowing with eagerness. "And how do you do, Lady Claire? I am pleased to meet you *at last*. Figured it would only be a matter of time before I found you here."

"I...I'm well, thank you." She placed the sketchbook upon the table, clasping her hands behind her back to keep from reaching for it again. "Your drawings are extraordinary. I've never seen anything like it."

"Thank you kindly." Rosanne's voice oozed with pleasure. "And just so you know, you'll not find the likes of these anywhere in Dragonwall. Now, how can I help you?"

Reyr stepped forward. "Lady Claire is in need of a wardrobe befitting of her position—the king's orders."

"Wonderful!" Rosanne clasped her hands together, turning her assessing gaze upon Claire. "His Majesty's wish is my command. Have you any designs in mind?"

She chewed on the skin of her lower lip. "Can I pick something from the books here, or do I need to come up with something all on my own?"

"Either! Or, if you need something immediately, there are several gowns on display."

She thought about the beautiful beige dress in the window and frowned. It would cost a fortune, surely. "Do I have a spending limit?" she asked, looking up at Reyr.

"Probably not, but let's be sure," he said with a wink before contacting the king. *"Beg your pardon, Your Grace. Claire wishes to understand the constraints of her new wardrobe?"*

Reyr's voice in her mind was as crisp and clear as if he had spoken aloud. It was an ability that had once shocked her. She could hear and communicate with the drengr—all of the drengr. Only Reyr and Saffra knew of her secret.

The king's response was immediate. *"There are no constraints. Give her whatever she desires. Charge everything to my account."*

"As you wish."

She suppressed a smile. Sometimes, like now, her telepathic abilities were a blessing. Other times, they were a curse. Too many voices in her mind gave her migraines. She was learning to block them, an exercise she practiced daily, but it didn't always help.

Distance played a huge role. With the fort outside the city walls, the fort's drengr were easier to contend with. But when they were close, like Reyr standing beside her, they were almost impossible to ignore.

"I have spoken with the king," Reyr said to Rosanne. "Claire may have whatever she desires. Charge everything to his account."

Her skin prickled with excitement.

"Excellent! Just excellent." Rosanne looked overly pleased, for obvious reasons. "I will see that she has the very best."

"Good. I will leave you to it." Reyr nodded at both of them before walking out.

～

HOURS LATER, Claire left the shop in search of Reyr. He stood on the opposite side of the street, conversing with a well dressed stranger. When he spotted her he bid the man farewell and made his way over. "What are you smirking about?" he asked.

"Oh...nothing. Or at least, nothing *you* would take interest in."

"Hardly fair! I take a great deal of interest in many things. Try me."

She studied his expression, then shrugged and said, "If you must know, I commissioned Rosanne to make me some under-garments."

"Undergarments. Like...pantaloons?" He appeared thoughtful. "Women raved about them, but it was too damned hot in summer for the trend to stick."

"No, no. Not like that."

"Like a chemise?"

She smirked. "I was referring to *underwear*. Women here aren't keen on the idea. The bras I can live without. But undies? Nuh-uh." He frowned. "In my world," she explained, "undies are a small bit of clothing you wear around... Oh, never mind. I can see that I've already lost you."

He chuckled. "Well whatever it is, I am sure Rosanne was happy to oblige your request."

"It took some convincing, but yes."

"Good! Shall we, then?" He held out his arm for her. Together, they walked down a cobblestone street lined with storefronts. She shielded her gaze against the sun to study everything.

Eventually, they turned down a neighboring lane. Reyr pointed things out as they passed. There were apothecaries, cafes, black-smiths, book shops, clothing shops, jewelers, toy makers. Every-thing, really.

"Down there," he said, pointing, "there's a cozy tavern I enjoy visiting when I want to get out of the keep for a drink. On second thought, I would not recommend the locale for a lady such as your-self." She snorted, rolling her eyes.

They continued their stroll. It was easy to fall in love with the city. Kastali Dun was everything it should be—rambunctious, eclectic, and very much alive. Not to mention, the air was full of smells. Some of the odors were downright putrid, like those coming from the trenches along the roads. Others were delightful, like the bakeries with fresh bread and pies. They stopped at a street stand for a cheese bun, which she ate as they walked.

People rushed about in a frenzy of action. Everyone had something to do. She saw an older boy pushing a small cart heaped with carrots. Their long green stems dangled over the edge. He called out his price in hopes of a buyer—

"How much is a steely?" she asked Reyr, eyeing the cart.

"Not a whole lot," he explained, outlining their coinage system. Steelies were their lowest form of currency. Fifty steelies made a silver. Twenty silvers made a gold dragon. She'd already known about the gold dragons. She'd received her own little stack from Cyrus. She couldn't bear the thought of spending them...not now, not ever.

The boy with the cart passed. After him, several men rushed by atop their horses. A woman bustled by, leading two children who each cried and pointed. She followed their gaze to find shelves of candy sitting just outside a candy shop.

"Oh!" she gasped. "Let's go in here!" She grabbed Reyr's arm, pulling him inside. The smell of sugar permeated the air. She inhaled, smiling. "Is this where you got me that bag of sweets?"

"It is." Reyr's face glowed with boyish excitement. "It's my favorite shop, if you must know."

"I can see why!" With absolutely no reservations, she raced around to collect vibrantly colored pops, bags of toffees, chewy drops, and more. He watched her, his eyes dancing. When she dumped her goodies onto the counter, the clerk hobbled over to assist her.

He was a stooped, older gentleman, with white hair. His eager grin swallowed up his tiny eyes. "Pleased to meet you, Lady Claire. You may call me Duncan."

He already knew her name. Word must have traveled through the city that she was out and about today.

"Duncan Flynn has been caring for this shop since boyhood," Reyr explained.

"Indeed, I have," Duncan said, still smiling. "*Flynn's Fine Sweets* has been in my family for generations."

"They've owned this shop longer than I have lived, if that puts it into perspective for you," Reyr added.

Duncan set about writing down each item in her pile of candy. He recorded everything by hand, one at a time. There were no cash registers; she had to remind herself to be patient as she eyed everything, her mouth watering.

When he finished, Duncan said, "That'll be four silvers and thirty-five steelies."

A slow grin spread across her face. "Please charge it to the king's account."

The old man nodded, unsurprised. "Of course, my lady. It will be done." He bagged everything up before handing it over.

Her cheeks hurt from grinning.

They made their way back up the streets to the keep, walking shoulder to shoulder. "Something tells me you're eager to do that again."

"No idea what you're talking about." She popped a toffee into her mouth, offering one to Reyr.

"Oh, I think you do," he said, taking her proffered offering. "Tomorrow, I shall find the entire royal treasury spent."

"What kind of girl do you think I am?!" She feigned her best glare. He only chuckled.

"Are you sure we can't go down to the market before heading back?" It was the second time she'd asked.

"As I said before, the streets are no place for a lady after nightfall. You'll have to go another time." She exhaled to make her disappointment known, but dropped the subject. Instead, they continued up through the city towards the keep.

Reyr broached the silence and said, "Are you nervous for tonight? It will be your first time dining with the nobles."

"Thanks for reminding me." She resisted the urge to groan.

"You cannot hide from the public forever. People are eager to know you. The surest way is through conversation. Let them see the true you, and you will win their hearts."

She frowned. "I don't even know what to say to them—like, how to talk to them. What if they ask me things that I'm not comfortable with answering?"

"No need to be nervous. Just be yourself."

"Easier said than done," she scoffed. "Besides, isn't it *more* important for me to focus on learning magic than socializing? When will I begin my training?"

There were many reasons for her eagerness, but the biggest was because of the promise she'd made a few days prior. Unbreakable promises were no small thing in Dragonwall. Unlike mundane promises, which were bound by honor, these were bound by magic. To fulfill hers, she needed to defeat Dragonwall's most dangerous sorcerer, an asarlaí by the name of Kane. The only way to do that was with magic. Except, she had no idea how to use hers.

Reyr was quiet for several moments before saying, "You are correct. Learning to wield your magic *is* important. So is your sanity and welfare. King Talon had hoped to give you a few days to adjust to your new position first. Are you sure you're ready?"

"Ready or not, every day wasted is a day I fall behind."

"I admire your strength, but I am hesitant. You have been through a lot in a very short period of time."

She barked a laugh. "You aren't kidding! But I've got to roll with the punches. There isn't much of a choice."

"Very well. I will speak to King Talon."

They reached the keep's outer wall as dusk was approaching. The keep's guards spotted them and opened the main gate. Dinner was promptly held at nightfall, which would leave her just enough time to prepare.

"I've got a few things to check on before the meal," Reyr said. "May I take my leave? Will you be all right?"

"Uh...I think I'll be fine. Yes, go ahead."

He paused to make sure she wasn't going to change her mind. When she remained silent, he said, "Good. I will see you at dinner." His footfalls died as he retreated into a nearby corridor. Behind her, the portcullis clanked closed. After several long moments alone in the courtyard, she made her way to her quarters.

She was delighted to find a cluster of brown packages waiting for her. She collected her goodies and marched into her bed chamber, barely managing to hold everything before it tumbled onto the bed. She opened the first bulky package. A silky heap of fabric tumbled out like a waterfall. This was the beige gown she had admired. She picked it up, letting the material caress her fingers, then smiled.

Moving to stand before her mirror, she held it up to her body. It was simply perfect. As quickly as she could manage alone, she slipped it on over her chemise, struggling with the corset and ties. It was no wonder that women who wore these gowns had servants and handmaidens.

Sighing with exasperation, she finally got it properly into place. The fabric looked lovely against her skin, and the blue brocade of the bodice perfectly contrasted her green eyes. Pleased, she glanced outside. Her stomach gave a nervous jolt. Darkness had all but fallen.

Reyr's voice sounded in her mind. "*Are you coming to dinner? Do not be late!*" Throwing everything aside, she scurried from her chambers. She had avoided the courtiers for long enough. There was no more hiding. She was royal now. It was time to start acting like it.

CHAPTER 2
BEST FRIENDS

Kastali Dun

Claire stepped through a pair of wooden doors and into the great keep's dining hall. Heat flooded her body. She froze as hundreds of eyes fell upon her. Everyone was silent. She searched for a friendly face, for an empty seat, for some direction, trying not to drown under the intense scrutiny.

She wasn't late, technically. The hall's door closed when dinner began. Latecomers were not permitted. But now, she wished she hadn't dallied—

"Lady Claire! Over here!" She exhaled at the sound of Saffra's voice, rushing forward.

Proceeding down the central aisle, she felt the regard of a certain pair of silver eyes. The hairs on the back of her neck prickled. She glanced up to find King Talon at the head table, on a raised dais overlooking the hall. There were three chairs to his left and right. Only one remained empty.

The king held her gaze. She dared not look away, even as her heart began to race. Instead, she squared her shoulders and continued until she was forced to deviate down an aisle to reach Saffra.

"I saved you a seat," Saffra said, beckoning her over.

She sank onto a wooden bench, glad to be free of King Talon's scrutiny. After several deep breaths, some of her tension fled. With nothing more to see, the courtiers slowly returned to their conversations.

"Thank you for rescuing me," she whispered. "I've been dreading this moment all day."

Dread was a strong word, but adequately described how she felt. Attending dinner with high ranking members of the court was something she'd rather avoid, especially since many were openly opposed to her new title. She had gone from outsider to royal, and in the eyes of high society, that did not sit well.

"You have nothing to fear." Saffra leaned in close, keeping her voice low. "People owe you their respect."

"That may be true, but they look at me with scorn—"

"Claire—!"

"No need. I've heard the rumors. I know what you did for me during court and I wanted to thank you. I also wanted to thank you for not telling everyone that—" She glanced around to make sure no one was listening. "Well, for not mentioning the part of your vision about me and Kane. I can only imagine how King Talon might have reacted."

"It was the least I could do. Truly, you do not need to thank me." Saffra grabbed Claire's hand and squeezed. "The rest of the world will come around. I am sure of it."

She appreciated the gesture.

A loud echo captured their attention. The doors leading into the dining hall grumbled as they swung shut. Servants poured in from servant entrances carrying platters of food.

She looked for Desaree but didn't find her. Soon enough, her gaze fell upon the head table. She breathed a sigh of relief. The king's attention was occupied elsewhere. Perhaps she was paranoid, but he seemed to scrutinize her more than necessary. She rolled her eyes and looked away. He probably still distrusted her.

Reyr's amused voice sounded in her mind. *"Glad you finally made it. And what an entrance, I might add."* She glanced up to find him grinning at her from beside the king, who was now focused on his food. Despite Reyr's smiling face, she shrugged and looked away.

As the food was served, the courtiers at her table took the opportunity to introduce themselves, making every effort to flaunt their wealth and importance, as if court positions might impress her. She recognized most of their names already. Hating it, she did her best to feign politeness, knowing they were the same people who'd called for her death not long ago.

Eventually, she and Saffra settled into light conversation, careful not to reveal anything private. She told Saffra about her day in the city exploring and dress shopping. "I've never seen so much fabric in one place. And so many beautiful designs, too."

"Rosanne's work is incredible," Saffra agreed, sighing. "I cannot get over how beautiful your gown is tonight."

"Isn't it *stunning*?! And this is nothing special compared to the others. It's just one of the ones she had on display. Wait until you see the gowns we designed together." She pictured them as she glanced around the hall, looking at the other women. Many of their designs paled in comparison to those she had commissioned.

A frown formed on her face.

Since when had this become a competition for best dressed? What did she care about having the fanciest gowns in the court? Was she getting too carried away?

She shifted uncomfortably in her seat, her excitement evaporating. "Now that I think about it, I'm afraid to know how much of the king's money I spent. Probably too much."

"Nonsense!" Saffra grinned. "After what you have been through, I recommend going easy on yourself. King Talon owes you —we all do. Live a little." Saffra nudged her gently in the ribs.

Dinner flew by. Before long, dessert platters were cleared away. The double doors opened, and everyone rose to leave. She turned to Saffra and said, "We definitely have some catching up to do—about *you know what*. Can you come by my quarters tonight? I'll fill you in on everything. Oh! And bring Desaree, if you can."

"I'll be there," Saffra said, before hurrying away with a gleam in her eyes.

~

She returned to her chambers to find the wall sconces lit and a fire burning in the grate. Someone had been by to tidy up. Her gowns were unwrapped and hung in the wardrobe, the brown paper discarded, and even her bed was turned down. This wasn't something she was used to, but she couldn't help her glee, feeling pampered.

She placed additional candles around the living area until everything was blanketed in a relaxing, yellow glow. It was a temperate night, so she opened the glass doors leading to her balcony. The sea breeze filtered in, rustling the sheer curtains. A breathy sigh left her chest.

She went to her wine cabinet and uncorked a bottle. In her previous life, she had worked as a bartender to make ends meet. She'd wanted to work in government. She'd even gotten a degree in political science. Unfortunately, things hadn't gone as planned. Finding the right job proved impossible, and she'd been forced to move back in with her parents, albeit temporarily, to continue her search.

When Cyrus dropped into her life, everything had changed. She could have turned her back on Dragonwall. It would have been easy after the way King Talon had treated her. Instead, she'd made the decision to be a part of Dragonwall's future.

Knocking brought her thoughts to a halt. She rushed to the door to greet Saffra and Desaree. They entered, admiring their surroundings, and gladly agreed to some wine. Once they were settled in, curled up in front of the fire with wine goblets in hand, she said, "Okay, let's get down to business. Whether you guessed it or not, I've got a hard road ahead of me. That's where you come in. I'm going to need a lot of support." Desaree and Saffra nodded eagerly. "*But*," she added, wagging her finger for emphasis, "I need both of you on the same page."

While Saffra already knew about Claire's ability to hear the drengr, Desaree did not, so that was the first thing she talked about. Desaree's sharp intake of breath was accompanied by, "All this time? No wonder you were having headaches! I would too with dragon voices in my head."

"Reyr has been coaching you though, hasn't he?" Saffra asked, turning to Claire, eyebrows drawn together.

"He has, thank goodness. For the most part, I'm getting better at blocking." She shrugged. "I wouldn't say I'm a pro. Not yet. But I'm improving. Cyrus is helping, too."

They talked about Cyrus's gift, how he'd given it to her. How his act might play a role in explaining her magical abilities. What it might mean for their future.

"Cyrus's gift explains why you were holding his sword during my vision," Saffra mused, putting a few pieces of the puzzle together. "If you have his soul, you can use his sword."

"What vision?" Desaree asked, trying to follow.

"The one about me and Kane," Claire answered.

Saffra told Desaree every detail of what she'd seen, from Claire's quarterstaff crossed with Cyrus's sword, to the way Claire had defended herself against Kane's magic. It was Saffra's vision that had ultimately prompted Claire to make an unbreakable promise.

"And based on this vision," Desaree squeaked, her face going pale, "she must kill him?"

"I think so," Saffra mused. "Although, I never saw the end. I only saw her stand against him. The gods rarely offer certainty."

"What Saffra *means is* that a lot can change between now and then."

"But…" Desaree's voice was shrill. "But you could *die!*"

Claire's insides squirmed. "Yes. There *is* that possibility. But Cyrus made one thing *very* clear. I am Dragonwall's best hope."

"But…" Desaree looked at Saffra in disbelief. "Claire doesn't have to do this, does she? She doesn't even know how to use her magic yet." There was a long pause before Desaree turned to Claire and added, "Just because you think it's your responsibility, doesn't mean you have to go through with it."

A hot ball of guilt dropped into Claire's stomach. "Actually, I kind of do."

Desaree scowled. Saffra set her wine on the coffee table and said, "I don't like your expression. Should we be concerned?"

"Um...probably?" She sagged in her chair. Only a few days had passed since making her promise, and in its wake, she found herself overly anxious. Every minute spent dragging her feet was another minute the promise pulled against her. She was overwhelmed, scared, and even regretful.

"Well?" Saffra said. "You'd better tell us."

"A few days ago, I made an unbreakable promise to destroy Kane."

"Oh, Claire!" Saffra squeezed her eyes shut and shook her head. "You cannot be serious." Desaree chose to say nothing at all. She sat rigidly, her back straight.

Seeing *their* fear made her more afraid too. Tears sprang into her eyes. "I wish I were lying," she whispered at last. "I don't know what I was thinking. I can't take it back now. I made my bed, and all that."

Saffra folded her hands in her lap. "Tell us everything. How did you word it?"

She explained exactly what had transpired during the day of the execution. She had been alone in her room when she'd had a strange conversation with Cyrus. Eventually, she'd made the decision to ensure Kane's demise. "My journey into Dragonwall began with a promise," she said. "It needs to end with one too. It's hard to explain, but it just felt right."

"Maybe I fail to understand," Desaree said, "but what makes you certain that the promise will make a difference? Why not make a simple pledge or resolution? Why bind yourself with magic?"

Claire sighed. "The promise acts as a guide. Its strings push and pull me in the correct direction like a silent beacon. By invoking the power of it, I have made it harder to fail. Think of it as...insurance."

Desaree and Saffra did not immediately speak for some time.

They were both quietly staring at her. Finally, Saffra said, "I am at your service, Claire. Whatever you need from me, I will be there every step of the way."

"And me, too," Desaree added. "Tell me what you need, and I will do it."

She was so overwhelmed, she burst into tears. Soon, Desaree and Saffra did too. They sat crying and hugging each other, reassuring one another that everything would be okay. She wasn't going to take this journey alone, even though it sometimes felt that way.

"I just wish I could get straight to work," she admitted, once they calmed down. "Reyr has helped me control the voices, but what I really need is to learn how to use my magic. He said he would talk to the king, but I should have started my training days ago."

"Maybe I can help speed things along?" Saffra wondered. "My training as a mage is complete."

"Really?" Hope seeped into her chest, warming her insides.

Saffra is wise and powerful, you would do well to accept her offer, Cyrus said, offering his two cents. Since she'd made a new promise, he'd been especially close, giving unsolicited advice in the form of a disembodied voice within her mind whenever he felt it prudent to do so. A side effect of his gift, she'd learned.

"If you are willing to learn," Saffra said, "then I am willing to teach. Why wait for King Talon to work out the details with the grand mage? We can get started right now."

"Now? As in, right this minute?" Claire's heart began to race.

Saffra smiled. "There is no time like the present."

"Oh, goodness!" Desaree's face lit up and she clapped her hands together. "I have always wanted to learn how magic works! The knowledge is a guarded secret."

Claire squared her shoulders and pulled her feet up into a cross-legged position. "I'm ready to learn," she said. "More than ready."

"Good, then let us begin." Saffra started by explaining the theory behind the world's magic. "Each race has its own magic, though little is understood about them. Dwargs have their magic —they weave it into their metalworking. The sprites have powerful magic too, but like the dwargs, they guard their secrets fiercely. Even the goblins have magic, not that I know what it is.

"The magic *you* will learn once belonged to the asarlaí. It was their race who created the old language—the Aldinn Malasarlaí—which is now the language used by mages across the kingdom. Tell me, what is the root word of *malasarlaí?*"

Claire was silent for a moment before answering, "Um… asarlaí?"

"Yes, good. It is no coincidence. That is something you will be expected to know very early in your lessons. The asarlaí crafted the language and even used it to bring the dragons to life. Then they mixed with those of non-magical abilities, and through their offspring, they created the magoi, a lesser race of magicians. That is why I am a mage. A small bit of blood from the first sorcerers runs through my veins. It gives me the sight, and the ability to work magic."

"Were your parents mages too?" Claire asked.

Saffra shook her head. "No, and neither were my grandparents, nor any other of our relatives that we know of."

Claire frowned. If magic was blood based, why didn't Saffra's whole family have abilities like hers? "Magic skips generations," Saffra explained. "It chooses when to show itself. Blood is simply the door, magic is the lock, and a person's capability is the key. Now, shall we get started?"

Claire nodded, eager as ever.

"Good. Let's start with something simple. Magic takes a lot out of a person in the beginning." Saffra fell silent before she said, "Let's start with the first thing Marcel taught me—the power of warmth."

"Warmth?" Claire frowned. "That seems mundane, doesn't it?"

"You never know when you'll need it." Saffra lifted her goblet and poured a small amount of wine in before saying, "*Varmar…et!*"

Claire watched but nothing seemed to happen.

Saffra smiled. "There, touch it."

Claire and Desaree both reached out to touch the goblet. She immediately gasped and jerked her hand away. "It's hot!"

"Indeed. That is the power of *varmar*." Next, Saffra said, "*Kaldar...et!*" She then held the goblet forward. Again, Claire and Desaree both touched it. The goblet was ice cold.

"So, *basically*, if I say the proper word it changes the temperature of the object? Is there anything else to it besides speaking?"

"Oh yes, there is more. Now, take your goblet and try simply speaking the words. See what happens. Say '*varmar*' and then end your magic with '*et*.'"

Claire glanced between Desaree and Saffra's watchful faces before saying, "Varmar." She looked so intensely at the goblet, it felt as though her eye's bulged. "Nothing is happening," she said at last, admitting defeat.

"Good."

"Good?" She looked up. "How is that good?"

Saffra laughed. "It is good because I haven't taught you the rest of the theory. If it happened easily for you, I would have been suspicious."

"Let me guess, I've got to clear my mind and imagine I can do it? All that mumbo jumbo stuff Reyr and I discussed when he taught me to block drengr voices?"

Saffra's eyes twinkled. "Something like that. The old language was constructed from the desire for power. The owners used it to command the world and shape it according to their will. When you speak the words, you can say them in two different ways. You can speak them conversationally, as a language is often used, or you can command them. Only when you command the language, does it obey."

"It sounds as though I must think of it as a sentient being."

"Yes, you may if you like. There can be no question in your voice. Just like you and Reyr discussed, you must truly believe that you were *meant* to perform the action. The thing which you control has no say in the matter, not once you have commanded it. You are the master and it bends to your will."

"I am the master," Claire repeated. It sounded slightly barbaric.

"The asarlaí were power-hungry control freaks," she muttered. Once more she looked at the goblet. She was *meant* to do this, she told herself. There was no other way but to bend the goblet to her will. "*Varmar*," she commanded. As she spoke it, the word felt wrong.

The goblet responded immediately as it began to heat. "Ouch!" she yelped, dropping it.

"Do not forget to end the magic!" Saffra cried, warning her. "Say '*et*' and treat it like a finality. Otherwise, it will continue to heat."

"*Et!*" Claire cried, releasing the magic. A wave of exhaustion crashed over her. She began panting as she slumped back against the couch. Good thing she was already sitting. "Is it supposed to... Why do I feel...?" She felt as if she were coming down with the flu. Her shoulders grew achy, her head pounded, her body labored for each breath. "Why do I...?"

"Why do you feel tired?" Saffra asked.

"I was going to say *exhausted*."

"That's normal in the beginning." Saffra stooped down and retrieved Claire's goblet. "*Herinsia sem skiru*." The stain of the wine on the rug disappeared. "I think that is enough for one night, unless you have the energy to try again?"

Claire could barely speak, let alone issue any further magical commands. "No, I think... I think I'm done." It frustrated her to give up so easily. Only one command and she was already steamrolled! "How will I defeat Kane if I can barely perform one word without collapsing?"

"You must practice every day. In time, the exhaustion will begin to fade."

"You can do it, Claire," Desaree said. "I know you can!"

"Thanks, Des." Claire gave her her warmest smile before turning back to Saffra. "How long did it take you to get over the exhaustion?"

"It took weeks before I stopped feeling the need to sleep the entire day."

She sighed. "I think I might have to sleep for an entire week."

The thought of her bed was enticing. With what little strength she had left, she rose from the sofa and bid her companions good night. Then she stumbled to her sleeping chamber without bothering to remove her gown, put out the wall sconces, or blow out the candles. She was asleep the moment her head hit the pillow.

In her hand she held the blue dragonstone. As she gazed at it, she felt a sense of déjà vu. This dream wasn't new.

An underground lake stretched out before her. This stone would be safe at the bottom—safe from all those who might try to take it from her. She rolled the precious object over in her palm, feeling its power pool up inside of her. She hated to part with it, but it was necessary. The future was too uncertain.

It would be safe here, in this underground lake where humans and creatures would never find it, until the day she could call upon all five. A thrill shot through her at the thought. How she longed for all five. How she longed to destroy King Talon and his regime. How she longed to defeat the race of drengr—!

HER EYES FLEW OPEN, breaths ragged and harsh. All that found her was the soft glow of her candle lit room. It was still night. She wasn't off hiding dragonstones in the wilderness, she was here. In Kastali Dun.

CHAPTER 3

A BARGAIN

Vallahurst, Eagle Lake

Kane surveyed his surroundings. The dark nook and hooded cloak allowed him the anonymity necessary to go unnoticed. In front of him sat a flagon of ale, hardly touched. He didn't have a taste for the stuff, yet the bar wench had insisted.

Three days had come and passed in much the same way. All the while he grew more certain—he had chosen well—Eagle Knight was the man for the job. What a stupid, boisterous name for an assassin, but he came with a reputation and unquestionable credentials.

He watched the man whilst he drank with his friends, analyzing his behavior. There was calculated caution in his every movement. To his associates he appeared at ease, but Eagle's eyes moved discretely around the room as they took note of each happening in the *Eagle's Nest*. What came first, he wondered, the tavern name, or the assassin who frequented it?

It took him a week to track Eagle's shadow from Mistport to Vallahurst. In that time, he had learned a fair bit about the man and his dealings. This assassin covered his tracks well, moved quickly, and surrounded himself with the right people.

His territory was limited to Eagle Lake, and his patrons were often rich nobility. He knew the region well, and there was no need for business to take him elsewhere until now. Kane planned to present the assassin with an offer he would not, could not, refuse.

"I will give my terms tonight." He sent the information to Wrath. The dragon waited for him in the Vallahurst Forest. *"When I finish, I will meet you on the outskirts of the city. Wait for my call."* They had a long journey ahead of them. They were to head east, all the way to Pavv.

Walking among humans reminded him of why he lived in seclusion. He was eager to be away. Already, he risked a great deal. He could not afford to ruin his cover.

Eagle's eyes suspiciously studied him. Twice the assassin had scrutinized him.

One of the tavern's wenches deposited another drink before him. This time Eagle caught her arm and whispered into her ear. Fortunately, Kane was a sorcerer. His inhuman ears picked up every word.

"My fair lady, tell me the identity of the hooded man in the corner."

"I don't know his name, Eagle. But I'll tell ya one thing. He paid me a gold dragon to ask no questions."

There was a moment of surprise in Eagle's eyes, quickly hidden as he nodded to the wench who then returned to her tasks. A gold dragon was a fair amount of money—far more than any tavern wench saw in a week. This would pique Eagle's interest.

It did.

Eagle rose from the table, taking his flagon with him, and made his way over. "Greetings, kind sir." He stopped before the table. "Mind if I buy you some ale?"

"Cup's already full." He picked it up, tipping some of the nasty liquid into his mouth.

"This, I know. I've scarcely seen you take a drink." It was in the man's nature to be observant. Merely another reason why he was a perfect fit for the job.

"Sit. Let's talk," he said, motioning to the empty chair across from him.

Eagle narrowed his eyes. He was about to protest. He would have, were it not for the bag of gold tossed at him. Assassins were predictable. Money made them tick.

"What is this?" Greed was written all over his face as he picked up the bag and weighed it in his hand.

"Sit," he repeated, this time less patiently. Eagle sat.

"I see you got a job for me," the assassin said. "Which noble you want dead? I can only assume your target is of the blood, else you wouldn't offer me so much gold."

"No nobles and no death," he answered, setting his cup down.

"Case you ain't noticed, I deal in death."

"Obviously. I will pay you three times what you have there if you are successful."

Eagle's eyes widened. "Who are you?"

"That is unimportant. Do you wish to hear my terms or not?"

"Aye, I'll hear them." Eagle glanced around the tavern, keeping his awareness intact.

"Very good." At that moment the bar wench passed by, stopping briefly at their table. "Another flagon for Eagle, if you please," he said to her, passing her a silver, far more than what the drink cost.

"Right away, sir." She took the money and scurried away. He watched her fill the cup. Only after she had placed it in front of Eagle and retreated, did he begin.

"There is a certain person of interest, a woman, who is important to me." It was no longer within his goals to kill her. Especially not after the rumors of her power. "Bring her to me alive and unharmed, and I will make you rich beyond your wildest dreams."

"You want me to kidnap some lassie? You must be barking!" The assassin crossed his arms and eyed him doubtfully.

"I do not jest. The task is not as easy as it may sound. Far from it."

"Who is she?" Eagle asked.

"Her name is Lady Claire, and she is well protected." And indeed she would be now that she was the king's ward. "Which is why I selected *you*."

"Fair enough. How do I find her?"

"Go to Kastali Dun. From there your search will be easy."

"Kastali Dun!" Eagle's face darkened. "That ain't part of my territory. Who do you think I am?"

"I know exactly who you are, and I know you are perfectly capable." He clenched his cup. "But if you are not up for it, I will gladly retract my gold and peddle my business elsewhere." Eagle stayed quiet, considering the offer. "Can you do it, or not?"

"Course I can do it," Eagle muttered darkly. "It is a matter of whether or not I want to. You are good for the gold?"

"I am good for it. Deliver the woman and I will pay you three times what you have there. You have my word."

"All right, then. I will do it. You have my word." Eagle held out his hand to seal the bargain. The word of an assassin. He wasn't sure how much it counted for. Reluctantly, he stuck his pale hand forward and grasped Eagle's, shaking it briefly. Humans disgusted him. Touching this one was not favorable.

"And how will I get her to ya?" Eagle glanced about the room again.

"Bring her here, to this pub. I will know when you arrive." With that, he left. He'd greatly underestimated Claire. Not anymore. Her time would come, same as the rest of them.

CHAPTER 4
A PROPOSITION

Fort Squall

Tamara sat with her eyes fixed in front of her, fighting the urge to glance sideways at Byron. Her mate. He sat comfortably upon their bench, leaning back so that his elbows rested behind him atop one of many trestle tables arranged in Fort Squall's dining hall. His long legs stretched out before him and crossed at the ankles, muscles straining against his trousers. Even sitting, he was a whole head taller.

Her gaze darted towards his face, stealing nothing more than a moment's glance. She saw his golden hair and amber eyes. He looked so much like his father, Lord Davi, though there was a little of his mother, Lady Emmy, which could be seen in his fine straight nose and prominent cheekbones.

Byron caught her gaze and winked. Heat flooded her cheeks. She returned her attention to the front of the room and made an extra effort to focus on the matter at hand, Lord Davi and his speech.

Davi was Fort Squall's leader. His mate, Emmy, stood beside him. "Our recent loss has been devastating for everyone," Davi was saying, his modulated voice permeating the hall. "Something must be done. I have decided to call a kingdom-wide meeting, and representatives from each fort are to attend."

Death hung over the fort like a dark cloud. Losing five pairs had been a heavy blow. No one deserved to die the way they had, torn to shreds and eaten by wild dragons.

As Lord Davi's voice washed over her, calming her, her mind began to drift again. She strained to see more of Byron beside her. She saw so little of him these days. As the fort leader's son, he had numerous obligations, and with her special lessons, she too struggled to find the time.

She'd been taking private lessons with Emmy, learning all about Dragonwall, its politics, its history, its secrets.

So much had changed in the last few weeks. She had gone from being a lord's daughter to rider-in-waiting, or so she called herself. Her father, Lord Redwynn, the lord governor of Warslie, had intended to marry her against her wishes to Lord Rahl. He was the lord of Squall's End and lord governor of Shaldorna. She'd fled her family and her home, seeking out Fort Squall, posing as a volunteer with a fake identity.

As luck would have it, she'd discovered a bond after touching Byron's scales.

Now, if only they could already be mated. She continued to ruminate over this. Once they were mated, their minds would be connected. She would always know what he was thinking, where he was, what he was doing—

"One thing is certain," Lord Davi's voice cut through her thoughts. "We must prepare for war. Dragons will attack, and we must be ready."

Chills skittered down her spine. If the dragons attacked before she and Byron were mated...

Scenarios flashed through her mind. What if they became separated during the attack? What if he flew out to meet the dragons without her? What if he died in the battle?

Oh, gods. She couldn't think about it—

The sound of scraping benches made her jump. The hall's occupants were rising to their feet. The buzz in the room increased as voices greeted one another to discuss recent developments. Was the meeting over already?

She looked at Byron. He sat watching her with a knowing expression. Once more, she blushed.

"Care to share your thoughts?" Pursing her lips, she shook her head. Perhaps it was a good thing they weren't mated...yet. "Very well. You won't *always* have your mind to yourself." The corner of his mouth turned up. Her eyes latched on his mouth, studying his crooked smirk. He had fine lips. They opened to say, "I thought I might ask you something, Tamara. Perhaps you would indulge me in a walk tonight?"

"I—oh. Of course. Right now?"

"Actually, I was thinking next month." Her eyes fell to the ground. "I'm teasing. Gods. Come on." He took her hand and tugged. Together they stood and made their way from the hall. At the feel of his skin, tingles erupted across her own.

"It is a beautiful night," he said, casually. She agreed. "How are you finding your lessons with my mother?"

"They are going well, I think. Your mother is a blessing. "

"Good. I'm glad the two of you can spend time together. Once your true training begins, we will be busy."

They fell into a comfortable silence. Once more she found herself stealing glances at him. He brought them to a stop overlooking the city of Squall's End. The glittering of lanterns and torches made the place look like a jewel in the darkness.

Byron dropped her hand and turned to face her. The look in his expression had her stomach dropping as waves of anxiety pulsed through her. "What's the matter?" she found herself asking.

"We need to discuss your family."

"My...my family?" It was the last thing she'd expected from him.

"Your family. Both your mother and father wish to see you."

Ice trickled down her spine. "How can you know that?" she demanded, her tone changing. "My father cares nothing for me. He would have sooner sent me to live with a man I do not know, and my mother did nothing against it."

Byron exhaled. "I *know*, because they have sent multiple requests to my father."

"Do you not see it?" The ice she'd felt melted, turned to heat, until it raged in her belly. "Do you not understand their motives? *Why* they wish to see me?"

"They miss you, Tamara. You are their only daughter. Can a parent not miss their child?"

"That is not why," she snapped, surprising even herself.

His brows lifted. "I had thought you would be gladdened by their request. Surely you miss your home?"

A lump rose in her throat. "I...I do miss my brothers. Perhaps even my mother. But..."

But never her father. After what he had done, giving her up without a care, she'd never forgive him.

"But *what*?" He took a step closer, eyes darting between hers.

"If I go home to visit, everything will be ruined. That is the way of my father. He wishes to bring me back so that he can lock me up, so that he can steal me away and force me to marry Lord Rhal. He will trick you and convince you that he misses me, only to see me returned safely to him."

"Tamara." Byron's voice was a warning. Why couldn't he understand? Or at the least, take her word for it.

"I worked so hard to get here," she whispered, heart kicking up a notch. "He...he would take it all away. He would never allow me to return to you, and I would never see you again. I would never become your rider."

Byron's expression changed. He grabbed her hands and lifted them, kissed her fingers. It made her heart race for an entirely different reason. "Your father could *never* keep us apart. Besides, I will be with you the whole time. You think I would send you alone?"

"I—"

He huffed, eying her with amusement. "You have much to learn about me. About the drengr race in general. I don't plan to let you out of my sight."

"You...you would come with me?"

"I intend to. How in the name of the gods do you expect to get there if not upon my back?"

Her mouth dropped open. Then, the most glorious feeling trickled through her body. "We would...we would fly there? Together?"

A shiver raced down her skin and she found herself grinning so hard her cheeks hurt.

"Ah." Byron's amber eyes sparkled in the darkness. "You hate the idea of paying your family a visit, but by bribing you with flying, I will convince you to accept."

She bit the inside of her cheek. Was flying worth seeing her family? Gods! She dearly wanted to fly.

"Come now, what do you say?"

"Will it please you if I do this?"

He was quiet for a moment, considering. "Yes. But only because I think it is the right thing to do."

"And...you are sure my father will not separate us, since we are not yet mated?"

"A smart man would never come between a drengr and his beloved. If he so much as tries, he will have me to contend with." The fierce protectiveness in his voice made her toes curl.

"How long would it take to fly to Redport from here?"

Byron chuckled. "You are weighing the benefit of flying with me. Fair enough. If I told you that it takes a full day, might I convince you to say yes?" A full day of flying?! Two, if she counted there and back. "What is your answer?"

"And...I only have to see them this once? I need not go back again?"

"If that is your choice, I will never ask it of you again."

"You truly believe they miss me?"

"Tamara, from the look of their letters, they were worried sick. Your mother thought you had died. I believe they do miss you, yes. Come now, give me your answer."

"All right. I will do this. But only because you will be with me. I do not think I could brave them alone."

"I will be with you every step of the way, *mate*." He placed his hand in hers and captured her fingers, twining them together, then tugged her along the battlements to continue their walk.

She was glad of his words. Of his optimism. No matter what her father wrote in his letters, she had a sinking suspicion that he had something up his sleeve. They would soon find out what it was.

CHAPTER 5

THE SOCIETY

Kastali Dun

Claire's eyes flew open. She winced at the blazing sunlight streaming in through the windows. "Wake up, sleepy." Reyr threw open the remainder of the chamber's thick curtains. She groaned and smashed a pillow over her head, dragging her blankets higher.

"What, no friendly greeting?" The corner of her bed suddenly sagged under Reyr's weight.

"Too tired. Want sleep," she slurred. Her sluggish memory drifted over the previous night, then her eyes flew open. She had performed magic. *Real* magic! She bolted upright, rubbing her bleary eyes.

"Excellent, you have changed your mind. Welcome to the world of the living." Reyr stood and tossed something at her. A chemise and gown that had been draped over a nearby chair. "Get dressed. You're still wearing what you wore last night. *And,* you missed breakfast in the great hall."

"Who cares? I'd rather sleep."

"Would you rather sleep than meet the grand mage and begin your training?"

"What?!" she cried, jumping from her bed. "Why didn't you say so before?"

Reyr shrugged, but his grin abolished any guilt. Satisfied, he turned on his heel and left the bed chamber, shutting the door behind him.

She removed her gown and went into her bathing chamber. It was a blessing that the castle had *some* semblance of modern technology. Plumbing was used for their bathing pools to keep the water warm and well circulated, almost like a hot tub. The toilets, however, weren't nearly as sophisticated. They were fancy pit toilets, so the waste dropped down chutes and out of sight to some unknown place.

She bathed and dressed before entering the living area of her quarters. A tray of food sat on the table. Reyr sat beside it, picking at it, waiting for her. She smiled and rushed over to grab a bowl of porridge. "No time for that," Reyr said. "Grab something for our walk. We must be off." She gave him a scowl before plucking up two bread rolls, stuffing them into her mouth in a very *unlady-like* way.

Reyr escorted her through the keep.

"I spoke to the king last night," he said. "He agrees that you ought to begin your training straight away, if you're ready for it."

"I am."

"Aye, I know." There was a long silence before Reyr said, "Just so you know, His Majesty visited Marcel late last night. He rarely does that. He wanted to ensure that your training began immediately simply because *you* wished it to."

She snorted. "I'm flattered that he's so concerned with what I want."

She wasn't.

"He cares more than you would guess," Reyr said. She lifted her brows, which made him shrug and add, "Maybe he is trying to make up for...you know."

"Right!"

"Yes, yes. Nothing beats a genuine apology, believe me, I know exactly where you stand."

It angered her that the king had not yet apologized for his behavior. "So, my training...?"

"Ah, yes. Marcel will see to everything. I should warn you though, it won't be easy. You have a great deal to learn in a short period of time. If Saffra's vision comes true, and you play a large part in the war to come, then we must prepare you as best as we can."

She bit her tongue to keep from telling him exactly what Saffra had seen. Exactly *what* role she was to play. "It's a bit much, isn't it? Playing an *important* role..."

Reyr chuckled. "If anyone can do it, you can."

"Thanks for the pep talk."

"Just trying to help." His eyes sparkled. "I *am* here to help, you know. If you need anything, you need only ask."

"Great! You can start by telling me about the society."

Reyr chuckled. "All right, then. They're an ancient order, built upon the very foundations of this keep. Those who belong to it, the mages, rely upon the magic of the old language, the same language used by the asarlaí. When King Eymar the First selected Kastali Dun to be his capital, he insisted that a college be built along with it. That is where I am taking you now."

They passed several courtiers who gaped, then hurriedly bowed. She wasn't sure if they were bowing at her, or Reyr. Probably Reyr.

"The college was established nearly fifty thousand years ago, around the same time as the monarchy."

"Fifty thousand years..." she echoed. "That's a long time."

"I suppose so. To a human, yes. Not so much for the mages, who often live much longer than humans."

"How long?"

"Not as long as the drengr. Five hundred years, give or take."

"Huh."

"Since its creation, the society has presided over the magical community, sitting just under the rule of the monarchy. Its creation was monumental in bringing order to the harsh treatment of others. Those with magic have a tendency to, at times, look down upon those without. The society keeps everyone honest."

"So...everyone was okay with them sweeping in and taking over?"

"They were opposed at first. In time, none could deny their importance. King Eymar's mages were placed around the kingdom to ensure those with magic behaved."

"Huh. Interesting."

They passed into one of the large courtyards on the third level of the keep. Her mind was writhing with questions. What kind of order did the mages keep? Did young children submit themselves when they discovered their magic? Did they have mage representatives in every city throughout Dragonwall?

"The purpose of the society is to teach those with magic to control and use their powers. Most established settlements have a mage who trains others who are new to the art."

"It sounds as if the mages have their own government."

"Aye, they do. All those with magical abilities must attend training. They are registered and tracked...usually."

She arched an eyebrow at him.

He shrugged. "No establishment is perfect. As you can guess, those in smaller settlements can slip past the watchful eyes of the society. You can imagine the problems it sometimes creates."

"Probably something like when I lost control with Lady Caterina."

"Exactly like that, but oftentimes worse."

"All the more reason to begin my training as soon as possible."

"Indeed."

"It is a lot to digest," she said, sighing.

"Yes, I can see why." He stopped in front of a door. "This is where I leave you."

"So what about—"

He held up a hand. "No more questions. Save them for another time."

"Okay, but—"

He winked, gave her a pat on the back, then hurried off.

She exhaled, bracing herself. There was so much she still did not know. So much to learn.

Blinking, she took in her surroundings. The college had its own wing in the castle located on the easternmost side of the third level. Much of it overlooked the Bay of Bandu. Everything here was overseen by the grand mage. She stood before his door, hesitant.

A click made her jump. Before she could knock, the door opened. She found a squat, older man with sparkling grey eyes and a shaggy beard. His manner of dress was drab. He wore plain black robes that were belted at his waist. This, she decided, was probably Marcel.

"What are you waiting for, dear girl? I might die of old age if you do not enter!" Despite his snippy words, his smile was friendly.

"My apologies, sir."

He ushered her into a large room. It was oddly decorated with strange glass and metal instruments. Tall bookshelves at least two stories high lined the wall opposite her. There were a few random wooden tables scattered around, along with armchairs, and two fireplaces, one on each end of the room. Several interior doors were closed. She assumed they led to his living quarters.

Marcel motioned for her to follow him, leading her to a large wooden desk dominating the back of the room. She took a seat as he took up the large chair opposite her, grunting as he pulled it in.

His long exhale permeated the silence.

She waited for him to speak, but he didn't. He sat there looking at her, smiling. In fact, his smile grew larger and larger. Did he find her amusing? Or was he sharing a silent joke with himself?

"I have been curious to meet you, Lady Claire. A woman worthy of Cyrus's gift."

She opened her mouth to speak, then decided against it.

"The king spoke with me late last night, so no need to explain. Let us jump to the point. As a result of Cyrus's gift, you now possess magical abilities. I have no experience with gifts, and there is little written about them, so we must proceed with caution.

"In the king's court, Saffra mentioned her vision and that you have an important role to play in the war to come. What part? Who can tell? Perhaps not even Saffra. However, I believe we can begin your training regimen at an advanced pace, and from there, we might get your magic where it needs to be. Sound good?"

She could do little more than nod before he forged ahead.

"From this day forward, you will be a mage-in-training. Until you either become an apprentice, or take your exams. Your training will cover everything from diction, cantrips, incants, and incantations with Mage Targa, to brews with Mage Sepia, history and magical theory with Mage Joren, and everything in between with me. There are other mages who teach here, but they cover advanced topics. We will not dive into those quite yet."

"I...see," she managed.

Marcel smiled, almost as if he knew how overwhelmed she was. "With the others—Mage Joren, Mage Sepia, and Mage Targa—your training will be regimented. With me, it will not be. Our time together will be devoted to better understanding your strange curiosities.

"Now, let us move on to your schedule. You will report to me every morning after breakfast. Do not be late." He arched an eyebrow at her, as if he knew she liked sleeping in. "When you arrive, we will spend our time studying the mystifying aspects of the world, including your capabilities. Thereafter, I will direct you to either Mage Joren or Mage Sepia. They will work with you privately, which is rather unusual. Our students generally work together. After the midday meal, you are to report to Mage Targa. For that portion of training, you will join other students. You will each be at different levels in your training, so do the best that you can. The second half of the afternoon is your time. I recommend you use it to study."

Mage Targa. Mage Joren. Mage Sepia. She began repeating the names of each in her mind and the lessons they taught, trying to keep everything straight.

"Mage Targa has an excellent mastery of the old language, as you will discover. It is especially important for you to develop the correct habits of diction when using magic, but more on that later. Targa is a fine teacher. Do you know where to find him?"

She shook her head.

"Well enough. Why not go see him now? The morning is nearly over anyway. No point in sending you to Joren or Sepia. Targa's study is located out that door,"—he pointed at the door she'd come in through—"and to the right, four doors down the corridor. Think you can find your way?"

"I think so."

"Good. Go and see him. When you have introduced yourself, stop by to see me again." Marcel rose, so she followed to the door, thanking him profusely on her way out.

Moments later she found herself standing in front of another closed door, and once more, she was too overwhelmed to knock. She took a deep breath and tapped on the door. Shortly thereafter, she found herself face to face with Mage Targa. He was a thin man, bald, with bold eyebrows and dark eyes. His face was solemn—a direct opposite of Grand Mage Marcel's. The only thing they had in common was their drab attire.

"Mage Targa?"

"Yes. Who is asking?" He studied her with a narrowed gaze.

"Oh, I'm Claire." She extended her hand. He did not take it. Instead his dark eyebrows rose briefly in recognition, then his face went back to its previous expression. She lowered her hand and said, "The Grand Mage sent me to meet you. I'm to begin my lessons today?"

"Fine, all right," he acknowledged, sounding slightly reluctant. He moved aside and invited her to enter.

His study was different from what she had expected. It was much smaller, and far emptier than the grand mage's. Everything about it was dark and uninviting. She disliked it immediately.

"Sit," he commanded, motioning to the chair opposite the sofa. She followed his instructions. "First things first, let us go over some ground rules."

"Oh...of course."

"I take my class very seriously. I expect you to attend daily and treat your lessons with the utmost regard."

She nodded.

"There are four other students aside from yourself. I demand that all of my students get along and behave maturely, no matter what." His gaze narrowed again. "Everyone is treated the same, so there will be no exceptions made for you despite your...status."

"Of course, I wouldn't expect special treatment—"

"Class will commence after the midday meal except on Sundays. We meet in the royal library, so I do not expect you to dally on your way from the dining hall. Each day we will practice the words necessary to perform magic. The pronunciations can be challenging, as the language is not like our own. I expect you to study and practice diligently. You will be tested." She was nodding along. "I believe that covers everything. Do you have any questions for me?"

Her heart kicked up a notch and she scrambled for one. "Uhm. Should I bring anything to our class?"

"Yes, occasionally you need to take notes, so quill and parchment should be fine." She exhaled. "No other questions?" he asked. She shook her head. "Very well then. I will see you after the meal."

"Thank you, Mage Targa." She all but jumped to her feet and fled.

She made sure to stop by Marcel's quarters on her way back. When she told him of her supply requirement, he gave her some writing materials, which included a feathered quill, an ink pot, and parchment. She studied them, intrigued.

"I suggest you pick up some supplies in the city when you have the chance," he advised. "The market by the docks has a number of booths with a unique selection if you are looking for something inexpensive or exotic."

A smile stole over her face. At least *now* she could petition Reyr with a good reason to visit.

"See you tomorrow, Lady Claire." He ushered her from his room.

She rushed back to her chambers to prepare for her afternoon lessons with Mage Targa. Perhaps if she worked hard enough, she might change his opinion of her, whatever that opinion happened to be. It clearly wasn't a good one.

CHAPTER 6

MAGE TARGA

Kastali Dun

Claire finished lunch then walked arm in arm with Saffra, holding on to her like a lifeline. Her stomach was a ball of nerves. "Is it too soon to pretend I'm sick?"

Saffra chuckled. "Mage Targa *can* be intimidating."

"Intimidating? He's downright terrifying."

"I know what you mean, but really, he is not as bad as he seems."

"Agree to disagree, friend. Don't even get me started on his appearance."

"Yes, he is quite awful to look at, isn't he?"

They burst into giggles, their voices echoing down the corridor, though hers was more of a nervous laugh. Mage Targa's ugly sneer swam into her mind. She might have pitied his frightening face, except his disposition seemed to match.

Saffra led the way up another sweeping staircase. They took a left turn and continued down a wide hallway lined with paintings. She froze mid-step—

"What...?" Saffra stopped beside her, following her gaze. "Oh."

"I've seen her before," Claire whispered, brows furrowing. The painting was of a woman with golden hair, not so different from her own. She had sprite markings and glittering blue eyes. "Is this—?"

"Queen Isabella, yes."

Chills raced down Claire's arms. "I saw her in the marble dragon's mind. I didn't realize... She looks so much *like* me."

"Indeed, she does." Saffra's head tilted, then her gaze bounced between Claire and Isabella. "The similarities are...uncanny."

"Who's the girl beside her?" Claire reached out as if to touch her, then pulled away at the last moment. She was young, with sandy brown hair and hazel colored eyes—eyes only slightly darker than her own. "They have the same thin nose," she realized. "Same shape of eyebrows... Is she...? Did Queen Isabella have a daughter?"

"Princess Irelia," Saffra said. This time, the back of Claire's neck prickled. Something about that name. "Hers is a sad story. I will tell you sometime, but for now, lessons. Targa does not tolerate lateness."

"Oh, yes. Right." She gave the painting a final, curious glance.

They rushed off, hurrying through the castle until they reached the large oaken doors to the library. Each was carved with little vignettes of men on horseback, riding into battle. "Try to relax," Saffra said. "You have Cyrus's magic now. That counts for something."

"Okay." Her throat thickened, making it hard to swallow. "I'll try."

You will be fine. Magic is in your blood, Cyrus's voice was a whisper in her mind.

"Deep breaths," Saffra added, taking her hands and squeezing them.

"I don't know what I would do without you," she said, holding the seer's brown eyes.

"I meant what I said last night. I am at your service. Whatever you need."

"Thank you," she croaked.

"And I...I'm glad we're friends," Saffra said, grinning.

"Me too," she breathed.

They shared a quick embrace before Saffra rushed off.

She turned to the doors, staring apprehensively at them. Her servant duties had never included the library. It had its own dedicated caregivers.

Taking a deep, fortifying breath, she pushed past the doors and stepped inside. The light was different here. Bright and airy and open. Generous amounts of daylight found even the darkest spaces.

She inhaled and a smile crept over her face. The decay of old books, the scent of varnished wood, the lingering hint of musk. It smelled like impossibilities and imagination, of all the things libraries ought to be. Most importantly, it smelled like home.

A pang of sadness pierced her heart. She missed her parents, her friends, the simplicity of her old life. She shook her head, pushing those thoughts away. She couldn't afford to think like that right now.

The library's entrance chamber was filled with alcoves. Some with tables, others with plush armchairs. Just beyond, she could make out the vast rows of books in the main chamber, ceilings hidden from view.

She spotted Mage Targa and his students in a nearby nook. Quickening her step, she hurried over. A far too familiar face had her jaw clenching. Caterina was sitting among the group.

"Ah. There she is." Mage Targa nodded in her direction, as much of a greeting as she was likely to get. "We have a new student joining us. Everyone, this is Lady Claire."

Four faces stared at her. Two males and two females. She gave an awkward smile and wave, avoiding Caterina's gaze entirely.

"How about some introductions?" Mage Targa decided. "This fellow is Jaycel. He is in his third year of instruction with me."

"Call me Jace," the young man said, jumping up to offer her a bow. He couldn't have been more than sixteen. She was instantly taken by his outgoing nature. He had dark brown skin and hair that was tightly braided along his scalp. His eyes were a brilliant blue.

"Nice to meet you, Jace," she said, grinning as he sat back down.

"This young woman here is Renna," Mage Targa continued. "She recently completed her sixth year of instruction."

Renna looked to be around twenty. She had pale skin, dark hair, red lips, and delicate features. She did not stand, but she *did* plaster a fake smile onto her pretty face. "Pleased to meet you, my lady." Her voice matched her cool expression.

It took a moment to click, but she recognized her. Renna had been one of the women with Caterina during their little spat the other day. That explained the frosty greeting.

"Nice to meet you, Renna," she said, keeping her voice light.

"This is Lady Caterina." Targa gestured. "She is in her seventh year of study and has proved to be a most proficient student. Especially given her circumstances." Mage Targa looked briefly conflicted, then added, "She did not join me until she was seventeen. Better late than never." His dark eyes darted between Claire and Caterina for a few brief moments. "I believe the two of you have already met."

Caterina's eyes flashed dangerously back at her, but she acknowledged her with a nod.

Mage Targa ignored the animosity between them. He quickly moved on and said, "And this young man is Devmont. He is in his fourth year, though some days it seems he is back in his first." He offered Devmont a glare, which the young man ignored.

"Call me Dev, my lady, as my friends do." He stood and bowed. He had tanned skin, brown eyes, and hair the color of sand. She greeted him with a friendly hello.

"Now, please take a seat so that we may begin." Targa also sat back down upon the padded chair he'd recently vacated.

She grabbed the empty seat beside Jace. His grin did not go unnoticed. Out of the corner of her eye, she caught him staring at her. She was growing used to the curiosity from other courtiers.

"Very well, let us begin. Having a new student affords us a wonderful opportunity to review old material," Targa said. "All of you need a refresher anyway. Tell me, Renna, what is the most important aspect of performing a cantrip, incant, or incantation?"

A deep blush spread across Renna's pale cheeks. "Um...the mind?"

"Yes, but why?"

"Because you have to own it," Jace said, his rich tenor voice taking over. "You must exhibit dominance over the language. The mind of a mage is powerful, but it must be exercised."

"Very good, Jaycel. It is one thing to speak the words. To command them is entirely different. A mage must have a strong mind, a dominant mind, and that is what sets him or her apart. We are masters over the words we speak. Our power of command is the reason magic chose us when it could have chosen others, instead. Many have the blood but few have the control."

Claire's forehead furrowed. Something did not sit well with her. Her mind went to the asarlaí. "I have a question," she said, interrupting the class.

Mage Targa's mouth twitched as if holding back a frown, but he nodded.

"If the old language is used to perform magic, and we must exercise dominion over the words, we must command them such that they obey, won't we become just like the asarlaí?"

Mage Targa choked. "Gods above! Do the mages strike you as evil people?"

"No! Well, that is...it's not what I meant. I just thought..."

"We do not use magic for evil purposes, Lady Claire. Even if we did, our blood is not as pure as the asarlaí blood was in days of old."

She clenched her jaw in frustration, ignoring the fact that most of them were gawking at her.

"Now, moving on, once you have placed yourself in the correct frame of mind, what comes next?"

"The magic words—the old language," Caterina said. "You must have a thorough knowledge of the old language so that you can string together the correct phrases for the things you want."

"Wonderful!" Mage Targa cried, as if she'd achieved some

immeasurable success. "Can you tell me more about the old language?"

Caterina grinned widely, sitting up straighter to speak, "The old language, or *Aldinn Malasarlaí*, was invented by the ancient sorcerers before dragons. They used it to perform magic. They even used it to bring the dragons to life."

"Well aren't you a right Hermione Granger," she muttered, unimpressed.

"Excuse me?" Caterina rounded on her just as Mage Targa clapped his hands together and cried, "Excellent!"

She turned away and pretended to have said nothing. Mage Targa also appeared oblivious as he said, "And who can tell me the root word of malasarlaí?" He looked around at each of them.

"The root word is asarlaí," Claire said, studying her nails as if bored. All eyes snapped in her direction.

Mage Targa gave her a curt nod but offered no praise. "The rest of you ought to have remembered that as quickly as she did."

They moved on to diction. Mage Targa had Devmont recite all the words he knew in the old language. Dev did not mind getting called on, though he was frequently corrected for mispronunciation throughout his recitations. She got the impression that he did not take these lessons seriously. She couldn't afford the same luxury, though it was entertaining to watch him at it.

"All right, enough! Enough of your painful recitations." Mage Targa waved his hand, bored of Dev's display. "Let us move on. Time to practice. Since you are new to our group, *Lady Claire*, you may go first." Her skin crawled under his scrutiny. He picked up a book and held it out on the flat of his palm. "Without touching it, I want you to open this book to a page of your choice. Do you remember the word?"

"Uhm." Dev had just spoken it earlier. "I cannot remember it, sir."

Targa's expectant gaze turned to a sneer—

"*Reyr?*" The king's voice sounded in her mind. "*Are you free before dinner? I need your advice.*"

"*About?*" Reyr's voice sounded curious.

"The word, Lady Claire, is *hinga*." She almost didn't hear Targa. *"I'd rather discuss it in person."*

"I was planning to meet Claire," Reyr said. *"Can it wait?"*

She clenched her teeth, trying to focus.

"Very well," King Talon said.

"Well?" Targa barked. "What are you waiting for?"

She blinked. "I apologize for my confusion. You said the word is *hinga*? But what about ending the magic after I've performed it? Like, with the word *et*?"

"Ah, I see what you mean," he mused. "The cantrip is a closed form of magic. It has a beginning and an end. When you tell something to open, it will not repeatedly open if you feed magic into it. Once it is open, it is open. For other magic, magic that is open ended, yes, you would need to end the magic or else it will continue to flow. Do you understand? Good. Please proceed."

She took a deep breath and remembered Saffra's instructions. "Hinga!" she cried. The word made her cringe. The pages of the book fluttered. For a brief moment, she feared it would not open, but at last it did. She exhaled and slumped back against her chair.

"Very good." He snapped the book shut again. "Now, open it to page two-hundred."

Her lips parted in surprise. "I..."

Targa huffed, then turned to Caterina. "Would you kindly demonstrate?"

"Of course," Caterina purred, throwing her a malicious grin. "I would be happy to. *Hinga tivi-draun*." The book flipped open, pages fluttering, coming to rest on page two-hundred. *"Hinga ein draun eindra."* The pages fluttered backwards, settling on page one-hundred-and-eleven. *"Lagar."*

The book snapped closed.

Mage Targa chuckled, pleased. "Always one to go above and beyond."

Caterina's smile widened. "Perhaps, sir, I should demonstrate something that actually requires some skill?"

Claire rolled her eyes and caught Jace smirking. Their gazes met and they both shared what felt like a moment of simultaneous disgust. She liked him even more after that.

"I have no doubt that you are capable of far greater feats. I have witnessed a few of them myself," Targa said.

Claire made a gagging motion and Jace covered his mouth to keep from laughing.

The rest of the class took turns showing her single word commands. They used various objects Targa had brought along, until everyone grew bored with the simplicity. She learned that these simple displays were called cantrips. Everyone made them look effortless.

Magic that required more than one word, such as a full sentence, was an incant. Magic that took multiple sentences was an incantation. And Caterina was especially eager to show off how good she was at both.

It was simultaneously fascinating and frustrating.

Claire wanted to keep up with the group, but she didn't have the energy to try anything else. Saffra had warned her that it would take a while. But, what if she was the one person who never got over the feeling of wrongness and the exhaustion that came with it?

"All right, I think that is enough for today." Targa brought everything to a stop. "My, my, where did the time go? Tomorrow is a rest day, so I will see you all the day following."

They thanked him for his lesson and departed.

She was the last to leave the little nook, dragging her feet. She'd hoped to explore the library, but it would have to wait. Reyr was supposed to drop by just before dinner. If she hurried, she might squeeze in a nap.

A body stepped in front of her path. "You had no right to attack me the other day," Caterina hissed.

"Excuse me?" Heat immediately boiled to the surface of her skin. "I had every right. Now *move*."

"Every right?" Caterina sneered. "You're nothing more than an outsider. An outsider who needs to learn her place. No one wants you here, so stay out of my way."

"Lay off, Caterina!" one of their male classmates called from down the corridor.

"Yeah. Lay off, *Caterina*," she parroted. "And maybe you're blind, because right now, *you're* in *my* way. Unless you'd like another smack against the ceiling, I suggest you move."

Caterina scoffed. "Am I supposed to be frightened? You can't even perform more than a single cantrip. I could kill you right here with just a few words. No one would miss you."

Her lips parted, but she refused to rise to the bait. "Are you *serious* right now?"

"You wouldn't be the first to die by my hand."

She schooled her features and said, "Fine. You win. But just so you know, somewhere beyond this keep there's a tree diligently producing oxygen so that you can breathe. I think you owe it an apology." With that, she stepped around Caterina and walked away smiling.

An angry voice cried after her. "This does not end here! Stay out of my way, and stay away from King Talon. He's mine!"

~

SHE COLLAPSED INTO BED, exhausted. Caterina had been right. She couldn't perform more than a single cantrip. If she wanted to, Caterina could have attacked her right there and she wouldn't have had the energy to fight back. How was she supposed to defeat Kane?

SHE WAS on the back of a red dragon, flying south. This time she protected a different dragonstone. It was nestled within the folds of her tunic.

Stretched out beneath her, all the way to the horizon, was a large bay spilling into the South Sea. The Eastern Barrier Range was at her left. There was Zaikar Bay. It had a unique appearance, not easily forgotten. Mountains rose up steeply like walls to one side. To the other, desert as far as she could see.

She untucked the green dragonstone and gazed down at it. Power surged, flowing into her. It would be a shame, but she'd part with it. For now. It would be safe until she needed it again.

As Wrath descended in lazy circles, she caught sight of a cave entrance. Her destination. She was certain this place would be an excellent location until the time was right—

HER EYES FLEW OPEN. This time, she remembered more of the dream. There'd been a body of water. A bay. Something that sounded exotic as it rolled off the tongue, but she couldn't quite remember the name.

She'd been in Kane's head. Nausea clawed at her stomach, lifting into her throat. She dashed to the bathing chamber and spilled her guts, then settled on the marble floor until the last of it subsided. Something was very wrong.

CHAPTER 7

CONFLICTING EMOTIONS

Kastali Dun

Reyr made one final sweep of Kastali Dun's perimeter. The air current caught his wings and propelled him forward. He stretched them to their fullest, easing the muscle strain and growling with pleasure. Nothing compared to flying, to that feeling of riding the wind, except perhaps mating.

He wasn't the only one in the sky. There were other drengr, glittering with color, making their way towards the fort's walls. Today's drills were finished.

He looked out over the horizon, watching the sun sink towards the water. It cast shimmering rays along the surface of the sea, dancing with gold. It would be dark in an hour.

"Claire?" he called, waiting for an answer. Her consciousness was a bright spot against his mind—had been since he'd discovered her ability. *"Claire?"* he called again.

"Reyr?"

Amusement rushed through him. *"Have you been sleeping?"*

There was a hesitation and then, *"Yes? I needed a nap."*

"No judgment," he said, chuckling. *"Just letting you know that I'm finished with drills."*

"*Oh!*" She sounded happy. "*Okay. See you soon.*"

Their contact ended.

His gums pulled away from his teeth in the semblance of a smile. To a human, it probably looked more like a snarl, pointed teeth and all. If he wasn't careful, he'd grow addicted to the sound of Claire's voice in his mind.

Gemma had been the only other woman capable of invading his consciousness. Only riders spoke with their mates, yet Claire had the ability to speak with all of them. It was unbelievable, something he'd never imagined possible.

Guilt needled him, making his heart squeeze. Talon ought to know about it. Hiding the truth didn't sit well, but it was her secret to tell, and betraying her trust could ruin them.

He caught sight of the remaining drengr disappearing behind the walls of Fort Kastali. It sat north of the capital, a half a mile away. Today's drills had gone well. He'd played the role of wild dragon, preparing them for what it might be like.

Except, none of them knew how to defeat a dragon. They were similar in size. Flames wouldn't work. Scales were nearly impenetrable. So, *how?*

He descended towards the keep's lowest courtyard, then shifted and made his way to Claire's chambers. He walked right in. She whirled around in surprise, hand pressing against her chest. "What's the point of knocking if you're just going to storm in?" Her pout was far too endearing. "What if I had been dressing?"

"Had you been dressing, I would have been graced with a glorious sight. My lady," he added, bowing to greet her. His mouth twitched.

"I should start locking the door," she grumbled, throwing him a glare.

"Oh yes, because a locked door would be impassable." He crossed his arms, amused.

She rolled her eyes and threw herself onto a nearby sofa. "Whatever. So, guess who *I* had to deal with today?"

"Hm...let's see?" He tapped his chin. "Does she have raven black hair and a bad attitude? Must have been Caterina."

"Ugh. Yes. I can't stand her. I'm going to have to start calling her *Miss Witch*."

He laughed, taking a seat across from her. "I take it Miss Witch interfered with your day?"

She exhaled loudly. "Sort of, yes. She's in my diction class with Mage Targa. Speaking of, I dislike him almost as much as Caterina."

"That bad, huh?" He'd spoken to Mage Targa on occasion, but never found anything wrong with him.

"Anyway, after our lesson, Caterina had the audacity to corner me outside the library with a death threat—"

"Wait, what?" He sat up straighter.

"She also told me to stay away from King Talon. As if I'm interested in him!"

"Caterina threatened you?"

"She said she'd kill me if I didn't stay out of her way. That I wouldn't be the first person."

His skin prickled and he thought back to Verath's behavior during the execution. Surely it was a coincidence. He sighed. "Caterina may be reckless, but I highly doubt she has the means to kill anyone, including you."

Claire shrugged. "Maybe you're right. I'm trying not to let it bother me. I just don't know how I'm supposed to attend lessons with Targa breathing down my neck while Caterina secretly envisions ways to kill me."

He relaxed against the sofa, eyeing her. "Perhaps I will speak with Marcel—"

"No! I—I'll try to handle it myself. I don't want Caterina to think she's won, or that she has any power over me."

"But it appears that she does. If she makes you uneasy—"

"I can deal with it," she assured him. "I'm stronger than you think. But...why did she tell me to back off King Talon?"

He chuckled. "I'm not surprised she said that. Though, I would have assumed she'd given up on that after the execution."

"Wait...does Caterina have *feelings* for him? Here I thought she was interested in Mage Targa, the way he fawns over her."

"Caterina's been trying to woo the king for years. There was even gossip that he'd take her as his wife."

"*What?*" She gaped at him. "You're joking, right? Caterina—Dragonwall's queen?"

He huffed. "I wish I were. Rest assured, King Talon would never have her as a wife for many reasons, the most obvious being her inability to give him an heir. That can only happen with a mated pair."

"So, it's true then? King Talon never found his mate?"

"Unfortunately not."

"But...it's not too late for him to keep trying, right?"

"I think he sees it that way. He stopped searching a long time ago."

"Why?"

"His scars. He believes no one could bear them."

She huffed. "His scars aren't the problem."

"Well, yes, there is the matter of his temper."

"And what about you? I remember Jovari and Koldis mentioning something about a woman named Gemma. Was she your mate?"

His mind skidded. He took a moment then said, "Yes, but I would rather not talk about it."

Claire worried at her lower lip, her expression conflicted. "I... I'm sorry, Reyr. I didn't mean to upset you."

"It's all right." His voice was barely a whisper.

"On a separate note," she said, brightening. " I've got something else to discuss with you."

"Oh?" Warm relief washed over him. He hated that the mere mention of Gemma's name brought back old hurts. He wanted so badly to share that part of his life with Claire, but he simply couldn't do it yet.

"I need you to help me with my dreams."

"Your dreams?" He blinked.

"Yes, I keep having these strange dreams. At first, I wasn't able to remember what I was seeing, but now I think I'm seeing inside of someone's head."

"Visions?" His scowl deepened.

Claire shook her head. "I don't think so."

He considered for a moment. "Cyrus was a Mind Bender. With his soul and his magic, you ought to possess the same abilities. Perhaps that is it."

"But I'm not trying. I'm not standing in front of someone breaking into their thoughts. Besides, this person does not seem to know that I'm there."

The hairs on the back of his neck prickled.

"Whose mind are you seeing?"

"Kane's." Her eyes fell to her skirt and she picked at the embroidery.

"Kane? You are sure?"

"I'm sure." Her voice was barely a whisper. "The worst part is, when I'm in his mind, it's like I become him. I become this horrible person and I don't mind that I do. I want the same things he wants, to possess all the dragonstones and steal the monarchy."

"Claire..." He shook his head, uncertain of what to say. He didn't want to let on how disturbing it was. That would only frighten her.

"You don't think I'm...I'm not an evil person for wanting those things, am I? I don't *want* to want them. I can't help it. But...how is it even possible?"

He sighed. "You are not an evil person. But, this is concerning."

"You're not going to tell *him,* are you?"

"The king?"

Claire nodded, rubbing her palm on her gown. "I don't like him knowing stuff about me."

He made a sound in the back of his throat. "You're going to have to move past that if we are to work together. Like it or not, he is your king now."

She groaned. "It's not like I need him to thank me for all the sacrifices I've made, but maybe if he would apologize, things would be easier. He tried to kill me and never even bothered to say sorry. Now I'm just supposed to forget it happened? He needs to get over his stupid pride."

"Yes, he ought to apologize. I will speak to him about—"

"No! Don't tell him. It doesn't count if the apology doesn't come from his heart."

He exhaled. That was the second time he'd tried to come to her rescue and she'd refused him. He needed to step back and stop letting his emotions cloud his judgment. "You're right. It's not my place to interfere."

"Thank you."

He nodded, then stood. "We had better go down for dinner," he said. "May I escort you?"

His words had the exact effect he was hoping for. Her serious expression dissolved into a smile that left him feeling warm all over. She nodded and jumped to her feet, eagerly taking the arm he offered. Together, the two of them left her chambers and went downstairs.

CHAPTER 8
CLAIRE'S NEEDS

Kastali Dun

Talon watched Claire enter the dining hall. His eyes homed in on the place where her hand wrapped around Reyr's elbow. His jaw tightened.

Reyr leaned in and whispered something. She tossed her head back, laughing. The sight of it made his stomach flop. He couldn't tear his gaze away from the bright expression on her face, even knowing he wasn't responsible for putting it there.

Her powder blue gown was cut low on her chest, showing off elegant embroidery and beautiful beads along the cuffs. She wore her golden hair pinned back, elongating her long neck. Anyone seeing her for the first time would never guess she was an outsider.

He tried to remind himself of that, too. Tried, and failed. Especially as Reyr guided her through the busy hall.

He pictured their roles reversed. Pictured leading her down the central aisle, the feel of her hand looped around his arm, her eyes smiling up at him. His grip tightened on his goblet and he pushed the image away. It was so easy for Reyr to be around her—so *effortless*. He wasn't blind. Reyr had feelings for this woman, even if he hid them.

He released his goblet, but not before he caught a flash of his reflection. A low scoff escaped his lips. It was pointless, careless even, imagining himself in Reyr's place. Imagining a reality where she'd look at him the same way when most people couldn't bear the sight of him.

It was better that she hated him.

Reyr settled Claire before striding up and rounding the high table. "Good evening, Your Grace," he greeted, grinning. He took a seat at Talon's left. "You look miserable, as usual."

He snorted. "Only because I must suffer *your* company." On his right, he heard a snicker from Koldis.

Reyr grinned, bumping their shoulders together in affection. "What is it you wished to discuss?"

Talon glared down at his empty plate. "It's nothing. Forget about it."

"I can always tell when you're lying," Reyr sing-songed.

He heaved a sigh. "Claire looks well this evening. How is she?"

"And here I thought you would be more interested in this afternoon's drills. They went well, just so you know."

"I already received updates from Verath," he snapped. "You know that."

"Yes, yes, I know," Reyr huffed. "Just giving you a hard time."

"As usual. Answer my question."

"She's...adjusting. Better than I had expected."

"That's good."

"Indeed." Reyr's eyes darted in Claire's direction, a flash of concern edging his features.

Talon frowned, studying him. "What is it?" he asked. "Why are you looking at her like that?"

The doors to the dining hall closed with a grinding thud. Servants poured in, filling the room with mouth-watering aromas.

Reyr glanced away almost guiltily. "She had an eventful afternoon."

Heaping platters of food were deposited before them. He ignored them and said, "Eventful, how?"

"You should discuss the matter with her."

He snorted. "We both know she hates me."

"Do you blame her?" Reyr turned to meet his gaze. "You have hardly atoned for your behavior."

"I gave her the nicest accommodations in the keep," he bit out. "She's been elevated to *royalty,* her every want and need met. What more can I do to make her happy?"

"Firstly, *my king,* how can you possibly know her wants and needs if you never talk to her? And secondly, perhaps all that is needed is an apology."

He opened his mouth to protest, then closed it. Reyr was right. Except, he'd rather fly into battle. "I don't *do* apologies, Reyr," he grumbled.

"Fine. Suit yourself," Reyr said, shrugging, as if the matter made little difference to him.

Talon reached for a serving spoon, quickly dishing up food to put an end to their discussion. When he looked at the succulent meat, grilled to perfection, the steaming rice, the seared vegetables, he found he no longer had any desire to eat. He stifled a curse under his breath—

"So, what did you wish to discuss earlier?" Reyr asked again, pressing the matter.

He exhaled. "It's not important."

"Seemed like it at the time."

"That's because it was a time sensitive matter." His words were clipped.

"Oh?"

"It doesn't matter now. She's already off sitting with Saffra."

"This has to do with Claire?" Reyr's brows lifted, and a knowing grin spread across his face. "Will you just spit it out?"

"Fine. I was going to ask if we ought to invite her to sit with us at the head table. She's royal, after all. We'd need to add a chair, but..."

Reyr stared at him, then blinked. "You're serious. That's really what you needed to discuss *in person?*"

"Well, yes." His skin flushed hot, which only served to irritate him. "I don't exactly..."

A laugh burst from Reyr's chest. "Ahh...that's what you meant by *we*. You were going to have *me* invite her because you can't even talk to her."

"So?" he snapped.

"Talon..." Reyr pinched the bridge of his nose. "You have to get past this. The two of you can't be enemies. Just go talk to her. I'm serious."

He made a sound in the back of his throat, then ignored Reyr for the rest of the meal.

When the guests rose to exit the hall, he kept an eye on Claire. She left the room with Saffra. The two of them spent a great deal of time together. It was probably a good thing.

When the hall emptied, he exited through one of the well-disguised servant doors, stepping out into an empty corridor behind the dining hall. He nearly turned away three separate times before he found himself outside her door.

He stood there, clenching and unclenching his fists. There were sounds within. Shuffling, and rustling.

How would she react upon seeing him?

He hesitated, then knocked louder than intended.

"Come in," Claire's voice called. He exhaled and opened the door. She was sitting near the fire, a book in one hand, and a goblet of wine in the other.

A small gasp fell from her lips. "You." She set her things down and rushed to stand. "I mean, Your Grace—I didn't expect to see you tonight."

She offered him a surprised, sloppy curtsey. His mouth twitched. He fought the urge to smile.

"Sorry about...my attire." She cleared her throat. "Had I known you were coming, I would have worn something more appropriate."

His gaze darted over her. She wore only her white, lacy chemise. He flushed and quickly turned away. "There is no need to apologize. I didn't mean to intrude. I will come back another time."

He was relieved to have an excuse to leave.

"Wait!" she cried. He stopped but did not turn back.

"I didn't mean to scare you away," she said. He heard her rustling around behind him. "It's just a nightgown. Can I get you some wine?"

Tempted, he glanced over his shoulder to find she'd donned a silken robe. "I—no, no wine. Thank you for the offer."

"Have a seat then." She gestured to the sofa across from hers as she sat back down. A book lay open and flipped over beside her, its cover facing up.

He sat but remained aloof, his back straight. This way, he could bolt for the door if necessary. Claire slouched back against the sofa, sipping her wine, curiously regarding him. It both thrilled and terrified him to have her unflinching attention entirely on him. He tapped his fingers on his knee, looking around her chamber, until at last, his gaze settled on the book beside her. "What are you reading?"

"Oh." She picked it up. "Something from the bookshelf, children's tales I believe."

"Hmm..." he said, then inwardly cringed. A long, awkward silence followed. He cleared his throat. "Did...did your first day of lessons go well?"

She set the book on her lap and shrugged. "I suppose. As well as they could have."

That was clearly all she intended to say on the matter. He was tempted to push, but stopped himself. When the silence stretched on, she picked up her book and pretended to read. He was certain her eyes didn't actually move across the page. She sipped her wine, casually.

He used this opportunity to study her. Her captivating green eyes were hidden beneath long lashes. Her mouth was set in a slight frown as she concentrated on the pages. Her golden hair, now removed from its pins, fell in tresses around her face.

He noticed the gentle rise and fall of her chest—

She suddenly looked up at him and arched an eyebrow. He quickly turned his gaze to the fireplace, feigning interest in the flames. She cleared her throat. "So...is there a reason for your visit tonight?"

His eyes snapped to hers. "Yes. Now that you are royal, I'd like to add an additional chair to the head table—"

"Oh. That won't be necessary. I prefer to sit with Saffra."

"Is that so?"

But of course she did. Why wouldn't she, when *his* company was the alternative. Then again, it also meant she wouldn't be near Reyr, or any of his other shields. That *did* offer a small measure of satisfaction.

"Yes." She set her book down and crossed her arms.

He was tempted to argue, if only to exert his will. Instead, he recalled what Reyr had said, about working together. About moving on. "How are you adjusting?" he blurted, before he could stop himself.

Her mouth opened, then closed. "Oh. Fine, I suppose."

Another clipped answer. Another desire to avoid details. How in the name of the gods was he supposed to practice talking to her, if she refused to actually talk?

"Is there...is there anything that I can see to? You have all that you need to be comfortable here?"

She cleared her throat. "Actually, there is something." He stilled, then leaned forward to look at her, surprised that she would need him for anything. "Marcel recommended that I pick up a few supplies from the market for my lessons. I thought I would go tomorrow afternoon, since it is a rest day."

His anticipation heightened. Was she about to ask him to join her? Why did the thought make his heart race—?

"Saffra offered to go with me. I figured it would be fine."

He reared back, his inner thoughts shattering. "Absolutely not. You may not leave the keep without adequate protection."

"That's bullshit!" Her skin flushed pink with irritation. So did his. "We will be back before dark. You said that as long as I have an escort, I can go into the city."

"I know what I said," he bit out. "I specified that it was to be one of my own guards."

Or himself. But he certainly wouldn't reveal that. Not now.

"Well I asked Reyr, but he's busy tomorrow. Bedelth is flying sweeps. And Jovari and Koldis just left for Fort Squall."

"What of Verath? Did you forget about him?"

What of me? he was tempted to say, then cursed himself.

"I...I'm sure he has better things to do than to escort *me*. Why should I inconvenience him?" She huffed, eyes flashing with anger.

His shoulders bunched with tension. "When I set rules, Lady Claire, I expect them to be followed. You would rather risk your life than simply ask Verath?"

"Yes," she snapped, jumping to her feet. "I'm not a five-year-old! Saffra and I will be fine. We're both grown women."

His jaw clenched. He had half a mind to forbid her from visiting the market altogether. Instead, he reached out to Verath. *"I need you to escort Lady Claire and Lady Saffra to the market tomorrow afternoon."*

"As you wish, Your Grace."

"Verath will escort you," he said. "There will be no further arguments on the matter."

"I don't appreciate being treated like a child. Has anyone ever told you you're controlling?"

"It is my job to be," he snapped, jumping to his feet. "You can go with Verath, or not at all. The choice is yours."

"Fine," she hissed. "Is that *all*, Your Grace?"

He flinched. "Yes, that is all."

"Good. Then thank you so very much for seeing to my needs."

He flinched. She may as well have slapped him. He could have had the last word, or said something cutting. He was tempted to keep this going, if only to vent his frustration. Instead, he pressed his lips together and stormed from the room.

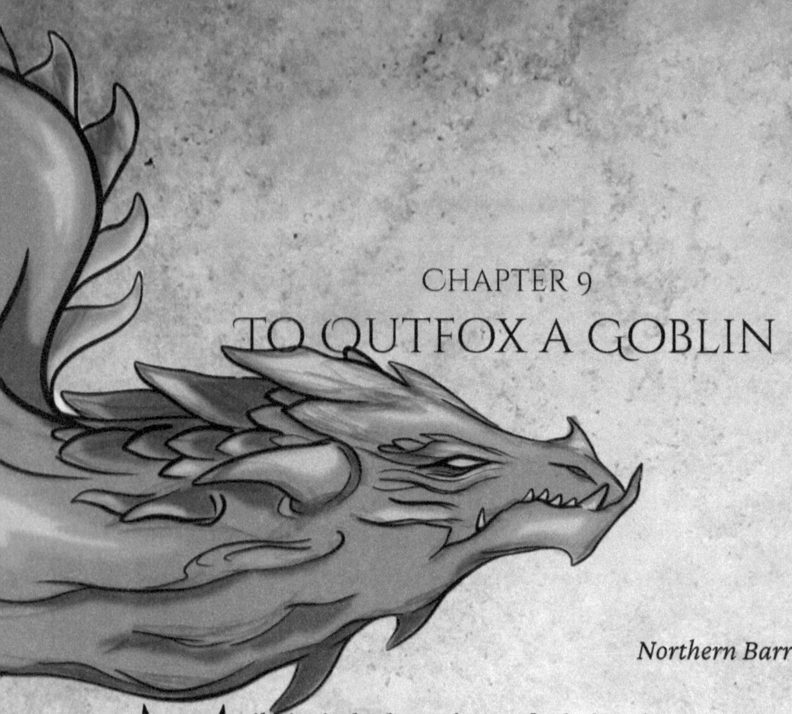

CHAPTER 9

TO OUTFOX A GOBLIN

Northern Barrier Range

Mikkin jerked awake to find the sharp prod of a blade against his side. Goblins swarmed his camp. He nearly gagged, his eyes watering against the putrid smell of them.

"Up!" shouted a guttural voice, followed by a swift kick. He sat up. It grunted something to the others, and several of the little urchins rushed forward to bind his hands. He looked over at Jamie. The lad's wide eyes met his.

He and Jamie were in the forest of the *Northern Barrier Range* in search of dragons. When his home and family had been reduced to ash, he'd struck out in search of the beasts who destroyed his happiness. While he cared little for his life, he cared for Jamie's.

This certainly complicated things.

He strained against his bindings but they didn't budge. His gaze darted around the camp, taking count of his captors. There were twenty of them, and who could say how many more out patrolling. His shoulders slumped.

Their packs were confiscated. He eyed his belongings, exhaling. Grunts sounded as the little urchins discovered the three short swords he'd taken from goblins he had previously killed. These were passed around and argued over.

He winced, hoping they wouldn't know where the blades had come from.

The leader shouted something harsh and the goblins calmed down. Pointing at the swords, it looked at Mikkin. "How you got these?"

"We found them," he said almost too quickly. "In the forest down there." He motioned in the direction they'd come from. Weeks had passed since they'd killed the owners.

"Lie!" hissed the goblin.

"I do not lie," he said. "Jamie, would I lie?"

The poor lad was too terrified to answer coherently. "N-no. You...you would...not."

"And this?" the goblin asked. He held forth the coins and rubies they'd also taken from the bodies.

"Those are mine," he insisted.

The goblin laughed, showing its pointy teeth. "Not yours *now!*"

Everyone knew goblins coveted jewels and gold. Knowing this, a plan began hatching in his mind. "Fine," he said, shrugging. "Since you like them so much, keep it! I already have a huge chest of riches. I buried it three days ago for safekeeping. What do I care about a few precious jewels? Once you let us go, I'll still have plenty."

The goblin's little mind was working hard. Its face scrunched in concentration. Then it began to laugh. "Let go? Let go! Ha-ha-ha. I no let you go. Why you bury this?" It held up one of the coins.

"To keep it hidden from little people such as yourself."

"Where? Where you hide it?" it eagerly demanded. Mikkin pressed his lips together, unwilling to answer. "Where you hide it?" it repeated.

"Why would I tell you?"

"Tell or die!"

"Okay, okay." He held up his bound hands in submission. "I

cannot describe the location. I only know in my mind. Here." He tapped his temple.

The goblin began conversing rapidly with the others in its mother tongue. Several of them got very excited. A few started hopping up and down.

"What are you doing?" Jamie hissed.

"Remember the tale of Redcote the Fox?"

Jamie's eyes widened. It was all he needed to say. The lad understood.

The forest fell silent. The goblins all turned to face him. "Show!" commanded their leader. "Show us treasure."

He put a grave expression on his face and said, "Very well."

With bound hands, they retraced their steps from the day before. He made things up as he went along. It was an unfortunate setback, but better this than their lives. As they walked, he considered his next move. Facing off against twenty goblins wouldn't be easy. Impossible, even.

Why were so many goblins in this part of the forest anyway? That was the better question. They were creatures from the east, from Pavv, beyond the borders of Dragonwall.

As night began to fall, their leader prodded him with a spear and said, "How much longer?"

"Two days. I told you I buried it days ago."

"Two days?!" it barked, stopping them dead in their tracks. Once more it began to converse with its comrades. More arguing followed.

The raised voices gave Mikkin a chance to whisper to Jamie. "We will have to overpower them."

"How in every gods' name will we do that?"

"I am not sure yet. Perhaps tonight when they sleep. We cannot hope to outrun them." At his words, Jamie's jaw dropped. "I will need my bow back. It is the only way."

"You cannot shoot all of them!" Jamie hissed.

"Can you climb a tree?" he asked. Jamie nodded. "I thought so. When I give the word, we will take my bow from that one there." He motioned with his head towards the goblin carrying his quiver and bow. The little wretches continued arguing, oblivious. "After I take it, we will climb a tree and shoot them from above. I think it might work."

The possibility was promising as long as they could climb fast enough. He felt something brush against his ankle and glanced down. He had almost forgotten about the knife hidden beneath his trousers. Jamie had one too. The goblins had forgotten to search them in their excitement for gold. He could cut their bindings.

"I don't know, Mikkin." Jamie's eyes were on the ground in front of him. "It sounds reckless."

"It is the best plan I have. I'll keep thinking and let you know if I come up with something—"

"No talk!" the leader shouted, finally taking notice. Mikkin pressed his lips together. "Two days?" it clarified.

"Yes," Mikkin confirmed, yet again.

"Fine! Move."

They marched onward, navigating rough terrain littered with boulders, trees, and undergrowth. When night fell, the goblins halted and began preparing a fire. They had very little to eat, and even less to share. It explained why they were not prepared to make the two-day trek to his treasure. An argument broke out, which abruptly turned into a fistfight. One of the goblins pointed at Jamie.

His stomach dropped.

A larger goblin moved forward, sword raised towards Jamie.

Adrenaline flooded his senses and he rushed into action. "Whoa!" he shouted, jumping in front of the lad to protect him. "What is the meaning of this?" He looked angrily at the leader for answers.

"We hungry!" the leader answered. "Want meat."

"The lad is not to be harmed," he said, disgusted. "If you touch him, you must go through me! All your *precious* gold will be lost. Without me, you will never find it!"

The leader fell silent, perhaps considering his options. Then he shouted something at the others. He held his breath, tense. The goblin lowered its weapon. An exhale fell from his lips.

When he next looked at Jamie, it was to find his face pale as snow. "Do not fret, lad. I will get us out of this soon enough."

He settled down and took a seat beside Jamie. Several goblins went off into the night. They returned later with three rabbits. The meat would scarcely feed half of them. The party of goblins knew it, too. It was almost satisfying to watch them argue over their dinner, but it was distraction enough.

"I am going to cut our bonds," he whispered, looking at Jamie. Firelight danced over them as the lad's eyes went round. "Once I slit them, we will pretend they are still there. This is our chance for escape."

Goblins were rumored to have horrible eyesight; hopefully, nighttime would give them an advantage.

The arguing grew more heated. One of the goblins forcefully snatched a rabbit from the hunter who held them. Quietly, with as little motion as possible, he slipped the knife from under his trouser leg.

The ropes around Jamie's wrists cut cleanly. The lad returned the favor. He then slipped the knife back to its position and arranged the ropes about his wrist such that they looked uncut. Jamie did the same.

They waited and watched.

The spectacle *was* entertaining, even despite the language barrier. A fight broke out. He kept his eyes on his quiver and bow, urging the goblin closer so he could grab it.

"That tree there," he whispered to Jamie. He motioned with his head towards a large oak. It looked climbable. Its branches started low enough that he and the lad could reach the bottom limb with a decent jump.

Another fight started between a smaller group of goblins. This time, the leader got involved and began shouting and pulling fighting pairs apart. Several of its soldiers grunted angrily.

This was their chance. The carrier of his bow and quiver was an arm's length away, trying to detach from the group with a plump rabbit of its own. Jumping silently to his feet, he grabbed his bow and quiver, forcefully knocking the surprised goblin to the ground. Its cry was drowned out by the fist fights and shouting near the fire. Mikkin and Jamie reached the tree before anyone in the camp noticed, but when they did notice, they roared with anger.

He already had the quiver and bow slung over his shoulder. Jamie was on his heels. "Jump to the lowest branch and swing yourself up," he cried.

Jamie followed orders and deftly pulled himself up. The boy had strength, thank the gods. He followed, though he was not as quick to get into position. Together they climbed. Both of them scrambled up the branches as if wraiths haunted their footfalls. They were near the top before either had the courage to look down.

To his relief, the goblins had not successfully cleared more than the first branch; they were too short.

"Jamie, it's time!" he called up to the lad, positioning himself. He prayed to the gods, hoping he had enough arrows in the quiver to take out the majority of them. He nocked an arrow and let it loose. The closest goblin had already cleared several branches. The arrow struck true, hitting the green creature through the top of his head. The goblin fell, taking out another along the way.

Jamie cheered.

They were like ants, clambering over each other to gain ground. They screamed and hollered in fury. He discerned their emotion through their harsh voices. Those on the ground issued commands to the goblins climbing above.

"Do not forget your knife, lad," Mikkin called up to Jamie. "If it comes to that, use it!"

He nocked another arrow, then took aim. The second goblin fell as quickly as the first. Several others were closing in, climbing from branch to branch.

He loaded each arrow with absolute focus. Over and again he released, carefully removing one goblin at a time, sometimes two, if the falling one knocked another off balance. There were fewer and fewer.

Eventually, only two remained, lingering at the base of the tree. They argued, the sounds of their harsh language floating up. He studied them, breathing hard as his muscles strained to maintain balance. The final two would be easy.

He reached behind him for more arrows—

He grasped nothing but air. There *were* no more arrows. "Gods above!" he swore under his breath. "You down there," he called, raising his voice. "How about you come up and make this easier for me."

Their arguing stopped. He wasn't sure they understood his words, but his meaning was clear enough. They sprang from the ground and began climbing.

Mikkin looked up into the tree above. "Jamie," he called, "come down. We will need that second knife of yours after all."

Jamie complied, climbing down beside him. "I can hardly believe it!" the lad said. "Every mark you struck was true."

"Rejoice later. I will take the bigger one, the one closest to us. You take the smaller one down there, if you can."

"I'll try," Jamie said, apprehension filling his voice. The goblins were close.

Mikkin clambered down to the branch below, meeting the first with his knife. Given his position—lower than Jamie's—he had no choice but to take them both. Neither goblin had weapons, but they tried to grab him and yank him from the tree.

He grunted and held fast to the branch above, stabbing the closest in the neck with his knife, removing the blade quickly to go in for a second jab. The goblin howled and did not immediately release its grip upon his tunic. The other made another attempt to wrench him from the tree.

Jamie let loose a battle cry. The lad jumped to the branch below, positioning himself behind the second goblin before stabbing it in the back. The goblin shrieked, the sound setting the hairs of Mikkin's arms on end.

He stabbed the closest goblin several more times. The wretch finally lost its footing, but still grasped his tunic. He gave a shout of surprise as his foot slipped. His knife fell from his hand, clattering against branches as it tumbled to the forest floor below. He worked to remove the dead goblin's grip, peeling open its stiff fingers. At last, it dropped out of sight.

He looked up in time to see Jamie push his wounded attacker from the tree. Jamie yelped as he did it, as if surprised by his accomplishment. He doubted that the lad had ever killed anything like a goblin before.

When the last body hit the ground, they fell quiet. The only sound was their heavy breathing as they clung to the branches of the tree. He pressed his forehead against the bark, thanking the giant sentinel for being exactly what they'd needed.

He regained his voice and chuckled. "Well, how's that for trickery? Come, let's get out of this damn tree. I need some water."

They descended much slower than they had ascended. His muscles were screaming. His nerves still lingered on the edge of fear; he knew little about what they would find in the camp.

Once on the ground, he looked around. There wasn't a goblin in sight that was not dead, but he had a bad feeling. "Jamie, count them—count the bodies."

The lad did as he was told. "Nineteen. How...how many were there?"

"This morning, I counted twenty. One's missing." He looked over their faces. It was difficult to distinguish one from the other. Their ugly green skin and stunted features looked all the same to him. The smell was ripe, but he got over it quickly after his capture.

"The leader," Jamie said, getting his attention. "Their leader is not among them."

He looked over the faces again. Jamie was correct. The leader was nowhere to be seen.

Northern Barrier Range

Mikkin wandered around the pile of goblin bodies pondering his next move. His plan had worked. They were free, but the goblin leader was unaccounted for. "Where do you think it went?" Jamie asked, traipsing around as if he might find it hiding in the bushes.

"Don't know, lad. Maybe it ran away." The noise of their fight had already alerted the forest of their presence, so he cupped his hands and shouted, "You there! Goblin? If you're hiding, come out. We will not harm you. You have my word."

He waited, but no answer came.

"Well, we had better not let these rabbits go to waste." Jamie held them up, grinning.

He laughed, tension fleeing his shoulders. "We had better not! But first, let's move those reeking bodies, reclaim our arrows, and arm ourselves. I do not like the idea of an unaccounted for goblin lurking about. We can take turns on watch. I will take the first tonight. You may take the second."

They got straight to work, and stinking, disgusting work it was. The bodies reeked of garbage, rot, and dead fish. It was a miserable chore to remove the arrows and clean the guts from them. When they finished, they too smelled of death.

"Gods!" he cursed. "If it was not so dark, I would go find a creek for a bath."

Jamie heartily agreed.

They set about skinning and skewering the rabbits. He tried once more to tempt the goblin out of hiding, keeping his voice lower this time. If it lingered in the area, then it would hear his call. Part of him had a tingling feeling that the creature was watching them from the darkness. "We will share our food with you," he called into the night. "If you come out, I promise we will not harm you. Surely you are hungry."

Still, there was no answer. He shrugged his shoulders. Perhaps it was better this way—more food for the two of them.

He took a whole rabbit to himself and gave Jamie another. They saved the third for breakfast. The excitement of the day had generated an insatiable appetite. When they finished, they both stretched out and lay back to gaze upon the little bits of stars visible from the forest floor. Together they pointed out as many as they recognized.

There was Elduin, the north star, always visible in the north. Then there was Orym and Elmar, two stars that made up points of a bull's horns named Katar, lord of all the bulls. Katar was one of Elduin's guardians. They also spotted Lhoris, Sylvar, and Gaelira, bright lone souls in the vast night sky.

After a time, he heard Jamie's snore and chuckled. The lad had seen enough bloodshed this evening to last him a lifetime. This journey was a good opportunity for Jamie to do some growing up. A young man of nearly twenty should have experiences that shape him. This one had certainly done the trick.

Gods only knew he had experienced his fair share of maturing moments. Memory took him back to his fifteenth name day—the day his father insisted he prove his manhood. He'd been tasked with going into the mountains alone and bringing back meat fit for feeding his family. At that age, the idea of an independent conquest excited him, but it also scared him. He dared not show his father his fear.

"A smart man fears the right things," his father had often said. He knew the forest wasn't one of those things smart men feared, so long as those smart men knew how to behave in a forest. At fifteen, he'd believed himself to be a smart man. He'd even been eager to prove it.

"Once you have returned with a kill worthy of adulthood, you have my blessing to marry," his father had said. "If you come back empty handed, best you not return at all."

Perhaps people brought up in easier circumstances would have considered his father's words harsh. Harsh words were sometimes necessary in life. Harsh words—an even harsher reality. It was what he'd needed at the time. He knew the tricks of hunting in the forest. His father had taught him young, explaining the types of game often found in various regions, and how to kill it. He knew the right berries to eat, and even the right greens, should it be necessary.

Providing was a man's responsibility. He'd never seen it any other way because his father had raised him that way. "Food for the table will always be our duty," his father'd often said. "A woman's lot in life is hard enough. You remember that when you take a wife, *boy*." Many of his father's words had stuck with him throughout life.

As he sat with his father that day receiving his name-day instructions, he'd understood that this was his one chance to prove himself. Besides, he'd had no other choice. Mardra, the beautiful red-headed girl he had been seeing, would not want him if he failed.

It was a rough three days in the mountains. All that he'd been given was a bow and three arrows. He'd been determined to pass this daunting test. On the first night he'd gone hungry. He'd failed to kill the cottontail he had spotted. The second day he'd succeeded with a small one. Famished, he roasted it and ate it immediately. The animal was hardly a worthy token of manhood. No, he wanted something greater. Before nightfall that day, with a full belly, he'd spotted a large buck feeding in a clearing. It was as though the gods themselves placed it there for his taking. The buck's side was exposed, lining him up for a perfect shot. Fate had been in his favor.

The following day, he had returned with a mighty trophy that would feed his family for a month. His father and mother had been proud. Mardra had been even prouder.

One year later, after he had built a home worthy of a wife, he'd married Mardra. He still recalled her gold gown and the way she'd kissed his lips during their ceremony...

He pushed those memories from his mind. She was so much a part of him that it was nearly impossible to ignore the continuous thoughts of her. He saw her face and the faces of his two sons. Images of them writhing in flames plagued his dreams. Dragon fire was horrific. No one deserved to die like that.

Somewhere out there, a goblin lurked. He wished it would come out. Was it watching him from the dark depths of the forest? Waiting for the opportune moment to strike? In truth, part of the reason he wanted to speak with it was because he hoped the wretch would have useful information.

Eventually, his watchful eyes grew heavy. He woke Jamie and instructed him to take the second watch. The lad rubbed his tired eyes and positioned himself next to the fire.

"Keep this sword with you and watch the shadows," he warned. "Do not hesitate to wake me, even if you have the slightest gut feeling that danger lurks. Otherwise, rouse me at dawn."

The lad nodded.

He hardly trusted him, but he badly needed a few hours of rest. He positioned himself comfortably next to the fire then looked at Jamie one last time. "If I catch you sleeping, lad, I will skin you alive." Then he drifted off to sleep.

Jamie woke him just as the sky was turning pink. His stomach grumbled. A night of fighting off goblins had taken its toll. He certainly wasn't as young as he once was.

"In my eyes, you grow more handsome with age." Mardra's words came floating back to him. She was there in the sunrise, in the oranges and reds. He picked out the perfect hue to match her hair. His chest tightened.

"I gathered some wood and got the fire going again."

"There's a good lad," he said, looking Jamie over. "Thank you." To fight off the morning chill, he held his hands over the fire for warmth. Summer was nearly over. Each morning the air grew colder. "How did your watch go?"

"It went well, I think. It was hard to keep my eyes open, but I managed."

"It'll get easier. I find that a little movement and a stretch of the legs often wakes the body." Jamie nodded before layering more wood onto the flames. "I want to get an early start today. We have a lot of ground to make up for."

"I can be ready shortly," Jamie said, and set about packing his things.

They ate their breakfast hurriedly and set off back the way they'd come the previous day. They carried their reclaimed packs, along with all the goblin's weapons. Everything of value was removed from the camp. It was not wise for the lurking leader to raid the camp after they departed. As a result, their load was burdensome, but the precaution was unavoidable.

His anger rose as they retraced their steps. A whole day the little beasts had cost them. Now they were covering this ground for a *third* time.

"Did you hear that?" Jamie stopped and looked around.

"What is it you hear?" he asked, quieting his breaths.

"I swear I heard something—someone following us." The lad glanced over his shoulder, a look of paranoia upon his face. "I think it's the leader."

He studied their surroundings but saw nothing, so they continued onward without interruption. He paid careful attention to the forest sounds as they moved. Though he was probably imagining it, it did seem like they were being followed. But each time he looked over his shoulder, the forest appeared as it ought. They were being overly paranoid, and this was no way to travel.

By midday they were exhausted. They needed baths, too, so

they took a break next to a picturesque creek. They had traveled along it for some time. It was hardly deep enough for washing, but the water would work well to remove some of their stink.

"You go first. I will keep watch," he said to Jamie, who gladly stripped and followed his orders. While the lad bathed, he examined the forest around them. He always kept his ears open for any odd sounds. He heard plenty of them. The occasional snapping of a stick or the crunch of leaves. Perhaps it was only his imagination.

They switched places, with Jamie taking watch. The creek was icy cold but glorious. He felt refreshed once he washed his stink away.

"I have an idea," Jamie told him as he climbed out.

"Go on...?"

Jamie leaned in close and began to whisper a plan. He listened, stroking his shortly trimmed beard as he considered the idea. There were two of them and only one goblin, though it was highly unlikely that the creature would fall for it.

They managed to hunt several birds and rabbits that afternoon. It slowed them down, but they ate well that night. When they were finished, they hung the remaining meat on a line. Jamie volunteered for the first watch, so he found a place to sleep. He kept his bow at his side and closed his eyes, steadying his breathing. After some time, Jamie actually began to snore, but he remained awake and on guard.

As he lay there, he almost laughed at the lad's silly idea. A good deal of time passed, and the moon was halfway across the sky. If the goblin wanted their food, it would have come. A snapping twig silenced the forest. He cracked open an eyelid and looked at the line with the dangling food. Again, he heard a noise—leaves crunching—this time closer.

His fingertips were already touching the bow, but he dared not grab it. Not yet.

Several minutes passed. He almost feared his imagination had run wild until the little wretch emerged. It crawled from the forest foliage, glancing about with caution.

"Well I'll be…" he muttered. Jamie's cool intellect had come in handy after all. They had created the perfect goblin trap.

The line was just out of reach for the little thing, which was surely frustrating. He'd insisted that they hang it at eye level. Given that the creatures stood chest high and had short arms. The poor thing was trying mighty hard to reach the ties.

At that moment he snapped up the bow and took aim. "Do not move, or I'll shoot!" The goblin spun around and gave a little grunt. "I swear it. I will stick you with this arrow right between your eyes."

"No!" it pleaded. "You promise! You promise no harm!"

"That is correct," he said. "I will not harm you if you stay still. One move and you will be dead."

"No dead!" the goblin said, wringing its hands together. "No dead!"

"Fine, then you must agree not to run," he warned. "Do you agree?"

"Agrees!" it howled. "I agrees!"

He looked at Jamie, who was now standing beside him. "Get the rope, lad."

Jamie did as he was instructed, saying to the goblin, "Not so tough now, huh?"

The goblin didn't respond. It merely sank to its knees, defeated.

CHAPTER II

THE MARKET

Kastali Dun

Claire sloppily finished the ties on her gown as a knock came. She wrapped herself in a shawl. "Just a moment," she called, stepping from her dressing area and striding through her suite.

Golden rays of light made sparkling patterns on the floor. It was especially cool this morning, so she kept the doors to her balcony shut. The first day of fall was a little over a week away, bringing them closer to the famed tournament happening in the middle of the season.

She'd heard about it. Each year, competitions took place in the city's arena. The events were open to the public. Most highlighted physical strength and ability, involving things like fighting, archery, and obstacle courses. Celebrations also accompanied the events. But best of all, a fair was set up with booths for merchants and stages for performances—everything from dancers to acrobats. There was sure to be something for everyone.

This year was especially special, because it was a *fifth year*. A ball year. Held right in the heart of the great keep.

She reached for her door only to find—

"Desaree!"

Desaree's chocolate-brown eyes and warm smile greeted her. "Good morning, Lady Claire. I brought your breakfast."

"Oh, come on, Des! None of that *lady* stuff. Just Claire." She led Desaree through her suite.

"Claire it is, then," Desaree said, depositing her breakfast tray on the dining table. She turned, grinning, and said, "I have been waiting for an excuse to come visit you. We hardly get to see each other."

"Why don't you stay and dine with me? We can catch up on everything."

Desaree's eyes glowed. "I'd love to!"

They sat down to a generous breakfast of oatmeal, boiled eggs, fruit, warm spiced bread, honey, and juice. Claire used the opportunity to tell Desaree everything that had happened the day prior, about her lessons and Caterina's threats. Desaree's golden skin lost its color. "Pardon my surprise," she said, "But why aren't you more upset about her threats? That is a serious infraction."

"I..." Claire swallowed. "I know it was inappropriate"

"Inappropriate! Claire, you are a *royal*."

"That didn't stop her."

"None but the king is higher than you. She should have kept her mouth shut. She's lucky there weren't guards around to hear her."

Claire shrugged. "I am sure she will get what's coming... eventually."

"I would not be so sure." Desaree shook her head. "I do not think she has suffered a single consequence of her actions in her entire life."

Claire frowned. "How do you know so much about her?"

Desaree sighed, setting her utensils down. "There is something I should tell you. I...I should have told you before." Claire waited. "When I was younger, Caterina was my stepsister. Judging by your expression, I imagine you are as shocked as Verath was—"

"*Verath knows?*" she shrieked, completely blindsided by the revelation.

"He does now," Desaree said, looking sheepish. "As of recently. Listen, Claire, you need to watch yourself around Caterina. She's dangerous."

"So, wait. If Caterina *was* your step-sister, then Lord Stefan Rosen was...your *stepfather*? I'm struggling to keep up. How did...?"

"It's a long story," Desaree said, her skin flushed. "It was suspicious *and* reckless for Caterina to act the way she did, yesterday. To claim she'd killed before. Because my mother mysteriously died a few years after Stefan married her. That is how I came to be here in the keep. Bad things happen around her. She...she ruined my life... my happiness."

Claire blinked, momentarily stunned to silence. "Are you...are you insinuating that she *killed* your mother?"

"I—I never said that," Desaree quickly said. "It would be a dangerous accusation given that she's a noble and I'm...just a servant. Especially without proof."

"Was there any?"

"Proof? None that I could find—not at the time. I have often wondered..." Desaree's voice grew strained.

"Maybe Caterina is just like her father." Claire gripped her fork harder than necessary. "At any rate, she doesn't deserve to get away with her behavior—any of it. I hate the way she treats you, Des." Her muscles were tight with anger. "She needs to be held accountable. I don't know how I can help, but I will do what I can."

"Thank you. That means a great deal. The gods only know *she* has plenty of supporters..." Desaree sighed and pushed her plate away. "Just promise me you'll be on guard."

"I will watch out for her, I promise."

"If it happens again, tell the king."

Claire nodded, hoping whatever animosity was between her and Caterina would simply fizzle out. Better that, than having to go to Talon with her problems. She'd rather not go to him for anything. Just *thinking* about their encounter last night left her hot and itchy.

Desaree stood to leave. "I wish I had more time with you. This has been too brief."

"Way too brief. Maybe you can deliver my breakfast every morning?" Claire grinned, trying to lighten the mood.

"You may request me. Verath does." The moment the words were out, Desaree's face turned a deep shade of red. She gave a quick curtsey then strode to the door.

"Oh, Des, I almost forgot! Saffra and I are going to the city's market today. Would you like to come along?"

Desaree's face lit up. "I would be delighted to." Then her face fell. "Only, I am not permitted to abandon my daily duties."

"But it's a rest day!"

"Yes, well, I don't always get my rest days to rest. There is always work to be done...as you well know."

"Surely Tess will make an exception? Tell her I insist! If she has a problem with *that*, she can speak with me about it. You're coming, and that's final!"

A slow grin enveloped Desaree's lips. "Very well then. If you will have it no other way, I am sure she'll have no choice but to permit it. When and where should I meet you?"

"The lower courtyard, just inside the portcullis, after the midday meal. If I don't see you there, I will come and find you. There's no getting out of this."

"See you there," Desaree said before taking her leave.

THE AFTERNOON SUNLIGHT was warm and welcome on Claire's skin. She found herself grinning as she and Saffra made their way from the dining hall to the lower courtyard. They were joined shortly thereafter by Verath.

He strode briskly towards them and said, "Good afternoon Lady Claire, Lady Saffra." Of all the king's shields, he was the least familiar. Four additional guards stood at a safe distance. She gave them a strange look. Verath said, "They will be shadowing us to ensure your safety."

"You yourself aren't safety enough?" She raised an eyebrow.

His mouth twitched but he said nothing.

Moments later, Desaree appeared, her skin flushed, eyes darting in Verath's direction.

"I hope Tess didn't give you a hard time?" Claire asked, noting the way her friend had reacted to the shield's presence.

"Not at all," Desaree managed. "Good afternoon, Lady Saffra. Lord Verath." Desaree curtsied and Verath only eyed her, giving a brief nod. His eyes lingered, though, and that made Claire grin. This was going to be the *perfect* opportunity to play matchmaker.

Desaree cleared her throat. "Uhm, shall we get going?"

"Yes! Let's!" Claire linked her arms through theirs, pulling them away from Verath. They burst into a fit of giggles, leaving the shield to trail behind them.

They made their way deep into the city. Saffra and Desaree pointed out various districts and shops, some of which she'd seen with Reyr. Soon, the houses got shabbier. Roads gave way to muddy streets, and each of them had to pick up their skirts to keep from dirtying their gowns. When they reached the market near the docks, she paused to take everything in. The air smelled of brine. Ringing bells mixed with the cries of seagulls and merchants' voices, advertising their wares.

A sea of booths and stalls and tents stretched out before them, crisscrossed with colorful bunting. Almost like a carnival. Food stalls, glass trinket booths selling figurines and jewelry, chandlers with tents full of scented candles, and everything in between. A person could find whatever they wanted in a place like this. She shared a glance with Desaree and Saffra, grinning wide before stepping into the chaos of it.

The crowd swallowed them up like a swift current, sweeping them into the mass of bodies. They were surrounded by a mix of rich and poor, everyone looking to spend their coin. Pickpockets slipped between wealthy patrons, hoping to steal items of value. Personal guards kept their eyes in constant motion, ensuring that their patrons weren't taken advantage of. No wonder the king had insisted on sending skilled chaperones along.

Verath kept an unusually close watch on them, never more than a few steps away, and behind him, the other four. They stepped into a tent selling beautiful shawls. The fabrics were beautiful and luxurious—bright orange silk with embroidered silver flowers, turquoise brocade with diamond-pattern stitching, lavender lace...

They rushed around in a frenzy, admiring the various shawls, trying them on over their gowns. Claire acquired a handful before she realized that the smaller merchants, such as this one, probably didn't use the credit system. Her shoulders dropped. She wasn't going to be able to use the king's account, which meant she had no money—

"Here." Verath stepped up beside her. "This is for you—from the king," he said, handing over a leather pouch. It clinked, full of coins.

An excited shiver raced down her spine. "Thanks!" she said, only to find that Verath had already stepped away.

Saffra had two shawls draped over her arm and was considering a third. Her eyebrows pulled tight as she gazed at the dark green fabric. Desaree stood admiring a shawl she'd been eyeing since their arrival. A robin's-egg blue wrap of lightweight fabric, with little tassels dangling from the ends.

"Oh, Des," she gushed, "that one brings out your beautiful eyes."

"Really?" Desaree turned to her, flushed. "I do love it!" She draped the shawl around herself yet again, turning this way and that in the large mirror. Her smile widened with delight.

"It looks amazing on you. Doesn't it, Saffra?" Claire turned, speaking louder than necessary. She shot a furtive glance in Verath's direction, pleased to see him watching Desaree keenly. When he noticed her scrutiny, his face changed to blank indifference and he turned away.

"It certainly suits her well," Saffra said, coming over to stand with them. "You should get it! Claire and I insist, don't we?"

Claire smiled and nodded. "We do."

She finished picking out the shawls she liked and paid the merchant. Saffra stepped up to do the same. When it was Desaree's turn, the man gave her the total and she gasped. "*Fifteen* silvers? I... Never mind. I changed my mind."

"Very well, miss," the merchant answered, holding out his hand to take the shawl.

Claire stepped forward. "I will get the shawl for her."

"No, Claire. It is fine. I do not need it," Desaree said, trying to appear modest.

"Yes, you do too need it. It looks exceptional on you. I'm getting it. Besides"—she added in a whisper—"it's not my money, it's the king's!"

Desaree's cheeks turned bright pink, but she did not argue. When they finished paying the merchant, they ventured back into the market proudly carrying their wares. She made sure to take note of Verath's overly pleased expression as they set off again.

When she slowed at the next booth, he stepped up beside her. "That was very kind of you—what you did for Desaree. It is a gesture I will not soon forget. You have my thanks." His voice was low to keep from being overheard.

"Desaree deserves the best," she said, looking back at him with a sly smile. "Don't you agree?"

"She certainly does," he answered. "And I intend to see that she gets it."

Her brows lifted. "Then we share a mutual desire?"

"We do."

"Good." She offered him a quick smile before slipping away to rejoin her friends. Desaree had more than just her friends looking out for her. She had Verath, and there was definitely something there between the two of them.

CHAPTER 12
THE WATCHER

Kastali Dun

Eagle stalked Lady Claire and her entourage as they enjoyed the market, keeping a safe distance. She and her ladies strolled from merchant to merchant, browsing goods, giggling and chatting happily. Guards trailed behind, keeping a safe distance. They were far too restless, too observant. The king's shield was the most vigilant of them all.

Side-stepping a puddle, he pulled his wide brimmed hat lower over his eyes. His contractor had not been entirely forthcoming about who she was. Abducting a royal? It wouldn't be easy.

He exhaled, knowing better than to have gotten his hopes up. No matter how badly he wished to be done, to return to the north, he wouldn't capture her today. Instead, he'd use this time wisely, to learn about her.

He continued trailing her, grinding his teeth until a headache formed. His contractor should have been more truthful. He might have been better prepared. Then again, that had been intentional. Eagle never would have taken the job had he known, but...he was here now. He wouldn't waste this opportunity.

It had taken nearly two weeks on horseback to reach the capital. He'd traveled alone, leaving his associates behind, planning to make new connections. His pockets had gold dragons enough for that, thanks to his handsome deposit.

He'd only just arrived yesterday. It had taken no time whatsoever to learn *exactly* who she was. The city was bursting with gossip—how an outsider had come to be royal, a position usually only obtained through blood or marriage.

He'd need a good, solid plan. People he could rely upon. People who weren't worried about getting their hands dirty. He'd spent the previous night moving from one drinking establishment to another. Usually he worked alone, but not this time.

As he kept her in his sights, ignoring the loud sounds of the market, he plotted. He would need a place to work out of, a headquarters of sorts. Somewhere he could stash her after he captured her, just in case leaving immediately wasn't an option. He'd need a way to transport her. A wagon, horses, a few travelers to accompany him. And a cover story. He'd pose as a merchant, departing the city with his wares, back to wherever he'd come from.

Claire smiled, her face lighting up as she stopped to speak with a merchant. His gaze never left her. He swooped towards the nearest stall, showing a great deal of interest in the fruit on display. He selected an apple, paying the merchant two steelies before taking a crisp bite.

Laughter drifted to his ears. He watched from a safe distance as Claire's party entered an especially large merchant's tent. After waiting a few beats, he followed them in. Two of the four armored guards remained stationed outside.

The tent was full of writing supplies. He found quills, ink pots, books—some empty, others filled with writing—stacks of parchment, wax, seals, and the like. Feigning interest in a display of quills on his left, he watched the activity in the tent.

He took another bite of his apple.

Feminine voices drifted towards him as he brushed his fingers over the quills on display. "Tell us again how Commander Daxton proposed? It's such a romantic story," one of the girls said. He sighed. It was all he could do to keep from rolling his eyes.

He felt the shield's gaze linger over him—

"Can I help you, sir?" A voice said behind him.

He turned and came face to face with the merchant. "Greetings." He gave the man a quick bow of his head. "I was wondering about the price of these quills and perhaps an ink pot to go along with them. I have several letters to write."

From his peripherals, he noticed Lady Claire as she made her way towards him. His heart began racing. "Pardon me," she said, reaching around him for a dark brown, feathered quill. Her arm brushed his, but only barely, as the fabric of her gown rubbed against that of his tunic.

 Gods, what if he simply snatched her now? Tossed her over his shoulder and took off with her? Could he evade her guards? Run fast enough to spirit her away?

He almost snorted. She had a drengr in her presence. A *king's shield*, he reminded himself. Lord Verath would use his inhuman speed to catch up, and there'd be no mercy for him after abducting a royal.

Claire paid him little mind as she removed the quill from its holder, studying it. He clenched his jaw and looked away from her. So close yet so far...

"These here are five steelies each," the merchant was saying. "And these on top are of higher quality. Two silvers each. Depending on the ink pot that interests you, they start at a single silver and range up to five silvers for the larger sizes—"

"Pardon me, but why are these more expensive?" Claire interrupted the merchant, pointing to the larger quills.

He looked at her with a wide smile. "My lady," he said, removing one of the more expensive products from its holder and rotating it between his index finger and thumb. "These are made from larger feathers, particularly swan feathers. And they have nib attachments which are gold."

What a *farce!* Who needed a gold nib on a quill?

"Of course," she replied, making a grab for one of the more expensive options. This time he stepped out of her way, moving aside to get a better look at her. She was rather tall for a female.

The top of her head reached his nose. Her hair was golden blond, cascading down her back. The gown she wore must have cost a steep price. It was all frills and fabric.

The merchant eyed her for several moments before turning back to him. Quickly, Eagle removed one of the cheap, black-feathered options, and asked for an ink pot. After paying for both, he retreated from the tent. Spending too much time in the lady's company was dangerous. If he was suspected, his mission would be at an end.

Placing his wares into his satchel, he made his way to a booth across the lane. This one served ale. Stalking was thirsty work, so he ordered a tankard and sat to watch the folks going about their business.

It was a while before Claire and her entourage emerged from the tent. The ladies in attendance were all smiles, chatting enthusiastically and throwing their heads back in laughter. She looked happy. He wondered why his contractor was so interested in abducting her. A secret love interest perhaps? There was no denying her beauty. She had charm. Given her rise to fame, it seemed a likely scenario.

He turned his thoughts elsewhere. Like every job, it was not his business to meddle. He'd killed many without a second thought. Asking questions was dangerous—it could get him into trouble. A man needed to make a living, so he completed his missions without hesitation. As long as there was gold enough to pay him, there was work enough to be done.

His scrutiny followed her until Claire rounded a bend and continued out of sight. He was unable to do anything just yet. But, if it came down to it, sneaking into the keep might be his only option. For now, he would bide his time.

CHAPTER 13
SECRET MISSION

Kastali Dun

Reyr hurried through the city on foot. He could have flown, but walking felt good. It allowed him to soak in the sights and smells, the chaos all around him. Gave him time to think. To ruminate over Claire's dreams.

She'd been sneaking into Kane's mind, enough to fool her into thinking she was turning into him. Sharing his thoughts and desires. He didn't like seeing her distraught over it. Perhaps if they found an explanation, it would put her at ease.

The bells grew louder. Kastali Dun's port was monstrously large, sprawling along the bay. As usual, it was a frenzy of activity. Dockhands loaded and unloaded cargo, carting goods about, calling out instructions to each other.

He set off in search of the dockmaster. He found him overseeing a batch of cargo in massive crates. He cupped his hands and called, "Master Arden!"

Arden whirled and spotted him, rushing across the maze of docks. They grasped forearms. "My Lord Reyr! I was wondering when you would be back. Looking for news?"

"Good to see you. And yes."

"Come! Let us speak in private." Master Arden led him through the hustle and bustle.

"How fares your wife?" Reyr asked.

"Better 'n ever. She's due by the next full moon." Arden's voice reflected his excitement. This would be their fourth child.

Arden was a tall, lean man with a grizzly beard and sparkling brown eyes. His forehead had deep-set lines, his skin looked like tanned leather from years in the sun, and though he wasn't much older than forty, he looked closer to fifty.

They entered the dockmaster's office and settled at his desk. Arden reached for two cups and a bottle of amber liquor. He poured them generous amounts.

Reyr sipped his, letting the smokey liquid roll over his tongue. He swallowed and said, "Good stuff."

"Indeed." Arden smiled wide. "Now, I have a guess as to why you're here."

Reyr nodded. "Have you any updates for me?"

"Aye. Preparations are well underway," Arden said, swirling the contents in his cup before taking a swig. "After we last spoke, I selected my best merchant captain. We can rely on him for discretion, I promise you that. He insisted the mission be carried out with his current crew, so I allowed it. Could be dangerous, and he'll need men he can trust."

"Good. When did he depart?"

"Little over a week ago. I s'pect he should be at the destination sometime in the next week, collecting the...cargo. After that, he will be havin' a dangerous journey home."

"Because of the pirate attacks?"

"Aye."

"Tell me," Reyr prompted.

Arden hesitated before saying, "It's getting bad, Lord Reyr. Real bad. I consulted all the records"—he pointed over his shoulder at a case filled with rolls of parchment—"and there's only a few mentions of pirate attacks at this frequency, this destructive."

Reyr took a deep inhale. "Any idea who's behind them? Could it be Kane?"

Arden shrugged. "I might have a guess or two. There was a reference I found dating back some forty thousand years past. Just before King Gallant and Queen Lena, when pirates attacked up and down the coastline."

"Huh." Reyr rubbed the stubble along his jaw. "Go on."

"Turns out the attacks were all driven by Oshea. Greed most likely."

"Oshea?" His brows lifted.

"Like I said, Lord Reyr. I ain't got solid proof, just records to go on. They may be driven by the pirates...but it makes me wonder, who's paying them?"

"How bad is it?" He'd need a full report for Talon. Not that he wanted the details. He was almost afraid to know.

"Pretty bad." Arden refilled his cup. "Bad enough that half my ships are fighting sea battles on their voyages. I make sure to send 'em out well-armed."

He swore. "Those are bad odds, Master Arden. Chances are, our sea captain is going to encounter some problems on his journey home, especially if word gets out about what he is carrying. Who did you send, by the way?" He knew nothing of Dragonwall's merchant captains. He had met a fair few in his day but he rarely remembered their names.

"Captain Bennett. He ain't got no surname that I know of, so for most, he just goes by Bennett. I trust him more than any o' the others. If pirates attack, he'll know what to do. I warned him o' such. It wouldn't be his first time, either."

"Fine. And how long, by your calculations, until we can expect this cargo?"

"If all goes well...?" Arden fell silent for several moments before saying, "Two—three weeks, if the sea gods are good to us."

REYR LEFT MASTER ARDEN'S office with more concerns than when he'd arrived. There was just enough time to visit Claire—if he hurried. *"May I drop by for a few minutes?"* he asked.

There was a slight pause before her response came. *"Sure."*

This time he did not bother walking. He jumped into the air and transformed. It took less than two minutes for his wings to take him up and over the city. He few around to the keep's back face, to Claire's terraced balcony, and descended towards it. Her doors were thrown open to allow the sea breeze entry. He transformed and landed on human feet. "Knock-knock," he called before striding through the open doors.

His appearance was met with a clatter and a screech. Claire and Saffra were at the table, drinking tea. Saffra's teacup lay shattered on the floor. Saffra glared at him. Claire, however, looked less than surprised.

He grinned. "Forgive the sudden intrusion, ladies. I did not intend to frighten you."

"You did not frighten me Lord Reyr, you merely surprised me," Saffra said. She bent to repair her cup.

"Wait!" Claire said, grabbing Saffra's wrist. "Can I try? I've not yet mended anything."

Reyr watched this exchange, hiding his amusement.

"Good idea." Saffra smiled. "There are several ways to mend broken items. The easiest—place your hand over the shards and say, *malí gler ahlasem.*"

"Malí gler ahlasem," Claire said, repeating the words. As she spoke, her face contorted with disgust. "It just seems so..."

"You will get used to it," Saffra assured her. "Learning the language is hard for everyone."

Claire did not appear convinced. Nevertheless, she held her hand over the shards and repeated the words. The pieces reassembled, leaving the perfectly formed teacup behind. Claire studied it until she was satisfied, then handed it back to Saffra. After that, she slumped back against her chair, groaning loudly. "I *hate* magic."

"Oh, come now, you will get the hang of it," Saffra said, encouraging her.

Reyr pulled up a chair. "It seems your lessons are going well."

Claire huffed. "I'm not so sure. Like I said, I hate magic. The words are so...wrong. They feel *wrong.*"

He tilted his head, uncertain.

Saffra said, "To what do we owe the pleasure, Lord Reyr?"

"I had hoped to speak with Lady Claire regarding some interesting theories I had about her dreams. Perhaps some privacy, if you wouldn't mind?"

"Oh, it's okay." Claire put her hand on his forearm. The long sleeves of his tunic had been rolled to the elbow, so he felt her warm skin against his. He immediately tensed, taken aback by her touch. She pulled her hand away and awkwardly said, "Uhm. Saffra already knows about my dreams." She then looked away from him, her cheeks flushing a slight pink. "I would like her to stay. I'm sure she would be interested to hear your theories."

Reyr hesitated, glancing at Saffra before he nodded. His mind replayed the feeling of Claire's skin against his. He tried to forget the sensation. Tried, and failed. "Well, I've been thinking, and I believe that seeing inside of Kane's mind has something to do with Cyrus."

Claire offered him a disappointed look. "I thought we already discussed that possibility."

"We did, more or less. But what I mean is, Cyrus left remnants behind when he broke into Kane's mind. Back in the forest, he overpowered Kane. Ultimately—he beat him. That's how he saw Kane's plans."

"Right..." Claire continued to gaze at him, frowning.

"What if some of Cyrus's connective threads remained?" Reyr didn't know a whole lot about mind bending, but this theory felt right.

"Hmm..." Claire chewed on her lower lip. "So you think that by beating Kane, Cyrus formed some sort of permanent connection? I suppose it is plausible." She fell silent, thoughtful, then cried, "I've got it! Cyrus became a permanent master of Kane's mind. Now that he shares my mind, I have access to that same connection."

She looked both excited and relieved.

"Did Cyrus just tell you that?" he asked.

"Yep." She nodded. "Convenient...sometimes."

Reyr smiled.

"So...I'm not *really* becoming like Kane. I was...well, never mind."

He stared at her, wondering what she'd been about to say. When she remained silent, he turned to Saffra. "What are *your* thoughts on the matter? You have had more experience with Cyrus and his abilities than any of us."

"Cyrus once said that in order to enter my mind, he had to establish a connection. Maybe you are right. Maybe Cyrus is connected to Kane."

"Do you realize what this means?" Claire whispered. She looked between them.

Reyr frowned. "I cannot say. I certainly do not think it is good for you to be connected to such a twisted creature."

"No! That isn't what I meant. I saw him hiding the dragon-stones—the blue one and the green. What if...?" Her eyes were very round now. "What if I can figure out where he hid them based on what I saw? What if we can get them!"

"Gods, Claire!," Saffra said, equally as excited. "We could steal them right out from under his nose!"

"We can find each one without Kane knowing!" Claire said.

"Think of how surprised he would be to realize they are all gone," Saffra added, grinning widely.

"Without the stones, he won't be able to feed from the power of possessing them." Claire looked victorious.

"Then you will have a better chance at defeating him!" Saffra cried. The moment the words were out, her hand flew to her mouth. She looked over at Reyr and her eyes widened.

He lifted his hands to bring their excitement down. "Let's not run away with ourselves. Claire is *not* going to defeat Kane. There is no way anyone would allow her to place herself in that kind of danger."

"You—you are correct, Lord Reyr. I was...I merely got excited." Saffra pressed her palms against her flushed cheeks. After a brief pause, she began fussing with her teacup.

"Kane aside," he said, "I think you are both right about the stones. By winning them back, we place ourselves at an advantage."

He waited for a response but none came. Both Claire and Saffra had grown overly quiet now. They quickly glanced at each other. What were they hiding?

"Goodness me," Claire cried in a high pitched voice. She turned to look outside. Yes, she was definitely hiding something. "If we don't get going, we are going to miss dinner."

He snorted. Now he knew for certain. Gods, the woman loved secrets.

"Yes, we had better get going." He refrained from saying anything more about his suspicions as he stood. The three of them left Claire's quarters. He'd get the truth one way or another. He had to. Because whatever secret she was hiding, he did not have a good feeling about it.

CHAPTER 14
JOURNEY TO REDPORT

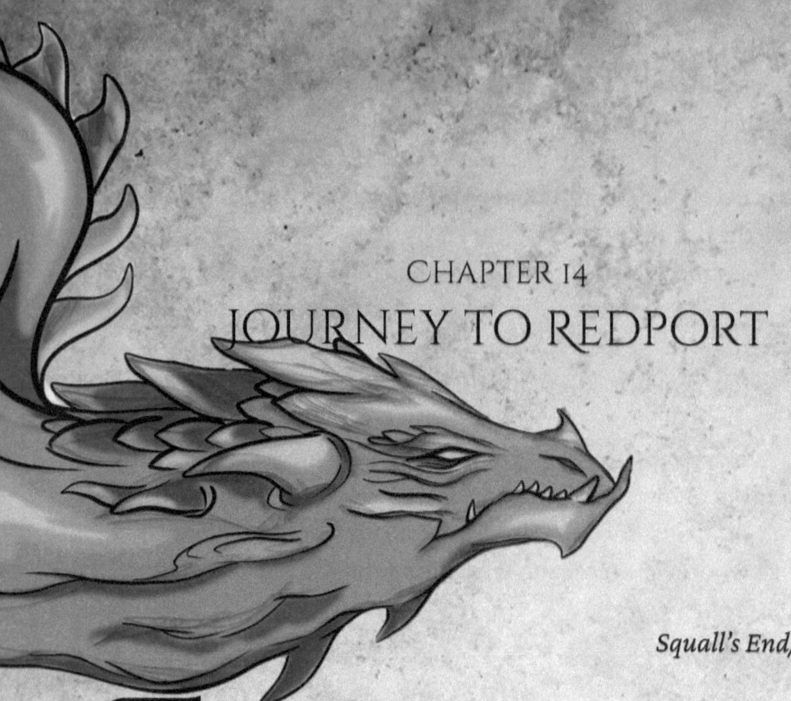

Tamara stood alone, waiting anxiously in the corridor. She shuffled her weight from foot to foot. She'd pictured it so many times—flying on the back of a dragon. Today, that dream was coming true, soured by the price of seeing her family. By the dread pooling in her belly.

She hadn't seen them since the night of the search, just before she'd run away. Now it was time to make peace with them. She heaved a sigh.

The fort leaders' door opened; people began filing out. Wing-leaders and wing-seconds, mostly, finished with their meeting. They were in the middle of preparations for the conclave Fort Squall would be hosting, bringing representatives from all four forts together to discuss the current state of matters.

She chewed on the inside of her cheek. Perhaps it was selfish that she wasn't more worried. That she was so wrapped up in discovering her mate bond, her mood tended towards happy more often than not. People were dying, and here she was, dreaming of flying, worried about what her family would do—

"You look well today, Tamara." Lord Davi appeared before her, hand in hand with Emmy.

"Oh!" She composed her thoughts and immediately dropped into a curtsey.

"Are you ready for your journey?" Emmy asked. "It is a fine day for flying."

She lifted her chin. "Yes. I believe I am."

Lady Emmy sighed. "If only we could join you." She planted a quick kiss on Davi's cheek and added, "I must be away, my love. Duties await. Take care of my son, Tamara, and have a good trip."

Lord Davi watched her depart, his gaze tender.

Byron emerged into the corridor. She heard him before she saw him. He quickly grasped arms with his fellow wing-second, bidding him farewell. His eyes fell upon her and he said, "There you are." Her belly bottomed out, nerves ratcheting up a notch. He came beside her, placing a hand against her back, leaning in to plant a kiss on her forehead. Her skin flushed hot at the gesture. Gods!

Davi cleared his throat. "Have a safe journey, you two." He gave them a brief nod and departed.

Suddenly, the corridor was empty and they were very much alone.

Byron took Tamara's hand in his, lifting it to kiss her palm. His eyes were trained on hers, and the intensity of them stilled her heart. Each breath was a struggle. Was it just her? Did others go to pieces when paid this kind of attention?

"Still brooding about your family?"

"No. Why would I be?" Her voice sounded a little *too* defiant. She had spent the better part of the day wrapped in anxiety, filled with apprehension about her decision. Yet, things seemed better now with Byron here.

He studied her a moment longer then said, "Good," and gave her hand a little tug, setting them in motion. They headed for the open courtyard beyond. "Have you packed everything you wish to bring?"

She nodded.

"Very well. I only need to grab a few things."

They crossed the open courtyard and arrived at Byron's quarters. In a matter of minutes, she found herself within. Curious, she wandered around the space, looking over his possessions. He gathered up what he needed, stowing it in a travel pack.

His accommodations, while not overly generous, were tidy. Almost too tidy. She was tempted to set something off kilter.

Upon one wall there were shelves of books and other knickknacks. She picked up a small dragon, no larger than the palm of her hand. It was carved from blue stone, nearly an exact replica of his dragon form. The blue was slightly darker than his scales, but everything else, from the neck spikes down to the arrowhead tail, was identical.

It was beautiful—

"A gift from my uncle." Byron's lips nearly brushed her ear when he spoke, sending shivers across her skin. He stood just behind her. How long had he been watching her?

He lifted the dragon from her hands and gently placed it back on the shelves, perfectly straight as it had been before. Yes, he was definitely tidy.

"I've only ever seen my reflection in water. Is...is it a true likeness?"

"Yes," she whispered, suddenly caught within the intimacy of the moment. She could feel the heat radiating off him, smell the sharp scent of his aftershave, mixed with something...other. Something draconic—smoke and earth and life.

"Uncle Reyr carved it for me after my first transformation."

"How old were you?" She whirled to look at his face.

"Fourteen." He cleared his throat then stepped away to finish packing. She wanted to reach for him, to pull him back, to reclaim the heat she'd felt, but kept her arm at her side.

Perusing his bookshelves, she asked, "Have you read all of these?"

"I have."

She ran her fingers over the bindings. She recognized several of their titles. *Beyond the Dragonfire Sea.* A very worn copy of— "*Sir*

Galadhal's Fables! This was one of my favorites as a child." She removed the copy before thinking better of it. The pages were in a similar condition as the cover. "Its owner has loved it well."

She glanced at Byron. He stood near his bed, fussing with his travel sack. Her gaze snagged on the bed and her skin warmed. It was quite large, far too big for a single person, and covered with plush sleeping furs.

"That is the most precious book I own," Byron said, distracting her with a sheepish smile. "My favorite story was *Lord Bernard and the Red Dragon*."

"Oh!" Her heart fluttered. "Mine too. *Kathika and the Dwarg* would be a close second." She cleared her throat, slipping the copy back on the shelf.

"What about *Redcote the Fox?*"

She huffed. "I loved that one too."

His eyes sparked at her, and heart stopped beneath his gaze. "We should get going," he said, striding across the room with his travel pack. "It is a long journey today."

"Must we really go?" She gave the bookshelf a final glance then turned to him.

"My dear Tamara, why the sudden change of heart?"

She hesitated. "My father—"

"Your father will be happy to see that you are hale, as will the rest of your family."

She bit her tongue to keep from arguing. Instead she simply nodded. He took her hand and led her away as a deep sense of reluctance settled over her.

They went to a grassy courtyard at the edge of the fort, a popular place for pairs to launch into the sky. Sometimes, when she had free time, she came here simply to watch them. Flying fascinated her.

Byron dropped her hand and said, "I had a leather harness made for you. Master Winston, the leather-crafter, placed it upon my back earlier while I was in dragon form. I will be wearing it when I transform." He handed her the pack he carried. "If you wouldn't mind securing this for me?"

"Of...of course."

He hesitated, then frowned. "Is it the sky you fear, or your parents?"

She swallowed against a suddenly dry throat. "Both, I suppose."

He exhaled. "You have nothing to fear, Tamara. No harm will ever come to you in the sky. As far as your parents are concerned, I have already told you, they are eager to see you. Trust me. After the search they conducted for you, it is clear they care for you deeply."

"I hope..."

"Come." He motioned for her to follow him to the center of the grassy area. "I am going to transform. When you next touch me, we will be able to communicate with ease, remember?"

Her belly swooped. She did. Of course she did.

Byron gave her a reassuring smile before transforming. His body grew in size. There was scarcely time to blink before a hulking dragon filled her gaze. His icey blue scales glistened in the sunlight. She blinked, recovering.

Oh—right. She was supposed to be doing something. Standing on her tippy-toes, she tied his travel pack to his harness. She double checked to make sure the straps were tight. They held fast with each tug. Then she moved over to his extended forearm and eyed it.

When she tilted her head back, the dip at his wing joints and neck seemed a long, long way up.

She pressed her hand upon his warm hide, felt the hard, glassy surface of his scales against her skin. As soon as she made physical contact, she felt his easy presence in her mind. It reminded her of how empty she felt when he wasn't there.

"What is the best way to do this?" she asked aloud, hoping he couldn't sense her embarrassment.

Byron gave a draconic chuckle, but there was nothing judgmental about it. Only excitement poured from him. He was thrilled —eager, even—to show her this part of his world. *I recommend placing your dominant foot onto my forearm. From there, you can work your way up my back.*

She listened carefully to each of his instructions. He paired them with images, thoughts that explained what he was saying. When she was ready, she gave it her best effort.

Getting to his forearm was not difficult, but the first time she tried to pull herself into the harness, she failed. Her body slid down his scaly hide, and her feet returned to his forearm.

"It is all right. Try again," he said. *"No one gets it the first time."*

She tried again. Her second attempt was met with success. She managed to place her left foot in the foothold and use it to hoist her body up. From there she swung her right leg over and settled into the harness. The leather under her was lightly padded, not hard like a horse's saddle, though it reminded her of one.

"Well done!" Byron said. *"It will become easier, believe me."*

She settled down and felt the jolt of movement as he stood from his crouched position. He walked several laps around the grass.

"There are straps to hold your legs if you feel uncomfortable. But as I have said, I will do nothing to dislodge you."

In her mind, she told him that she understood.

"Are you ready?" he asked, although he did not wait for an answer. He knew from her thoughts that she was. *"Good. Hold on tight."*

Without further hesitation, Byron's powerful legs and forearms vaulted from the ground. The wind whooshed past her ears. Instinctively, she reached for the straps as the ground shrank away. Her body was heavy; she could hardly keep her head upright.

Her heartbeat roared in her ears. An embarrassing squeal escaped her lips. Instead of fear, all she felt was excitement. Joy. Bliss. Whether Byron's or hers, she didn't know—didn't care.

She grinned, spreading her arms wide. "This is incredible!" she screamed. "I can hardly believe it! I'm flying!"

"I told you, did I not?"

"It's…unbelievable," she whispered, trying to take in every part of the experience.

They were above the fort now, climbing higher into the sky. Byron turned on his wing tip. They circled around the city, taking in a grand view of Squall's End. It was huge—much larger than Redport—stretched out beneath them in miniature. She saw the large town homes, Lord Rahl's castle, the marketplace, the docks, hordes of sailing vessels, and beyond all of that, Stormy Bay.

After completing his flyover, Byron turned northwest and began flapping his blue wings in the direction of Redport, towards her family, towards her old home...

Her heart thudded. Every flap brought her closer to her dread.

"Stop fretting. This journey is important. You cannot start your new life on bad terms with your old one."

She agreed with him, but that did not make it easier.

"Fine. Then let us think of something happier."

"What do you suggest?" she asked.

"How do you like flying?"

He knew the answer before she spoke it. She offered her thoughts anyway. *"It is the best sensation I have ever experienced. It feels like floating, but also like falling."* She admired his powerful wings and the ease at which he controlled them. *"I wish we could spend every day doing this."*

"Soon, we will." She saw his meaning. When they completed their training, they would be assigned to a wing. With their wing-mates, they would patrol the territory. Fort Squall's wings often ranged into the north for weeks at a time, flying by day and camping by night. The adventurous idea thrilled her.

"I wish we could begin training now."

"This, I know."

"Why not start early?"

Byron said nothing in response, but she knew that he was considering the matter. It was unconventional. Still, she hoped she might sway him.

She left him to his thoughts, turning her attention to Stormy Bay. She watched it sail by beneath them. When she began to feel dizzy, she rested her cheek against the warm scales of Byron's neck and shut her eyes, allowing the sensations of flight to take hold.

***

The day passed in a blur. Byron stopped once they reached the other side of the bay so that she could stretch her legs and relieve herself. But for the most part, they stayed in the sky.

The sun had dropped low on the horizon when Redport sprawled beneath them. She gazed upon the city and realized that from the sky, it was hardly familiar. Her father's castle sat near the middle of Redport's epicenter, slightly elevated above everything else. Once more, her stomach gave a tense jolt.

"We will get through this together." Byron made a wide circle around the castle's battlements, looking for a landing place large enough to fit his form. He descended towards an upper courtyard. Surprised cries lifted upward on the wind.

How grand Byron must have looked to the people below! And what would they think when they saw her arriving on his back? He was the son of a fort leader, after all. Lord Reyr's nephew.

"I imagine they will be quite impressed," he chuckled. *"You have done well, capturing such an important drengr for yourself."*

Her face heated and she released a nervous laugh.

Byron landed on all fours, tucking his wings tightly to his body. *"You may dismount now,"* he said. *"Once you have removed my traveling things, I will shift."*

It was common knowledge that when a drengr shifted, whatever was on them at the time stayed with their other half. Their magic made it possible. So, he'd be wearing the same exact clothes from this morning. And when he turned back into a dragon again, the leather harness would remain strapped to his back.

Reluctantly, she dismounted, coming to rest on Byron's extended foreleg. The back of her neck pricked, alerting her to watchful eyes. She tried to be as graceful as possible. Her fingers trembled as she undid the ties holding Byron's traveling pack in place. Then she hopped down to the ground.

Her contact with Byron was broken, his reassuring thoughts swept clean from her mind, making it painfully obvious just how much his strength had helped her. Moments later, his hand found hers. "Just relax," he whispered against her ear. "I am right here."

She swallowed down her nerves and nodded.

"Lady Tamara!" A woman rushed forward. Kenna Josephine. A

relieved breath burst from her lungs, surprising even her. Perhaps she'd missed her old nursemaid more than she'd realized.

Kenna Josephine swept her into her arms, giving her the only hug she had ever received from the woman. She sputtered, then pulled away. The woman was all smiles.

Byron was right there to take her hand again. Others rushed forward to greet them, too. The steward was not far behind. He gave her a warm welcome, a low bow, and informed her that her family was not long behind.

A few moments later, her brothers rushed forward.

Jonah swept her up into a big hug, lifting her off the ground and shaking her before setting her back down. She embraced Daniel and Brandon the same way. Again, Byron reclaimed her hand when she finished saying hello.

"Our own sister! A rider!" Jonah cried. "You must be her mate," he added, appraising Byron.

"Aye, I am." Byron stepped forward to grasp Jonah's forearm. She introduced her three brothers, explaining that Jonah was the eldest, followed by Brandon, who was three years younger, and Daniel, the youngest, only fourteen.

"You gave Mother and Father quite a fright," Jonah explained, lifting his brows. "They searched endlessly when you went missing."

"We all did!" Brandon said. His heated tone did not match the twinkle of his eyes.

"Not I," Daniel said, snorting, as if he knew more than his brothers. "I knew where you were all along. Anyone with a bit of sense would have known you went to Fort Squall."

"Is that so?" Byron asked, curiously eyeing the lad.

"Yes," Daniel said. "I always knew Tamara wanted to be a rider. She never shut up about it."

Byron smiled, looking down at her. Her cheeks flushed from the intensity of his gaze. Her brothers noticed too, eyes darting between them.

"My darling girl!" a woman shouted, rushing forward. Her mother had finally arrived. "Oh, my dear heart!" She threw her arms around Tamara, holding her there, sobbing into Tamara's hair.

"I'm sorry, Mama!" she apologized affectionately. Her mother's tears were contagious. She found herself crying too. Together they wept in each other's arms.

She never would have guessed her mother's touch was so missed until she felt it. It took time for them to calm down, but when they did, she wiped her tears and turned to Byron. "Byron, this is my mother, Lady Astra Redwynn, wife of Lord Aaron Redwynn of Redport."

Speaking of...where was her father? A sinking sensation filled the pit of her stomach. She glanced around, but he was nowhere to be found.

"It is a pleasure to meet you, Lady Redwynn." Byron took her mother's hand and kissed the back of it, honoring her. "We have flown many leagues today. Tamara is both tired and hungry. I hope we may see to her needs?"

Tamara blinked. Byron's request sent warm tingles through her body. That he would put her needs above all else.

"Of course!" Her mother beckoned them into the castle. Byron led her behind her mother. The crowd trailed behind them as everyone, servants and highborns alike, filed into the castle. They had attracted quite a crowd.

"How long will you be with us?" her mother asked.

"Oh... Uhm..."

"We plan to stay a fortnight," Byron said. "We can remain no longer than that."

A fortnight?! She nearly stopped dead in her tracks. She gave him a pleading look, but he ignored it, pulling her along.

"Two weeks?" Lady Redwynn was jubilant. "I did not think I would be so lucky."

I did not think I would be so unlucky, she thought to herself.

They entered the dining hall. Her mother barked orders for the servants, who scurried off to fetch refreshments, then turned, finally taking in her daughter's appearance. "My dear heart, we must use this visit to ensure you have proper attire for the fort. You left all of your beautiful gowns here."

She refrained from rolling her eyes.

They took their seats at the head table. Her brothers sat next to them while her mother bustled about, instructing servants who brought food and drink.

"Where is Father?" she quietly asked Jonah. A strange look passed over his face.

Her mother overheard and said, almost *too* quickly, "Your father has business. He cannot be here at this time."

She saw right through her mother's words. Her father had not wanted to welcome them. It was just as she'd suspected. Knowing that left her feeling the same deep unease that had warned her to stay away. There was no telling what she'd gotten herself into by coming here. Whatever it was, it was too late to turn back now.

CHAPTER 15

A GATHERING OF FORTS

Fort Squall

Davi stood in the corner of the packed conference room, surveying the attendees for their conclave. The space comfortably sat twelve, with its high-backed chairs and mahogany table. There were far more than that in attendance. Fourteen stools were brought in for the remaining drengr and riders.

The crowded chamber was growing more cramped by the minute.

The turnout was both unanticipated and welcome. Representatives from each of the forts were in attendance, including some of the king's own shields. Davi could not have hoped for better, though he wished Reyr had come. His twin brother still owed him a proper visit. His presence would have made everything easier, especially given the state of things.

"My love, we both know he wanted to come," Emmy reminded him.

"I know," he groused, still disappointed.

With each passing day, the city of Squall's End grew more crowded. Refugees from the northern villages were pouring in at an unusual rate. Fear of wild dragons had sent many south. Davi could hardly blame them. These were frightening times.

He gave the chamber's occupants a few more minutes to settle down before taking his position at the head of the room. He cleared his throat. "Thank you all for coming. I know that for many of you, it has been a long journey. You have my gratitude."

Some of the members from Fort Lin and Fort Edge nodded.

"I will not waste your time on small-talk. We are here because wild dragons have invaded our homeland." A few shifted uneasily in their seats. "The purpose of today is simple. We must devise a plan to defeat the beasts. In the meantime, we need to observe protective measures. We need to keep our people, our *kingdom*, safe."

Silence soaked up his words. This meeting should have happened weeks ago. They were running out of time.

"As you've heard, the north is already under attack. Belnesse was the first. There've been several since then, the last of which killed ten of our own. You felt it when they died—the same as I." A room full of grim faces stared back at him. "Aside from these crippling attacks, there are strange rumors in Vestur...rumors of unnatural creatures stalking the land.

"We have sent teams to evaluate these claims and should have answers soon. Closer to home, here at Fort Squall, our infantry have been training twice as long. Our forge fires are lit day and night. They have produced extra weapons, shields, and the like. Our siege masters have successfully mounted dragon-lance throwers on the walls of the city and the fort, should there be a direct assault. The commander has his men working alongside our drengr using iron spearheads on their dragon-lances. Their aim has improved greatly. The only problem is, we need ice metal if we want to pierce dragon scales."

The room erupted into murmurs.

"Finally, we have our infantry training in combat against our drengr. We must prepare for the possibility that they will be forced to fight wild dragons on the battlefield. Unfortunately, we all know the likelihood of human survival in such a scenario. Our infantry stand little chance should dragons take the fight to them. We must hope they remain in the skies. That is where *we* come in. That is where we must defeat them."

He looked around the room, making eye contact with several of the representatives from Fort Kastali. They had already started training for a sky battle.

"Today, We're joined by two of the king's closest." He nodded respectfully at King Talon's Shields. "I am told by Lords Jovari and Koldis that new tactics have been implemented over the skies of Kastali Dun. I believe each of our forts should follow suit. Our pairs need practice with aerial combat." After a long pause, he added, "This war is coming, whether we like it or not."

There were several murmurs of agreement.

"Now, enough talking on my part. Let us begin this discussion. Everyone has a voice. I want to know your thoughts on the matter. But understand this, we are not leaving here without a plan of action. Our serving staff is on standby with food and drink, should it be needed."

He pulled up the single remaining stool and sat down. As he did, his gaze circled the room, looking from drengr to rider. All were reticent, but not because they were shy or reserved. He understood that their silence was a result of helplessness. They were at a loss.

"Well?" Davi looked around the table. "Has a wraith got your tongues?! Speak up."

Zarel, one of the wing-leaders from Fort Edge, was the first to talk. "What does the king say on the matter?"

"King Talon has many things to say on the matter," Koldis answered, shifting in his seat. "You will have to be more specific." He appeared rather bored, evidenced by the sarcasm in his voice. Zarel didn't seem to notice. Thank the gods. Today was not the day for petty bickering against old rivals. Koldis and Zarel had known each other for a long time.

"How does the king expect us to *prepare?*" Zarel clarified. "What precautions would he like us to take?"

Jovari said, "The king expects each fort to train in the same way as Fort Kastali. Everyone needs adequate experience in aerial combat. More detailed information will be relayed in writing to each of you. Also, regarding the safety of the people, sweeps should be conducted more frequently and in larger groups. If you wish, you may assign pairs to temporary stations in larger cities. This might ward off possible dragon attacks and discourage another case like the *Belnesse Massacre*. It will also allow for relay communication."

"Do we know what kind of numbers the enemy has?" someone asked. Davi looked around to see whom.

"Very little is known," Jovari said. "The king's prophetess saw over one hundred in her vision. A single witness also confirmed the number."

"What about Kane?" Shaila, a Rider from Fort Lin, asked. "Is it true that he flies with the wild dragons?"

"How do we know what Kane is planning?" Carith added. He was Shaila's mate.

"Short of seizing the dragonstones and wreaking havoc on Dragonwall, we do not know exactly what else Kane is planning. We know that the dragons answer to him, but I believe they also have a clan leader. It is likely that this leader answers to Kane—"

"All the clans had leaders, did they not?"

"That is correct," Davi said. "Assuming—"

"Have any of you addressed the *real* problem?" A commanding voice silenced everyone. Davi knew it belonged to Lord Avraean, the only fort leader in attendance aside from himself. Lord Avraean was over eight hundred years of age, and far wiser than most. Not to mention, he had witnessed a great deal in his lifetime living so far south before moving so far north.

Avraean continued, "How, in the name of all the gods are we supposed to kill these beasts? They're fire resistant, just like us. It seems we are equally matched. Short of scratching their eyes out, which would simply heal, how do you propose we stop them?" Fort Edge's leader looked around the room. His eyes settled on Davi's.

There was a prevailing stillness. No one spoke a word. As far as Davi knew, no solution existed.

"Ice metal and poison." Everyone turned to Koldis. "Ice Metal in its purest form, laced with poison. That is how we will defeat them."

Whispers broke out around the room. Even Avraean was taken aback. The king indeed had a trick or two up his sleeve. Thank the gods. It was brilliant.

"Brilliant and dangerous," Emmy said. He felt her apprehension. Their bond connected them such that they shared minds, feelings, and thoughts.

"Ice metal in its purest form—not mixed with steel like our sveraks—will be strong enough to pierce dragon scales," Jovari said. "The poison will ensure they die a quick death."

"True poison, poison capable of exacting a quick death, is made with dark magic, is it not?" Emmy asked.

"It is," Koldis said.

"It may be the only way," Avraean told everyone, quickly jumping on board with the idea.

"For now, it is the best we have," Jovari said. "As you all know, ice metal is hard to come by, but the king has a massive shipment heading down to the ports of Kastali Dun, from the dwargs."

"And the poison?" someone asked.

"The mages are already brewing cauldrons of the stuff in the capital. In secret, of course—"

"It should be coming here," Davi said, interrupting. "It should *all* be coming here. Squall's End and Fort Edge are the first line of defense, but we are not ready. Should there be an attack tomorrow, we will fall."

"Be that as it may, I am told the ship has already set sail for Kastali Dun. The matter can be taken up with King Talon as soon as we return."

Davi rocked his jaw side to side, trying to calm his ire. If Reyr were here—

"Peace, my love. They are doing their best."

"Very well," Davi said, giving Jovari a compliant bow of his head. "Please see that the matter is attended to with haste."

"Davi, I have plenty of connections with the dwargs," Avraean said. "I will see to the purchase of any available ice metal from the mines north of my fort. We have coffers enough for that. I will gladly send a portion of it over."

"Our forges stand at the ready," Davi said. "My blacksmiths will attend to it the moment it arrives, though some will need proper training for such a material. There are few who know how to adequately deal with it."

Lord Avraean gave him a brief nod and then turned to the shields. "Please have your mages send their recipes to ours, so that we may brew our own poison. We must act quickly, lest we be taken unawares."

"Understood. Consider it done," Koldis said. "I will see to it as soon as this meeting adjourns."

Unfortunately, the meeting did not adjourn until much later that day. Hours were spent discussing strategies. Ideas were tossed around and solutions proposed. But, by the end of it, Davi had something to hope for.

DINNER WAS A BOISTEROUS AFFAIR. The dining hall was packed with visitors. Minstrels sat in the corner strumming instruments. Wine kegs emptied. Voices grew louder. Soon it was difficult to hear one's own conversation. Under any other circumstances, he would not have allowed the indulgence, but everyone needed a distraction.

The head table was not large. It seated only six. King Talon's two shields sat on Emmy's right while Lord Avraean and his rider, Evelyn, sat on Davi's left. Those of the highest status sat up near the front of the hall, while occupants of lower distinction sat farther away. The servants attended too, sitting closest to the door.

"I am happy our discussions went well," Evelyn mused in an off-hand way.

"Aye," Avraean said, affording her a tender glance. After a thoughtful pause, he began again, keeping his voice low. "I would like to add, Lord Davi, that defense should not be our only focus.

Have you given any consideration to our other options? Looking for allies, perhaps?"

"Aye, I have," Davi said. "Now that our strategy is shaping up, I am inclined to think beyond."

"I thought so," Avraean said, almost whispering. "I had hoped we might see eye-to-eye. If you ask me, we need to find out where this sorcerer is hiding, perhaps even visit the dwargs while we're at it."

"I agree. What have you in mind?"

"If we can get a small party to track the dragons back to their source, we may be able to suss out his hiding place. Could work to our advantage if ever we take an offensive stance.

"Is it safe to assume that if we find the dragons, we find Kane?" Davi asked.

"I think that's a safe bet," Avraean said. "And I think I know where to find them. When word of Belnesse reached Fort Edge, I was certain the dragons came from the mountains. It is the only way, the only possible way the beasts could go undetected. I went deep into the library. As you know, ours is the oldest of the forts, founded by King Eymar himself. I found geographical maps of the Northern Barrier Ranges. Our teams once explored far north, back when we had more dealings with the dwargs, thousands of years ago. I found one in particular dating back to the year two thousand of the third age—"

"Truly?" Davi's eyes rounded.

"Aye. The ink has faded with time, but not entirely. The date was clear. I noticed one stark difference upon the old scroll." Avraean paused to drink from his goblet. "There are three ancient fortresses listed. All three belonged to the Ice Clan, that much is certain."

"You think Kane is using one of them?"

Avraean chuckled. "That, too, was my question. I looked at the locations of all three. Initially I thought each might be a possibility. I ruled out two—Darknest and Forsaken Hold—based on their location with respect to Belnesse. The third however, Shadowkeep, has caught my attention."

"Please tell me you brought these mysterious maps with you?" Davi asked, his voice falling to a hush.

Avraean gave him a triumphant smile. "Aye, I have brought them. I think it is time you and I had a private chat. Perhaps it is time to arrange an expedition."

Davi couldn't have agreed more.

CHAPTER 16

WOMANHOOD

Redport

Tamara looked with wide eyes between her bloodied bedsheets and her handmaiden, Leena. "You've nothing to be ashamed of, my lady," Leena said. "'Tis only a bit of blood."

Ashamed?! She could care less about shame. What was she to make of this disgusting mess? And the pain! Surely something was wrong with her insides, for it to feel like *this*.

It was still dawn. Leena had roused her just moments before. She'd been able to tell something wasn't right, even then, but it hadn't been until Leena helped her out of bed that the dull ache in her belly intensified. She hunched over and took several gasps of air. Seeing the mess only made the situation worse.

"Why didn't my mother warn me it would be like this?" she groaned. A painful spasm ripped at her belly. Her fingernails dug into the bed's bannister for support.

"Mothers often make light of the situation," Leena tsked. "They do not wish to frighten their beloved daughters."

"Well!" She took a steadying breath. "I promise you, I am frightened now!"

"Come now, my lady. This is a part of becoming a woman. You will get used to it. For most, the pain only lasts a few days."

"A few…" She groaned, hunching over further, clutching her belly.

"Your mother will be so pleased to hear the news. I shall go and fetch her."

She considered stopping her, arguing against her departure. She did not want to be alone. But perhaps having her mother here was for the best.

Leena was halfway across the room when her door opened. Byron stood in the doorway. His gaze took in Tamara's doubled-over posture and widened. "What is going on here?!" he demanded, striding forward.

It didn't matter that she felt like dying, she wished a pit in the floor would open right up and swallow her. The bloodied mess was unmistakable. "What are you…you cannot be here!" she hissed through clenched teeth.

"I sensed your distress and came at once." His brow furrowed.

"You should not see me like this. Please…go!"

"But you are in pain." Byron hesitated, blinked, then looked at her handmaiden and said, "She has reached her womanhood."

Not a question.

Still, Leena said, "Aye, sire."

"Byron, go!" Tamara pointed at the door.

He did not move.

"I will fetch your mother now, my lady." Leena rushed from the room, making matters far worse. Now she was alone with her mate. Her heart pounded against her chest and her breathing turned rapid. Gods, how utterly embarrassing.

Byron took several steps towards her. She held out her hand to stop him from coming any closer. When she noticed that her hand was bloodied, she swore under her breath and hid it behind her back. "Please," she whispered, putting her forehead against the cool wood of the bed's bannister. She closed her eyes and clenched her jaw, biting hard on her teeth. "I will be fine. I…I am told that this is perfectly normal."

"Normal? Seeing you this frantic is not normal. Blood is not foreign to me, Tamara. You need not be abashed."

"My word!" Lady Redwynn's cry silenced everything. Thank the gods! She'd never been so happy to see her as she was now. "Lord Byron," her mother said, "this is *not* the time for a visit. You must leave at once! Leena, bring Josephine and fetch some fresh bedding. I daresay you know how to handle this. Go quickly."

She exhaled, all her relief infused in that one breath. Her eyes remained closed. She felt her mother's cool hands upon her face, comforting her. When at last she lifted her head and opened her eyes, Byron was no longer there.

"Come now, a bath will be drawn. You must be rid of this sleeping gown. Take it off while your bath is prepared."

Several servants filed in behind Leena and Kenna Josephine—she thanked the gods that they were all female. The ladies chatted happily, as if this was a joyous occasion. It most certainly was not!

It took some time to get cleaned up. She felt much better after the hot bath they had drawn. It helped to ease her belly pain and relax her muscles.

"I am afraid the pains will come and go," her mother said. "Sometimes they will be short, and other times longer. I found that for me, they grew worse after having children, but everyone is different." None of this was reassuring. "Here. Drink this. It will ease your pain."

She was handed a cup of hot tea. "What is it?"

"Aegan leaf, made into tea. Drink it when the blood comes. It will help. It is expensive, so use it sparingly. I have placed a small pouch on your bedside table."

She did as she was told and drank the whole cup. Within minutes, the pain disappeared, and she felt much better. The only thing the aegan didn't do was eliminate her blood. She felt disgusted with herself. How could she possibly stay clean under such circumstances? And this was to happen monthly?!

The women spent most of the morning in her room, instructing her on how best to handle these monthly nuisances. She was thankful that they had so much good advice to offer up. For the time being, layers of linen cloths were used beneath her gown, and she was ordered to bed rest for the remainder of the day. No complaints were given, as she had little interest in leaving her room anyway.

***

She didn't see Byron again until later that evening, right around suppertime. Leena permitted him entry, departing to give them privacy. He rushed to her side, fussing over her. "I'm sorry I was short with you this morning," she said, feeling only a thimble of guilt.

"It was my fault for barging in on such a private moment," he assured her. "I admit, it was selfish of me. I understand that reaching your womanhood is a turning point in your life—a *female* affair. I only wanted to ensure that you were well. Keeping you safe is the greatest responsibility I will ever bear."

Her skin flooded with heat and she turned her gaze away.

The servants brought up enough supper for two. She was happy to have him all to herself. For a little while, they ate in silence. Then, she said, "Have you seen much of my father today?"

He set his plate aside and said, "I have. Why?"

"He still avoids me."

It was an understatement. In fact, in all the time since her arrival, he hadn't spoken a single word to her.

"Your father has been cordial with me," he assured her. "In fact, when I spoke to him today, he requested our company in four days' time. He wishes for a private meeting."

She frowned.

"Perhaps it is nothing—perhaps it is something. I cannot be sure as of yet, but I will look into the matter. You are right though, it seems as if your father is avoiding you."

"Which is why I find it odd he's requesting a private meeting, don't you?"

Byron frowned. "Perhaps he wishes to make peace with you."

She offered Byron a slow smile. She wanted to believe him, to adopt his optimism. "I hope you are right. Unfortunately, where my father is concerned, I have nothing but distrust." She shook her head, her feelings souring. "Today would have been a glad day for him—me reaching my womanhood. He will never forgive me for weaseling out of his grand plan. To think"—she closed her eyes, picturing the path her life might have taken—"I might have been planning my wedding now..." Her heart raced for several moments. She felt a warm touch upon her hand and opened her eyes to Byron. In that moment, everything she felt, changed. Her emotions were soothed, her heartbeat slowed, she relaxed.

"Your bravery saved us. Lord Rhal would have whisked you away to live forever in his castle as his lady. It is not a bad position—though it is not a position meant for you. I imagine many maidens would gladly take up such a life."

"Not this one." She shook her head as she thought of the women who would be happy as Lord Rhal's lady. "I am not like them..." she said at last. "My purpose is not to sit and look pretty. I do not wish for a life of begetting children to ensure that my lord's legacy will win out."

Byron frowned, hesitating before he asked, "And what of *my* legacy?"

Her eyes widened. "I did not..."

"You do not wish to have my child?" His voice was low, surprised.

"I did not mean it like that." She looked away from him as she picked at the embroidery on the bedspread.

"My family's line is an ancient one, and I am the last living heir. Reyr will never have children. As you know, only one child is born..."

She was well aware of Queen Isabella's Price—disgusted by it, even. How could she deny Byron a child? She gazed up at him, intent on making this known. "For you, Byron, I will take pride in bearing a child."

Byron studied her a moment longer before his face relaxed.

Her chamber door opened and her mother entered, several handmaidens in tow. They sent Byron on his way. Supper dishes were cleared away, and Tamara was prepared for bed. Her mother fussed over her, as she had done since her arrival. She tolerated the attention, knowing it would be a long time before she saw her mother again.

"Mother, might I ask you something?"

"Anything, dear heart." Her mother helped her with the remainder of her nightgown, and then helped her back into bed.

"Jonah once told me, when I was younger, that you nearly died giving birth to me. Is that true?"

After a brief silence, her mother answered. "It is true. You were the most difficult to bring into this world. But how I longed for a baby girl, and how I rejoiced when you were born. Perhaps such gladness brought me back from the brink of death. I cannot say."

"I fear the idea of having children. I fear death and—"

"You would be silly not to fear, my dear child, to some extent. But the gods made us for such a purpose. Asjaa smiles upon you. But do not fear needlessly. The act itself is painful, yes, but it is the most beautiful event you will ever experience. Besides, once you are a rider, you will not be as weak as humans are. You will have Byron's strength."

"I do not think I wish to have children, but I could not bring myself to say it to Byron. I know he longs for an heir."

Her mother chuckled. "I daresay you will not have much of a choice in the matter, my dear. When you love a man, as you will love Byron, making such a choice does not come easily. While there are magical remedies to keep a woman barren, I doubt the magic of the drengr will allow outside forces to interfere with fate."

"Oh...I had not thought about that." Once again, she inwardly cursed herself for being so oblivious.

"I suppose I sheltered you far too much, but I had hoped to explain things like this to you before your wedding day. I admit that the manner of explanation was not as I had hoped. Now, to bed. You have had a taxing day."

Her mother bid her goodnight, and at last she was left alone. As she lay beneath the covers she imagined many things, including what it might be like to make love to Byron. In the darkness, she decided that perhaps a small child in the likeness of her mate was a thing she could cherish rather than fear. With Byron, fear was more difficult. Perhaps once they shared minds, there would be no need for it. She smiled at the thought, then drifted off to sleep.

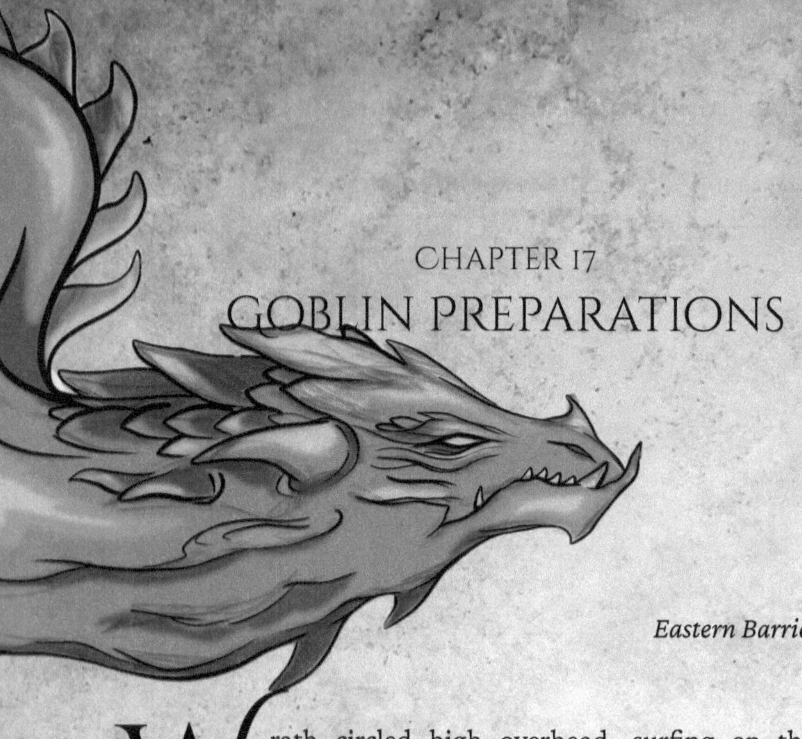

CHAPTER 17

GOBLIN PREPARATIONS

Eastern Barrier Range

Wrath circled high overhead, surfing on the wind currents, letting his crimson wings stretch to their full length. Below, hordes of nasty green goblins assembled in packs. Wretched, disgusting things, goblins. He resisted the temptation to bathe them in his flame.

They were camped below in the forest awaiting Kane's orders. Soon, they would march on Dragonwall. He secretly hoped they would all die in the process.

Long ago, when his ancestors first conquered these lands, goblins had hunted dragons. They stalked them in their lairs, trying to locate their caches of gold and precious jewels. People had believed dragons to be greedy creatures, but goblins were just as greedy, if not greedier.

Despite their frequent raids, they'd never had much luck in besting his kind. Their stench was often warning enough. If not that, then their stupidity did the rest.

Once Dragonwall finally belonged to him, he'd slaughter every last one of the little nuisances.

Besides, it wasn't as if Kane cared one way or the other. He cared for nothing beyond his own desires. Except, perhaps, the stones, which he coveted.

Wrath snorted. For too long he had stooped low, agreeing to work with the sorcerer to achieve his own means. He would play along for now, but Kane's games were getting old. It was only a matter of time before the sorcerer met his end.

His sharp eyes looked below as he circled yet again. Kane stood among the goblins, bargaining. It was taking some time. Not that he minded. Carrying the asarlaí was heavy work. After a week of it, his wings felt much better free of the added weight, so did his mind. With no one else for company in the sky, Kane often wanted his thoughts on attack strategies. He was careful not to share much. Kane was, ultimately, his enemy.

He turned on his wing-tip, making another circuit. At least here, the stench from below didn't reach him. Small mercies...

He recalled the stories of his forefathers, when he'd been a young hatchling. Stories of the ruthlessness of goblins, of their greed. It was one thing to seek wealth for political reasons, for need, but to desire riches simply for the joy of hoarding? That was pure folly. What good was treasure if never spent?

Selfish creatures.

He entered a bank of clouds. The cool mist sizzled against his burning scales. Too much time had passed since his last attack upon Dragonwall. The pent-up fire in his belly would not hold forever. He longed to return to his clan. He ached for battle, which would soon come. Fort Squall would stand no chance against his mighty force. His fires were hot enough to melt the city, to kill its people. He could cut off the entire north from the south, if he wanted.

He imagined the attack upon the fort, rumbling with glee as he pictured his force sweeping in and taking the fort's drengr unaware. They wouldn't even see them coming. But only if his planning played out properly.

For now, he would bide his time. The goblins had been ordered to make the first move against the kingdom. They would begin their attacks on the eastern part of Dragonwall, in Austar. Its unsuspecting inhabitants would have their hands full. Simultaneously, ships would increase their attacks upon the coast. Dragonwall would be struck from all sides.

Once the north was cut off, his clan would take control. They would force the people of the north to swear allegiance to Kane. From there, they would begin their assault upon the South.

"Negotiations are complete." Kane's voice was an unwelcome intrusion into his contemplations. *"The goblins will begin their strike at dawn, the day after tomorrow."* Kane's thoughts were laced with excitement.

"Good. May we leave?" He was eager to be away.

"We may."

He turned on his wingtip and returned. He had flown much farther from the goblin army than intended. When he landed in the forest clearing, his nose was met with the all too familiar stench of rotting filth.

Kane spent several minutes longer in discussions with a commander before making his way over to climb upon his back.

"I cannot stand the smell of them," he complained.

"Neither can I," Kane said, *"but we need them."*

Just as Kane needed *him*. Just as *he* needed Kane. But that would not last forever. As soon as he had the opportunity to turn on the sorcerer, he would. His powerful legs and forearms launched from the ground, sending them high into the air, and they were off.

CHAPTER 18

PIRATES ATTACK

Dragonfire Sea

Bennett was called from his slumber by a loud trumpet blast. Another sounded immediately thereafter. At the third, he hoisted his lanky frame from his cot and reached for his pants, scrambling to do up the ties.

One blast meant land lay ahead. Two signaled the approach of another ship. Three calls of the trumpet meant only one thing— "Pirates, Captain Bennett! Pirates!" His cabin boy shouted through the locked door, banging his fist upon it.

"Gods above!" he swore as he pulled on his boots and fastened his belt, which contained his sword and other personal items.

Beaky squawked sleepily from her perch, protesting against the interruption to her sleep. The damn bird slept too much. "Let's go, ya bleary-eyed bird." He tapped his shoulder and Beaky gave another protest before spreading her wings and flapping into position. She was aging. Then again, he wasn't exactly in the prime of his youth, either. Birds like her lived a few decades. He'd been a young lad when he found her in the southlands, on the islands of the *Great Delta*. She was only a hatchling then and had since become his companion. At times, she was a downright nuisance. It didn't help that she picked up far too many words. When she began mouthing off, the name *Beaky* had stuck.

With Beaky on his shoulder, he rushed to the deck above. His first mate met him, ready with an update. "Two pirate ships, Captain. George spotted 'em from the nest. They came upon us quick. Lorchas from the looks of it. Fast ones, at that."

"*Pirates! Pirates!*" Beaky repeated in her high-pitched voice.

His first mate led him to the poop deck, talking all the while. "The wind is in our favor, Captain Bennett, but with sails let, we're maxed out at six knots. These pirates though, these are doing eight at least." Jonah handed over the spyglass.

Taking the scope, he held it to his eye and had a good, long look. There were indeed two lorchas, the pirate ship of choice in these parts. Lorchas were speedy by nature, depending on the cargo they carried. In this instance, his own cargo greatly weighed down his vessel. His ship, the *Lady Faith*, was one of the fastest in the merchant fleet. Unfortunately, *Lady Faith's* precious goods weren't doing them any favors. "Sink me! It's too soon for this!"

"*Sink me! Sink me! Sink me!*"

"Quiet, Beaky!" He gave Beaky's head a pat and returned the spyglass. "There is no escaping them, Jonah. If they get close enough to use their rams, our voyage will be at an end. That being said, if they are after us for our cargo, they would not dare sink us. No...they'll want to board us and kill every last man. Then they gain a ship and her cargo."

Jonah shook his head in disbelief. "Perhaps we can use the oars to outrun them? Perhaps we might make it to the nearest port?"

"No, that's doubtful. At their speed, they will run us down long before that."

They'd been at sea a mere six days after departing Port Ice. He'd known there would be problems on the journey back to Kastali Dun, but he hadn't anticipated them this soon. He swore under his breath. One of the damned dwargs must have let it slip. Like it or not, disaster was upon them. Fortunately, this wasn't his first sticky situation.

"Jonah, we must prepare for the worst."

"*Prepare for the worst. Prepare for the worst,*" Beaky began to chant. They both ignored her.

"I agree. What'll ya have me do?" Jonah rolled up the sleeves of his tunic.

"Send the rowers below deck—arm 'em first, mind you."

"It'll be done."

"Right now, we need all the speed we can get. I'll steer us towards Stormy Bay, and in the meantime, I already have a plan brewing."

Jonah nodded and left him. Bennett moved away from the ship's rear. From his position, he had a good view of the crew. Already the rowers were passing around weapons and making for the oars below deck.

He cupped his hands around his mouth. "Ho! Men of the *Lady Faith*!" he called. "Pirates be upon us!"

"*Pirates! Pirates!*" came the bird's rejoinder.

"I chose you to accompany me on this voyage for a reason. Every one of you likes a good fight, and every one of you does it well. You're the best damned seamen the seas have ever seen. Every one of ya's stood true before the mast."

Cries of "Aye" and "Too right," echoed through them.

"These pirates will give us no quarter. They will try to board us with the intention to kill. We got mouths of our own to feed, so we will do the same. No hostages." His crew echoed their agreement.

Sweat beaded his brow, making his palms sweaty. The lorchas were getting frighteningly close.

"Arm yourselves!" he shouted. "We cannot be taken. Dragonwall's very existence depends on it. Today, Válkar rules in our favor, and Asjaa watches over our souls. Pray to Hafunger if you must. Perhaps our sea god will hear us." He paused to take a breath then added, "Bowmen, report to me! The rest of you, step to!"

"*Man your stations...Man your stations...*"

The deck erupted into organized chaos as men jumped into action, rushing around to their positions as several others distributed weapons. The eight bowmen—guards he had brought for this very purpose—were making their way up the ladders to the poop deck. They assembled before him.

"I began this mission with the intention of keeping it secret. Not a single one of my crew knew the purpose of this journey when we set out. Well, damn it all to hell! Thank the gods I brought you." He looked at each of them, sizing them up, looking for signs of fear—there was none. "I know there are few of you, but even the smallest numbers can count for many."

"Aye," they said in unison.

"Separate yourselves—longbows here, and you four, there." He pointed and coached, getting his longbow men into position, followed by his archers. The longbowmen had the most important job as they would act first. Once all of his archers were in position, he went to each group and relayed his intentions, detailing his plan.

The *Lady Faith's* oars extended from both sides of the vessel, paddling with heavy strokes. Little good the rowing did. The lorchas tailing them also utilized the same tactics, and they were gaining at a rapid rate.

"Remember my instructions," Bennett added, turning to the longbowmen beside him. "We must wait until they are within range. If we fire too soon, our plan will be obvious."

"Understood, Captain Bennett."

He did not remove his gaze from the approaching vessels. The unease of his men radiated outward as they all watched in silence. It didn't matter that they were good fighters. For many, this wasn't their first time dealing with pirates, but it was their first time dealing with two boats' worth.

A deathly calm permeated the air, making each creak and groan from the *Lady Faith's* woodwork shriek. Even Beaky was as quiet as the dead. Waiting...

The lorchas put space between them, with the intention of bracketing the *Lady Faith*. "Strike the sails!" he called. They needed the speed of the sails, but the last thing he wanted was his own plan used against him. His deckhands burst into motion, handling the ropes and pulleys with deft ease. As soon as the job was finished, they slowed a great deal, bringing the pirates right up behind them. The men on the enemy decks became visible—

"Light your arrows." Bennett's voice was quiet. With extreme caution, the longbowmen nocked arrows and lit them in the cast-iron fire pit. It was dangerous to bring fire on deck. Even now, if their ship rocked too violently, the pit could overturn, igniting the deck.

The longbowmen were quick to draw. "Fire!" he hissed. Several gasps from his own crew rent the silence as four flaming arrows shot through the air. None of his men expected this tactic. Two arrows hit the left lorcha's foremost sails, and the other two hit the right lorcha's foremost sails. To his great luck, the arrows each stuck in the cloth. Immediately a crackling sound met his ears as the flames took to the fabric and the fire spread. Once more, the longbowmen reloaded and took aim.

These lorchas had three sails each. With a few more flaming arrows, the task was done. They quickly tossed the cast-iron pits into the sea.

The pirates began shouting orders, running around their decks, climbing the masts, attempting to extinguish the flames. It was a great distraction, for without their sails, their lorchas would lose speed.

His own men shared quiet smiles of relief as they waited silently. Unfortunately, the battle was not yet won. Already, the pirate ships were nearly close enough for the grapples.

"Withdraw the oars," he said loud enough for Jonah to hear him below. The oars would splinter and break once the pirate ships were beside them. Like all orders, this one was echoed among several loud voices that carried it throughout.

"*Burn in flames. Burn in flames. Pull the oars. Pull the oars.*" Beaky squawked with agitation.

"Arrows!" Someone warned.

A stream of arrows caught his attention, whizzing through the air before they hit the deck. Several of his men called out in alarm. Three of his own collapsed. "They are readying the grapples,"

George shouted from the crow's nest. The lookout trumpet sounded in warning.

"Prepare to be boarded," he commanded. "Thomas, Aaron, Peter!" he called, getting their attention. "Cut every damned grapple you see on the starboard side. I want them cut the moment they hold. Regan, James, you handle the port side."

"Aye, aye, Captain." Peter grabbed Aaron and Thomas, making for the right side, as Regan and James headed for the left, their swords at the ready.

Grapples flew over the railing from both sides. After that, pirates began pouring onto the *Lady Faith*'s deck.

Bennett looked at his archers. "Do not hit any of our men," he warned. "I want every damned pirate who touches the wood of my ship *dead*." With that, he bounded over the railing and descended the ladder to assist with cutting the grapples away.

It was a mess of shouts and chaos.

Clanging swords, shouts, flying arrows. He made his way along the port side, cutting every grapple he saw. They were far outnumbered, but his crew would never back down. Knowing that did a number on his pride.

His oarsmen poured onto the deck from below. Their assistance couldn't have come at a better time. They threw themselves into the foray, swords lifted, faces lit with determination.

"The grapples are cut on our side, Captain." Peter rushed to him a few minutes later, breathless. Shortly after, the ropes on the right were cut too.

"Set the sails," he shouted, his impatience growing.

"Set the sails!" His first mate cried the command even louder than he. Those men who could afford to dodge combat, jumped into their positions.

He aided where he could—bringing down pirate after pirate—darting between them with his own sword raised. Several of his prized ropes of hair were cut off by his attackers. He let out his anger on every godsdamned pirate that got in his way. Beaky had already taken flight as she circled the ship, squawking and squeaking insults, "*Nasty pirates. Burn them. Filthy pirates!*" Every so often she dove, to claw out enemy eyes.

The sails were unfurled to catch the wind. Bennett hoped that the pirates were occupied enough to forget his fire trick. As the sails fell into place, Asjaa must have answered his prayers for speed. A huge gust of wind, unnatural in strength, struck the sails. He thanked Asjaa, he thanked Válkar, he thanked Hafunger, he thanked every godsdamned god he could think of. Hopefully they were saved from this mess.

"We need more grappling hooks!" he heard an enemy pirate captain shout. The accent was rough—different. His ears perked up at the sound of it, recognizing it. "Hurry up you scoundrels!" They were definitely not from Dragonwall.

The *Lady Faith* caught the wind. With most of the pirates otherwise engaged, there were few to follow the enemy captain's command. However, several new grapples flew over the railing. He sprinted to them, hacking at each rope as it took hold. They were nearly a full ship's length ahead of the two lorchas, whose flaming sails were all but shreds. In fact, the fire had spread to their masts, but the pirates were too distracted to notice.

"They are getting away, you sons of whores!" one of the pirates shouted from the enemy ship.

He spotted a particularly large pirate as he cut down two of his crew. He dodged and thrust his sword at the man, attempting to take him out. The brute managed to slice his arm wide open, but he hardly felt it. The rage of battle was coursing through his body.

Just in time, an arrow struck the brute right in his heart. He fell upon the ground. Bennett glanced up at the poop deck where his archers stood. One saluted him before nocking another arrow. He gave the man a quick nod of thanks and moved on to the next pirate. Still more pirates came.

Did it ever end?

He looked around, surprised by what he saw. The *Lady Faith* was well away from the two lorchas, whose oars were extended as they rapidly paddled to catch up. That was never going to happen.

Without their sails the pirate ships had no hope of gaining on the *Lady Faith*. Not now.

But...there was still the matter of pirates on board his own vessel. Their numbers were dwindling, but his men were growing tired. Growing sloppy. He moved through the mess, stabbing several pirates in the back.

"All available oarsmen below!" he called when he felt they could be spared. Only a handful of men rushed below. Moments later, they began picking up more speed.

It took nearly an hour to eliminate the remaining pirates onboard. When they did, his crew still had the strength to give up shouts of victory. "Hip-hip-hurray!" they repeated, aided by Beaky, who joined her voice with theirs. She circled above the masts where she sought refuge.

"Well done!" he shouted at the top of his lungs. "Well done indeed! Tonight, we celebrate our victory! Rum for all!"

The pirate ships were shrinking from view. There might be more, he had no doubt of that. It was imperative he get his wounded men the treatment they needed. It would delay their arrival to Kastali Dun, but if he didn't, they might never arrive.

He had the pirates' dead bodies mercilessly thrown overboard. His own fallen men were wrapped in cloth and given a respectful burial—a traditional sea burial. Each was sent below with their most prized possessions and words of recognition. It was a sad time for them. They lost too many friends.

"What now, Captain?" Jonah asked loud enough for the remainder of his crew to hear.

"We make for Stormy Bay, to the port of Squall's End." He saw several of his men nod in agreement. "I must get word to the drengr—to Lord Davi—that our cargo is no longer safe."

The secret was out. They could no longer rely on stealth to get them where they needed to go.

CHAPTER 19

REYR'S PAST

Kastali Dun

Reyr hesitated at Claire's door. It was midafternoon, and he had just come from Fort Kastali. His muscles were still tense. It had been another day of drills, and yet another reminder of how unprepared they were for an aerial attack.

He knocked, then entered without waiting—

"I'm beginning to think you're doing that on purpose," Claire said, eyeing him from the sofa.

The fireplace beside her was empty, so he went to the grate and threw several logs in before starting a fire. Then he collected himself and turned to her, taking note of her mussed hair and drowsy expression. "Napping again?" he teased. "You've been sleeping a lot these days."

She scoffed. "We both know why."

"Your magic is still troubling you? Has there been no improvement?"

She sighed. "Improvement, yes. It isn't as bad as it was, but I still feel tired. But that's not what's bothering me."

"The magic still feels wrong?" he asked. She confirmed with a nod. "What's there to feel wrong about? You simply speak the words and command what you will."

"Easy for you to say," she groused.

"Perhaps you just need to get used to the language." He took a seat opposite her and leaned back, stretching his arm over the top of the sofa.

She rolled her eyes. "I wouldn't expect *you* to understand. You're old. You've been using the language for a long time."

He chuckled. The rumble in his chest sounded more draconic than anything. "I will have you know that I am young by common drengr standards."

"And how *old* would that be?"

"Hm. I seem to have forgotten. Perhaps I lost count..." The corner of his mouth twitched. She stared at him, waiting. "Oh, all right. I'm three hundred and seventy-nine years old. Four years younger than King Talon, if you must know."

Her jaw dropped. He lifted his brows. "Is this how you reacted when Cyrus told you his age?"

"Pretty much." She shut her mouth. He realized he'd been staring at her lips for far too long. He looked away and silence fell between them.

She'd made changes to her living space, made it more her own. The furniture had been rearranged, with several gowns and other clothing items draped across the backs of chairs. He almost chuckled. Most women in her position had handmaidens or ladies-in-waiting to clean up after them. Perhaps he ought to speak to the king about getting her some help.

He cleared his throat. "Aside from your lessons, how are you doing with all else? Are you adjusting? Are you happy?"

"I suppose. As happy as I *can* be in this kind of a situation."

He regarded her, trying to read beyond her words. "What about your rocky relationship with King Talon? Any luck on that front?" She snorted and rolled her eyes. "Fine. I'll take that as a *no*."

"Every time we speak—which is rare, mind you—we argue."

"Have you not spoken since that last time?"

She scoffed and said, "Nope," popping the *p* at the end. "It's like he doesn't know how to hold a decent conversation. He's always so awkward and quick to anger."

"How about I tell you a little secret?"

Her eyebrows rose and she leaned forward. "What kind of secret?"

"One about King Talon." Something like eager desire flashed in the depths of her gaze. "Our dear king is terrible at conversing with women, specifically the single, pretty ones. He's been that way for a long, long time. It is not you, or anything you have done."

"Is it because of his scars?"

"In a way, yes. He lost a lot more than his vanity that day—the day he got his scars."

"What happened?" She frowned, her brows pulling tight.

He opened his mouth, then hesitated. Her question left his insides squirming, but he said, "War. War happened."

Gemma's death was directly tied to the war. Talking about one meant talking about the other. But he wasn't a coward. He told her about the great battle to end all battles. How everyone flew north to defend the kingdom against the Kalds. How many lives were lost and the toll it took.

"When King Talon saw his parents fall," he explained, "he went straight for the giant who'd killed them. The fight lasted well into the night, or so I am told."

"Weren't you there?"

A familiar pain squeezed his chest. "I was there, but I was only half there. That was the day I lost Gemma."

Claire's lips parted. "She died in battle?"

He gave a curt nod. "The lucky ones were those who died *with* their mates. Cyrus and I? We were forced to endure without our other halves. To know love, but be forced to live without it, is the cruelest trick that the gods have ever played upon my soul."

Her eyes welled with glittering tears. "Reyr, that's...that's terrible. I'm so sorry."

He ran a hand through his golden hair, unsure if her tears—welling up on his behalf—pleased him or made things worse. It was obvious that she cared for him, yes. But, was he selfish to wish she cared as more than a friend?

He cleared his throat. "No need to apologize. It is in the past."

Perhaps he shouldn't have said anything.

"What about King Talon?" she asked, her voice husky with emotion. "Did he defeat their leader?"

"Obviously, but at a great cost."

"His scars? That's how he got them? The ice giant?"

"Aye. Black rock ice can be lethal in the same way poison from a vodar's blade is. It burns what it touches. Fortunately, it does not spread."

"I never...I guess I grew so used to seeing him with scars that I never thought about it. Drengr are self-healing. Your scars are supposed to heal under normal circumstances. My wound from the vodar never fully healed because of poison, so it makes sense about his scars. I should have realized." She sighed. "What a terrible thing to endure, and in the wake of seeing his parents die. It's...kind of sad, actually. I might even feel a little bad for him now."

"I once told you that King Talon has suffered more hardships than most. Now you understand."

"Is that why he never, you know, found his mate? Because of his scars?"

He snorted. "No. He failed for other reasons. There are no scars, no matter how deep, no matter how devastating, that can defeat the kind of love shared between mates. Talon simply did not find her. Or perhaps she never existed. Some of us are just unlucky, I suppose. It is rare, but it happens."

"The idea of mates is so...I don't know...romantic?" Her voice came out soft. "One soul exists in the world for each drengr, and the two of you are meant to be together forever. It almost sounds too much like a fairytale to be true."

"You mean, it almost sounds like *magic*?" he teased. "A drengr's mate—a thing of fate. Every drengr knows the words."

"Was that how it was for you and Gemma?" As soon as the question was out, her eyes widened. "No—I'm sorry. I shouldn't have brought her up again. I know it hurts you to talk about her."

"It is all right. I can tell you if you like. It is a much happier story than the one of her death."

She hesitated, then nodded, pulling her legs up beneath her as if preparing herself for a great tale. He supposed it *was* a great tale, the story of their love, or a good one, at the least. He delved back hundreds of years, into the midst of his memory. There he saw it in his mind's eye. "It was the perfect day outside," he began. "I was in the market with King Talon when I spotted her."

"Wait, you and Talon were hanging out? But weren't you really young then? How long have you known each other?"

"Our whole lives." They'd been friends since childhood, their parents being who they were. As they grew into adolescents and then young males, they often visited each other. "The prince was an incorrigible flirt and found it easier to bed women outside of the watchful eyes of his parents. Which was why he often visited Fort Squall."

"You're kidding?! King Talon? A womanizer? I thought you said he didn't know how to talk to women?"

"In those days he did, believe me. The market at Squall's End was his favorite place to meet lovers. King Tallek and Queen Ahlessa hated it when he behaved like that. He was Dragonwall's prince, and as such, he was supposed to possess dignity and self-control. He was lacking in both, but...he was young."

Claire stared at him in disbelief.

"Fate was in my favor that day when I spotted Gemma—when *we* spotted her. The sunlight fell upon her just so. It was as if the gods illuminated her for our notice. Or perhaps it was divine fate. Talon knew immediately that he wanted her. In fact, he took off to speak to her without saying a word to me. Just left me standing there. But I knew what would happen if he reached her; once a woman caught the prince's eye, he pursued her to no end, and they rarely refused him. For the first time, I was jealous and overprotective. Angry, even. I stopped him—*restrained* him."

"Did he get mad?"

"No. He found it amusing." A chuckle burst from Reyr, recalling that day. "He was surprised that I took such an interest. 'Well, this is a first,' he said. 'By all means, my friend, let us see your charm.' Perhaps he found my sudden regard for her amusing. He allowed me to take the lead. In truth, I was too fearful to speak to her. I was no Prince of Dragonwall, like Talon. And I was too much a coward to put myself in her path."

"Because she was your mate?"

"I certainly didn't know it at the moment."

He remembered everything from that day. The scent of meat pies and perfumes wafting through the air. The dazzling sunlight. The cool, crisp air. The slight breeze. His desperation to know the young woman who'd instantly consumed his curiosity. "Talon followed me as I followed Gemma through the market. I watched her from afar as she went from booth to booth. Gods! How beautiful she looked with each smile she paid the merchants, and each time she spoke, each time she laughed...I wanted those smiles on me, for myself."

Claire grinned.

"When it appeared that she was leaving, Talon gave me a rough shove between my shoulders. I think he was trying to tell me that if I did not go after her, I was going to lose my opportunity. He would have picked up where I left off, so I mustered my courage and introduced myself."

"What—what happened next?"

"Well, she must have sensed Talon and I for what we were."

"That you were drengr?"

He laughed. "No. Lustful troublemakers. She was smarter than that. She refused my invitation for a walk. It wasn't until I watched her walking away from us that I knew she'd be mine some day."

"But eventually, you won her heart?"

"Oh yes. I won her heart...among other things." He grinned.

Claire burst into laughter. Then they both began laughing, until tears streamed from his eyes and his ribs hurt.

"What was she like?" Claire asked after they'd calmed down.

He got up and went to her wine cabinet, pouring a goblet to take the edge off. "Gemma was quite intelligent as far as most go.

Women of this world are not like those of yours. They do not go to...what did you call it?"

"School?"

"Yes, that is it. A place of learning. Most live at home with their families performing domestic duties. They don't read or write. They are content to find husbands and bring children into the world—not that there's anything wrong with that. It's simply how life is, here. Anyway, with Gemma, there always seemed to be some private joke lurking behind her eyes. She was headstrong and persistent. She was also incredibly stubborn and argumentative. I learned to concede to her in all things."

"As you should!"

"As I should," he agreed. He leaned against the wine cabinet to regard her. Gods, she reminded him so much of Gemma. As if sensing his thoughts, her face flushed and she looked away.

"Anyway," he said, "we spent many happy years together." He turned his back to her then and poured an additional goblet, which he took over to her. He sat back down and took several large sips.

"How long did the two of you have before...?"

"Forty-five years, and glorious years they were. When she was taken from me, I wanted to turn my back upon the world and find some way to die."

"Why—why didn't you? What kept you here? What kept you fighting?"

"King Talon."

"Oh." Her eyes widened.

"It was my love for Talon and our enduring friendship that kept me rooted to this world. I believed that by serving him, by helping him overcome his adversity, I would find a way to heal my own sorrow. How wrong I was. Gemma will always be a part of me the way stars belong to the sky. I must go on without her, forever alone."

"Sometimes we don't know how strong we are until we are forced to be. I'm glad you kept fighting, Reyr. The world is a better place with you in it."

His chest tightened. The way she looked at him—as if he meant something to her—was too much. "Maybe you're right, maybe you're not." He shook his head. "Sometimes I curse my stupid self for choosing to serve the king. Most days I wish I would have died with Gemma. And then there are days that go by, especially now that the years have passed, where I find myself passing each minute without a single thought of her."

"Time heals wounds."

He shook his head. "Not this kind of wound. And not now that *you* are here. The two of you are too much alike." He regretted the words almost immediately. Especially when a look of understanding crossed Claire's features. Godsdamn it. Knocking back the remainder of his wine, he stood. "I think I ought to go. See you at dinner." He strode across the room.

"Reyr…" There was a hesitance in her voice, even regret.

He kept his back to her, unable to turn around. Instead of waiting to see what she might say, he didn't. With every bit of self-control he possessed, he opened her door and walked out, closing it behind him. He never wanted to speak of these things again.

CHAPTER 20

STORMY BAY

Stormy Bay

Bennett paid no heed to the angry sky. Normally the weather had a greater effect on him. He was a seafaring man after all, but today, he was too focused on getting to shore. He kept his attention on the task at hand. The port of Squall's End stretched out before the *Lady Faith*. It was a grand sight to any man of the sea eager for the comforts of land: a good washing, strong spirits, hearty grub, tavern wenches, and a soft bed. The bay waters were full of ships today—barges laden with grain and fish, cogs with their sails furled, and even a few hulks to ferry passengers about the bay.

Familiar sounds carried out over the water. Ringing bells on the docks, clanging as they bobbed back and forth. People shouting as they loaded and unloaded their wares. Cawing from the ever-present seagulls, swooping beneath the clouds.

Since the pirate attack, three of his injured had died. They hadn't been fast enough. Now, his first matter of business was to entrust those in need of care to the healers. It would cost him a fortune, servicing their wounds, but he would pay it.

"Ready to go ashore, Captain?" His first mate gazed at him with eager eyes.

"Aye."

Very carefully, the injured men were hoisted down into the ship's rowboats. Some were well enough to climb the ladder, others had to be lowered, moaning with each movement of the ropes. Only when they were comfortably set did he follow them into the small boats. The remainder of the crew was ordered to guard the cargo.

The water on the bay was choppy today. The wind whipped about them, but it was nothing a good seafaring man couldn't handle. It took them some time to get their little boats to the docks. As they finished securing them, a dock master appeared. It started to rain. "Where is your captain?" he asked, a pompous air of authority obvious in his voice.

Bennett took a deep breath. With all the patience he could muster, he said, "Yer lookin' at him." He refrained from saying *boy* even though the dock manager looked green as grass.

"Ship name, please?"

"*Lady Faith.*"

The young man pulled out his ledger, which immediately began absorbing water droplets. "Oh, drat this rain! Let us get under shelter where I can do this properly." He stuffed the ledger back into his coat.

They rushed over the wooden planking and found cover beneath a warehouse awning. Bennett instructed Jonah to take the wounded directly to the town's healers. The dock manager looked as though he might protest. All men coming and going were to be documented in the ledgers before entering the city.

Bennett shoved a gold dragon into his gloved hand. "I will handle the business with you, let them be."

The man gave him a nod and began scribbling. "Reason for port?"

He exhaled. This was always a pain. Ports kept records of everything to cover their backs, should suspicious persons enter their cities. They also tracked the cargo and goods that entered within their domain. He was not going to divulge the details of what he was carrying.

All in all, it took longer than he wished, but at last, he finished running through names and reasons for entry—which were entirely made up—and was free to enter the city.

He found himself trudging through the streets of Squall's End, his rubber boots splashing through every puddle as he made his way towards the other side of the city. When he reached its edge and exited its walls, Fort Squall dominated his view. It was a sight to see. Its massive walls rose above the marshlands surrounding much of Squall's End. If he squinted, he could discern men standing upon the battlements.

He scanned the skies. Every so often he caught a flash of color as drengr swooped beneath the clouds or descended down to the fort. Dragons always made him uneasy.

He crossed the grass pasture that separated the fort from the city. When he reached the fort's gates, he was a sopping mess. But he was a man of the sea—a little water never frightened him—so he tolerated it as best he could.

"Who are you and what business have you?" a guard shouted above the rain.

"I am Captain Bennett. I have urgent business with Lord Davi. Can you tell 'em I am here?"

The soldier looked skeptical as he shared a nervous glance with his comrade. No doubt Bennett looked very much like a vagabond. "Very well," the soldier said. "I will be back shortly."

Shortly, it seemed, was greatly optimistic. The guard returned nearly three-quarters of an hour later. Patience was already a fragile thing, and he was not adept at waiting around.

"I am sorry, sir, but Lord Davi is unable to see you at this time."

In his frustration, he released a string of foul words.

The soldier cut him off mid-sentence. "He did say that he is willing to meet with you first thing in the morning. Is this favorable, Captain Bennett?"

"It'll have ta be, then. I'll be back tomorrow." There was no hiding his irritation as he turned away from the gate.

At least it wasn't raining anymore.

When he re-entered the city, he noticed that the city folk were making their way back outside. He asked a few passersby for directions to the healers and then made his way there.

"That was speedy!" Jonah's spirits seemed improved. The land often did that for a sailor. "How fared your meeting with Lord Davi?"

"There was no blasted meeting," he growled. "I'm ta see him first thing in the morning."

"Well, that's good, isn't it? At least he'll see ya. I don't imagine he knows who you are, how important your mission is, or what cargo is carried by the Lady."

"You are likely correct. It was my understanding that the king hadn't planned on telling more than those directly involved. I wonder, will Lord Davi be happy or not when I tell him what lies just outside his fort? And how will he react to my request?"

"Let us hope he is reasonable." Jonah leaned against the building behind him, arms crossed with ease.

"How goes it in there?" Bennett pointed at the healers' building.

"Goes well, I'd say." Jonah pushed himself away from the wall and moved forward. "There's nothing we can do for the moment. The healers have assured me they will live. Can't say how long their recovery will take. Might as well head down to the docks for some good grub and ale."

"And...women?" Bennett knew as well as everyone that Jonah never turned down a pretty lass. Given his handsome features, the lasses didn't complain.

"Women *and* a good scrubbing. Haven't bathed in over a week and I still smell like them dead pirates we disposed of."

They both heartily agreed to that. They were halfway to their destination when Bennett felt a familiar pressure on his shoulder. "Found me did ya, you *cheeky* bird?" He gave Beaky an affectionate caress.

She squawked in return. *"Found you! Found you!"* She was obviously pleased with herself.

"I think that bird woulda spotted you anywhere, sir," Jonah said. He was right. Beaky often left the ship well before him to explore, but she always found him on land, even if it meant waiting on the roof of an inn or tavern. Speaking of which, the Docking District of Squall's End stretched before them now, full of every indulgence a seafaring man could wish for.

The familiar sound of hornpipes called to Bennett. "This place sounds jolly tonight."

Jonah chuckled. Bennett knew exactly what was going through his first mate's mind. "How 'bout here?" Without waiting for an answer, Jonah ducked through the door of an alehouse they had frequented many a time before. Squall's End was one of the largest port cities in Dragonwall. They had been through enough to know every establishment open to seamen.

Bennett followed Jonah into the Swaggering Thief. A blast of hot air mixed with the familiar stench of pipe weed and cheap rum overwhelmed his senses. The roaring sounds of merrymaking lent a welcoming atmosphere to the place.

"Well hang me from the mast! If it ain't Cap'n Bennet!" the local barman roared. Several women rushed to him, to cling to his arms. "Be on your best behavior, you seadogs!" yelled the barman to everybody in the establishment. "We got the greatest captain o' the seas in our midst." Then more quietly the barman added, "First round is on the house, eh, cap'n?" He tilted his cap in respect as Bennett approached the bar with Jonah. And indeed, Bennett took the barman up on it, making sure to pay the man well after each consecutive round he and Jonah put away.

THE FOLLOWING MORNING, his pounding head tried to keep him down. He'd had far too much fun. The image of Tabitha swam in and out of focus in his mind. He looked beside him. She was no longer there in the bed. It shouldn't have surprised him. She often snuck away in the wee hours of the morning.

He checked his personal belongings and sure enough, she'd

pocketed a few of his coins—nothing more. He chuckled. She never took more than she deserved, and he always felt that she deserved quite a lot. He had his favorites in every city. She was one of them.

He was a man of responsibility and he took his appointments seriously. Therefore, despite his splitting headache, he rose just as the sun was coming up and made his way through the quiet streets and then the fields to the fort. There were different guards at the entrance this time. He informed them of his meeting.

It didn't take long before he was taken to Lord Davi's private chambers. He gazed upon everything with wonder. The drengr folk lived distinguished lives—lives of luxury—but they were hard workers too.

He looked down at his manner of dress and immediately felt out of place. It was very clear that he belonged on a ship—not in a fort. But what did he care? He was proud of who he was. The stuffy life of a land-lover wouldn't have suited his adventurous soul. He was a seaman; looking the part was simply another facet of the job.

"Captain Bennett!" Lord Davi greeted him warmly, rising to grasp his forearm in customary drengr fashion.

He returned the greeting, "Lord Davi. Thank you for agreeing to see me on such short notice."

"The pleasure is mine. Please, sit and dine with me."

He welcomed the offer, as did his hungry stomach. Lord Davi was gracious and gave him a good deal of time to eat before bringing up business. Not long into his meal, a beautiful woman entered the room. Her long hair hung in cascades around her. He couldn't help but lose his composure for a few moments. When he looked away from her, he found Lord Davi's suspicious gaze. Before he could make anything of it, Lord Davi said, "This is Lady Emmy, my *mate*. She will be joining us this morning."

Worried that his regard of such a pretty woman might have offended his company, Bennett quickly rose and bowed, an honor he had not given to anyone in a while. True ladies were scarce in his business. In fact, being at sea most of his life warranted few distinguished meetings, but he knew his manners. "It is a pleasure to meet you, Lady Emmy. I apologize for my manner of dress. I have been at sea for sometime. That can chip away at the manners of even the best men, but especially the worst."

She bowed her head in return. "I am pleased to meet you, Captain Bennett, and I take no offense. Please be seated."

When they were all sitting, Lord Davi said, "I cannot say I know the true purpose of this meeting. I doubt it stems from any desire to pay the leader of Fort Squall your respects." Lord Davi gave him a curious look. "I admit, I had a few men look into the matter of your identity and purpose for visiting the port. They went down to the docks late last night. Likely whilst you were..." Davi paused to give him an appraising look, "enjoying yourself." The side of the leader's mouth twitched.

Was it that obvious? No doubt he reeked of tavern rum and sex.

"The dock manager said something to the effect of treating your injured crew. I know pirates have been giving all of our merchants problems. No doubt you have encountered what is befalling many these days. However, something tells me you are not here to simply treat wounded men."

He hummed and said, "Perhaps my being here is more telling than I realized. I need your help."

"Oh?" Davi's brows lifted.

He told the leaders of his commission from the king, of his trip to Port Ice, and of the attempted robbery of their precious cargo. "*That* is why I have so many wounded men."

"So you are the one I recently heard about?" Lord Davi exchanged a triumphant look with Emmy. "Well, this is fortunate news. Good favor has smiled down upon us once more." He drummed his fingers upon the surface of the table and appeared lost in thought.

"I am not sure I follow," Bennett said, frowning. "You know of my voyage and cargo?"

"Aye. As of recently—a private meeting held with members of our forts and the king's own shields—."

Tap-tap-tap. A sound on the window interrupted them. Emmy's eyes widened.

Bennett swore under his breath and said, "Apologies. Don't

mind her." He waved a nonchalant hand. "That's just my blasted bird." Emmy opened her mouth as if to speak and then closed it again. "Do you mind if I...?"

"Not at all, Captain." Lord Davi beat him to the window and opened it wide.

Beaky rushed in, flying straight to his shoulder. *"Found you! Found you!"* she squawked, nipping affectionately at his ear.

"Clever bird!" Emmy gasped. "May I?"

Bennett chuckled. "You may, yes."

She rose and gave Beaky several pets before they got back to their matters of importance. Lord Davi was more than pleased that Bennett had come to the port of Squall's End. In fact, he insisted upon procuring fifty percent of the cargo.

"I will speak to the king directly. He has already agreed to give us half of the cargo upon delivery in Kastali Dun. Looks like this will save his merchants a trip."

Bennett considered this. It was convenient. "Normally I would refuse such a request, my lord, with all due respect. Cargo is to be delivered in full as part of my contract. Seeing as your brother is Lord Reyr the Gold, who arranged my mission with Master Arden, then I will agree to your proposal. I admit that I am eager to be rid of this accursed metal—more trouble'n it's worth, if ya ask me. I will let you handle the politics of it."

Lord Davi nodded. "Very well. I am glad we are in agreement. In return, I will grant your other request. I will send six pairs to escort the *Lady Faith* for the remainder of her voyage to the port of Kastali. You needn't fear pirates with such protection."

"Thank you. Truly. Your assistance is very much appreciated."

"How long until your wounded are ready to sail?"

Bennett could not say. It might take several weeks before the worst of them were capable of boarding the *Lady Faith*. He told Lord Davi as much.

"We cannot delay. The ice metal must reach the ports of Kastali. Are these men essential to continuing your voyage?

He thought the matter over. He agreed with Lord Davi, but didn't like the idea of leaving men behind. "I suppose not. We can manage without them if we must. As you say, the drengr will be there to protect us."

"I will cover the healing costs of those who remain," Lord Davi said, overly generous. "And I will see that they are well taken care of. When they are recovered, I will take it upon myself to book them passage back to the capital."

Bennett was grateful for the offer. The three of them spent a few minutes discussing other matters, specifically the kingdom's latest news. Being out at sea meant he was often deprived of such things. The most surprising was that of a young woman who had recently been named the king's royal ward.

All too soon, the meeting came to an end, and he found himself profusely thanking Lord Davi. With the protection of Fort Squall's drengr, he was confident that he could get the remainder of *Lady Faith*'s precious cargo to its destination.

It took the better part of a day to divide the *Lady Faith's* cargo in half then transport it. They had to ferry it from the ship to the fort. In the meantime, they made repairs to the ship. Those with minor wounds were returned for the voyage, while goodbyes were given to those who would stay behind.

The drengr-rider pairs who would accompany them were afforded the nicest accommodations aboard the vessel. Bennett did not mind giving up his cabin to them and decking with the crew in their hammocks below. Beaky had something to say about it, but he ignored her as he usually did.

He was eager to be back on the sea where his mood would be at its highest. Sometimes he wondered if his blood was more seawater than anything else. Why else did the sea feel like home?

As the ship was prepared for departure, his spirits soared. He walked up and down the deck inspecting the ropes and making sure everyone and everything was in place. Beaky flew high above him, making wide circles through the sky.

"All is secure below, cap'n," Jonah informed him.

"Good. Raise the anchor."

"Weigh anchor!" Jonah called, relaying the command to the men on deck. His voice was a booming roar.

Bennett's happy mood drove him to lead their first sea shanty, as the men gathered around the capstan. He settled on a favorite of theirs called, *Turn and Then Go*, because it would take a number of turns of the capstan before the anchor was free of the water. Like all shanties, his voice rang loudly as he called out the first line, "What time is it, men?!" The men answered with the chanting chorus:

It's time! We are ready to sail the seas.
Aye, aye, turn and then go.
Our rum and our grub are all safely below.
Hey, hey, turn and then go.
Heave and ho and crank her full.
Aye, aye, turn and then go.
Get the anchor on board and the cables all stowed.
Hey, hey, turn and then go.
Say goodbye to the lasses and wenches, yo ho.
Aye, aye, turn and then go.
You'll see them again 'pon returnin', you know.
Hey, hey, turn and then go.
Man the capstan forthwith and give 'er a tow.
Aye, aye, turn and then go.
Soon we'll be movin' away from here.
Hey, hey, turn and then go...

THEY CONTINUED LIKE THIS, singing and chanting, as the *Lady Faith* sped on her way out of the bay, out to the vast sea beyond.

CHAPTER 21
THE GOBLINS ARE COMING

Kaljah

Jeanine rose from her cot, grabbing her bow and quiver of arrows. She was careful not to make a sound as her bare feet crept over the dirt floor. She threw on her boots and left her cottage behind, heading deep into the hills. Stars still dotted the night sky, but in little more than two hours, the sun would be upon her.

Dawn was the best time to hunt wild game and she intended to get a decent head start. She followed the same trail she always did, though she had never taken the trail to its end. It led up into the Eastern Barrier Range. Some said it would take you all the way into Pavv if you desired to go the distance. She shuddered. A person would need a death wish.

Following the trail, her feet stepped in all the right places, the path ingrained in her mind. It hadn't always been that way. She'd once been an immigrant to these lands. Nearly eight years had passed since then. Before that, she had been a city girl. Her mother and father were well-off during those days.

Her father was once a prestigious commander in the king's army, living and working with the kingdom's eastern troops. He'd been sent to these lands during the goblin wars. She'd been young at the time, only five. They'd stayed behind in Lincastle where she witnessed the hardships war brought upon her mother. The separation, the uncertainty, the fear.

Four years later, the fighting ended. They'd rejoiced, until news arrived in the form of a disastrous letter. Her father had lost his right leg in the final battle. She would never forget her mother's face, or the way she'd sobbed on the floor in the corner of their home. A woman she'd believed so strong, reduced to a heap of frilly fabric.

The following day they packed some of their belongings and sold the rest. Her mother hired a sell-sword to escort them to Kaljah, the village where her father was stationed during his recovery. It was a difficult journey. They were forced to take the cheapest route, which was also the fastest route, directly through the desert. All she remembered was the thirst, but sometimes sharper, more detailed memories came back in the form of nightmares.

As a child, everything had been an adventure, including the first few days after they arrived in their new home. Kaljah, with its population of less than three hundred, was completely different compared to the life she'd known. Surrounded by harsh terrain, it took very little time for her to learn the dangers of the wilderness. She grew up quickly after that.

Terrible as fate had already been to their family, it had one last thing in store for them. The gods let her father live whilst taking her mother. Though she loved him, she would have given quite a lot to switch their fates.

The child her mother birthed did not survive. Had it lived, she would have grown up with a brother. Her father would have had his wish, for he always longed to have a son. What did it matter now? That was many years ago.

He didn't talk about her mother anymore—it was a forbidden topic. After she'd died, he never remarried. What woman would want a man who'd been crippled? Jeanine was the only one in his life now, and a hard life it was. She did most of the heavy work, though he helped where he could: gardening, cleaning, and tending to their cow.

She was left to the other tasks that required two legs, like making repairs on the cottage roof and hunting. She scorned everything but the hunting. It was the only time she had away from her hardships. As she got older, and with much practice, she began to claim superiority in tracking and killing wild game. None could fell an animal as effectively, or track a wounded one into the mountains to finish it off.

Everything she'd learned, she'd learned out of necessity. Hunting big game brought a steady income. And when she didn't sell her surplus, she gave it to hungry mouths. Her father wasn't the only injured war veteran in the village.

She often wondered though, if they'd gone home to Lincastle, if her mother might have had the healing help she'd needed. If her mother might have lived—

"*Psst!*"

She froze, then spun around. Jahl's face poked out of a bush, a lopsided grin on his features. She exhaled, unsurprised to see him.

Jahl was her best friend. Not many were close to her age of seventeen and those who were, were already married. She and Jahl loved hunting together, but she was much better at it. His real skill was his swordsmanship. Everyone knew that he wanted to leave Kaljah and become a soldier in the king's army. His parents promised him that when he turned seventeen, he could. His seventeenth name day was but three weeks away. She feared the day when he would leave her behind, but she knew he had to forge his own destiny. Until then, they continued with their tradition. In the morning they hunted and in the evenings they sparred.

"Seems a bit *too* quiet this morning, doesn't it?" Jahl afforded her a quick glance. Their gazes were largely fixed on the landscape around them. The trees increased as the hills grew steeper, until they were surrounded by the forest. She supposed that it was rather quiet, but her mind had been otherwise occupied, so she hadn't noticed. They continued, quietly placing their feet.

Just as she was about to move forward to the crest of a hill,

Jahl's arm shot out in front of her, halting her progress. She glanced at him, only to find an expression of alarm upon his features. An unsettling feeling tumbled into the pit of her stomach.

They crept behind a tree, both holding their breath as they strained to listen. There was no noise—none at all. It was an odd occurrence for a forest that was usually alight with the sounds of birds and other creatures.

It took no time for her nose to discern the most horrid stench imaginable. At first, she thought it might be a spoiled carcass, but then she decided that it was worse than dead flesh. She had been this way two days ago. A scent like this one would have taken far longer to fester.

"Can you smell that?" she whispered. Jahl nodded, his eyes wide.

Colors were creeping into the trees as the sun began to shed its first rays. It was just enough for them to see their way into the growth. There was still some time yet before it would peep over the horizon.

Jahl tugged on her arm, taking her with him as they dodged around a few trees, making their way to a better vantage point. Once more, he stopped short. Hiding behind a large tree trunk, he positioned her to the right of him, and with worry upon his face, he motioned for her to peek around the tree.

The source of the smell was revealed.

"Oh gods," she whispered, the blood draining from her face. There were scores of goblins! They moved about in the forested valley, assembling into formations. Fear gripped her insides. Jahl pulled her away, guiding her back the way they'd come. She was glad he led her, because her mind was too clouded with terror to place one foot in front of the other.

"We need to alert the village!" She kept her voice low. Jahl nodded. He did not stop. They both understood what this meant.

As soon as they were far enough away, they abandoned all caution and broke into a sprint. Taking her hand in his, Jahl set the pace. Their harsh breaths were the only sound they made.

They ran until they could run no more, trying to cover two

hours of distance in a fraction of the time. Every muscle in her body screamed as the hills flattened. They were forced to stop. She took a drink from her water skin, choking on half of it, then said, "Even if we warn them, what good will it do? There must be hundreds!"

Jahl was doubled over, his hands on his knees supporting his weight. Just as he opened his mouth to respond, an unmistakable sound split the silent air. Not far in the distance there was a strange horn blast. She looked over her shoulder, half expecting to see the goblins right behind her, but she only saw a large, tree-covered hill.

"They're coming." Jahl's voice wavered.

"Let's go!" she cried, despite the heaviness in her limbs. They both took off again.

Her father's cottage was the farthest from the village. The moment she saw it, she began screaming, calling his name. He hobbled around the corner, moving with haste.

"Father!" she screamed, now that she had his attention. "Goblins! Goblins are coming!" Though she wasn't close enough to see his face, she knew the fearful expression he wore. Immediately he turned and fled back to the house.

"Tend to your father and meet me in the village square," Jahl shouted without stopping. "I must warn the others." Before she could say anything, he split away from her. She raced into the cottage and grabbed the only important items she owned, which were held in a leather case she tied to her belt. Her father was busy throwing things around, searching for something.

He thrust an object into her arms. She looked down to see his prized war sword. "No, Father!" She shook her head and tried to give it back. "You need this more than I."

"Pig shit! I'm no longer fit to fight. I'll use the axe. You use that."

She swallowed against the dryness of her throat. How could this possibly be happening? She didn't want to believe it.

"How many are there? Damn it, girl, get your wits together!" He took hold of her shoulders and gave her a rough shake.

"Five...five hundred?" It was hard to speak. Everything felt like a dream, and she almost found herself waiting to wake up. "They nearly outnumber us two to one..." she whispered, caring little for the hopelessness in her voice. "We are all going to die!"

"That isn't going to happen. We've got to get the women and children out of the village. You will protect them. Take all the horses you can. Steal 'em from the Averys—I don't care—they won't either if they got sense. Get everyone you can out."

"But..."

"Don't you worry 'bout me. My time's coming whether it's later or sooner."

"Father...I..."

He shook his head, silencing her. She hugged him—something she never did. It was a short embrace. He pushed her away moments later to gaze into her eyes. Then he shoved a bag of coins into her hands and said, "There is no time for goodbyes. Go!"

Without another word, she fled the cottage. The village bell began to ring. As she made her way to the square, people emerged from their houses. They were wholly confused. Some were shouting the warning of goblins, others hardly believed it.

She rushed to the stables. These were owned by the Averys— another military transplant family like hers. Jahl was their son. The Averys had more horses than any other family in Kaljah. After saddling a chestnut mare, she moved to saddle Jahl's stallion, Storm. Her fingers fumbled—it was taking too long. Abandoning her task, she instead threw a bridle around Storm and left the saddle on the floor. It would have to do. She did the same to a third horse, another chestnut mare nearly identical to the first.

Jahl's parents entered, both terror-stricken. They had the same idea in mind and did not question her actions. "Grab as many horses as you can and get out of the village!" she said. "My father plans to stay and fight. We must get the women and children out."

She moved with lightning speed as she mounted Storm and took hold of the two chestnut mares, chirping and encouraging them. She led the horses out of the stable.

Spurring her heels into Storm, she prompted the black stallion to increase his pace. As she neared the town square, she discovered it in a state of panic. Villagers rushed back and forth. The town's constable, Phillip—another military transplant—stood in the middle of the square, directing people. His voice carried over the panic, "Women and children: carry only—"

A horse squealed. She caught sight of Ronan, the town drunk, trying to lead one of her chestnut mares away. She wrestled with him, struggling to overpower him. A sword appeared at Ronan's throat. Jahl stood behind him. "Touch that horse and you die, Ronan." Ronan dropped his hands and stepped cautiously away from the blade. A moment later, he disappeared into the crowd.

Jahl mounted the saddled mare. "I am in charge of organizing Kaljah's defense with our fathers. Phillip will handle the women and children—he is directing them to flee. The daft man was going to hide them in the village hall until I talked some sense into him. We must get them out. Help him in any way you can, but quickly. Then you must run for your life."

Jeanine was too stunned to respond, and instead gazed at him, dumbfounded.

His attention shifted to those around them. He circled a couple of times shouting, "Those of you who would stay and fight—with me!" He motioned to the other side of the square to where other men were assembling. "The rest of you, flee with the women and children!"

She snapped out of her trance. "Wait! Jahl!" She galloped Storm to his side, dragging on the bridle of the other chestnut mare. "Jahl, we must leave together. Those who stay will die."

She couldn't lose him.

"We need to give everyone a chance," he said, clearly unwilling to budge. "If we do not slow them down, those who flee will die. You think the goblins won't pursue?"

She didn't answer. Instead, they both glanced at the hills looming over their little village. The goblins could be seen now, cresting the top of the nearest hill. "Look at the swarm of them. They will pour over our empty village like river water over rocks. We must give them something to break on."

A distraction forced Jahl's attention to a small girl named Cissa. She stood alone and confused, frantically crying for her mother. He jumped from his saddle and scooped her up, placing her upon the bare back of the other mare. "Take her and go. If you do not leave now, you will never get away in time."

"If you stay and fight, I want to fight with you, Jahl. I am no coward."

"You are no coward—that is the truth. But who will protect them when we fall?" He pointed to those fleeing the village. "Your time for heroism will come soon enough."

She had never seen him this unyielding—this insistent. He was always soft spoken, with a quiet firmness about him that she admired. Now she saw him for the man he had become, and fierce pride welled up within her.

"Where will we go?" she asked, more to herself than anything. There were so many people fleeing the village. West of them there was only the dry desert—they would die of thirst. East of them were the mountains, teeming with more goblins. There was no doubt that the South would be just as dangerous.

"Go north. Take them to the forest. Oh, and take good care of my horse, Jeanine! You know how I care for him." With that he slapped Storm's flank. Storm reared high in the air. Jeanine had to squeeze her legs tightly to keep from slipping off. Just as suddenly Storm bounded forward. The chestnut mare followed in his wake. They left Jahl behind and she felt her heart break a little, knowing what would soon befall him.

"With me!" she cried to the remaining women and children fleeing. "Follow me! We must escape!"

Once she was outside of the village, she took a moment to gaze at the mothers and children fleeing. Their progress was too slow! They would never cover enough ground at such a pace.

Something grabbed a hold of her leg. Her chest tightened with fear before she looked down to find the pleading face of a woman, Ashka. "Take her, Jeanine. Please—take her." Ashka held up her young child high over her head.

She took the child and passed her over to Cissa. "Hold on to her tightly. Do not let her fall."

Wide-eyed, Cissa nodded.

Goblin battle horns broke through the cries of the frightened villagers. The piercing sounds sent chills down her spine. The noise told her one thing. Goblins had reached the village outskirts. She dared not look over her shoulder. Any moment now, they would be descending upon her father's cottage. She couldn't bear the thought of him fighting them off, one-legged, weak in his old age. Instead she focused on the task at hand, leading the throng of people from the village.

"Run! All of you!" she cried. "Run until we reach the Gable Forest!" They would never be able to run that far, or that long. The forest was days away, but she had to motivate them somehow.

Those on horseback were already galloping far ahead of her, but she remained with the group of villagers on foot, keeping to the back. Most of the men remained behind. For that she was grateful. If Jahl died, he would not die alone.

She did everything she could to hurry the women and children forward. The village began to shrink away from sight. Next to her, on foot, she saw another struggling child. This one was a young boy. She lifted him and placed him in front of her. Then she picked up an infant from a woman's arms and told the boy to hold the baby.

She was unsure of the weight Storm could carry, but he was a powerful horse. She would take as many children as she could. At the pace they were moving, the mothers were going to be left behind. That was the harsh truth of it. Their children fled faster. Unfortunately, the goblins ran faster than everyone.

And then she heard the sound of metal on metal—a faint echo that rang of brutality. That was the moment she felt hot tears streaming down her cheeks. She wiped them away with her sleeve and kept her face still and emotionless. When she had the courage for it, she looked over her shoulder. Her father's cottage was no longer discernible. The village had become a single, dark smudge. All she could pick out now were wisps of smoke rising from the cottages. Without being able to see it, she knew two things with certainty. The goblins had reached Kaljah, and her father was dead.

CHAPTER 22

ON ONE CONDITION

Kastali Dun

Claire was sharing breakfast with Desaree and Saffra four days after their trip to the market. They had been nearly inseparable since. The challenge was thinking up excuses to keep Desaree from her duties. Fortunately, Tess was lenient and Desaree was largely influenceable.

They had a delightful spread of eggs, sausage, fruit, and spiced apple bread.

"So, Des," Claire said, licking her fingers, "are you and Verath official yet?" Desaree choked on a mouthful. "It's obvious you both have feelings for each other."

"We're merely good friends."

Claire and Saffra shared a look. "*Just* friends?" Claire arched her brow. "Then why did he say you deserve the best? That he intends to give it to you?!" She pitched her voice low and did an impression of Verath, repeating exactly what he'd said.

Desaree blushed. "I doubt he meant it like *that*."

"I think he did." Claire sat up straighter, grinning.

Saffra huffed, entertained by their back and forth.

Desaree was in denial, obviously. Lord Verath cared for her as more than a friend. Still, Claire said, "Well, I bet when you came to the keep, you never expected someone like Verath to single you out."

A bitter laugh burst from Desaree's lips. "You're right. I had very different expectations. Different dreams. Until I learned to hope for nothing."

"Des!" Saffra cried, mouth dropping open. "That's a little extreme, don't you think? You've never seemed the hopeless type. You're always smiling, always happy. What's going on? Are you... not?"

"I..." Desaree shrank down in her chair.

Claire squeezed Desaree's arm, gentling her voice. "What sort of aspirations did you have?"

Desaree worried her lower lip. "I wanted to be a handmaiden."

"A...a *handmaiden*? Seriously?"

"Serving as a handmaiden is a prestigious job," Saffra amended. "In Kastali Dun, people in the middle class train their daughters for such."

"Oh...I...I guess I had no idea."

"It was my mother's wish before it was my own," Desaree explained.

"But, I don't understand." Claire frowned. "Wouldn't those of the middle class be better off working rather than serving? Wouldn't they rather have careers of their own? Look at Madame Rosanne."

"Madame Rosanne was trained as a Mage," Saffra explained. "Besides, being a handmaiden is a job of its own, no different from any other, merely more prestigious. Look at Jocelyn. She has done quite well for herself."

Jocelyn was Saffra's handmaiden. Claire didn't know her well, didn't see much of her, mostly because Saffra was so independent.

"Did Jocelyn aspire to be a handmaiden when she was younger?" Claire asked.

"I do not think she could afford to entertain the idea—not in the social sphere she had originally occupied."

"What do you mean?"

"I rescued her from the *Pauper's District*," Saffra said. "She was too poor to consider becoming a handmaiden."

The Pauper's District was the poorest district in Kastali Dun. Many of its laborers were employed at the docks. Others were fishmongers, midwives, housekeepers for the middle class, chimney sweeps, peddlers, thieves, tavern wenches, prostitutes, and the like.

"I was walking through the market one day and I saw Jocelyn selling pears from a basket. She was dressed in rags, but I admired the way she had done her hair. Her hair—it was just like mine, you see. Having been so young, I struggled to do my own. I certainly could not do to my hair what my mother had done for me. I knew immediately that Jocelyn would do well living with me in the keep. She was several years older, but that did not matter."

"Wow…" Claire exhaled. "I never realized you had rescued her from poverty. She certainly doesn't look the part. All the times I have seen her, she always looks as if she were highborn."

"She has adapted, I think." Saffra looked proud.

Claire chewed on her lower lip, thinking. How might one acquire a handmaiden? Did they need to be a certain age? Was a woman permitted to choose her own handmaiden, or was she assigned one? Could anyone have one? Was it a matter of wealth, status, or both?

She voiced her questions.

"Any woman who can afford a handmaiden may hire one," Desaree explained. "Most often they serve those of elevated social status, but only because those are the women who can afford them."

"A handmaiden does not necessarily need to be a certain age," Saffra added, "but those with more experience, and those who come with higher recommendations, are always more expensive."

"Handmaidens do not usually go through any formal training." This, from Desaree. "Nor do they always serve the same woman for life. They are permitted to move up and down the social ladder if they want, based on their skills."

"And," Saffra said, "if they decide to increase their price based on their growing experience, it sometimes becomes difficult for their mistresses to increase their salaries. In those cases, they seek jobs higher on the nobility ladder. More often than not, however, they stick with a mistress for a long time."

"*Apparently*," Desaree whispered conspiratorially, "King Talon's mother had three ladies-in-waiting *and* three handmaidens, all of whom stuck with her for the duration of their service. It was also known that she retired each at the age of forty, and did not allow them to mother children until that time. When they retired, she offered them a large sum—and whatever else they desired—to happily carry out the rest of their lives. It must have been hard to see them age so quickly, you know, considering she lived nearly seven hundred years before her death. But anyway, she always kept *six*. No more no less."

"Six?" Claire's brows lifted in surprise. "How could any one person need so much assistance? Don't handmaidens just help you get dressed and whatnot? I've managed fine by myself."

"Hah!" Desaree laughed. "Hardly. The handmaiden's primary role is to serve her mistress, but generally, she is more of a companion. She does a wide range of tasks. Yes, she helps her mistress dress, but she also draws her baths, unless the woman is lucky enough to live in the keep where our baths are always full. She performs light housekeeping, manages her mistress's correspondences, writing letters on her behalf, and attends court, or any other function with her mistress, should she want company. Furthermore, she is expected to know art, proper etiquette, music, wardrobe care, and much more. Handmaidens are respected and paid well, especially in Kastali Dun."

Claire hummed. It sounded nothing like what she'd imagined. "So, if being a handmaiden was what you always wanted, why didn't you?"

"Caterina." Desaree made a sound in the back of her throat. "She ruins everything." When Claire frowned, Desaree elaborated. "She went to every lady of nobility and soiled my name. She ruined my chances of getting chosen. She told them that I was a thief, that

I was disrespectful, and that I would dishonor anyone who might choose me."

Claire's jaw dropped.

"It's true," Saffra confirmed. "I heard the rumors myself, but I never believed them. I always knew Desaree was honorable."

"How could she?!" The heat of anger burned Claire's skin. "Desaree would never do any of those things."

Desaree slouched in her chair. "Tell *that* to the women of the court."

Clair at up straighter. "If you could—if Caterina had never ruined your name—would you still want to be a handmaiden?"

"Yes," Desaree breathed, setting her fork down. She gave a long sigh. "But, I don't have time for wishful thinking. Speaking of which, I am afraid I must return to my other duties." Claire's stomach hardened into a knot. She hated seeing her friend like this. Hated that Caterina had done something so cruel. "Until next time, I suppose..." Desaree stood and pushed her chair in.

Claire jumped to her feet, giving her a fierce hug. "I will make this right. I promise," she whispered.

"Lady Claire." The guards outside of King Talon's tower greeted her. "His Majesty is occupied with an important meeting. Best you return later."

"Isn't *every* meeting with the king important?"

They exchanged a look. "Yes?"

"Exactly." She lifted her chin. "Let me through."

They didn't move. Her smile faltered. "Fine. I will let myself in." She reached for the doorknob. Their spears crossed in front of her, barring her entry. "If you do not move, *sirs*, the king will hear of it. Step aside."

This time, they looked uncertain.

"I do not wish to tell him about this, but I will if I must. I daresay he will not be happy."

They shared another look, contemplating, then nodded. They stepped aside.

"Thank you." She let herself in and closed the door behind her.

The entry chamber leading into the main tower looked exactly as she remembered it. This was her second time coming here. The first had been when she'd learned about Cyrus's gift. Opulent rugs, a spacious sitting room, a marble fireplace, doors leading...who could say where?

She heard voices coming from one to her right. She moved towards the sound, putting her ear against the wood.

"...goblins attacking the border along the range...doing it for a reason."

"Organized, too..."

"...divide the troops from Lincastle...strategically in each settlement...protect the people."

"Aye."

"How many losses...?"

"...cannot be sure yet." King Talon's voice. She smiled at the sound of it, then wiped her expression clean.

"...numerous villages...Kaljah among them."

"...thought we defeated the goblins...war."

She pressed harder, trying to hear more than just snippets. The door was too thick.

"...eight years ago, Lord Royce."

She pulled away, glancing around the room. It sounded like a serious meeting, and yet, she had no idea how long it might last. Marcel was waiting on her. She was already late for her morning lessons.

Biting her lower lip, she contemplated. What would happen if she simply walked in? Perhaps the king would be angry with her. She kind of liked that he would.

Taking a deep breath, she grabbed the door's handle and pulled it open. Silence fell.

It was a cozy room with a large table in the center. Stretched across the dark wood was a huge map. She quickly recognized

Dragonwall's geography. The lower council was gathered around it —some hunched, others standing further back.

"My lady!" Greetings echoed around the room as the king's council began bowing. She found King Talon. If he was surprised to see her, he gave no sign of it.

"Pardon my intrusion, Your Majesty, but may I speak with you?"

He stared at her, his expression unreadable. Then he blinked and cleared his throat. "You may—of course." He turned to the others. "Leave us."

Everyone rushed out. When the door closed, she gravitated towards the map. Some of the landmarks were easily recognizable. The Gable Forest, various mountain ranges, the four forts, even several cities. Clusters of figurines were scattered like enlarged pieces on a chessboard.

The king was silent, watching her. She felt his gaze like a phantom touch. She shivered, looking up at him. "I hope I wasn't interrupting anything important?"

"Yes, and no." His eyes darted from her to the map and back. "It's probably for the best. I was growing tired of this"—he gestured towards the map—"and you being here saves me the hassle of tracking you down myself."

She blinked. "I wasn't aware that tracking me down was such an inconvenience—"

"Forgive me." He took a step towards her then halted. "I worded that poorly. I just...that is to say...I had something to tell you."

"Oh?"

"I am leaving for Fort Lin tomorrow. I shall be gone a week, perhaps longer."

"I see..."

"While I am gone, I expect you to behave yourself. My shields will be here if you need anything. All I ask is that you do not venture into the city without them. I'm familiar with your propensity to defy me. I hope you don't see this as an opportunity for it."

"You're right." A slow, wicked smile formed on her lips. "I do so *love* breaking your rules. Were they anyone else's, I might follow them more diligently." He blinked, quickly regaining his composure. "That being said, I'll be on my best behavior, follow every single rule, stay out of trouble...on one condition."

His eyes narrowed. "And what, pray tell, is that?"

"I want a handmaiden."

His lips parted. Realization spread across his features. He threw his head back and laughed.

She gaped at him in disbelief. Was he...was he *laughing* at her? The sound was rich and decadent. It left her skin flushed.

"If that is all it takes to tame you, then you may have a hundred of them!"

The way he looked now, his face all but glowing, was a direct contrast to his nature. He was almost a completely different person. What was *happening*?!

"Are you...do you mean that? I can have a handmaiden?"

"Yes. Take whomever you wish, however many of them you'd like, so long as I have your word that you will behave."

"So, I can have Desaree?"

"Yes. I'll see to it she has a fine salary. We can formalize the matter of her payment upon my return. You have my word. Do I have yours?"

She blinked. Was it really this easy? Instead of screeching with delight, or fist pumping the air over her win, she composed herself and said, "You have my word as well."

CHAPTER 23

THE ROYAL GARDEN

Kastali Dun

Desaree smiled, placing her last item of clothing—a chemise—into her wooden trunk. She couldn't remember the last time she'd been this happy. She closed the latch on her trunk.

A knock sounded.

"Come in," she called, knowing Claire had wanted to help. "I think I got most of it already—" Her eyes went wide. "Verath! I had not—I did not..."

He filled the doorway, blinking. "You're leaving? I don't understand."

"Leaving?" She frowned. "Oh! *Oh!* Then you do not know yet?"

She sat down on the edge of her cot.

"Know what?" he nearly growled.

"It is not what it looks like, I promise."

"Then what is it?" His voice was softer this time. He closed the door to lean against it.

She twisted her fingers in her lap. "I have been offered a position as Claire's handmaiden."

172

"Then you are not leaving? I almost thought...never mind." His expression shifted to one of relief. "A handmaiden, you say?"

"Isn't it the best news?!" she asked. He smiled, and for a moment, she was struck speechless by it. Then, she frowned. "Did you think I would leave without...without saying goodbye?"

"It crossed my mind."

Her chest tightened, almost hurt. "Have a care. You know me better than that."

"It was silly." He fell silent, then cleared his throat. "Will you be living with Lady Claire?"

"I am to have my own accommodations." Her chest swelled with pride. "I have been given a chamber across the hall from her."

The chamber in question was not entirely unique, nor was it the best, but it was better than most. There were a number of these chambers along the corridor. They lined the inner side, which made sense, because the outer rooms were occupied by Dragonwall's royalty and highest-ranking individuals, which offered ocean views with large sweeping balconies. The inner rooms were intended for those who served, most often handmaidens and elevated servants.

"And when did this development come to fruition?"

"Just earlier." She grinned, over-eager to tell him exactly how it had come about. He listened patiently. "I never imagined I would become a handmaiden for royalty," she sighed, still struggling to believe it.

"Your mother would be very proud of you."

Her eyes watered. "Thank you, yes." She blinked, then brightened. "Can one be *too* happy?"

"You deserve to be happy," he said, moving towards her. He took a seat beside her and they both fell silent.

The silence stretched on. When he still didn't say anything, her eyebrows pulled together. "Is...is something wrong? Are you unhappy?"

He glanced at her, brow furrowed. "Unhappy? Hardly. Just brooding, I suppose."

"But...why?"

He exhaled. "There's something I wanted to discuss with you—that was the reason I came. We can talk about it later."

"But—no. Please, tell me!" If he didn't, she'd end up obsessing over it.

"Something has been on my mind since you shared your past with me. Forgive me, I would rather not upset you."

She frowned, trying to anticipate his intentions. He knew how much it upset her, talking about her past—even thinking about it. Yet, she could not bring herself to stop him. Instead, she sat frozen.

"Desaree, I want you to reclaim your title."

Ice settled into the pit of her stomach. "My...my title?"

"Yes. It was taken from you. I want you to take it back. People should be calling you *Lady* Desaree."

The use of her title had a strange effect on her. "Lady Desaree..." she whispered, trying the words out, letting the sound roll off her tongue. Her cheeks flushed. She stole a glance at him.

The way he looked at her made it impossible to think. His eyes were heated. Completely focused on her. Of all the males in Dragonwall...she'd fallen for this one.

"Lady Desaree." Verath's purring voice gave her chills. "I insist that you take back what was once yours."

Her heart fluttered—all irritation forgotten. Now she was merely befuddled. "But...how would I...? I do not... What would I...?"

"It will require some effort, but it will be worthwhile. You will need my support—I will back you."

"What must I do?" An uncomfortable foreboding settled over her.

"First, you must present yourself to the king."

"In...in court?" Her eyes widened. Did she have the courage for such a thing?

"In court, yes. I know it sounds intimidating—believe me. But you must open an investigation into Lady Caterina's past. Until we can prove what happened, we do nothing. Once we have the king's permission, we will carry out the investigation and then move against her. For now, all that is needed is a request."

"But…it would require me to go against Lady Caterina," she said, stating the obvious. She picked at her fingernails. The idea was terrifying.

"I suppose this must feel daunting, but it is something we will get through together." When she said nothing, he said, "Tell me you agree. Say the words and we will make it happen."

She allowed her silence to buy her time, considering the prospect of it. "What about becoming a handmaiden?" she asked. "Will I be expected to take up some other mantle if I become a lady?"

"My dear," he said, his voice low. "You may do anything you wish. As a court lady, you will have a great deal more freedom. Besides, you deserve the respect of the court." He hesitated before adding, "I want this for you, Desaree."

My dear. She let the endearment ring in her mind. Flushed.

"What if…what if I say no? Would you still want to be friends with me?"

"Gods, Desaree!" He sprang from the cot beside her and began pacing. "Do you take me for a shallow, heartless fool?"

"Of-of course not." She shook her head, taken aback.

"I will care for you regardless of your decision. You ought to know that." He returned to the cot to kneel before her. Then he took her hands in his, which left her heart hammering. "Just to be clear, I should hope that we are more than simply friends. Now, about your title—what say you?"

Blood rushed past her ears, a roar, as if the sea's waves were inside her head. His warm touch, his question, the way he was looking at her, it was all overwhelming. She was forced to close her eyes and exhale, allowing the waves to grow docile. As her mind cleared, she began to think.

She had spent many angry years agonizing over what was taken from her by the wretched Rosens—by Caterina. This was her moment to fix things. What if there was never another chance such as this? Could she let such a thing pass her by? It was time to step up and look her fear in the face. "I will do it," she said at last.

Verath visibly relaxed. "You deserve to have what they took

from you—what Caterina took from you." He wanted to see justice as much as she did. "Now, let us take a walk before you finish packing. I could use some fresh air." He held out his hand to her. She did not move to take it. "Why is my request so shocking?" he asked.

"You...you do not mind being seen together in public?"

He scowled. "Why should I?"

Wasn't it obvious? She wanted to tell him why. She was a mere servant and he was not. Yet, how could she deny him? How could she say no when he looked at her so insistently? She thought about what Claire might do?

Smiling, she took his hand. "Very well. Let's take a walk."

They left her chamber, her arm linked through his, making their way through the keep. Her insecurity did not ruin these perfect moments as she had expected. She worried that shocked gazes would distract her. She quickly discovered that in Verath's presence, only *he* mattered. She forgot to look at anyone else.

The royal garden in Kastali Dun's keep was perfectly romantic. Its rows of rosebushes and elegantly manicured hedges—all overlooked by looming trees—made an ideal escape for any couple wishing to avoid scrutiny. It happened to be a lovely day, so they were not the only ones enjoying the outdoors. They avoided everyone else by meandering down a path that took them to a quiet tree-inhabited corner.

"When I first moved to the Great Keep, I used to pass many hours here," Verath told her as they rounded the trunk of a large eucalyptus. They moved further into the shelter and shade of the overhead foliage. "It reminded me of the Vallahurst Forest—a place I often visited in my younger years."

"How old were you when you came here?"

"Eighty-six. I had no mate, and King Tallek was looking for a new shield to join his ranks."

"I often forget that you are much older than you appear."

"Four-hundred-and-eighty-two."

"So many lifetimes... What is it like living for so long?"

"Lonely—most of the time."

"I can understand that. When you are with me—"

"When I am with you, I am never lonely."

Her skin burned and she grew shy.

"Come this way." He took hold of her hand and pulled her behind a large pine, secluding them from view. Her footing felt unsteady, so she grabbed hold of his arms to regain steadiness. Her chest was flush against his, and when she next looked up, she found his questioning eyes. He chose that moment to speak, "I know you find it incomprehensible..."

"Find...what?" She could hardly think. Her heart hammered against the insides of her chest.

"You find it incomprehensible that I take an interest in you." His voice was low. "I have seen your doubt. You believe yourself unworthy of me."

"I...that is to say...I..." She swallowed against her dry throat several times.

"I have pursued you diligently, Desaree, only to be greeted by more reserve than I am used to. Even now you are silent, leaving me to wrestle with my own words. I have all but thrown myself at you. Still you hold your regard for me captive. You are either denying your feelings or have none. Am I a fool to pursue you?"

"We are both fools," she whispered. "At least we are fools together. Verath, I..."

"There is no correct answer, Desaree. I can see that you are searching for one—I see it on your face. All I want is a simple answer. Do you care for me?"

"I...yes."

"We are not banned from love, though you fear it. Sometimes when I think about it, I fear it too."

"You are a king's shield. Won't our love get you in trouble?"

"Yes, I daresay it might, but not in the way you think. If by trouble, you mean helplessly lost and ever in want of your affection, then yes, loving you has already gotten me into a great deal of trouble."

"Are you saying..."

"I am saying that I love you, Desaree. I love you."

"But, you hardly know me!"

"I know enough."

Her eyes dropped. Why did she feel undeserving of what he offered, especially when he offered it so freely?

"Look at me," he whispered. "Tell me that you love me."

For a moment, she froze. There was only one answer, wasn't there? Anything else would have been a lie. "I do love you, Verath."

His expression brightened. He smiled widely, his eyes narrowing into slits. Then he took her face in his hands and put his forehead against hers. Her heart pounded and she felt hot and lightheaded all at once. He kissed her. At first, she went numb with surprise. The feel of his hot mouth against hers, moving, turned her molten.

She kissed him back. Her lips were hesitant at first but grew more confident. She didn't dare breathe, holding her breath until she was dizzy, until she was forced to push him away.

"Forgive me. I did not mean to get so carried away." He held her shoulders at arm's length and inspected her.

"It is my fault," she gasped, her chest rising and falling in rapid bursts. "I could not breathe. I—I'm better now."

"I see. In that case, may I kiss you again?"

"Yes," she whispered.

The side of his mouth twitched. His eyes twinkled with mischief. "As you wish, *my lady*." With that, he took her into his arms once more.

CHAPTER 24

PASSING TIME

Kastali Dun

Claire rushed through the keep's corridors, anxious to return to her chambers. She had just finished her lesson with Mage Targa. While she was tired, she wasn't as tired as she used to be. She was getting stronger.

Over a week had passed since Caterina's threat. Fortunately, she hadn't tried anything else. She did, however, take every opportunity to glare at her and utter snide remarks under her breath.

She reached her quarters and breathed a sigh of relief.

"Welcome back, my lady." Desaree rushed to greet her.

"You know, you don't need to call me that."

"But all handmaidens call their ladies '*my lady*.' I take my position seriously."

"I am starting to understand all too well." Claire's lips twitched.

Today was Desaree's first official day as handmaiden. Out of pure excitement, she had far outdone herself. She had brought Claire breakfast, insisted on dressing her, and then insisted on putting her hair up in an elaborate style fitting for a royal woman.

Claire wasn't used to this kind of pampering.

"How was your first day as a handmaiden?"

A dreamy look passed over Desaree's features. "Absolutely wonderful!"

"Oh?"

"Well, after you departed for your lessons, I went to the market to collect more writing supplies for you. I also stopped by Rosanne's to pick up your latest gown. You will never believe what happened while I was there." Claire's brows lifted. Desaree's smile grew wider. "When Madame Rosanne discovered that I was your handmaiden, she was in an uproar! You should have heard her. 'A handmaiden to Lady Claire *cannot* walk around dressed like that!'"

Claire giggled. "That's good! Really good! Maybe you should be an actress instead of a handmaiden."

Desaree's smile was shy. "Anyway, I could hardly say no after that, could I? Anyone in my position would have felt conflicted."

"Conflicted?"

"Oh come now," Desaree tsked. "Madame Rosanne's gowns cost a fortune. Everyone knows that." Claire's lips parted in surprise. "Forgive me. I did not mean to sound so..."

"It's fine. But...I will gladly pay for whatever you need. Besides, the king said you would have a good salary. There's nothing to feel guilty about."

Desaree sank onto the sofa, exhaling. "I suppose after living without indulgences for so long, I have become rather miserly. There is nothing I can do about it now. Madame Rosanne was more than accommodating, believe me."

"So...you decided to accept her offer?" A hopeful excitement fluttered her chest.

"Oh yes." A wicked grin spread over Desaree's face. "She outfitted me with two new gowns from the display window and had my measurements taken to commission two more. She put everything on loan. I am not to pay her until it is convenient."

A squeal erupted before Claire could stop it. "That's so great! You deserve it."

Desaree smiled widely and said with a dreamy voice, "I can hardly believe it. New gowns...and from Rosanne no less. I will wear one to dinner tonight—" Her eyes grew round. "Oh. My. Gods! I get to have dinner in the dining hall! Me! Won't that be grand?"

"Wait until Verath sees you!" Claire said, conspiratorially.

Desaree had already filled her in on everything that had happened between her and Verath.

"I suppose you are right. I still cannot believe..." Desaree trailed off, blushing.

There was a knock at the door. Desaree jumped to her feet and rushed over. Saffra entered carrying a recurve bow and quiver of arrows. "Hello ladies." She smiled at them.

Claire gaped at her. Saffra's gown, which was made of a plain, lightweight fabric, looked more rugged than anything. Her skirt was gathered and hiked up in front, held in place by what looked like a leather strap, showing off a pair of cream pantaloons and black boots.

"You're dressed like...like a brigand!"

Saffra laughed. "How would you both like to keep me company at the practice range? I'll give you a few lessons?"

Claire and Desaree shared a look before eagerly nodding.

They helped Desaree change into one of her new gowns, a light blue and gold brocade. It felt good to fuss over her, especially knowing all she'd been through. When they were finished, they headed to the lower levels of the keep.

"With the Fall Tournament approaching, I hope to take first place in my events," Saffra explained as they reached the second level. It was ovular because half of it jutted out towards the west. The western half was covered in green grass and hosted a large practice ground for the king's soldiers. Claire often saw it from afar, but she had rarely visited.

The late afternoon was a popular time here. The swordplay area was packed with bodies. Most of the men had ditched their shirts as they danced around with swords, spears, and a number of other weapons.

For the first time in a long time—since her breakup with her ex-boyfriend—she found her eyes lingering longer than necessary over the muscled chests. Her relationship with Jake hadn't ended well. After he broke her heart, she wasn't eager to give it away again, and aside from her feelings for Cyrus, she had not allowed herself to so much as look at another. Only now, she couldn't help her gaze.

She stopped dead in her tracks, letting out a little gasp. Bedelth and Verath were on the opposite side of the sparring area. They fought each other with a ferocity that left her gaping. After blinking several times, she nudged Desaree, whose eyes immediately found Verath and became transfixed.

"He certainly moves well, doesn't he?" Desaree whispered.

Almost as if the shields had heard them, Bedelth and Verath slowed their movements. "*It looks like we have company*," Bedelth warned, his words echoing in Claire's mind. Both Bedelth's and Verath's eyes snapped in their direction. They looked quite out of place amidst all the men. They giggled and scurried over to the archery range.

Desaree's gaze continued darting towards Verath.

"This will do," Saffra said. She pulled her bow from her shoulder and began fussing with the strings. She explained each of the steps, how she notched the strings, making sure they were firmly attached to the bow limbs. She selected an arrow and showed where to place it, how to stand, and how to hold it while pulling the bowstring tight.

Claire knew some of what she was taught, having grown up in a rural hunting family.

When Saffra sent a perfectly aimed arrow straight for the bulls-eye, both Claire and Desaree clapped with excitement. After that she fired several more, explaining her movements as they watched her. She made it look easy.

They each took turns. It took them a while to get over the difficulty of pulling the string taught. "I had no idea it took so much strength," Desaree managed, her voice strained.

"I think I've been spoiled by compound bows," Claire muttered.

"What is a compound bow?" Saffra asked.

"Oh. Well, it's similar to a regular bow, but with lots of pulleys and things to make it easier. I suppose it is a modern version of this."

"Pulleys? On a bow?" Saffra's brow furrowed.

Claire tried to explain the mechanisms, which earned more looks of confusion from both Desaree and Saffra. At last she said, "Oh never mind! It's all too complicated without a pen and paper."

Desaree surprised them by having a good aim for a beginner. Two of her arrows hit the edge of the target. Claire didn't hit the target a single time, but she was challenged in a way that left her invigorated. While she had shot her father's compound bow many times on their hunting trips, this was entirely different. She had to use her strength to hold the bow tight while aiming it. With each miss of the target, her weakness grew more apparent.

"It is a good thing I did not bring my longbow today," Saffra joked when Claire missed the shot by a great distance.

"Yes, good thing..." Claire muttered, scowling. She hated exposing her weaknesses, and clearly archery was one of them. Her inability to hit the target left her feeling helpless.

As the sun set and evening approached, they were forced to bring their practice to an end. Desaree was the most reluctant, having immediately fallen in love with the sport. "I never imagined it would be so much fun."

"Now you know why I have passed many hours here," Saffra said, "especially when I am overwhelmed with my other duties."

"Perhaps I ought to do the same." Claire thought about all the stress she was under. "I could definitely use an outlet for my frustration."

"That would be a grand idea. And I am sure Commander Daxton would also lend his assistance to your training."

Claire and Desaree burst into laughter. "Oh, I am sure Dax would *love* any excuse to spend time with his betrothed," Desaree said. Saffra blinked before giving them a shy smile.

～

THEY ENTERED the dining hall and went to Saffra's favorite spot. Claire's eyes happened to fall upon Lady Caterina. She was deep in conversation with her friend. The moment she spotted them, her talking stopped and her eyes narrowed. Little patches of red emerged on her cheeks. Seeing Desaree so finely dressed must have been a shock.

Seeing it brought more satisfaction than Claire cared to admit.

A quick glance to the head table showed it unoccupied. With Talon away on his trip, only a few of the shields were in residence—

"Good evening, ladies." Lord Verath stood beside their table. He only had eyes for Desaree. "I do hope you enjoyed yourselves this afternoon. You look especially lovely tonight, Desaree." She blushed beet red. "Have a pleasant dinner."

He bowed and departed, leaving them wide-eyed.

"He's absolutely smitten with you, Des." Claire nudged her shoulder. Desaree looked overcome and said nothing.

Dinner was especially fun. The three of them feasted while discussing wedding plans for Saffra's big day. Weddings in Dragonwall were very similar to those in Claire's world with subtle differences, such as the color of the gown and the phrases spoken.

For the drengr, ceremonies were quite different. They were not called weddings, but rather, bonding ceremonies, and several differences compared to weddings, the biggest of which was the involvement of magic and the gown color. For a bonding ceremony, the rider always wore a gown to match the dragon scales of their drengr.

For traditional Dragonwall weddings, women wore gold gowns and men generally wore the colors of their house. A formal ceremony was held to declare vows, and huge celebrations followed. In smaller villages, the entire village often took part. In larger cities, these celebrations were usually more restricted to those closest to the bride and groom's family.

"Madame Rosanne will design my gown, of course," Saffra told them, which sent them off on a long tangent about shades of gold, fabrics, and embellishments. Nothing made the time pass faster. It was the kind of conversation that left her feeling warm and giddy. The only time her heart felt heavy was when she witnessed brief flashes of longing that crossed Desaree's face. Shields were not permitted mates, and especially not marriages. Desaree's love for Verath no matter how deep, would not be sealed in matrimony the way Saffra's was soon to be. And although Desaree hid it well, Claire knew that this matter left her aching.

After dinner, Claire and Desaree bid Saffra goodnight and retreated to her chambers. Desaree was motherly in her attentions, helping her to undress and unbraid her hair. For Desaree it was a matter of principle. For Claire, it felt too excessive. She wanted Desaree to have some time to herself. Instead of saying something about it, she allowed her to fuss because it was clearly important to her.

After they had bid each other goodnight, Claire crawled happily into bed. Staring up at the canopy, she realized that her life was finally falling into place. Having both Desaree and Saffra by her side left her feeling more confident than ever. Somehow, she knew that having these two supporting her in the days to come was going to make all the difference in the world.

CHAPTER 25

TRUE INTENTIONS

Redport

Tamara entered her father's study hand-in-hand with Byron. She looked around. The room had hardly changed since her childhood. Tall shelves of aging books, a large fireplace, plush rugs beneath her feet, glowing oil lamps, and the smell of wood and paper were some of the many familiar memories that resurfaced as nostalgia washed over her. When she was a child, she had visited her father often, but as the years passed, she and her father grew apart. Even now she could not recall the last time she had entered this room in his castle.

He sat at a large oak desk, stained dark to showcase the wood's rich grainlines. Upon their entry, he stood. "Please, come and take a seat." He motioned for them to take the two chairs already positioned before his desk.

Byron offered Tamara's hand a gentle squeeze before they both took a seat. Once in her lap, her hands fidgeted out of nervousness. Her eyes did not know what to do either, so her gaze settled upon the sparse trinkets on her father's desk. Writing supplies, a small stack of parchment, and a little wooden boat her brother Jonah had carved when he was a boy.

She had anxiously anticipated this meeting for days.

"Thank you for inviting us to meet with you," Byron said. The moment he spoke, she was taken aback by his frosty tone. She knew him well enough to hear the strained formality in his voice. "At first, I considered myself honored that you would seek an invitation to meet with us."

"The honor is all mine, as you—"

"I said '*at first*.'" Byron's eyes narrowed. "I no longer consider myself honored. I know the reason for this meeting. Your men like to talk. I am a superb listener. I make it my business to be."

Creases appeared on Lord Redwynn's forehead. "And why should the reason for this meeting upset you?"

"I should think that is obvious."

Tamara's eyebrows pulled together. It was not obvious to *her*. She quickly hid her confusion.

Byron was not happy.

Lord Redwynn finally scoffed and said, "Then you must know, I have as good a right as any for hoping to make such a request. Better even. That is my daughter you're stealing."

"Stealing? Is that what you call it? Forgive me, *my lord*, but perhaps you fail to realize that drengr customs are steeped in tradition, and we certainly do not see it that way. Your daughter has chosen her path. She was never forced into it."

"Tradition?!" Lord Redwynn demanded. "Times change. Traditions change."

"Clearly, since you are reckless enough to demand that the fort hand over its most precious resource."

Lord Redwynn's face grew redder. "Ten drengr and their riders —that is all I request."

"All?"

"Gods above! That is my daughter you've got. This is the least you can do. Go to your father and insist upon it."

"You are brazen, my lord. Too brazen!" Byron crossed his arms. "What of the other strongholds? What of the other dragondoms? Have we enough to afford *them* the same...*luxury*? Or do you feel yourself above the rest?"

"To undirfold with the other strongholds! War is coming. I have villages to prepare. I can cut the preparation time in half with the assistance of your ki—"

"And how is *my kind* supposed to assist you?" Byron said, his voice a lethal calm.

"There are messages to be delivered. Meetings to be had. Have you any idea how much time is lost on travel? I have need of my lesser lords now, not when the crops are harvested or the weather improves."

"Is that what we are to you? Pack animals to do your bidding? To carry your messages? To ferry your lesser lords about for meetings? You must think we sit in our fort feasting and growing fat—that we have no responsibilities?"

"To hell with drengr dignity!" Lord Redwynn slammed his fist on his desk. "The war will come. Wild dragons will be on our lands before we know it. We must prepare. It is the duty of the fort to prepare its territory."

"Yes, but not in the way you suggest."

"Then you refuse my request?"

"Most vehemently, my lord."

"Then I will tell you this." Lord Redwynn straightened to his full height, tugging on the lapels of his jacket. "Do not expect our house militias to answer the fort's summons when war comes to you."

"You would dare break the law?" Byron showed obvious disbelief.

Tamara's eyes grew wide. Would her father really refuse? Truly?

It was the law that the lord of each dragondom was to send caches of soldiers if ever they were called upon. If the Redwynn Family refused to send their militia, they would be held accountable to the full extent of the law. Her father would not dare such ruin, would he?

"I will break the law if I must. I must look to the welfare of my people."

"Very well—we are done here. But I must ask, is there anything you would say to your daughter before we leave?"

Tamara's skin flushed as her father's gaze fell upon her. The silence was painful. Then Lord Redwynn turned back to Byron. "There is nothing I wish to say to her—nothing at all. Except, perhaps, that she has chosen dissociation. She will be welcome back as a rider, but never as a daughter."

It felt as if she'd been struck. The breath rushed from her chest. Hot tears pooled up in her eyes and her vision blurred. "You...you do not mean that."

Her father's gaze was stony. He said nothing.

"This is unfortunate, Lord Redwynn. I expected better. Tamara, come, we are leaving." Byron took her hand and gently pulled her from her chair. Lord Redwynn remained silent as they left his study.

"Slow...slow down, please," Tamara gasped once they were outside in the corridor.

At her request, Byron stopped and turned to her. She had never seen him this angry. "Please forgive my abruptness. I hope I did not frighten you."

She could do little more than shake her head. She was too shocked to say much else.

"Good. Now, let us be gone from here. I will be damned if I spend another two days near that man. Pack your things and bid those you love goodbye."

"Right...right this very moment?" She swallowed against the hoarseness of her throat, then she wiped her eyes.

"Immediately, yes. How much time do you need?"

"I...just an hour, perhaps?"

Byron took her face in his hands and gazed into her teary eyes. Perhaps he finally understood the reason she disliked her father. "I would not have you stay under that man's roof any longer than necessary!" With that, he gave her a brief peck on the lips and strode away.

She stood motionless and touched her lips. The tingles she felt were real. Aside from his kiss of trickery, he had not kissed her since. It took her several moments before her wits returned.

***

Her mother was frantic as she rushed about, helping to pack and muttering to herself in disbelief. Finally, she stopped to look at Tamara. "Surely your father's words were not so bad. I do not like this business of you leaving early. What could Aaron possibly say to send Byron away?"

"Mother, I can assure you, we have good reason to leave early. Father has done something shameful, something offensive." Tamara proceeded to tell her mother of the meeting. Poor Lady Redwynn was simply too devoted to understand the severity of the situation. She gave plenty of justifications for Lord Redwynn's poor behavior. In the end, nothing Lady Redwynn said could convince them to stay.

Tamara bid farewell to her mother and brothers. Before she knew it, she was on Byron's back, settled in where his wing joints met the base of his neck. They were sky borne in seconds.

It was not until her mind was melded with Byron's that she understood the full extent of his fury. It was not altogether her father's request that infuriated him. It was something else entirely.

Byron had been so certain that Tamara's family missed her—that her father missed her. In that, Byron had been very wrong. Tamara's father hadn't missed her at all. He never intended to make peace with his daughter. Moreover, he had all but demanded a bride price for allowing Tamara to become a rider. It was offensive.

Tamara winced under Byron's anger. She wanted answers. How had he known so much about her father's intentions beforehand? How had he discovered so much? She could have sifted through his memories. Instead, she asked.

"While you were indisposed, I met in secret with your father's servants and lesser lords. Men like to talk when you give them a strong mug of ale and make them feel good about themselves."

Byron had heard enough about her father's intentions to discover the purpose of the invitation. What was worse, those who also knew the truth thought nothing of it. Most believed Lord Redwynn was in the right, that he was merely trying to protect his people.

"He has always taken his position seriously," Tamara explained, *"even to the detriment of his family."*

"I am sorry for you, Tamara. It fills me with gladness to know that you will have a better life, away from him."

Her body felt heavy. *"I wish it didn't have to be like this."*

"Perhaps he will change in time."

"I hope you are right." There were so many things about her home she would miss. She tried not to think about it, instead, she thought about the future's potential. Becoming a rider was everything she wanted, but it had come at a cost. She was only just beginning to realize the sacrifices she was making.

The flight back to Fort Squall passed all too quickly. It heartened her to know that her company improved Byron's mood considerably. By the time he touched down in one of the Fort's large courtyards, he was much happier.

Because they had gotten such a late start on their journey, it was well past dark.

A few passersby, likely returning from the evening meal, noticed their arrival and rushed over. Byron had hardly transformed before they were approached. "We did not expect your early return," one of them said. "You had best go see your father. There's news from the capital."

Tamara was scarcely given time to drop off her belongings before Byron pulled her along to the fort leaders' chambers. When they entered, Lord Davi and Lady Emmy greeted them warmly. Emmy's embrace was sweet. She held Tamara for several moments and said, "My son told us about your womanhood. Please know that anything you desire, you need only ask."

"Thank you," she whispered, absolutely mortified that they knew. She couldn't fault him for revealing the news, though.

"Now, tell me of these attacks," Byron said.

Tamara felt the warmth drain from her body. More attacks?

"Goblins are raiding border villages along the Eastern Barrier

Range. It began after you departed for Redport," Lord Davi explained, leading them to a map. He pointed out several settlements. "We received word from King Talon, which reached us yesterday. By now, he has taken his leave of the capital and traveled to Fort Lin. They require his assistance in light of the continuing attacks."

"The attacks continue?" Tamara asked.

"They do. The goblins are attacking at random. Their movements have been unpredictable."

"The full force of Kane's malice has begun," Byron whispered.

"Aye," Lord Davi said. "Dragon attacks in the north, goblin attacks in the east. I hear that the pirates have increased their sea raids too. A fellow by the name of Captain Bennett confirmed this not but two days ago."

"Not to mention, rumors of increased vodar sightings," Lady Emmy added.

"I think it is safe to say we are truly at war." Lord Davi spoke with heavy finality.

Tamara's stomach dropped. It hardly felt real. *War?*

"Speaking of war..." Byron said.

He told his parents of the incident that brought them home early. After the initial shock wore off, Lord Davi decided that part of Lord Redwynn's request was not necessarily in poor taste. "The man does have a point in the overall scheme of things. Though, ten Drengr is just too many. Perhaps if we were to station say...two pairs...we would have a way of relaying messages quicker.

"Our forces would be spread too thin, Father. Perhaps when we boasted numbers closer to a thousand."

"I agree, which is why Lord Redwynn's request is impossible. But I do see some benefit of the idea as a whole, aside from attending to their absurd requests, like carrying deliveries for them."

"It is unfortunate that our numbers have fallen so greatly over the years." Emmy's words were sad. Tamara knew exactly what she meant. Tens of thousands of years ago, the fort had many more drengr than it did now.

"We must do the best we can with what we have, my love." Davi imparted a look upon his mate that left Tamara's cheeks flushed. "Now, let's all have a seat in my study, perhaps some wine, so that we might discuss the future."

When they were all comfortably seated, Davi broke the silence. "Lady Tamara, you are a woman now. I can no longer withhold your right to mate. You and my son may be mated at your earliest convenience."

A rush of something flooded her body.

"Father, please." Byron interrupted, looking from Davi to Tamara. "It is my wish that we might wait a little longer."

Tamara opened her mouth to speak. She was about to tell them that she was ready, when Emmy said, "You must understand, my son. For us riders, being parted is a burden, especially once a bond is discovered. I understand your hesitance, but you should know that Tamara will suffer for it. She will feel as if she is only half a person until the bond is sealed."

Tamara's chest tightened. Was that why she felt unpleasant when she was parted from him?

Byron sighed, glancing at Tamara. He did not wish to see her suffer, but he also feared mating with her at such a young age. But that was preposterous. She turned sixteen next week.

"I am ready," she said, looking him in the eye. "Besides, nearly every girl my age is already married. Some are even expecting babes."

Byron said nothing.

"War is upon us," Davi added, as if to drive the point home. "The time for waiting is over. If something happens to your mother and I, the fort will look to you to lead. They will respect you more if you are already mated. The two of you must present a united front."

Tamara's heart began racing. "You mean to say...there is a possibility he would lose the vote?"

"Yes, it is a possibility. As you know, there are many rules put in place at the founding of our great monarchy. That includes voting in new fort leaders. While it is nearly always the case that the offspring take up the mantle of their parents, it is not guaranteed. The fort must trust Byron enough as a leader to elect him. They will trust him more if he shows his maturity. He will appear more mature with his mate by his side."

"She *is* by my side, Father."

"Yes, but she is not yet mated to you. Do not feign ignorance. You know as well as I how the forts function."

"But surely the wild dragons will not come here," Tamara said. "We are too far south. They would not dare attack us. If they tried, we would know days in advance—they would never abandon the element of surprise, would they?" Tamara looked from Davi to Emmy for confirmation. When no one answered, she said, "I am too young to lead the fort with Byron."

"There is a reason Lady Emmy has taken you under her wing, Tamara," Davi's gaze was soft. "Nothing is promised in times of war. Those of us who lived during the war with the kalds know this."

Tamara's gaze dropped to her skirts. Earlier in the conversation, Emmy had poured them each a goblet of wine. She chose now to sip hers, to combat her nervous fidgeting. The idea of losing Davi and Emmy in battle made it hard to breathe, and the idea of ruling in their stead left her feeling unwell.

"You have given me a great deal to consider, Father," Byron said at last. "I cannot give you an answer tonight, but I will think it over. I must ensure my conscience is easy. I would not dare to live a life of regret. Yet, I understand the severity of my request and the potential pain it might cause. Grant me a short period of time to think it over."

As he spoke, Byron's gaze settled upon her. She returned his regard with fierce determination. A hot fire blazed up inside, along with a desire to prove a point. Regardless of how Byron felt, she was ready to seal their bond. If it came down to proving her readiness, she would do it. She would do whatever it took. Their time was coming.

CHAPTER 26
A CRACK IN THE WALL

Kastali Dun

Claire was relieved that the king was in Lincastle. His absence made everything feel more relaxed. Even the keep seemed to breathe a sigh of relief. While his presence no longer bothered her like it once did, she wasn't yet at ease with him, and running into him was awkward.

She did miss her time with Reyr.

Desaree made things better, filling the gaps Reyr's company left behind. As her handmaiden, she was on hand for her every need. She even accompanied her everywhere, with the exception of her magic lessons, which was a good thing. She wanted to keep Desaree as far as possible from Caterina. She also wanted Desaree to have some time to herself.

Four days after the king departed, a great storm struck Kastali Dun. Since her arrival, it had often rained to break the humidity, but never like this. She and Desaree went out past the overhang of her terraced balcony to enjoy the torrential sheets of rain and screaming wind, laughing and spinning with outstretched arms until they were drenched and dizzy. Despite the late summer's heat, they both needed a hot bath afterwards.

Once Claire was comfortably settled in front of her fireplace, Desaree took her leave, mentioning something offhand about reading a new book Verath had lent her. With Desaree's departure, she sat alone, watching the fire crackle, soaking up its warmth. It was a comfortable sort of night, with a glass of wine in hand, safe within the protection of the castle.

She sat for a long time, lost in her thoughts, until something strange caught her attention—a brief movement next to the bookcase. After studying the wall for several minutes, slowly sipping her wine, she saw another movement. It was subtle. She would have missed it, had she not been looking. Her gaze narrowed. It appeared as if the wall had moved, but that was silly because the walls of the castle were made of rock. What she had actually seen was a ripple of fabric from the giant tapestry that spanned the wall from the ceiling to the floor.

Like most rooms in the keep, the walls of her living quarters were covered with these decorative hangings. Some were floral. Others were landscapes. This one in particular was of a prairie that stretched upwards to meet the sky, with khaki grasses and wispy clouds. It reminded her of home. She often found herself staring at it, and sometimes she even got a little choked-up.

As the storm continued, she watched the periodic ripple of the fabric. Maybe it was a ghost. *Were* there ghosts in Dragonwall? Probably not. Had the timing of the movements been any different, she might have explained it as something supernatural, but the timing was everything. Whenever a particularly fierce gust of wind slammed against the castle's walls, the fabric fluttered.

A brilliant idea came to mind.

She got off the couch and went to investigate. She ran her hands along the fabric. Beneath it she felt the blocky stones that formed the foundations of the keep. She reached the edge of the wall hanging. Nothing felt amiss, but she wasn't convinced.

Taking hold of the fabric, she pulled it back. The stonework beneath looked normal enough. She studied it more intently, looking at the seams where the mortar had been placed. Only then did she see what she expected to see. Near where the disturbance was, the pattern of stonework was different. The stones lined up perfectly without a staggered arrangement. There was a crack in the wall. This wasn't the kind of crack that comes with aging stone and mortar. This was a seam, even in width, traveling from the floor upwards.

Her breathing hitched.

She put her ear against the seam. There was a faint whistling sound, a slight draft. Chills spread across her skin. This was a door, perhaps to a secret passage! A castle this size was bound to have one. But then, how did she open it?

She glanced around, excitement rolling off of her in waves. Her gaze landed on the bookcase. Dropping the fabric, she rushed over and began pulling books away, gently tossing them into piles upon the floor. Everyone knew that when it came to secret passageways, there was often a special latch in a nearby bookcase. She pulled books faster and faster until every single one was removed. The only problem was, there was nothing here.

Her shoulders fell. She glanced between the precious books now lying in a heap on the floor and the empty bookcase. She ran her fingers all along the shelves in hopes of finding something. There was nothing—no latch or button.

Exhaling, she collapsed back onto the couch and sipped her wine. After catching her breath, she replaced the books. She studied the wall again, the stones in particular. Was one of them the key? She pushed every single stone in the wall.

Nothing happened.

A small laugh burst from her chest. She probably looked ridiculous. She dropped her arms, and stared at the door. "Open Sesame," she said, lifting her arms like a magician in a magic show. "Abracadabra?"

Still, nothing.

"Okay," she said to it, thinking about her magic lessons. "What's the magic word for open? Hinga!"

Like usual, as soon as she spoke it, her gaze faltered, little pricks of light danced in her vision, and a gentle wave of fatigue washed over her. This time, she didn't notice. A low groan met her ears. Seconds later a jubilant smile spread across her face. Dust spurted from the seams in the wall as the rectangle of stonework moved backwards, grinding and rumbling. The door retreated into the darkness, disappearing from sight.

She gasped.

The doorway was blacker than black. She took a step backwards, exhaling. She was equal parts scared and excited. What would she find if she went inside? She walked forward and leaned into the blackness, straining to see. The space smelled damp and musky. There was a slight draft, probably what had caused the tapestry to flutter.

She grabbed one of the oil lamps from her chamber wall. A ferocious howl of wind sounded outside. The lamp flickered but did not go out. She illuminated the inside of the doorway, her hand no longer steady as excitement coursed through her. A narrow staircase led directly downward.

Thank the gods she hadn't stepped in without a light; she would have tumbled straight in!

She descended the stairs, moving slowly. Nerves gripped her. Her mind raced as she considered all the things she might find—all the ways this discovery might come in handy. The staircase continued downward for what seemed like an eternity. At last, she found herself on a flat landing in a tiny room. Holding her lamp forward, she was confronted with three pitch-black hallways. They presented a choice she was simultaneously nervous and eager to make. She chose the one in the middle, directly opposite of her.

She walked for several minutes in silence until the faint sound of voices could be heard. She came to an abrupt stop where she strained to listen. There were two of them—male—and they were growing louder. Perhaps there was a corridor spanning the secret passageway? When they were close enough, she could make out their words.

"...she's a right good lass."

"Of course you'd say that, Murn. Maybe if you weren't skipping guard duty so often, she would not be so kind to you."

"Bah! What are you talkin' about?"

"I see you leaving. Deny it all you like."

The voices continued like this, growing louder before growing quieter, then disappearing entirely. When silence returned, she continued on her adventure. Every so often, the walls of the passageways opened wider or grew narrower, and she was presented with the option of other hallways or stairways. Treating it as a game, she took whichever suited her fancy.

The longer she explored, the more she felt the magic of the keep. It reminded her of the Gable Forest, the way the trees had felt when she touched them, as if alive and sentient. She felt the same here, stopping to catch her breath as she laid her palm upon the stonework of the castle. Despite the darkness, she closed her eyes. There! She felt something, perhaps magic, radiating beneath her palm, buzzing with something akin to awareness. Queen Isabella and King Eymar were responsible for building the keep. Perhaps this magic was the same she'd felt in the forest.

A smile stretched across her lips. She had just discovered one of the best kept secrets in all of Kastali Dun. Did anyone else know about this? Did these passageways only navigate the keep? Did they lead into the city too? How extensive was this network she'd found?

She continued forward, twisting and turning, until she was forced to admit she was lost. Her hands turned clammy. She attempted to backtrack, but everything looked the same. In a place like this, she could wander for days before finding a way out. What would such an escape look like? Another door with light streaming through? A dark and hidden latch to the outside world?

How long had she been wandering, anyway? It must have been hours. She could feel the ache of her tired feet in their slippers.

Shutting her eyes tightly, she placed her palm against the wall. Calmness settled over her. Taking a deep breath in, she let the magic buzz against her palm. When she allowed herself a moment of thought, the answer became clear.

There was a way out, just ahead. The castle nudged her like Esterpine's trees had once done. She allowed her fingers to trail along the stones, keeping her eyes closed as she moved forward.

Yes, what she sought was just here. A door. She lifted her lamp high, examining the wall. It took several intense minutes of scrutiny, but at last she saw the familiar seams that indicated a moving door. She put her ear against one seam, listening. There was no noise.

She commanded the door to open, cringing as she said the word. It felt as if the stones around her trembled too, but that was merely the door responding to her. She stepped aside and waited for it to settle.

The faint orange light of dying embers met her eyes. She found herself in someone's living quarters. A spike of fear made her freeze. What if she was discovered?! She glanced about then heard a loud snore. Her eyes snapped in the direction of a closed door leading to a sleeping chamber.

Her shoulders relaxed.

She stepped through the doorway and said, "Lagar," to close it. She flinched at the noise. A loud snort followed by more snoring followed. She was safe—for now. Quietly, she crept from the chamber, shutting the door behind her. She didn't breathe easily again until she was strolling through the familiar corridors of the keep.

CHAPTER 27

THE VODAR ARE COMING

Kastali Dun

Saffra shifted her basket, readjusting the cloth that disguised its contents. A generous selection of dainties and a rare bottle of wine. Today was a rest day. The afternoon sun was high in the sky, sending many behind doors in search of cool darkness.

She was on her way to visit Claire and Desaree. They were slowly filling the hole that Cyrus had left behind. She was healing. Better still, in eight weeks she would be married to the man she loved. The king himself was to marry them in the throne room. She thought of all the plans to be made, and of her gown, which still needed to be designed. There was so much to do!

It was hard to believe that somewhere on the fringes of Dragonwall, an evil asarlaí was intent upon destroying their kingdom. The harrowing fact was always present in her mind. She had made it her job to help in whatever way possible, to prepare Claire for what she would one day face. But during times like these, when her happiness freely overflowed, she struggled to believe it.

Claire lived in the Hall of Kings, two stories above her. It occupied the top floor of the southernmost wing of the keep. These rooms were reserved for royalty, the king's shields, and the people who served them.

She knocked on Claire's door. A giggle sounded within. Desaree's face appeared, flushed with excitement. "Come quickly!" she whispered, glancing out into the corridor. "We have something to tell you."

She rushed in, depositing her basket upon a nearby table. Both Claire and Desaree were beside themselves with excitement. "You are not going to believe this," Claire said, rushing over.

Her brow furrowed. "What is it?"

"I think it's best if we show her." Claire and Desaree shared a look, grinning wickedly.

"Show me what, exactly?"

"Come here." Claire took Saffra's arm, leading her to a wall near the fireplace. Desaree pulled back the wall's tapestry.

Saffra frowned. "I am afraid I do not understand. Is this a joke?"

Claire's grin turned triumphant as she said, "Hinga!"

A loud grinding noise made her jump backwards with a yelp. The patch of wall before her disappeared into the darkness. All that was left was a gaping doorway. She opened her mouth but could not find words.

Desaree giggled. "Impressive, is it not? A secret passageway! Claire showed me earlier. She found it last night. I still cannot understand why you did not fetch us. There could have been something dangerous inside."

"And you could have protected me?" Claire's teasing tone was gentle.

"Well...no. But that is beside the point."

"You have been inside, then?" Saffra asked, turning to look at Claire. "You have seen what lies within?"

Claire nodded. "I spent hours down there last night. I got lost, actually. When I finally found my way out, I found myself in none other than Lord Glover's chambers!"

"Lord Glover's?" Saffra glanced between them. "And you did not get caught?"

"Ha! No. He was snoring way too loud to hear me." Claire did an impression that sounded more like a congested pig.

They all started laughing.

"Well, that sounds like a close call. I am glad you weren't discovered." Saffra turned from Claire to Desaree and asked, "Have you been inside too?"

"No!" Desaree crossed her arms. "I wanted to but Claire said we had to wait for you."

Saffra smiled and glanced back at the doorway. "I can hardly believe it. The entire time I have lived here...I never knew."

Her wedding plans were forgotten. The mere fact that a network of secret passages could lay disguised within the keep consumed her with curiosity. How many were there? Did her living quarters have a secret door, too?

Claire said, "Do you think anyone else knows about this?"

"If they do, they have kept it hidden."

Claire's eyes danced. "I suppose that's why they're *secret*. But, enough talk! Shall we?" She held out a lamp, illuminating the blackened doorway before disappearing into the darkness. Saffra and Desaree exchanged a final glance, plunging in after.

The stairway was narrow, forcing them into single file. There was a chamber at the bottom with three different hallways. "I think we need more light," Saffra said, examining the little room. "Dagar." A silvery orb appeared. She released it to follow in their wake.

The room was rather plain, seemingly forgotten in time if the thick layer of dust on the floor was anything to go by.

"I took the middle passage," Claire said. "If you follow it long enough, you'll find yourself in a maze. That's why I got lost."

"You did not think to follow your own footsteps?" Desaree asked. Claire blinked, as if only just realizing this. Saffra grinned, amused. "It's okay. I probably wouldn't have thought to, either. I would have been too distracted by my excitement. Perhaps we should take one of the other hallways?"

"I vote for the one on the right," Saffra said.

They set off, following its twists and turns. Sometimes there was a stairwell up or down. Some of the stairwells spiraled while others were straight. A few went down so far that they dared not take them all the way.

They spoke in whispers, afraid to lift their voices. Sometimes, the lack of noise was suffocating. Other times, they heard voices on the other side of the wall. Even entire conversations.

"Is that a light?!" Desaree gasped, bringing them to a stop. They'd been wandering for at least an hour.

"I think it is," Saffra said.

Up ahead, there was a faint green glow. Patterns of light danced upon the floor. The three of them rushed forward. They came to a small room, the oddest chamber imaginable.

"It looks like a shrine," Claire mused.

The room was circular, hidden within one of the many turrets of the keep. It had a high, pointed ceiling. There were no other visible entrances besides the one they came through. There were four pews facing the front, which held a large, stained glass window set into the wall.

"Well, that explains the dancing light," Claire said, her voice hushed with awe. "Do you think anyone still comes here?"

"I...I don't think so." Saffra moved forward with wide eyes. There was no dust in this room, as if protected by the ravages of time.

Glowing, green light emanated from the stained glass mural towering above them. Its brilliant colors looked as though they had been freshly stained. The panes made up an image of a majestic, lordly tree. There were pin pricks of light fluttering and dancing about it, as if in celebration. Simply looking upon the art left her feeling warm and happy inside.

They sat down shoulder-to-shoulder in the nearest pew. Several of the branches moved, swaying as if caught by an invisible wind. The panes of glass danced and rearranged themselves, creating a light show upon the walls.

"Did it just—" Desaree failed to finish her sentence.

"It did," Claire said, sounding just as awed.

"How?" Saffra managed.

"You know, now that I see it, I know exactly what this reminds me of!" Claire smacked her forehead. "I think it's a special tree in the Gable Forest, don't you?"

Desaree and Saffra could not confirm her suspicions, because neither had been to the Gable Forest. At length, Saffra said, "I suppose it would make sense. Queen Isabella *was* responsible for much of the magic in this castle. Perhaps she built this room as a way to remember her home, as a way to reflect?"

"I bet you're right." Claire sounded even more excited.

They fell silent. It felt disrespectful to talk in a place like this. They watched the branches on the window-tree dance and wave. Time seemed to lose all meaning.

"Shall we go back?" Desaree said at last, when the light behind the window had faded slightly, taking on a bluish glow.

They left in good spirits.

Saffra felt rejuvenated. There was strange magic in the castle, of that she was sure. As they made their way, they talked and joked, discussing how surprising the turn of events had been. They returned the way they had come, trying to closely follow their footsteps in the dust. As time dragged on, something seemed to be wrong.

"We're lost!" Desaree said, sounding a little panicked. "We are not even following our own footsteps anymore. Those are boots."

"I guess we know that others have used this place," Claire said. "I hope we don't run into them."

"These footprints could be thousands of years old." Saffra bent to examine one. "Is there a trick to getting out?"

"Surely we are close," Desaree added.

"I think there is a way." Claire glanced around. "Let me try something." She placed her palm upon the wall. For a moment, all was silent. Then her face broke into a radiant smile. "We are close. I'm quite certain."

"Which way?" Desaree and Saffra whispered.

"A door—just above. Not far from us." Claire started forward. "Up the stairs ahead on our right. This way."

They followed until their path ended at a dead end. Claire

placed her hand over the stretch of wall and commanded it to open. They were greeted by darkness. After waiting for several minutes, they each stepped through. Their arrival illuminated what looked like a private chamber.

"Whose room is this?" Claire asked. "It seems familiar, but I can't explain why. There's warmth."

"It looks quite nice," Desaree said, squinting into the dim light. "I have never cleaned it before."

Saffra faltered, sending her orb higher, bathing the entire room. Her shoulders tensed. There was no mistaking the painting above the fireplace. It depicted three large drengr breathing flame on an ice giant. "We should leave," she said.

"What is it?" Desaree turned to her with frightened eyes.

Claire was the only one who did not respond. She stood motionless, a strange look of recognition upon her features. Then she stepped away from the others and gravitated towards the painting.

Saffra cleared her throat and turned to Desaree, wetting her lips. "This room belonged to Cyrus. I think we should leave. Being in here...hurts." Her chest felt smothered.

"Of course, as you wish." Desaree grabbed Claire's arm and they fled, returning to Claire's chambers. After they calmed down, they set about Saffra's wedding plans.

Excitement over their discovery continued into the next few days. They explored more of the tunnels and narrow hallways. They familiarized themselves with various doors into and out of the extensive network. Saffra's eyes were now trained on the walls of the keep, no matter where she went. She looked for seams, cracks in the stonework that might suggest hidden doors. Each time she found one, she investigated it. The others did the same, although Desaree was the only one who couldn't open them with magic.

Claire even discovered a doorway into the king's tower.

"I was traveling from my room," she explained, "and I knew the left-most corridor at the bottom of the stairs ought to go beneath the Hall of Kings, so I followed it. I found none other than a door into a private parlor. You will never guess *who* it belongs to."

"Who?!" Desaree said at the same time Saffra said, "The king?"

"*Yes!*" Claire's face radiated with excitement. "Well, no! But technically, yes. What I mean is, I do not think he uses it. There are other rooms in the king's tower. A lot of other rooms. I had no idea until I found them. Anyway, I think this one belonged to his mother. It is a queen's parlor, a place for the queen to entertain her handmaidens and ladies of the court. The furnishings were feminine."

"Oh!" Desaree clapped her hands together, a look of longing on her features. "I would dearly love to see it."

"How did you slip past the tower's guards?" Saffra was worried. Claire could have gotten in a great deal of trouble, sneaking around.

"I got lucky."

They had started a collection of sketched maps detailing where they believed certain passages led. They kept them locked away in Claire's writing desk. After she found the king's tower, she picked through the leaves of parchment to present a freshly drawn map. It wasn't easy drawing these maps. They had to create them from memory and combine them with a significant amount of extrapolation. The extrapolating often got them in trouble, but it was worth it. They discovered a number of different chambers such as living accommodations, storerooms, and parlors, all integrated into the network of passageways.

"Soon, we will know the castle inside and out," Claire said, an odd gleam in her eyes.

"Perhaps one day our knowledge will come in handy," Saffra added.

Three days after first discovering the passages, Saffra announced, "I found another today." They were sitting out on Claire's balcony, gazing at the sea. "I found it beside the coat of armor near the royal library, just this morning." As she spoke, her gaze followed a small colony of seagulls that had taken flight from the rocks below. They often roosted in the cliffside beneath the keep.

The storm from earlier that week had long since departed, taking its clouds and leaving behind a brilliant, blue sky. With its departure, the first days of fall were particularly warm. Fortunately, the sun was nearing the horizon, offering a spectacular sunset for their amusement.

The three of them sat sharing a bottle of wine, celebrating their superior knowledge of the keep's secrets. While they had spent some time planning for Saffra's wedding, their plans had quickly given way to more conversations about the secret passages.

"We should sneak over to the library later tonight and see where your door leads." Desaree practically bounced up and down in her seat.

"Oh yes, let's," Claire said, nodding and smiling as she sipped her wine.

"Why not?" Saffra shrugged. "I, for one—" Her stomach lurched. The ocean faded from view, darkening at the edges of her vision. "Oh no!" she whispered. She was plunged into darkness. She felt her goblet slip from her hands, heard it clatter on the flagstones, and then there was nothing.

THE BLACKNESS GAVE way to twilight. She gazed upon the world beneath her. The Great Keep of Kastali Dun towered above the city. It looked spectacular from the sky. Like a pendant of a million diamonds, glittering in the darkness. She looked up at the sky again. She saw a full moon rising, still low upon the horizon. Her heart roared in fear as a score of black shapes soared across her line of sight. They were cloaked in shadow and smoke, flying without wings. She gasped in disbelief. They were heading straight for the keep. Oh, gods! She had to warn the others—!

SHE SUCKED IN A BREATH, coughing, nearly choking as she opened her eyes. Comforting hands pressed against her face. "There now," came a voice.

"It must have been one of her visions."

"I think you're right. Saffra, can you hear me?"

"Claire?" Her mind was foggy. Claire's worried face looked down at her. "I...I must have fallen from my chair," she mumbled.

"Are you okay?" Desaree bent down to look at her, feeling her forehead as Claire helped her to her feet. "I think she has taken ill. Shall I send for the healer?"

"No, not yet," Claire said. "Saffra? Was it a vision?"

"I...yes," Saffra croaked, and suddenly it all rushed back. "A horrible vision."

They helped her into her chair.

"Might I get you some water?" Desaree asked, bustling about.

"Yes, water would be welcome." She felt flushed. Her hands shook, so she tucked them in her lap, trying to hold still.

Desaree scurried away, back into Claire's room.

"What did you see?" Claire asked, her voice colored with worry.

"I saw *them*," she hissed. "The vodar."

Claire sucked in a sharp breath, "You, you're sure?"

"I am certain. They were here—here at the keep. But...how silly. Why would they be here?" She looked out over the sea. The sun was nearly beneath the horizon. The moon had not yet come up.

"I...I don't know? Maybe Kane...?"

"Your water, Saffra." Desaree returned, handing her a cup of water.

"Thank you." Saffra took a long drink. It settled into the pit of her stomach uncomfortably. Something was wrong. Even though the vision had ended, her insides churned. Her instincts were driving her into fear.

"What else did you see?" Claire asked.

"I saw them flying straight here. They were—" Her eyes widened. "Gods! What moon is it tonight?" She looked at Desaree.

"Tonight? It has not yet risen, but a full moon."

Saffra jumped to her feet. Claire and Desaree gave startled

cries. "They are coming!" Saffra hissed as terror seeped into her chest.

"What?" Claire shrieked, also jumping to her feet in alarm.

"We must warn the others." Saffra grabbed their arms, pulling them back into Claire's chambers.

Both Claire and Desaree bombarded her with frightened inquiries. "Who is coming? The vodar? What is going on?"

"Yes! The vodar," Saffra managed. "They are coming for the stones."

Without another word, the three of them burst into the Hall of Kings to warn the keep.

JOINING THE FIGHT

Kastali Dun

Claire, Desaree and Saffra raced through the keep. They ran as if the vodar were already nipping at their heels. Horrible scenarios flooded her mind, all of the things that could go wrong. As if on cue, her leg gave a painful twinge, remembering the last time she'd faced the wraths, the injury she'd received.

"We should warn Commander Daxton first!" Saffra called over her shoulder. Of course Saffra's mind would jump straight to him.

They plunged down a set of stairs and raced through an open courtyard. They reached the second level of the keep before she stopped them. "Wait. *Wait!*" she gasped, clutching her side. "Even if we find Dax," she said, "how will he know what to do? Where to go?"

"The vodar are after the stones," Saffra said.

"Right." Claire braced her hands on her knees. "That does not exactly help us. I don't know where..." The words died on her lips. What *had* happened to the stones? No one had ever bothered to tell her. "I don't even know where they are."

Fear gave way to frustration. After everything she had given for them, she'd never thought to follow up on their safety. She had merely handed them over. Her shoulders slumped.

"I saw the vodar flying into the castle," Saffra said. "That means they are hidden somewhere inside."

She stood to her full height. "Talon's shields. If the stones are in the castle, they will know where."

"You can warn them with your mind," Saffra said. "Use your telepathic ability!"

Her eyes widened. "I...I can't! The king doesn't know. If he finds out that I kept this from him..."

"You must!" Saffra said. "It will save us time. It could make all the difference in the world."

"I can't!"

Some secrets shouldn't be left to fester, Cyrus said. It was not reassuring. She felt dizzy. Her stomach hardened into a rock. The thought of Talon discovering her secret...

"It's nearly dark," she said, "which means the shields will be in the dining hall. Let's go."

Desaree and Saffra were forced to chase after her. The dining hall was on the main level of the keep. Its tiers were designed to withstand sieges by creating varying levels through which one could retreat to safety, beginning with the bottommost level. For them, that meant many flights of stairs.

When they arrived, they were panting, gasping for air. The dining hall's doors were already closed. By rule, they were not to be opened for late patrons. Before the guards realized what was happening, they pushed the doors open, ignoring their surprised protests.

They scurried inside and the hall fell silent.

Claire didn't care about the questioning eyes that followed them. She led the charge, racing down the main aisle towards the head table where Bedelth, Jovari, Koldis, and Verath sat. The four of them rose at once.

Whispers echoed through the hall.

Claire took the dais steps two at a time, hoisting her skirts to her knees. She stopped at the table, clutching her side. "The...dragonstones!" she gasped, trying to keep her voice low to avoid mass panic. "The vodar...you must...they are coming...Saffra's vision." She could hardly speak, and certainly not coherently. She stepped aside, hoping that Saffra might do better.

After several rushed exchanges between Saffra and the king's shields, the peril was finally understood. They rounded the table and fled the hall. The room erupted into loud speculation as everyone gazed at the three women standing before them.

Claire reached across the head table and discretely snatched up a carving knife. She turned to the others. "We're going after them. I'll be damned if I stand around and wait to see what happens."

"We are hardly fit to fight demons," Desaree cried.

"No, Claire is right," Saffra said. "We should go."

They raced from the hall, pausing to speak to the guards. "Which way did the shields go?"

"That way, Lady Claire. The king's tower."

"Good. Seal up the dining hall. Do not let the patrons leave until instructed otherwise. And one of you, round up more guards! Spread the word. There is danger lurking in the keep tonight!"

Without wasting another moment, they raced away. They reached the southern wing, preparing to take the first set of stairs. Saffra stopped them. "My bow!" she cried, then added, "How else will we protect ourselves?"

They diverted to Saffra's quarters.

Jocelyn was wide-eyed when they told her. "I'm coming with you," she said. "You are my charge to care for, Lady Saffra. I would not *dare* abandon my duties."

"I admire your honor, but this is too dangerous—"

"You think to dissuade me?" her handmaiden demanded. "I'll not have it. With all due respect, Lady Saffra, you need me." Claire, Desaree, and Saffra exchanged confused looks. "Your skirts!" Jocelyn added. "You have not bothered to hike up your skirts. How can you fight when you're tripping over them?! Here—" She sprinted across Saffra's chamber to a wardrobe, rustled around, then returned with a handful of leather straps. Desaree and Saffra took theirs without complaint.

"What is—?" Claire didn't know what to make of hers.

"It's a skirt chaser, my lady. One for each of you. Now hurry!"

"Skirt chaser?" Claire's eyebrows drew together.

"A skirt chaser is a skirt hike." Jocelyn moved over and began demonstrating on Saffra. The accessory consisted of a belt and accompanying strap. It fastened around the waist. The strap drew up a skirt to fasten it with a metal loop and pin.

"Jocelyn, you have proven your worth ten times over." Saffra sounded grateful. "Thank you. Are you sure about this?"

"I insist." Jocelyn began tossing pantaloons at them. "Here, put these on. They should fit well enough to keep you proper. Now then, let's go."

They set out for the Hall of Kings. The entrance to the tower was packed with guards, spilling into the open doorway, trying to get inside to replace their fallen comrades. The sound of clashing metal and panicked shouts echoed around them.

The hairs on the back of Claire's neck rose. "We're late," she whispered. "It has already started."

They tried to get closer but the guards stopped their progress. "Forgive me, my ladies. We cannot let you pass. You must retreat to safety."

"But we came to fight," Claire said. "Let us through." She had one hand on the handle of her purloined knife, which was still concealed beneath her sleeve.

Two more guards saw them and turned to dissuade them. "Please, Lady Claire. The king would have our heads. You must return to your quarters immediately."

"We are wasting time," Saffra hissed.

"The secret passageway," Desaree whispered. "Come on!"

They dashed to Claire's quarters and into the network of passages without bothering to find a lamp. Jocelyn gasped in disbelief. Claire led them to the queen's parlor. The sound of clashing steel was above them. A blast split the air and shook the walls. They squealed in surprise, moving across the room.

When they reached the stairway, Saffra turned to them. "The three of you must wait here," she commanded, nocking an arrow.

They erupted into protests. Why should they wait in the shadows when they might be of some use? "I am the only person with a weapon," Saffra explained. "Moreover, I have been trained!" With that, she disappeared up the stairs.

Claire pulled out her small carving knife and turned to Desaree and Jocelyn. "Wait here." Then she followed Saffra to the main floor. At first, all she saw was Saffra filling the doorway. When she caught sight of the scene beyond, she went rigid.

The main chamber was in ruins. Loud periodic blasts, clattering furniture, clanging swords. It was chaos. Shields and soldiers alike fought for their lives. Like something from a horror story, black figures glided around the room sending smoky tendrils to slither up the walls. "There were only six last time," she cried. "Only six!"

Now, there were more.

A giant blast shook the room. She screamed, throwing her arms over her head, ducking for cover. Her knife clattered to the floor. The walls rumbled around them, sending pebbles and dust everywhere. She coughed and covered her mouth.

Dust cleared and the fighting continued. No one noticed her and Saffra in the doorway. Another blast sounded. This time, different voices squealed. She turned to find Desaree and Jocelyn cowering behind them.

Verath appeared. His eyes widened when he saw Desaree. "All of you, get *out*!" he hissed. He might have said more, but a wraith descended upon him. He had little more than a moment to turn and lift his sverak in defense. After that, he threw himself back into the fray.

"Their blades are poisonous!" Claire cried to Desaree and Jocelyn, trying to convince them to turn back. "Verath is right! You're both human. You need to get out of here!"

Without waiting for their compliance, her attention was drawn away. Something pulled her like a magnet. Above the mantle, she found Cyrus's sverak ensconced in a glass case. Her heart quickened. Without a single thought for her safety, she threw herself into the chaos, dodging and diving.

She was panting and covered in sweat when she reached the sword. The case was swept to the floor, shattering into fragments that flew everywhere. She retrieved the blade and returned to Saffra's side.

Not a moment too soon.

Two wraiths detached and slithered towards her. Saffra was motionless, her gaze fixed on Dax. She was repeating an incantation over and over, her words barely a whisper. At that moment, an orb of crackling electricity blasted against an invisible barrier protecting Dax. Claire's eyes widened.

The two wraiths descended upon them whether she was ready or not. With Saffra distracted, she was forced to confront them alone. Sheer panic made her blood roar.

Relax and let me do the fighting. Cyrus sounded calm.

Swallowing against the sudden dryness in her throat, she did exactly that. Just as the two wraiths lifted their swords against her, Cyrus's sverak rose to meet them. The clang echoed in her ears, ringing and ringing. She twisted to the side, placing her feet deliberately like a dancer, one after the other, as Cyrus's sverak slashed through the air. It felt as if it were a part of her, an extension of her arm, each blade movement fluid. Before she realized it, she was fighting both wraiths while Saffra stood behind her, chanting.

Cyrus was fighting for her!

It was the strangest sensation. She had deliberately cut off her mind's ability to command her body's muscles. She had relinquished all control. Yet, her muscles tensed up and moved anyway. Without her mind's resistance, the movements were smooth and harmonious.

A short sword cut through the air. She met it while dodging the other. One wraith got too close. She kicked it away just as the other came down upon her. Cyrus acted *through* her, guiding her body as if it were his, as if she were the marionette and he the puppeteer. She spun in a circle, dancing away from both black figures. The sverak went with her. Its superior length gave her the reach she needed.

She removed one head in a clean sweep. Poof! The body disappeared. She did the same with the second wraith. In less than a minute, they were gone—

A high-pitched scream echoed in her ears. She whirled to find Saffra racing across the room, falling to the ground at Daxton's side. Crimson blood pooled up around him, spilling from the deep laceration on his chest. His assailant glided away to join the attack against the others. Skirmishes were taking place all around the king's chambers.

New guards poured in through the tower door. They fought sword to sword, trying to push the vodar back. The problem was, the guards were not mages. The vodar took every opportunity to utilize magic, weakening and wounding them.

King Talon's soldiers were no match for the demons of the underworld. Her resolve shattered when she saw their blackened bodies lying dead upon the floor, contorted into the awkward positions in which they had fallen. Each blackened face wore a look of utter terror.

Bile rose in her throat.

In the center of the room King Talon's four shields stood back to back, fighting with sveraks and magic. Bright flashes of light exploded in the air around them. They were an otherworldly force to be reckoned with.

Her eyes returned to Saffra, sobbing on the floor. Her stomach plummeted. Daxton was gasping for breath while Saffra held her hands against his wound using her magic to keep the poison from spreading. He would have died in seconds had it not been for her.

She was about to run to Saffra's aid when movement caught her attention. Two wraiths slipped through a side door, disappearing. A feeling of dread came over her. She gave Saffra and Dax a final glance before going after them.

She chased the wraiths down a curved staircase that ended at King Talon's study. She was met with more fighting. Tower guards dodged around a big desk in the room, attempting to fight a small group of wraiths. A whooshing sound drew her attention to the balcony. Several more joined the fight. "They just keep coming," she muttered. "Like cockroaches."

Sword in hand, she moved into the room. Just like before, she channeled Cyrus, throwing herself into the fighting. His sword was named Justice—a fitting name. A few moments later, she brought down another wraith. Then another.

Only two soldiers remained. When they noticed her, they put themselves in front of her, immediately becoming targets. The first was run through, his body blackening the moment the poison reached his blood. The other took a cut to the arm and crumpled beside his fallen comrade.

A small whimper left her lips. She was alone. Taking a step backwards, she hefted her blade.

A hiss filled the room. "Don't touch the girl. Our master wants her alive and unharmed. Take her and go."

The hairs on the back of her neck lifted.

Hands seized her from behind. She flailed, trying to free herself. The arms tightened, forcing the air from her lungs. She gasped, trying to breathe. Cold dread washed over her.

"Let me go!" she croaked, kicking and clawing.

"Drop your weapon!" A hiss against her ear. The wraith shook her like a rag doll.

"No!" she managed.

It shook her harder. Her grip loosened. Cyrus's sverak clattered to the floor. Oh, gods!

"Give up, *girl*. You have lost!" Another vodar wraith swept into the room. It went to the painting behind King Talon's desk, a ship navigating stormy seas set in a gilded frame.

She went limp.

The wraith began muttering words in another language. An audible click filled the room. The painting swung forward. It was a cubbyhole, and inside, an elegantly carved wooden box. The wraith made quick work of it, dismantling whatever magical protection it carried, lifting the lid. There, nestled on a bed of silk, was the familiar pouch of dragonstones.

Her stomach plummeted.

"Don't do this," she croaked. Everything she had sacrificed came crashing down around her.

The wraith turned its hooded gaze upon her. She couldn't see its face, but she could sense its smile. With quick movements, it snatched the pouch.

She threw her weight against her captor, struggling like a rabid creature. Something inside her erupted, a mixture of fear, anger, and disbelief. She began to chant, to sing, "Fallam nemaloh sasilo valandur ellohdar, geta ellohdar, geta ellohdar, geta…" The words slipped from her tongue as easily as any words should, as if she knew exactly what she was saying, as if this was the purest tasting water she'd ever had, or the sweetest honey to touch her tongue. Warmth erupted around her. A scream echoed in her ears. Her captor's arms fell away. She turned in time to see its body shrouded in green flame. It withered into a pile of ash, sword clattering down beside it.

The room fell silent for several long breaths. She heard her own gasps as she looked at the remaining wraiths in the room. They stood frozen, gazing at her.

"Drop the stones!" she commanded, feeling more powerful than she ever had.

A cackling laugh. "Take her alive," the wraith hissed, turning to the others. Then it glided towards the balcony. She tried to race after it but the others fell upon her. There was no time to think. The same song fell from her lips again. "Fallam nemaloh sasilo valandur ellohdar, geta ellohdar, geta ellohdar…" The enemies beside her burst into green flame. She did not wait around. She was already sprinting to the balcony. The final wraith turned to look at her. It took several steps forward, placing itself against the balcony's edge.

"My master awaits," it hissed, then it leapt. Without thinking, she jumped after it, closing her arms around its body. It was all she could do to keep it from escaping. The two of them sailed up and over the balcony wall. An angry hiss met her ears.

Her weight altered its trajectory. It began sinking towards the sea below, struggling to gain height. She clung to it, wrapping her arms and legs around its cloaked body.

The smell of its rotting flesh made her stomach heave. She

peeled away one of her hands and began groping for the pouch. It held the prize just out of reach. The sea below was approaching faster.

Once more, she began to sing. Flames erupted around her. They felt like warm tingles on her skin. The wraith's body ignited like kindling. It screamed, fighting to keep the stones out of reach, but its body was already withering.

"Gotcha!" she cried, her hand closing over the vodar's fist. It turned to ash in the sky, the pouch firmly in her grasp. She was flooded with relief, quickly followed by panic. She took a lungful of air just as her body plunged feet-first into the warm waters of the Bay of Bandu. Down she sank, into its dark depths.

She kicked, fighting her wet gown. The skirt twisted about her legs. She stowed the pouch in her clenched teeth then clawed at her gown, pulling apart the ties until the skirt and bodice floated away. Swimming hard, she broke the surface.

Her chest heaved.

The bay was calm here, moonlight glinting upon its surface. The wraith had taken them out over the water, a mile or more from the keep. She didn't bother shouting for help. She didn't have the breath for it anyway. She treaded water, simply glad to be alive.

The keep was lit up like a beacon. She squinted up at the magnificent castle, taking in its tall walls and windows glittering with candlelight. Beyond the peninsula, Kastali Dun's port was hiding just out of sight. There was no possible way she could climb to safety. She would just have to swim.

CHAPTER 29

CLOSE TO DEATH

Kastali Dun

Saffra finished her incantation as chaos reigned down upon her. The fight continued with Claire nowhere in sight. Her stomach sank with dread. Had she failed not one person tonight, but two?

"Saffra! Get him out of here!" Bedelth's voice was a distant echo. "We will keep them occupied. Now go!"

She snapped out of it, returning her attention to her beloved. "Can you walk?" she asked. Dax continued to writhe and moan. His eyes were fixed upon the ceiling, unseeing. "Dax!" she repeated. "Can you walk?" He nodded but otherwise appeared unresponsive. "Good. I've got to get you out of here."

She helped him to his feet, draping his arm over her shoulder and hobbling to the room's exit.

"Watch yourself!" Bedelth jumped in front of her, blocking an oncoming blow that would have ended her. The attacking wraith screamed like a furious wind.

Her skin crawled.

She broke free of the tower and its chaos. Desaree and Jocelyn rushed to her side. "We decided to wait out here," they explained, helping support Dax's weight.

"But...where is Claire?" Desaree cried. "We cannot leave without her!"

"I do not know, but I must get Dax to Marcel. If I do not take him now, he will die. My magic cannot keep him safe. The poison is spreading."

"But...Claire!" Desaree looked over her shoulder, as if Claire would burst into the corridor at any moment. "We cannot leave her. What if—?"

"Stay here and ensure that she is okay. Jocelyn will help me with Dax." She gave Desaree a final look and added, "Take care of yourself, Des, and do not do anything stupid."

Desaree nodded, moving back into a watchful position, peeking through the tower's door.

They reached the grand mage's quarters, pounding upon the door. Marcel opened it wearing a look of bewilderment that morphed into alarm. "The vodar!" she cried by way of explanation. Marcel paled and quickly ushered them into a chamber within his quarters. They laid Daxton's body upon a bed, positioning his arms and legs so he would be comfortable. Daxton moaned with each movement.

Marcel wasted no time. He began muttering an incantation. Then he turned to them and barked orders, none of which Saffra processed. She stood frozen, gazing desperately at the man she was supposed to marry in less than two months. Jocelyn rushed away, only to return shortly thereafter with supplies.

Her world fell into a dream state, images and sounds blurred and disjointed.

She felt Jocelyn's arms on her shoulders, ushering her into a nearby chair. She sat wide-eyed, watching Marcel do his work. She could have helped him. She could have joined her magic with his, but he never asked. Perhaps he knew she wasn't in a fit state.

Eventually, the fog of her mind cleared. She found Marcel crouched before her looking more exhausted than she had ever seen him. He took her chin in his fingers and lifted her face into the light. He assessed her. "I think you will be okay," he said at last.

"And Dax?" she asked, peeking around his portly frame.

"I have done all that I can. Humans never do well with poison."

"He looks so peaceful," she murmured. "May I go to him?"

"You may." Marcel stepped aside and helped her rise. He offered his support at her elbow as he guided her to the bed. She sat down beside him and ran a finger over his brow. A thin sheen of sweat blanketed his skin. "Is he asleep?" His breathing was steady. That was a mercy.

"Aye. A deep sleep. I cannot say when he will wake...or if. That will be entirely up to him."

"You mean, he could be like this forever? Until he dies?" It was too much. She wrapped her arms around her middle, hugging her body.

"He must fight what remains of the darkness. Rarely does one escape unscathed." Marcel fell quiet, then added, "Dax will either win or lose this battle of his. If he loses, then his eyes will never open again."

A sob escaped her chest and she threw herself across Daxton's body. "He can't. He can't! We are to be married...he..."

"My darling girl, let us pray to the gods that he wakes. Until then, I will leave you to your vigil. I...I must rest. I shall have some food brought along shortly. Jocelyn will be waiting for you in my study. If you should need anything, you need only call for her."

He left.

She gathered what courage she had and peeled back the blankets. Her eyes widened. She was forced to look away. Marcel had done what he could. The skin was already closed, however, the black pucker of the scar, the blackened skin surrounding it, and the thin blackened veins leading away from it would stay forever. No magic could erase the taint of poison, not entirely, anyway.

She swallowed back her tears and covered his wound. All she could do was to wait. The remainder of the fight against evil was Daxton's job.

Food arrived. She tried to eat, but every bite tasted like ash.

Food would never taste the same if he failed to wake. Her life would never be the same, either...

~

A LOUD COMMOTION jolted her awake. She must have drifted into a fitful sleep. She lifted her head, frowning. The chamber door burst open. Claire stood in the doorway, sopping wet, a blanket wrapped around her shoulders. Behind her stood the king's shields. Behind *them*, Desaree.

"I tried to give you privacy, Saffra," Marcel cried from the very back of the group. Saffra could just make out his bobbing head as he tried to get her attention. "I tried, but they insisted."

Claire rushed to her side, taking hold of her arms. "You're all right?" she asked. "You aren't hurt? And Dax?" Her voice was low, filled with concern

Every bit of her strength crumbled. She burst into tears, falling into Claire's arms. "He may never wake up!" she cried. "What will I do without him?"

Claire held her, arms wrapped around her heaving frame.

The shields worked their way into the room. Bedelth went to the opposite side of the bed, pulled back the blankets, then hissed. They posted themselves about the room, leaning against the walls. Meanwhile, Saffra collected herself. When her crying abated, she wiped her eyes and sniffled until she could breathe again. Bedelth offered her a handkerchief, which she graciously accepted.

Verath said, "I am sorry to see Daxton like this, Saffra." He dropped his head, eyes closed. "Kane has dealt us a low blow. We lost many tonight." When he next looked up, he said, "I need to better understand what happened leading up to this. King Talon expects a full report."

Saffra nodded. "Of—" She cleared her throat. "Of course."

"Let's start with your vision."

"I..." She steadied herself then recounted what she had seen in muddy detail. She could hardly remember the finer points. Her head was swimming. But she told him how she'd seen the castle from high above, and how she'd seen the wraiths flying towards it. How she'd felt their intentions.

"And how did you know it would happen tonight?" Verath asked.

Claire jumped to her rescue. "We didn't. Not until we connected tonight's moon phase with that of Saffra's vision. A full moon."

Verath nodded. "And you saw nothing else? No other plans or intentions? No other hints at what might come next?"

Saffra shook her head. "Nothing."

She certainly hadn't seen Daxton nearly die, or perhaps she would have forbidden him from participating—

"What about the king's tower?" Claire asked. "When we told you about the attack, how did you guys know where to find the vodar?"

Bedelth's somber voice filled the room. "We knew the stones were hidden there—everything the king does is our business. The demons were already there by the time we arrived, but only just. King Talon keeps at least twenty guards on duty."

"Little good they did," Koldis muttered, his expression stony. "Everyone died, except Dax. Which reminds me. You all had no business being there, putting your lives in danger. Taking such a risk—"

"We got the stones, didn't we?" Claire interrupted.

Saffra sucked in a breath. "You got the stones?!"

"Yes, she saved them," Koldis said, a hint of pride ringing in his voice. "The rest of us were too distracted."

"What...what exactly happened?" Saffra asked Claire. "Your clothes. Your gown—half of it is missing. What...?"

"Yes, Claire, *do* enlighten us," Bedelth said.

Claire shrugged, launching into her tale. She told them everything from her point of view. Of Cyrus's sword and how he took over her body. Of how she'd protected Saffra so Saffra could protect Dax. Of how she'd seen the vodar slip away and followed them to the king's study. "That's when everything went wrong." She shot

Saffra a look—some kind of secret message. "The wraiths wanted me alive, not dead. I cannot understand why."

"Kane gave you a death threat, remember?" Bedelth regarded her with crossed arms.

"Exactly. So why not just kill me there? I was alone with them. They had the chance. Why leave me alive and unharmed?"

"Kane must want her for something," Koldis murmured.

"Thanks, Koldis, but I think I already worked that out for myself," she said. "At any rate, I got distracted long enough to be captured."

"Oh, gods!" Saffra gasped. "I was fussing with Dax while they had you in their grasp? I am so sorry! I promised that I would be your ally—that I would help and protect you. My love for Dax clouded my judgment."

"You can't blame yourself for that," Claire said, laying a hand upon Saffra's. "You're engaged to him. Besides, he needed you more than I did."

"All the same, it was selfish of me, and I am ashamed."

"Then we can be ashamed together," Claire said. "We both did things tonight that we regret. I should have..." She fell silent and glanced at the king's shields. She was referring to when she had refused to use her secret ability. Her telepathy could have saved them time—perhaps lives too.

When Claire next looked at Saffra, her gaze was loving. "What am I saying is, apology accepted, and you're forgiven." Claire's words left Saffra's heart thumping. At that moment, she realized what true friendship looked like.

"What happened after you were captured?" Bedelth interrupted their moment.

"I..." Claire faltered, looking around the room. "Well...I sort of muttered some magic and set my captor on fire. It's hard to explain. I'm still struggling to make sense of it myself. In those moments of distress, I got so angry that a song came to me. Somehow, I knew that I needed to sing it. When I did..." She placed a hand on her cheek. "Now that I think of it, I never even got to finish the words."

"A song?" Bedelth looked perplexed. "You mean an incantation?"

"Oh no. I sang my magic, of that I am sure." Her voice was dreamy.

"Are you sure you did not hit your head during your fall?" Koldis asked, smiling, teasing.

"Fall?" Saffra stared at her. "What fall?"

"She fell," Koldis explained. "After her captor burst into *green* flames—"

"Green? But green is the color of—" Saffra's eyes widened.

"Claire then burned the remainder of the wraiths in King Talon's study, sending them up in flames." Koldis looked smug about knowing the rest of the story.

Wait, how did he know the rest of the story?!

"Is that true?" Verath scowled.

"It is," Koldis said. "Once she defeated them, she was brave enough—or *stupid* enough—to go after the thief." Silence. Complete silence. "She leapt upon the wraith's back and went tumbling over the edge of the tower's balcony. Isn't that so, Claire?" He pinned her with his knowing gaze. She nodded, lips pressed tight. "Figured I would double check." He winked at her.

"But..." Saffra was at a loss.

"Somehow, she managed to fight the wraith while plummeting towards the sea. She captured the stones, burned it to cinders, and survived the drop. That's why she's dripping wet, half her gown missing."

Saffra gaped. "And how do you know all of this?"

"I'm the one who collected her from the dockyard." Koldis grinned.

"When I finally swam to shore, I was spotted by the city guards on patrol. When they saw me, everything turned into a frenzy. They summoned the castle's guards. Apparently word was sent to the keep that a certain *Lady Claire* had come crawling out of the ocean missing half of her clothes. A great story for gossip if you ask me." Claire rolled her eyes. "Anyway, Koldis came straight down. I told him the whole story when we walked back together. I have the stones. Here—" She removed a pouch from beneath her blanket and opened it, letting them tumble onto her lap. "I don't dare touch them," she added. "I already feel their...essence. I had forgotten how creepy they are."

Saffra gazed, transfixed. "All this horror for two, stupid little stones small enough to fit in one's palm."

"You're telling me," Claire huffed, deftly scooping them back into the pouch without touching them.

"We can take them off your hands now, if you would prefer," Verath said.

Claire shook her head. "I will protect them, but they cannot stay here forever."

The rest of the room nodded. No more explanation was needed. Everyone knew Claire had earned the right, twice over, to decide what happened to the stones.

Saffra smiled. It was a sad smile, but a smile nonetheless. Claire never ceased to amaze her. Her resilience, her *luck*, her ability to scrape through every sticky situation. For a moment her mind rushed back to the night they'd first met, crouched together within a dark dungeon cell, exchanging scraps of hurried information. A lot had happened since then. She had enough confirmation now to know that Claire's role was as important as she had always believed.

CHAPTER 30

DINING WITH THE QUEEN

The Gable Forest

Jeanine urged the villagers of Kaljah onward to escape the goblins. "Run," she cried. "Run!" She looked at the distance they had yet to cover. They'd never make it. A cold panic set into the pit of her stomach. They had been running for little more than an hour and already her flock was scattered. Those in the back were far behind. The gap between them was growing larger.

She turned Storm sharply and backtracked, cantering to the rear. "Hurry!" she cried, waving her arms. "Hurry!"

A woman stumbled and fell, crying out in pain. Norah was middle-aged with four children grown and moved away. Jeanine led Storm over, jumping from the horse's back. She helped her stand.

"I canna go on," Norah cried. "I canna! Silah...Silah is back in the village. He's gonna die! We are all dead."

Her life had become a thing of nightmares.

"This is no time for tears," Jeanine said. "Keep running. Keep going for Silah, for your children." She gave Norah a push from behind, spurring her forward.

The villagers continued onward. Every time she counted there were fewer. Some of the older women were dropping like flies, scattered far *enough back that she could no longer see them. After a while, she stopped looking behind her, stopped counting. It hurt too much.*

By midday, even those in the lead stopped to rest. The children were crying for water. There was none. In the panic of escape, water—like so many other things—had been forgotten. She dismounted and lifted the young boy with her from Storm's back. He held the infant they had taken from a desperate mother, who was likely dead by now.

She bent over and took hold of the boy's shoulders. "What is your name?"

"Jorn, miss," he said, whimpering.

"Nice to meet you, Jorn. I'm Jeanine. Do not let the infant out of your sight. Do you understand?" She kneeled down to his height. His eyes were wide and scared. He nodded and stood there, too stunned to move otherwise.

Rising, she began to assess the others. There were no men with them. Most of the children were barefoot, still in their night clothes. Many were crying. The few mothers who'd made it were attempting to comfort them. Everyone was in utter shock.

The gently rolling hills held little life and no promise of quenching their thirst. Any further west and they'd be in the desert. She dared not take them eastward into the mountains, crawling with goblins. They needed to reach the forest. She could see the green smudge looming on the horizon. They were close.

Would they make it?

She climbed atop Storm's back, standing to her full height. He was old and patient and held perfectly still as he ought. Storm was a horse bred for war. Like much else in her slice of the kingdom, he was a remnant of the brutal efforts to protect Dragonwall's homeland, just like her father, Jahl's father, and so many others.

Shielding her hand against the sun, she squinted. Her heart stopped at the smudge growing closer.

"They're coming!" she cried. All around her, pitiful wails echoed from the lips of the mothers as they realized escape was impossible.

She squinted harder, surveying the goblins. They were moving quickly, too quickly. Were they truly so intent on catching the few remaining villagers who had fled?

"Oh, gods!" she hissed. Several men on horseback led the chase. They had managed to pick up a few stray women. They were the reason for haste. They were what the goblins pursued.

One of them was Jahl. She was half angry, half relieved to see him alive.

Nothing could be done now. Except run. "Go!" she cried yet again. "Hurry! Go now! Flee!"

She made a split second decision. Someone needed to buy them time. That someone would be her.

Grabbing Jorn and the infant, she placed them onto Storm's back, slapping his flank. He took off at a gallop. The others were already on the move.

She positioned herself atop the sloping hill to wait. The minutes stretched onward, until she heard the beat of approaching hooves. The distant snarl of goblins giving chase.

"Jeanine!" Jahl cried, spotting her. "We failed! They're coming!"

Yes, she knew that already. She counted the bodies, several hundred at least. Gods! They were doomed.

"What are you doing?" Jahl shouted. "Why are you standing there?"

"I'm going to fight. I will not die by a knife to the back. I will die fighting, and when I meet the gods, they will praise my valor."

Jahl gaped at her.

Her father's sword was belted at her waist. She would need that soon enough. Removing her bow, she nocked an arrow. She'd get a few hits before the goblin spawn was upon her. Aiming high, she released. The arrow flew skyward and out of sight. She did not watch it, already loading another. There was a commotion in the advancing numbers as a single goblin fell.

She released the next. Another fell. By the third, her chest was pounding. She drew her sword, choking back the bile in her throat. She almost failed to hear the horn, almost missed the roar from above. A strong wind buffeted her. Flames erupted right before her eyes. Dragon fire! Hammering hooves pounded behind her. A blur of white—

. . .

"Jeanine!" A pressure gripped her shoulder. "Jeanine! Wake up!" She opened her eyes, forgetting momentarily where she was. She tried to collect her thoughts. All she could see were goblins and imminent death. She shook her head, attempting to clear the nightmare away. "Hurry up and get dressed. The queen has summoned us. We are to dine with her for breakfast."

"The...the queen?" She jumped out of bed. "Why didn't you wake me sooner?!"

"I tried. You sleep like a rock. Gods!" He shook his head in amusement and retreated, leaving her alone.

She glanced around. Her dwelling was built within the base of a tree, its walls made entirely of glass. The single room was large, with several well-defined areas for dining, living, and sleeping. The bathing and dressing areas were the only separate spaces, with makeshift walls made of thin, elaborately painted paper stretched over wooden frames.

It was beautiful, magical, even, but it felt nothing like home. Her chest tightened. Memories of her loss resurfaced, heightened by the dream she'd just had. Her father's sword was propped up beside her bed. She glanced at it and a heavy pressure squeezed her, making it difficult to breathe. She and her father had rarely seen eye-to-eye, but he had sacrificed himself for her.

She should have respected him more—loved him more. She shouldn't have blamed him for so many years. Her mother's death wasn't truly his fault. Now that he was dead, she would never have the chance to apologize for her bitterness.

A single tear rolled down her cheek. Then another. She sat back on her bed, put her head in her hands, and cried. It felt good to let go—

Jahl knocked again. "Are you ready yet?"

She wiped her eyes. "Almost!"

She scurried into the dressing area and changed into pants, tunic, and a leather doublet. The sprites had left some of their own feminine garments, but she didn't have the heart to wear any of it. Her own clothes were comforting. Tattered as they were, it was all she had left. She glanced down at her boots, then decided to go without. Most sprites went barefoot. The forest floor was soft enough.

She washed her face in a crystal basin. The cold water erased evidence of her tears. It washed away her painful memories. Perhaps there was something magical in Esterpine's water.

After their rescue, the sprites had offered the survivors refuge in their forest. The villagers had taken a vote, whether or not they should remain. Most believed that they should. She did too, but only because they had no home left.

The sprites had guided them from Nilsa outpost, deeper into the forest. They'd traveled west for two days before reaching the spriten city of Ashvale, known for its ash trees, and more famously, the drink of enlightenment. From there, it had been a four-day journey to Esterpine, mostly spent in awe.

She'd done her best to learn snippets about their culture. Even still, nothing had prepared her for Esterpine. She'd spent the last several days wandering around the wooded city, exploring it.

Jahl was waiting outside. "Follow me," he said, turning on his heel. She frowned, then rushed to catch up. Something in him had changed after the attack, making his mood unpredictable. His parents, like her father, had perished. His mother had insisted on staying to ensure all the horses were put to good use. She never made it out of Kaljah in time. His father died protecting her, just before Jahl was forced to make his escape. They were all grieving in their own way.

They made their way through the city. She took everything in. While the dwellings were on the forest floor, the sprites took advantage of the forest's height too. Some trees had spiraling stairs, platforms, and rope bridges creating a network of passageways in the proverbial sky of mist made up of ethereal glowing lights and twinkling light bugs. It almost felt as if they had stolen the heavens and transplanted them here.

A movement caught her eye. She turned and gasped. "Look, Jahl! Look—" She pointed at a unicorn that had appeared, creeping onto the path from the foliage. She had seen a handful of them since arriving, mostly at meals.

"Mmm. Impressive..." Jahl said. He did little more than glance over. She sighed and allowed him his brooding.

When they reached the crystal palace, she stopped short. She'd seen it several times, always from afar. Up close, it filled her with awe. This was a place visited by invitation only.

Jahl led her up the palace's giant staircase to the large entrance doors. Even the stairs were made of crystal. She could see through them, down to the forest floor beneath. It was unsettling. When they reached the guards, Jahl announced their purpose. The guards permitted them entry. All too soon, she found herself wide-eyed within the hall.

"It...it's beautiful!" She sighed heavily, reminded of Jahl's indifference when he said nothing. Well, if he didn't care, she wasn't going to let that drag her down. She took several paces away to bask.

Plush rugs lay under her bare feet, warming the feel of the grand cathedral hall. Across from the entrance was an enormous throne atop a dais. A giant staircase carved into the wall circled around the perimeter, curling its way up to the top of the palace. Chutes from the staircase led to upper rooms.

"It's all one big hollow carving," she whispered, "but how is that possible?"

"Greetings!" A sprite appeared out of nowhere. "I am to escort you to the dining hall. The queen awaits. If you would follow me, please."

They trailed after him in obvious wonder. He led them up the turning staircase. Everything on the floor of the hall began to shrink away. Her stomach jolted and she stared ahead, focusing on the transparent steps in front of her. "It's rather unsettling, isn't it?"

Jahl didn't answer.

At last, they stopped at what must have been the fourth or fifth floor. There was really no telling, as doors were dispersed randomly all the way to the cavernous ceiling. They followed their guide into a room with a large dining table. Like everything else, it was made of crystal and adorned with gold platters and dining ware. Their guide announced their entry then exited the room.

Once she had a moment to look around, she saw that there were three people at the table. They stood to greet them. The woman at the head of the table was obviously the queen, but she was unsure about the other male and female.

"Good morning, Jeanine, Jahl." The queen's voice was rich and warm. It instantly calmed her nerves. "Welcome to the Crystal Palace, the brightest jewel of our forest. Please, come and take a seat."

They did as requested.

"I am Queen Jade. These are my children, the Princess and Prince of Esterpine, Taylynn, and Feowen. We are pleased to dine with you this morning."

The queen motioned to the serving staff who rushed forward carrying covered platters. When they removed the covers, she found herself presented with a colorful assortment of fruits, nuts, and breads. She kept her frown hidden, afraid to insult their diet. It was yet another huge difference between her familiar culture and their unfamiliar one.

Helping herself, she loaded her plate with various items, and they began to eat. The food was delicious, but it didn't quite fill her up. She missed meat and cheese, but they didn't eat such things here.

The queen looked up from her plate and said, "Jeanine, I am told that you faced the goblins alone before our aid arrived. Is this true?"

She was unprepared for the question. Nodding, she swallowed her mouthful.

Jahl beat her to it. "It is true, Your Majesty, I myself had every intention of fleeing. Jeanine would not let me. She told me, and I quote, 'I will not die by a knife to the back. I will die fighting, and when I meet the gods, they will praise my valor.'"

Prince Feowen made a noise that sounded suspiciously like a chuckle. She glanced at him. His eyes were on her, but they darted away to his mother. She studied his face, his unreadable expression. His features were beautiful and delicate, with angular eyes of different colors, and a pointed chin. He was almost feline in appearance. His blue hair was the most shocking piece of his appearance.

"Such a worthy statement from one so young." The queen set down her dining utensils and looked up at them. "I am impressed by your bravery."

"Thank you, Your Majesty." She tried not to grin in favor of maintaining a serious countenance, but it was difficult after such praise.

"My warriors tell me that you both fought bravely until the goblins were driven back."

"I saw it myself." Prince Feowen's voice was as musical as his mother's.

"You were there?" Jeanine's curiosity drove her to speak.

"I was. It was *I* who led the charge."

Her face burned. "I apologize. I got so caught up in the battle that I did not—"

"No need for apologies." Prince Feowen bowed his head then returned his attention to his food.

At length, the queen spoke again, "You are probably wondering why I have invited you both here this morning?" Her gaze was intent on Jeanine, though she addressed Jahl too. "There are two reasons. The first is to discuss leadership, and the second, how you might spend your time here."

Jeanine swallowed her food and tucked her hands in her lap. She was eager to make a good impression.

"Did any of your village leadership survive?" the queen asked.

Jeanine opened her mouth to speak—

"They did not." Everyone's eyes fell upon Princess Taylynn. Her voice was quiet, barely louder than a whisper, yet it held a strange power. It was as if her words permeated everything around them. Taylynn's eyes met Jeanine's, holding them. "Most of the survivors are children. There are a few mothers. A few males too—not worthy of leadership. As I have said, Mother,"—Taylynn's attention remained fixed on Jeanine—"it ought to be these two."

Jeanine's skin prickled. Something in Taylynn's gaze left her uneasy.

"You have seen this?" Queen Jade asked Taylynn, who did not respond. Instead, Taylynn returned to her food. Jeanine watched the interaction and frowned.

Queen Jade gazed at her daughter until she was convinced there would be no answer. Something unreadable passed over her features as her eyes lingered on Taylynn before returning to Jeanine. "Well then, are you willing to accept such a responsibility? Will the villagers accept you?"

"They will." Jahl squared his shoulders. His voice seemed to diffuse some of the tension still lingering between Queen Jade and the princess.

"Very well. Kaljah's survivors will remain here, and you will answer for them. It may be some time yet before you can return home. Attacks continue along the eastern border."

Jeanine's eyes widened. "Our village was not the only one?"

Princess Taylynn spoke again, "It was not. The goblins attacked others along the border. A coordinated attempt to undermine the monarchy."

Jeanine opened her mouth but could think of nothing to say. The room was quiet until Taylynn said, "Our forces arrived in time to assist your village. We went no further south than that. We do not like wandering too far from the forest."

Prince Feowen sat forward in his chair. "The drengr have stepped in to drive the enemy back, but goblins are relentless creatures. Only death hinders their progress."

"That is why we have invited you to stay with us," Queen Jade said. "You are welcome to our city until the fighting is resolved, after which our guides will escort you home."

"Thank you," Jeanine said. "I appreciate the offer. We will accept." Once again, she was caught off-guard by the queen's kindness. The behavior defied the ideas put into her head by her father, by history, by all the stories that made sprites out to be cold, prideful beings.

"I hope the food is to your liking?" Princess Taylynn asked. Her voice was suddenly lighter, more jovial. The corner of her mouth twitched, otherwise her face was unyielding as stone.

Jeanine and Jahl shared a glance then nodded, afraid to say otherwise.

"I have one last thing to add before we adjourn." Everyone looked at the queen. "I had mentioned that we might discuss how you will spend your time here in Esterpine. The Sprites are great warriors in their own right. You both witnessed that on the battlefield. It was suggested that you might like to train with our warriors while you are here."

Jeanine caught Feowen's twinkling gaze. His expression was smug. She got the impression that *he* was the one who had made the suggestion.

"Is this something that might interest you?" Queen Jade asked.

"Yes!" Both Jeanine and Jahl answered in unison.

"I told you," the prince said, turning to his sister who scowled back at him. Jeanine's brow furrowed. "My *sister* is not a fan of violence. She believed that you would not be interested. I disagreed. She did not see you on the battlefield as I did, so how could she know?"

Her face flushed. Something in Taylynn's expression hinted that the prince was behaving predictably, as if Taylynn had orchestrated this turn of events. Was there more to this offer than met the eye?

The queen clapped her hands together. "It is settled then. Our sparring grounds are open to you at any time. Please make use of them whilst you are here. You will find Master Orin, our weapons master, most helpful." As she spoke, the servants rushed forward to clear away the plates. "The three of us have matters to attend to." She eyed her son and daughter knowingly before smiling at Jeanine and Jahl. "I trust that you can find your way out of the palace whenever it pleases you. Stay as long as you like."

"Yes, thank you," Jeanine said. Jahl echoed the same sentiments.

With a brief farewell, the queen and her children departed. Soon they were alone. Jeanine looked at Jahl. He was staring openly at her. "What?" He shook his head. "Come on, *what*? You've been weird for days."

He grunted and mumbled, "Nothing."

"Does the queen make you uncomfortable?"

"No."

"Then what? Why are you staring at me like that?"

"Because *he* was."

"*He* was? He—who?"

"The prince! Gods, Jeanine. Could you be more oblivious? The prince couldn't keep his eyes off you." With that, he rose from his seat. "I've got something on my mind. I'll catch up with you later," he said before disappearing.

She was left to consider his words alone.

CHAPTER 31

A NEW GUIDE

Northern Barrier Range

Mikkin swatted a low hanging branch as he and Jamie continued their trek deeper into the mountains. The land was rugged and unforgiving. They had been walking for several days since capturing the goblin leader. Thus far, he'd gotten little information from it.

He'd promised that no harm would come to the creature if it surrendered. Now he regretted his words. Especially when they ran into impassable areas, rivers too wide to cross, sheer cliff faces, sudden drops, all requiring them to double back.

The goblin was hiding something.

They plodded along, the goblin tethered to a rope. Its short legs meant slow strides and even slower progress. It left him scowling and impatient. They'd never find the dragons at this rate. As if sensing his gaze, the goblin offered him a wicked grin. He turned, focusing on the path ahead.

That night, when they made camp, he presented the goblin with an ultimatum. "Unka"—for that was the creature's name—"I have a proposition for you. I believe we can both benefit from it, but that depends on your cooperation."

Unka blinked, staring at him.

"Where are the wild dragons hiding?"

"Unka not know." Unka looked away, pretending to ignore them.

"You're lying!" Jamie cried, frustration seeping into his voice.

"Jamie, let me handle this." The lad scowled, but he held his silence after that.

"Unka, we know the dragons have a lair in these mountains. We've seen them flying overhead. I'd reckon you know how to find them far better than me."

Unka squared his shoulders and grunted.

"I'll offer you a deal. You show us to their lair and I will set you free. I have lived up to my word thus far. I have not harmed you, have I?"

Unka's face puckered as his green skin pulled into wrinkles. Then he scowled. Goblins could be rather dimwitted creatures. He could tell that Unka was considering. At last the creature's expression changed. "Bad idea traveling to lair. More than dragons there."

"What do you mean?" Mikkin scowled. "Unka, tell me. What more is there?"

"A *sorcerer*." The word was spoken with a hiss. An evil glint appeared in Unka's eyes, which now glittered in the firelight like little black orbs. No soul liked captivity, and most liked their captors even less. The little goblin would be thrilled to see Mikkin and Jamie fall into the hands of a powerful magical being—especially a sorcerer.

He considered Unka's words. No dragon of legend cooperated with sorcerers. Some said that dragons killed all the ancient asarlaí out of cold-blooded hatred. "I don't believe you. Why would there be a sorcerer with the dragons?"

"I no lie. I knows."

"How? How do you know?"

"Kane."

Mikkin's skin crawled. Magic did things—made a person uneasy. Evil magic was even worse. If Kane was real, if hearing his name created discomfort, perhaps Unka *was* telling the truth.

"How do you know this sorcerer? This Kane?" he asked.

"Kane commanded goblins to patrol, so I patrol."

"Is that so? Is that how you found us?"

"Yes."

The little wretch seemed to be enjoying their discomfort. The dragon lair was one thing, a sorcerer was another. With dragons, the mission was all but impossible. With a sorcerer, it was beyond impossible. His stomach sank. "Does the sorcerer keep in close proximity to the dragons?" he asked. The goblin shot him a defiant look. "Do you wish to go free or not?"

Unka blew out a breath. "The sorcerer not live in lair. His fortress apart."

"Fortress?" Mikkin glanced at Jamie. "What fortress?"

"Shadowkeep," Unka spat.

He shuddered as a sense of foreboding settled upon him. Steeling his nerves, he said, "You will take us to this Shadowkeep place. If you do, you have my word that you will be set free."

"As you wish," Unka said. He wasn't sure if it was a trick of the firelight or not, but he saw a wicked gleam in Unka's eyes.

THE NEXT MORNING, the three of them set off. This time Unka took the lead. It was much easier traveling with a guide. Unka knew exactly where to go. The goblin had a knack for navigating. They didn't get lost or delayed a single time.

"Are you sure we can trust him?" Jamie whispered as they stopped for water. The river they followed was loud enough to mask their voices. Unka was given an extra length of rope to relieve himself in semi-privacy.

"I trust him as much as you do, lad, but what choice do we have?"

Jamie shrugged. "I fear that he will lead us astray, or worse, directly to the sorcerer himself." Jamie glanced over at the goblin with an expression of contempt.

"Yes, I have considered that." Mikkin frowned. Despite

enjoying the company of another, he regretted bringing Jamie along. Jamie was not a good fit for the upcoming task. He had a family and a good life. "Unfortunately, we don't have much of a choice."

They traveled for four days, guided by Unka, before Unka stopped and uttered the words they had been waiting for. "We here."

"Where is here?" Jamie growled. "I see no dragons."

"Easy, lad. No need to get worked up."

"Must creep careful now," Unka gestured sharply. "Dragons smart."

"Wait a moment, do you hear that?" Mikkin was hesitant. He picked up a strange beating noise, as if the sky had drums. They all froze. Then, from far overhead, several large masses flew by. Shadows flickered in the trees, dancing and jumping. His doubt turned to fear, then it turned to hatred. All too soon, the light returned. Everyone blinked, glancing at each other as if to confirm what had just happened.

Thank the gods the trees offered good cover.

"We sneak now," Unka said. "Then after I free. I go."

"You will be free to go once you have delivered on your end of the bargain." Mikkin eyed him. Unka offered a solemn nod.

They crept from tree to tree, silently placing their feet. He was too afraid to speak. Each time his feet made a noise, he cringed. The closer they got, the more his mind seemed to slow.

How much did he know about dragons, anyway? What weapon was sharp enough to pierce *unpierceable* scales? What fire was hot enough to melt their hides? What weak spots did they have? Only their eyes?

He was so intent on finding the beasts, that he had willingly ignored all other thoughts of strategy. He needed to figure out what came next. He needed a plan.

He would study them first, discover their routines, the times they slept, hunted, stretched their wings. Then he would use his knowledge. He would attack the red one first—the one responsible for taking Mardra from him.

"Shhh! No sound." The goblin turned to them, scowling. The forest trees had cleared, revealing a lake with a dark glassy surface. "It called Ice Lake," Unka said.

They hid behind a large pine tree to keep out of view. Mikkin's eyes flicked back and forth, captivated. Dragons of every color dipped and darted over the lake. Some dove in the water to catch fish, others glided in large, lazy circles. There were many.

Squinting, he scanned each of the beasts visible. There were a number of red dragons, but none of them were the exact shade of dark blood he was looking for. Beside him, Jamie's breathing was heavy. He glanced over and saw the lad's shocked face.

"Where is their lair?" Mikkin whispered to Unka. The goblin pointed to a rocky outcropping looming over the lake. It had a large cave entrance, with dragons. "And Shadowkeep?"

Unka pointed in the opposite direction to the other side of the lake. Resting atop a large peak sat Shadowkeep. Its giant rocky ramparts blended with the cliff below, making it hardly discernible. He might never have spotted it. There was no question in his mind as to why Kane had chosen it. The fortress was aptly named, too. Its cliff cast a long, dark shadow upon the ravine and lake below. Even looking upon it made him anxious.

He led them back into the shelter of the trees.

"I show you. Now I free," Unka said.

"Yes, it would seem so." He did not immediately untie the goblin. "How do I know that once I untie you, you won't go running directly to Kane?"

"I promise. I go other way." Unka pointed in a direction away from the lake.

Mikkin hardly believed the little wretch.

"I give word. Like you. You untie. I leave. Unka no like evil sorcerer."

"And you also know that if you so much as attempt to attack Jamie or I, that we will use your own goblin-made steel to slit your throat?" He figured that much would be obvious, but he threw it out there for good measure.

"No attack. Just leave."

"Very well."

Mikkin reached for his knife.

"You're going to let him go?" Jamie sputtered. "What if he tells Kane we are here? What if he tries to kill us? You actually believe him?"

Mikkin sighed. "No lad, I do not. But I gave him my word and I am a man of my word."

Jamie pursed his lips and shook his head.

With the ropes cut, Unka was free to go and go he did. He left in the opposite direction. Even still, Mikkin did not trust the tricky little urchin. It was only a matter of time before Unka worked his way around the lake and paid the sorcerer a visit.

He supposed that he could kill Unka. Part of his mind screamed for him to do it. All he had to do was grab his bow, notch the bowstrings, and load an arrow. The goblin, whose back was now turned, would be none the wiser. Mikkin shook his head. He couldn't bring himself to it. Moments later, Unka disappeared into the underbrush.

They sat for some time after Unka left. He was not eager to begin his observations of the dragons. Furthermore, he was even less keen to tell Jamie that the lad would not be participating. So, he stayed put and dwelled on his thoughts.

Jamie spoke at last. "We should find a safer place to set up our camp. Somewhere hidden."

"Smart lad, we should indeed." Happy to have something to occupy his mind, Mikkin stood and they set forth, making their way further from the lake. As luck would have it, they found a small cave with plenty of overgrowth disguising the entrance. Then they deposited their packs within. They both knew that there would be no campfire.

"I am going to go take another look at the lake," Mikkin said when they finished. "I want to study the lair."

"I'll accompany you, give me a moment to finish tying this together."

"No, I need you to stay here." The lad gave him a surprised look.

"I promised your father I would not risk your life. Until I better understand the dragons, I want you out of sight."

"Surely you don't mean that," Jamie said, growing angry. "I did not come all this way to sit and do nothing."

"You came to help me find the lair. We have found it. While I appreciate your company, it is best if you stay put, at least for now. This cave will offer a good hiding place for you."

"And what if I refuse?"

Mikkin sighed. "Look, lad, I know you are eager for adventure. Gods only know I was at your age. But this isn't something ordinary. We are dealing with beastly dragons here. I had half a mind to simply send you home before we found this cave. Now I am giving you the option to shelter yourself while you wait."

"We have been practicing with our swords nearly every night since we got them!" Jamie cried. "You do not think I am capable of defending myself?"

"No, I don't! Not against dragons. I will likely die when it comes time. Need I remind you again that I made a promise to your father?"

Jamie scowled before he stalked off to the corner of the cave and plopped down onto the ground.

"I will return soon. If I do not, you may assume the worst and leave this place." Then he turned and left the cave, hoping it wouldn't come to that.

CHAPTER 32

NEW PLANS

Shadowkeep

Kane gazed upon his wraiths in disbelief. Their failure shouldn't have surprised him, but he had allowed himself to hope. "Tell me again," he said, keeping his voice calm. "Tell me exactly what happened."

Two wraiths stood before him, another sixteen behind them. Behind all of them was the familiar backdrop of flames. Just recently, he had increased his numbers to twenty-five. That was how many he had used to attack Kastali Dun's keep. It took a great deal of strength to ensnare a single wraith, and each summoning took its toll upon him. It would be many days before he could replace those he had permanently lost. That alone was infuriating. How had this girl—*this outsider*—found a way to permanently destroy his assassins? The thought left him uneasy, which further served to anger him.

The two wraiths before him recounted their story, but this time in greater detail. They explained that once given their mission, they had gone south to Kastali Dun. Had converged on the king's tower while King Talon was away, confronting the guards and storming the interior. The king's shields had arrived shortly thereafter.

While the human soldiers were no match for the vodar, the king's drengr had put up a real fight. "We were forced to split up. Most of our forces remained on the main floor, while the rest went below in search of the stonesss. Just when we had the advantage, the girl thwarted us. You should have let us kill her and be done with it."

"No. I want her alive."

"She is a threat. She knew of our intentionsss, that we were after the stonesss."

Kane gritted his teeth. "Claire is still their protector. She may have handed the stones over to King Talon, but she never truly relinquished them." He rubbed the smooth skin on his chin, considering the matter deeper. Yes, that was the only explanation for it. "She is drawn to them. She sensed their danger."

"We did not realize her strength, my lord. We have failed you."

"Clearly, else I would have twenty-five of you instead of eighteen." He cursed under his breath. While some of his wraiths had been defeated, he still had enough. "Tell me again about the magic she used?"

"It is hard to *sssay*, my lord. All those present at the time of the girl's magic have been vanquished."

"But you said before that it was fire? You are certain of this?" Kane thought about all the types of fire he knew of. In most cases of magic, fire was not simply fire. Case in point, the fire he used to summon his assassins wasn't normal.

"*Yesss*, It wasss fire. We are certain without a doubt. Green flamesss. It turned our comrades to ash. We are most grieved to know they will not return."

"Most grieved?" He scowled. "And you are sure the flames were green? How do you know if you were not there?"

"I am certain, my lord."

He found it hard to believe the wraith. Had the flames been any other color, it might have been more straightforward. Vodar wraiths were curious beings, often capable of knowing things in a way that seemed unexplainable. In this case, all he could do was take them at their word. If what they said was true, and the flames Claire had used were genuinely green, then sprite magic was to blame. He swore under his breath and began pacing. This would not do. He could not afford to take any more risks. He would have to keep his vodar away from Kastali Dun, away from Claire. His nostrils flared in anger as he continued to pace, thinking.

His entire mission appeared to be a failure. What was worse, now Talon would know how desperate he was. Had there been any profit whatsoever? Yes, perhaps there was. The attack had not been entirely fruitless. "Tell me again about the king's soldiers." He stopped his pacing and turned to the vodar. "You killed all of them?"

"Yesss, my lord, all but one. He wasss well protected. We dealt him a lethal blow, but there was another girl—a seer. Her magic kept our poison at bay. Shortly thereafter, he was evacuated."

"The seer!" He knew immediately that it was Saffra and Daxton. "I should have known they'd be there..." He closed his eyes for the length of several slow breaths then his lips curled into a smile and he said, "Such a shame. Yes, such a shame for poor Saffra. Very well then. What is done, is done. Your misstep will require a change of plans. I hope you understand how inconvenient this is."

"Our deepest apologiesss, my lord."

"Yes, yes. I am used to such apologies by now." He went to his large map still spread over his monstrous ironwood table. His eyes slid over it, landing on a small dot surrounded by little notes written in his own scrolling handwriting. He bent over the dot and studied it. He had done the same thing several times that morning. It had become a daily habit, scrutinizing the map. He needed to be certain that this was *the* place.

He had hoped to send Wrath away. Had the attack on Kastali Dun been successful, he would have. The clan leader had plans to carry out their biggest mission yet, a battle to bring down Fort

Squall. Unfortunate as it was, now those plans would have to wait. He needed to hide the final dragonstone first. For that, he needed a dragon.

He turned to his dark assassins. "There's something I must do. In the meantime, I have a new use for you. Yes...one you will be most adept for." The Vodar stood silently, awaiting their next orders. "I have been too lax on King Talon. It is time for him to feel pain...closer to home. Travel into Eigaden. Begin killing the children first, then the women, then the men. One death each night. Let them feel terror." He smiled. "I dare say you won't complain about adding a few more souls to your tethers."

"We would be honored..."

"Honored?! Like you have a choice! Come." He called them to his side where he leaned over the map. "There, there, and there. Focus your efforts on these villages. Split into three groups so that you might attack each simultaneously. One death in each village each night. I will summon you back when I have need of you. Now go."

After a murmur of acknowledgement, they fled, turning into black smoke that filtered through the cracks in the rocky walls of Shadowkeep.

When he was finally alone, he went to his desk and took a seat. From a drawer he removed a box. When he ran his hand over it, it opened for him. Wrapped in silk he found his final stone. He had left this one for last because he liked the feel of it the most.

"Wrath—plans have changed. Our mission must wait. We will hide the final stone first, then you are free to carry out the attack."

Wrath was flying over Ice Lake. He did not sound happy about the change. *"I have already prepared my clan for our coming feast. Now I must wait?"*

"You must. Is that going to be a problem?"

There was a long silence—longer than Kane liked. *"We will wait. I will help you hide your remaining stone."*

"Be ready to leave at dawn."

"I will."

When dawn arrived, they departed south. In Kane's pocket, wrapped in silk, was the remaining dragonstone. He hated to give it up, but it would be safer this way. If he got caught with one... Well, he simply couldn't allow that to happen, and this would ensure that it didn't.

CHAPTER 33

THE KING'S RETURN

Kastali Dun

Claire kept busy in the days following the attack. She wasn't the only one. There was a frenzy within the keep. Everyone was worried about another assault. Guards had taken to patrolling the corridors, moving in small units. The castle's residents were frightened, keeping out of sight when they could. As glad as they'd been for the king's absence, they were even gladder for his return.

As was custom, the entire keep was set to assemble in the large courtyard just outside the royal garden. Claire had never taken part in a royal greeting, and wasn't exactly looking forward to it. "It seems like overkill to me," she groused as Desaree fussed with her hair. "Everyone forced to abandon their duties to simply stand there and gawk. Ladies and gentlemen in their finest attire and jewels."

Desaree huffed. "It's tradition."

"It's a bunch of peacocking."

"True. But it's also a reminder of what the king is coming home to."

"A court full of braggarts?"

"Oh, stop." Desaree shoved her shoulder. She'd spent upwards of an hour on Claire's hair, twisting it and braiding it into tight knots of pure artistry. When she finished, she stepped back, grinning from ear to ear.

"It's beautiful," Claire breathed, gazing at her reflection. She lifted her hand to fuss with a section, only to have it swatted away.

"I have one final touch. Stay here while I run to my room."

She narrowed her eyes with suspicion. "All right, then."

Desaree returned with a tiny bundle wrapped in cloth. "I got this for you yesterday in anticipation of the king's return." She looked immensely proud of herself.

"Des..." Claire's voice caught in her throat. "You did not have to get me anything. You really shouldn't have."

"Oh please! It was my pleasure. Besides, I know more about the capital's styles than you do, and I want you to look better than every lady out there today. This will be perfect."

Desaree handed her the small bundle. A delicate silver net tumbled into her palm. It was covered in tiny blue sapphires that glistened in the light. She gasped, holding it up to examine it. "Oh, Des! It's stunning. Where did you find it?"

"I snuck down to the Merchant's District yesterday. Verath escorted me. It was a secret because I wanted to surprise you. Here —" She took the net and delicately placed it over Claire's hair, pinning it securely. "There. What do you think?" She held up a small mirror.

"I'm speechless." Claire turned her head back and forth to gaze at the net's sparkle.

"Good! I knew you would love it. All that's left is your gown." Desaree smiled. "Quick! It's almost time."

She did as she was told. Her dressing area consisted of two full length mirrors angled toward each other. There was a small, elevated platform centered between them. Nearby, her large wardrobe gaped open, full of gowns designed by Rosanne. While Desaree shuffled around inside, she worked on getting undressed.

Naked, she studied her skin. Her lips pulled into a frown. It should have been impossible. The first time she had seen it, she'd freaked out. Even now, she felt panic rising in her chest. Just over her ribcage beneath her left breast was a mark. A tattoo of sorts, but it was unmistakable in nature, because she'd seen the exact same thing covering the bodies of the sprites in the forest.

The green fire that had vanquished the vodar hadn't been ordinary. No, it had been extraordinary. And now, she had a mark to prove it.

Her fingertips traced the lines, two connecting spirals with splatters of dots surrounding them. They were turquoise and glowed with luminescence, though it had faded some, which made sense. Luminescence was similar to *fluorescence* and *phosphorescence*. It was a spontaneous emission created by radiation. Or, in her case, sprite magic. Somehow, in doing sprite magic, she had made the mark appear.

Desaree came up behind her, holding a gown. "You need to tell Saffra about it, see if she has answers. Maybe it's linked to one of her visions."

She exhaled, dropping her hand. "I would, if Jocelyn would let me see her." Daxton had not yet woken up, and Saffra, in her grief, had requested to be alone.

"Tell her it's important."

"I don't know if I want to burden her with this right now, Des." She thought about what Saffra must be going through and her throat thickened. "I miss her. Our days are darkened without her presence."

"I miss her too," Desaree said, "but we need to give her time. It's her choice to stand vigil at Daxton's bedside until he wakes up and we need to respect that."

"I do. I just wish..." She swallowed the lump in her throat. "I just wish he'd wake up already. I hate seeing her go through this."

"I know. Now, arms up." Desaree helped her dress, pulling the corset tight enough to strangle the life right out of her.

"How do ladies stand it?" she gasped, clawing at the material. "Does it really need to be *this* tight? I never wear them this tight."

"Before I came along, you wore them incorrectly. Do not think I missed it, loose ties and all."

"Who cares!" She tried to take several deep breaths. "I can hardly breathe. It's ridiculous. Not to mention uncomfortable, restrictive, heavy..." She tried to move and nearly toppled off the platform. "They're probably unhealthy too, if memory serves me correctly."

"Lady Claire," Desaree hissed. "I insist you *stop* moving like a buffoon and hold still. The gowns are as they need to be. Besides, this is a special occasion."

"And what about every *other* day? I have to wear gowns then, don't I?"

"Yes."

"Why can't I just wear pants? Where I come from, people are allowed to wear whatever they want. Besides, riders wear pants." She'd seen several of them since coming to the capital. Their flying gear consisted of tight pants, boots, long sleeved tunics, and either padded or light armor.

"Firstly," Desaree tsked, "you are not a rider. Even if you were, it wouldn't matter. King Talon's mother never traipsed around the castle in flying gear. Secondly, you are the king's *ward*—you must dress the part, as a lady of the court."

"Lady of the court!" She scoffed. "I'm no lady. Don't let these fancy gowns fool you."

"Regardless, you have an appearance to maintain. This is your chance to prove yourself to everyone. You are not the dangerous outsider they believe you to be. Moreover, they expect you to make a fool of yourself. Prove them wrong! Show them how well you fit in." Desaree sighed, as if her lecture were getting the better of her. "Listen, your customs are not *our* customs. Fight them if you want, but if you don't win people over like King Talon hopes, what is the point of making you his ward?"

She opened and closed her mouth, hesitating. "I guess you're right. It isn't easy, you know, fitting in here."

Desaree nodded. "I think you're doing well so far. There. Finished." She backed away to admire her work.

Claire's smile faltered before turning mischievous. Her gown was made of royal blue silk brocade. A color reserved for the royal family. The same color as the sapphires Desaree had chosen for her hair net. There were several layers making up the skirt; it was heavy and full. The bodice was corseted, cut low to accentuate her breasts. Its long sleeves opened wide at the elbows and trailed down to the floor, as was a popular trend in the capital.

She looked like a romanticized version of Anne Boleyn from the Tudor era.

"You look *royal*." Desaree's voice was dreamy. "What will King Talon think when he sees you?"

"I can hardly wait to see his irritation."

"I highly doubt he will be irritated." Desaree seemed to believe that the king was fond of her, which was absurd!

She'd chosen the color on purpose, after Madame Rosanne had warned her about it. Royal blue was reserved for the monarchy; no one at court wore it unless they wished to risk punishment. While she was not part of the royal family, she was royal. It was a gray area, and she hoped it would irritate the king to see her asserting herself.

CLAIRE STOPPED to check in on Dax and Saffra. There were guards standing watch outside. They nodded at her respectfully. "Saffra," she called after gently tapping on the door. "I know you are in there!"

Eventually, the door opened.

Saffra looked unkempt. Her face was puffy from crying. It hurt to see her like this.

"Wow, Claire." Saffra looked her up and down. "You have truly outdone yourself."

"Blame Des. She's the one who trussed me up like a thanksgiving turkey." The joke was lost on Saffra. She smiled, but it didn't reach her eyes. Claire cleared her throat. "How are you doing? How's Dax? Is there anything I can do?"

"No, but thank you. I appreciate your concern."

"I would love for you to join us tonight at the king's return feast, but…"

A look of longing transformed Saffra's expression. She quickly glanced over her shoulder. "I do not have the heart to leave him."

"I understand. But you'll be missed all the same."

Saffra reached for her hands, giving them a quick squeeze. "Please, have a wonderful time. And tell Desaree to do the same."

"I will."

Saffra nodded and retreated inside, quietly closing the door behind her.

Claire found everyone already assembled in the courtyard, waiting for the king. They were organized by birth and rank. She pushed through the crowd, ignoring their whispered gossip, and took her place between the king's shields.

"Glad you could make it, Lady Claire," Koldis said, nudging her shoulder with his.

She kept her face forward. "Wasn't aware I had a choice."

"You don't," Verath said from her other side. "I was ready to drag you down here myself if you didn't appear in the next few minutes"

"I was checking on Saffra."

"Is she all right?" Bedelth leaned around Verath's frame to look at her.

She hesitated. "I think she's seen better days."

Bedelth's jaw hardened and he gave a curt nod, turning forward again.

Silence fell. For the first time in a while, she hesitantly opened her mind to the sounds of the drengr. Reyr's voice was immediately there. *"I do love the sight of Kastali Dun from the sky. It is good to be home."*

Verath replied with, *"See you soon, brother. You have both been missed."*

Several other thoughts pressed in around her and she quickly closed her mind again. While she had gotten better at handling multiple voices, she still preferred to take a deep breath and relax until she heard nothing.

She glanced about, growing more anxious. Lady Caterina stood one row behind her, several bodies down. Their eyes met and she was rewarded with a glare of disgust. She snorted and turned her gaze forward again, ignoring her obvious jealousy.

Blasting trumpets destroyed the silence, making her flinch. Shortly thereafter, bells began to ring. The city below erupted into noise.

Butterflies fluttered in her stomach.

Excited cries rose up through the courtyard as people lifted their gazes to the sky. The approaching drengr had already started their descent. She watched the king's hulking, iridescent black shape as the sun's rays danced across his scales. Reyr's large golden form was beside him. They were accompanied by a group of twelve.

Reyr and Talon detached from the group and began descending in wide, lazy circles. It was impossible to look away. Her shoulders began to relax at the sight of his arrival. She reached into her skirt pocket and felt the dragonstones, warm in their pouch. Carrying them around had kept her on edge. No wonder the king hadn't wanted to.

They needed a better solution, going forward.

Reyr and Talon transformed, landing perfectly on two feet with a muffled thud. They were dressed regally, their large sveraks belted at their sides. Naturally, the king was wearing a royal blue tunic the same color as her gown. His eyes immediately latched onto hers. She quickly looked away, ignoring the flush that coated her skin in response.

A wave swept through the court as everyone went down on one knee, paying their respects. Gritting her teeth, she did the same. She kept her head bowed, staring at the ground. Her hands fisted the skirts of her gown. Desaree knelt behind her, though she wished her friend could be beside her, instead.

Boots thudded on the flagstones, heavy and confident, heading straight for her. She stifled a gasp as her vision filled with the sight of them. "Walk with me, Lady Claire," King Talon said, voice ringing in the silence.

Eyes widening, she looked up at him and found his hand outstretched, waiting to help her up.

She remained frozen, all thought sliding right out of her mind. The king's hand twitched. She blinked, then reached for it, coming to her feet. The warmth of his fingers had a strange affect upon her. She glanced at his face, noticing his tightly drawn eyebrows, then quickly dropped his hand.

He turned to his court. "Rise." They obeyed the command and everyone's eyes fell upon on her.

"Come," King Talon said, turning back to her and offering his elbow. Like a gentlemen would. She blinked. It was on her lips to decline as she studied his face—so scarred, that she was reminded of his bravery. "Humor me, please."

There was something in his eyes. A measure of hesitance that wasn't normally there. She licked her lips, then nodded, taking his elbow.

"Your Grace." The steward appeared. She breathed a sigh of relief. Thank the gods, she was saved. "Your Grace, welcome home! There are several pressing matters we must discuss at once."

"Excellent! I'll just leave you to it, then..." she made to scurry away, but King Talon's hand came up to hold hers in place. The warmth of his skin made her falter.

"Not now, Mathis," he growled. "I will discuss business with you in an hour. I have more pressing matters at the moment."

Mathis looked at her, suspicion burning in his gaze before bowing deeply to the king. Then he melted into the crowd and disappeared.

King Talon returned his attention to her, his face as unreadable as ever. "Shall we?"

Her stomach fluttered. She cleared her throat and nodded. He led her away from the speculative crowd, whispering in her wake, straight for the privacy of the royal garden.

CHAPTER 34

ARGUEMENT IN THE GARDEN

Kastali Dun

Claire tried to ignore her tangled emotions. Before today, she and the king had never physically touched. Even when he'd tried to kill her, it was his dagger that had kissed her neck, nothing more. Now, her hand was wrapped around his elbow.

The royal garden sat within the keep's lowest level. It was a vast network of stone pathways that weaved through exotic flower beds, blooming shrubberies, and trees. It was empty, save for them.

Several minutes passed in silence, amplifying the sounds of the garden. Branches rustled in the breeze, bugs chirruped, birds fluttered about. It would have been magical, were it not for the tension of the king's presence.

She wished he would say something—anything that might explain what this was about. Maybe he finally intended to apologize. She almost snorted. Yeah, *right*.

His throat cleared. "Your gown is...beautiful."

Her lips parted. She quickly schooled her features. "I'm glad you like it, Your Majesty. I thought the color would look wonderful on me."

"It suits you, yes."

Her brain tilted on its axis, completely off balance. Her eyes darted towards him then quickly away. "Thank...you?"

A new and curious silence ensued. They came upon a bench. He led her to it and sat down beside her. He didn't look at her, as if he was determined to look anywhere but.

"Forgive me, but is there a reason we are here?" She tried to read him out of the corner of her eye. Something in his countenance hinted at nervousness, the tense set of his shoulders, the clench of his jaw, the way he fiddled with the golden coin in his right hand. He slipped it back into his pocket and angled himself towards her. "I was upset when I discovered what happened in my absence. Are you all right?"

She gaped at him. His eyes darted over her face, taking in her features, as if searching for some invisible injury. "I...yes?" Her brows pulled together.

He offered a curt nod. "I am glad. I would like to hear your version of what happened the other night."

She released a slow breath. "All right."

She recounted the story, starting with Saffra's vision and ending with her plunge into the sea. She left out a few things, like the keep's secret passages. She wasn't ready for him to know that bit of information yet. He listened in silence until she finished.

"Before I left, you promised me that you would stay out of trouble." His jaw tightened with irritation.

She huffed. "I had no other choice."

"And what of Cyrus's sverak? Throwing yourself into the middle of a fight with no training?"

"That was Cyrus, not me."

"And the fire? You cannot possibly expect me to believe you performed spriten magic."

Her mouth dropped open. *Take a deep breath,* Cyrus warned. *Be patient with him.* So, she took a deep breath and said, "I am positive about what happened. Check with Marcel if you don't believe me. It was spriten magic."

He watched her for a moment. "Fine. Regardless, if you ever do something so irresponsible as to throw yourself off a tower balcony again—"

"Are you kidding me?!" Her shout startled several birds nearby. The king's eyes widened before he schooled his features. "Should I have let the vodar take the stones? Do you *want* Kane to win? Is that it? Let's get something straight *right* now. Your entire kingdom was at risk. I had a single moment to make a split decision. Fortunately for everyone, I was willing to do whatever was necessary. Or, perhaps you fail to understand what that means?"

He scoffed. "You do not know me, Claire."

"You're right. I don't. All I know is that you did a terrible job of protecting the stones."

She waited for the explosion of his temper. The silence stretched on, punctuated by her frantic heart. When he next spoke, his voice was quiet. "I cannot decide whether to be furious with you, or grateful." He abruptly stood and took several steps away, keeping his back to her.

She made a scoffing sound. "I think you ought to be grateful—"

"Have you any idea how worried I was?" he roared, rounding on her. "After the attack, when they reported you missing? I was helpless to do *anything*. You were lost. I was left to wait until they found you. Until Koldis told me you'd crawled out of the sea." She stared at him, dumbstruck. "You put your life at *risk*, Claire. That is why I wish to be furious with you. Damn the stones, and damn you for making me worry."

Her breaths came faster. She buried her shock and donned a cloak of anger. "You have no right to be angry *or* worried!"

"I have every right," he growled, chest rising and falling in rapid bursts. "You could have died! You are my ward. *Mine* to protect."

Something inside her snapped. She jumped to her feet, no longer able to sit. Her fists clenched at her sides. "You're right! I could have died. But you don't get to suddenly care when you never cared before. You threw me in a dungeon cell! You had me dragged into your torture chamber! You put a blade to my throat!" Her voice cracked.

"You dare bring that into the fold? We can both agree that I acted rashly."

"Rashly? *Rashly*?! That's it? That's all you have to say for yourself? For what you put me through? You know, you never even apologized for it. Why is that? Wait—I will tell you. Because you don't give a damn about what you did to me. So no, don't pretend like you care."

His lips parted and he gaped at her, speechless.

"You know what? Forget it—all of it. You're the king. That makes you above apologies, right? I don't know why I ever even expected one. I'll see you at dinner, *Your Majesty*."

She left him to his shock and stormed away, unable to stomach another minute in his company.

SHE WAS STILL FUMING when Desaree escorted her down to dinner. She'd considered skipping the king's feast altogether, but Desaree had convinced her to put on a brave face and rise above. So, she forced herself into a pleasant expression. As they walked, Desaree chatted, filing the silence. It did little to calm her irritation.

They crossed the threshold into the dining hall. The room was already full. Reyr's voice sounded in her mind. *"Your new gown looks stunning on you. Oh...and interesting choice of color, too."*

She smiled a genuine smile. *"Thank you, Reyr. I'm glad you're back."*

And she was. She considered telling him how much she had missed him, but didn't.

The king was already at the head table. He had not noticed her yet. Would that she could slip past without his gaze landing on her.

They quickly made their way to their seats. "We should take Saffra some food, too," Desaree offered. "Perhaps she would like company tonight."

"We could try, if she'll have us."

The doors clanged shut and the serving staff poured in, arms filled with platters of food. They were deposited all along the trestle tables.

"What happened between you and the king?" Reyr asked as she filled her plate. *"He seems troubled...more so than usual."*

"Oh, really?" She drizzled gravy over her meat and potatoes. *"Fancy that."*

"What did you two fight about this time?"

She sighed. *"You know, the usual. He would rather scold me for risking my life than admit to being a pompous ass."*

A choking cough drifted over the noise in the hall. She looked up in time to see Reyr patting his chest, his face filled with mirth.

"What is so funny?" King Talon asked Reyr.

"Nothing, Your Grace. It is nothing." There was a slight pause, before Reyr said, *"While I do agree that King Talon can be pompous—"*

"Can be?"

"Very well." A mental sigh. *"I do not agree with his lack of apology."*

"But? I sense a but coming..."

"But, he made a valid point. You exposed yourself to a very risky situation—"

"Oh no! Don't you dare!"

"Hear me out. You have displayed undying bravery, yet again. I cannot fault you for taking action. The king may be incapable of thanking you, so I will. Thank you."

Her face flooded with heat—and surprise. After swallowing a mouthful of food, she said, *"I appreciate your thanks, Reyr, but it should come from the king, not you."*

"Do you think Saffra will want some of these?" Desaree held up a bowl of candied walnuts, unintentionally cutting into the conversation.

She turned her full attention to Desaree and said, "Sure, let's take her some of those. She'll love them." Then she glanced over at Reyr and added, *"We can talk about this later."*

Desaree snatched up an empty plate and began loading it with goodies.

"Very well. May I come by after dinner?"

"I don't think so. Des and I are going to visit Saffra tonight."

The real excuse was that she simply wanted to be alone, even if it had been a while since she'd seen Reyr. She still felt emotionally exhausted from her argument with the king. The best way to heal was with a hot bath, a mug of chamomile tea, and some sleep.

"Sure, we can discuss this tomorrow," Reyr said in an offhand way. When she looked up at him, he was intent on his plate of food, but his face mirrored his disappointment.

Her eyes locked with the king's. His expression may have been emotionless, but his eyes glittered with curiosity. She stared back at him with a blank face.

When he was the first to look away, she smiled, victorious.

CHAPTER 35

THE PRINCE OF ESTERPINE

Esterpine

Jeanine froze as the sharp edge of cold, spriten steel fell upon her neck. By now she was familiar with the blade's edge, especially the feel of it against her neck. She had felt it other places too, against her arm, her waist, her legs—

"Again. This time, quicker."

Holding back a snort of annoyance, she wiped beads of sweat from her brow before nodding. *Be quicker.* That was always Lykan's advice. She was beginning to loathe it. How could she move faster? She wasn't a sprite, so she didn't have their inhuman speed.

Lykan was one of many highly regarded sword masters living in Esterpine. He often frequented the sprite's practice grounds and had been recruited to assist Master Orin for her training. Like all sprites, his body was covered in glowing markings. His hair was as dark as darkness itself. His eyes were nearly the same shade of black. His face was angular, with high cheekbones and a pointed chin. He often looked stern unless he smiled, which caused his eyes to turn into friendly slits, but he didn't smile often. And unlike some sprites, he didn't sport a loincloth, but rather, pants and a tunic, as normal people ought.

She stepped away from Lykan and moved into position. A quick glance showed that Jahl fared no better. She suppressed her laughter as he landed flat on his back. Master Orin's blade point rested neatly against his throat. Red-faced and panting, Jahl batted it away and jumped to his feet to begin anew. Their morning had been much the same as they tried over and again to best their assigned opponents.

Schooling her features, she crouched low and then lunged, attempting another surprise attack against Lykan. His blade met hers and he parried the blow. They danced around, light on their feet, until it was obvious that Lykan could have bested her several times in that short span. "You're going easy on me," she accused. His mouth twitched. He stuck his foot out in a brief flash and sent her flying head-first for the ground. She landed with a thud and quickly rolled onto her back, sword at the ready. Just in time. Lykan's blade met hers.

"Very good. Almost thought I would have you there."

She offered him a brief smile. He helped her to her feet. She glanced around the clearing, a sudden feeling of being watched creeping over her. It wasn't the first time she'd felt it. Sometimes, she wondered if it was merely a byproduct of the forest, of its strange *otherness*. But, she had a feeling it was something else entirely.

She took a fighting stance, glancing at her father's sword gripped in her hands. It was slightly heavier than the practice swords she was used to, like the ones she had used in Kaljah. This was a soldier's sword—a sword for protecting the kingdom. It came from a time when her father had fought in King Talon's ranks during the goblin war. Inscribed upon the steel's flat blade were the words, *"Fight with honor,"* on one side and, *"Strive for glory,"* on the other.

Lykan came at her, rushing forward with sprightly ease as he had done a hundred times before, swinging his spriten blade above him. She raised her sword to block his—there was no time for anything else. Lykan never left her a moment for creativity. All she could do was focus on staying alive. She could count on a single hand the number of offensive blows she had successfully dealt him, and such successes were mere allowances. Lykan would never allow her through his barriers if she were a true enemy.

HIs blade swept around. She danced backwards, moving her feet gently in the way he'd taught her. "Do not blunder about," he'd scolded in a huff, back when he had first assessed her abilities. It had been a difficult practice. "Move quietly. Move quickly, but with ease. Know each footstep before it is made." It had taken time to learn the movements sprites preferred. Even now, she performed them poorly, but hopefully better than common swordsmen.

Lykan's blade came down hard, pulling her from her thoughts. It emitted a soft, pleased purr. Over and again she was forced to block as the sword sang its eagerness. That was how all spriten blades worked. She did not fully understand it, and they refused to share their secrets, but she was certain that some form of magic was worked into the metal itself.

Her frustration grew and her movements turned erratic, sloppy.

"Do not let your emotion overcome your skill." Lykan stopped suddenly to scold her. He was right. She exhaled, shoulders sagging. The tension in her body left her muscles screaming. "It should never get in the way. When you fight, you must clear your mind. Remember what I have told you?"

"Yes," she scoffed, blowing a chunk of hair from her face. While she was covered in perspiration and utterly exhausted, Lykan looked fresh as the morning.

"I think that is enough swordplay for today. Go and retrieve your bow, we shall see if you have been practicing."

"Thank the gods!" she muttered, nearly ready to collapse.

There was a large clearing on the outskirts of Esterpine popular for bow practice. This was where she and Lykan often practiced. Standing targets were no longer challenging enough, so Lykan insisted on moving targets. Today he carried a large sack of apples.

"Once I throw them, they might be hard for you to see. *Our* eyes are easily matched for tiny objects but I daresay..." He sighed. "Well, let us see how you do."

She ignored the dig. He frequently pointed out human short-comings, specifically hers. Sprites enjoyed their superiority, though it was never mean-spirited. They simply knew they were better equipped at most tasks. To argue otherwise was fruitless. In Lykan's case, it was clear that he enjoyed being a better swordsman. She enjoyed being better at things too, when the situation allowed for it. As far as she knew, everyone was guilty of such feelings.

For the remainder of the afternoon, she worked with her bow. Lykan spent his efforts throwing multiple apples into the air, sometimes all at once, other times, one followed by another. In each instance, she attempted to shoot them from the sky, or the trees, or wherever they flew.

He was correct in that the moving apples were damned near impossible to see. But after some practice, her eyes grew better attuned to spotting them, and from there, she let her instincts take over.

"That was nicely done," he said after she'd hit three apples in one go. Granted, he did not release them all at the same time, but his movements were quick, so he might as well have. She smiled and nodded, turning back to her bow. His praise was rare, but when it came, she appreciated it all the more.

Despite the intensity of her training, she had come to enjoy her time spent in the Gable Forest. More and more she found the idea of returning to her small village unsavory, not simply because there was nothing to return to, but mostly because she no longer wanted a simple life. The sprites of the forest were complex and full of depth. There was always something to offer up amusement.

When she wasn't training, she found herself exploring the wooded lands around Esterpine. Occasionally Jahl accompanied her, but she preferred to go alone. The silence of the trees was a welcome alternative to his moody behavior. Since their arrival, he had become somewhat distant towards her. He was working through the same kind of emotional loss as she was, but everyone dealt with loss differently.

Lᴇssᴏɴs ғɪɴɪsʜᴇᴅ ғᴏʀ ᴛʜᴇ ᴅᴀʏ, she found herself exploring more of the forest. She'd just found a nice clearing to occupy, a large boulder at its center, when she felt that niggling sensation between her shoulder blades. She was being watched.

She surveyed the lush undergrowth of the forest and this time, she found a pair of eyes staring right back at her. "You!" she gasped. "I mean..." She stood from the large boulder and curtsied. "Pardon me, Prince Feowen. I am surprised to see you here."

Her face flushed as she took in his distinct blue hair, which was tied back in a ponytail at the nape of his neck, his high cheekbones, and his glittering eyes, one blue, the other green.

He crept from the shadows like a prowling cat, every motion sleek and calculated.

"You've been spying on me this whole time, haven't you?"

He didn't reply, walking a large circle around her, like a predator sizing up prey. Chills raced down her arms.

"Well?" she asked again, placing her hands on her hips. "Are you going to answer my question?"

"Are all humans as curious as you?" His low voice caught her by surprise.

"Um..." All the witty things she might have said fled her mind. She simply stared back at him.

He took up the seat she had vacated, crossing his legs, propping his elbows on his knees. She moved several paces away, putting distance between them. His chin rested on his hands as he continued to study her.

As the moments stretched on, the silence grew awkward.

"All right. Well, if you're just going to sit there and stare at me like I'm some kind of strange animal, I'll just leave you to it," she said, turning on her heel.

"I asked your friend Jahl about you." She froze, muscles tensing. "The answers I sought were refused. Do you think he dislikes me? Perhaps he simply misses his home."

She whirled to face him, composing her thoughts. "I doubt it's his home he misses. His family, maybe. He was preparing to leave Kaljah when the goblin attack happened."

"I see. A man of his age must make a place and a name for himself in the world. That is how one discovers one's identity. Where does that leave you?"

"Me?" She gazed at him. He gazed back. "I suppose I was upset at the thought of losing him. But I always knew he would want to leave eventually. I could hardly fault him for it. I wanted to do the same."

"Then, you do not wish to return home? Humans are creatures of familiarity, are they not?"

"Some, yes." She pressed her lips between her teeth. "Others crave adventure. My coming here has opened my eyes. I could never be happy returning to Kaljah, even if it was rebuilt. Perhaps it is time I too find my own identity. Maybe I can do that here, maybe not."

The prince's head tilted. "You do not fit the picture I had painted."

Her eyebrows drew together. "What picture?"

A smile broke across his countenance. She found herself staring transfixed. "I can assure you it is a good thing. But perhaps it is still too early to tell. I shall have to consider it more."

He surged to his feet.

She blinked in surprise. Blinked again as he hopped lightly from the boulder. Blinked again, and he was gone. She gawked at the forest in his wake, at the place he'd disappeared.

Later, during the evening meal, she caught the prince's gaze. It was brief, yet it spoke of their secret encounter in the forest, like he was taunting her to press him further over what he had said. She felt her face warm and she was forced to turn her eyes upon her plate.

The sprites took their meals out in the open under the canopy of trees. These were always merry occasions. Large, low tables were assembled that allowed them to sit upon pillows on the ground. Each table was laden with food provided by the forest—fruits, vegetables, nuts, seeds, and mushrooms—and other delicacies obtained through trading, like grain for bread.

The unicorns were treated as equals. None were tied or stabled. They roamed freely through the city and often showed themselves during mealtimes for handouts.

They told stories or sang songs offered up as mealtime entertainment. She loved this the most. Because of their long lives, each of them was a walking, living, breathing, wealth of information. She was taking a bite of honey drizzled bread when Prince Feowen rose to his feet. A hush fell over the clearing. He caught her eye and her cheeks flushed. She quickly looked back down and took another bite.

A stringed instrument struck a tune and Feowen began to sing:

It gave us life when we did roam,
For roam we did aplenty,
A place that we might call our home,
For home still had no country.
Its waters which we all took part,
For they did quench our thirst,
Then steadied even faintest heart,
We no longer feared the worst.
And so in joy our voices lifted,
For song we did hold dear,
A gracious thanks as ever chanted,
To fill our world with cheer.
Then from our words did rise the trees,
The bushes, bugs, and birds, and bees,
The forest in our giant's likeness,
Took shape and form around us.
In its misty shade did we decree,
For our words were ever mighty,
To moniker the noble giant
A most fitting name of King Tree.
And still it stands 'til the end of days,

Protected by our peoples,
Its secrets lie within our hearts,
And will remain forever and always.

IT WAS a song about the king tree. The sprites had been a wandering tribe known as spirit singers. A single woman had embarked upon her own quest and discovered the lone *King Tree*. After speaking with it, the tree encouraged her to bring her people to it. When they came, they partook of its waters and uttered their thanks. The tree was much like they were, a lonely sentinel upon a barren landscape with only a pool for company. The spirit singers had no home of their own, so they began to sing for the tree. It rejoiced in their beautiful voices. Their song created the forest, which grew up around them, providing the King Tree with company. It was within this forest that the spirit singers built a home for themselves. Eventually, they became known as sprites, a new kind of people.

As Feowen took a seat, she couldn't help but wonder if it was truth or myth. Was there really a king tree? If so, where was it? She'd never found a tree different from the rest.

IN THE DAYS FOLLOWING, she kept an eye out for Prince Feowen. The watchful sensation that pricked her neck didn't disappear. She continued to wander the fringes of Esterpine's city, often pretending to search for the King Tree in hopes he'd show himself, though she doubted she would ever find it. "I know you're following me," she shouted into the forest's midst. "What is the point of hiding if I know you are there?"

All she ever got in return was a quiet snicker.

An entire fortnight passed before he appeared to her. Probably to laugh at her. She'd had a particularly unsuccessful day of training with Lykan, and had plenty of bruises to show for it. She was sitting at what had become her favorite place of contemplation, the boulder where she had originally encountered the prince, when he again materialized from the underbrush.

Her mood was too foul to utter a single word of greeting.

"If you let your emotions get the better of you, you will never master the sword."

Heat washed her skin. He could have chosen anything to say. *Anything*!

"You sound just like him," she snapped. Slipping off the boulder, she blatantly left him standing alone in the clearing. She called over her shoulder, "Maybe the two of you should laugh at me together," just as the trees swallowed her up.

Let him chew on that.

His laughter followed. It didn't help that she liked the sound of it. Especially didn't help that it lifted her mood. "Come now, Jeanine," he called. "I meant no offense."

She stopped at the feel of his watchful eyes upon her back. Taking a deep breath, she whirled to face him. "You have—"

"Lykan was my trainer once," he said, cutting her off. "He can be difficult, nearly impossible to beat with a blade. So, I can understand your frustration." His expression turned thoughtful. "Perhaps..."

"Perhaps what?" She crossed her arms.

"Perhaps I could give you a few pointers?"

She gaped at him. "*You?*"

His mouth twitched. "You do not think I am qualified?"

"It...it isn't that."

"I see. Are you embarrassed about losing to *a prince*?"

Embarrassed?! She scoffed and turned on her heel, marching away.

"Come now," he called again, his voice quietly echoing from tree to tree. "I was only teasing."

She stopped again, against her better judgment. Mostly because she hadn't expected him to tease her. Or to admit it.

"I promise I shan't tell a soul. It will be our little secret. I will even let you win—if you so desire." He came up beside her. The proximity made her breath hitch. He towered over her, a full head in height. His body was powerful, all lean muscle and pale skin and beautiful, luminescent swirls. There was no smile upon his face now, which leant a seriousness to him she wasn't used to. In fact, there was no emotion at all, making him impossible to read.

"If we're going to practice, then I don't want your—"

"My what?" He seemed even closer now.

She took a step back. "I don't want you going easy on me simply because I am human."

"Ah. Well, in that case, you must accept in advance your loss to a prince."

"Gods!" she cried. "You sprites are so full of yourselves." He simply shrugged, accepting the truth that she had given. She blew out a loud exhale. "I suppose I have done nothing but lose to Lykan, what's one more loss? I'm used to it by now anyway."

"Well then, shall we?" he asked, drawing his sword.

Hers was strapped to her back. She put her hand upon the grip and hesitated for several breaths before nodding. "Fine. Let's do this."

And thus began the strangest friendship she had ever chanced upon.

CHAPTER 36

BYRON'S DECISION

Fort Squall

Tamara and Lady Emmy entered Fort Squall's dining hall together, happily chatting about her lessons. It was mid-morning, so the breakfast dishes had long since been cleared. The hall's tables, except for one, stood empty with benches neatly pushed beneath. The room was quite airy when it wasn't full of bodies.

It was a common misconception that the hall's sole purpose was a place to serve meals or hold occasional gatherings. The hall was often in use during the entire day. When meals were not in session, it was used for meetings, group activities, training, and more.

Today, she was to be familiarized with a new task.

There was only one group in the hall currently. She and Lady Emmy approached a trestle table at the front of the room. There were a number of riders gathered about a large, open book. Her eyes widened when she saw how large it was.

The happy chatting stopped. Greetings were exchanged. She couldn't help but admire the way the other riders respected Lady Emmy. Their expressions mirrored fierce loyalty and love. She hoped that someday she might be respected in such a way, but respect was not given, it was earned. Lady Emmy had done well earning theirs.

Lady Emmy introduced her and the riders gave their names, even though she'd already met many of them. There was Amirah—Soren's rider. Soren was a wing-second to Alark, and Brylee was Alark's rider. She sat next to Amirah. Then there was Darya. They had spoken once or twice during dinner. Darya had a pleasant, dimpled smile, warm brown eyes, and a round face. Sandra was there too. She was Dagen's rider. There was also Valda, Maranda, Ellira, Sable...

All too soon, the names of those she did not yet know began slipping from her mind. There were seventeen riders in total, so it was a lot to remember. Later, she'd go through them with Lady Emmy to practice.

"Tamara will join us henceforth," Lady Emmy explained. "She may not yet be mated, but I see no reason to withhold these duties until then." The riders gave their approval with complacent nods and welcoming smiles before returning to their task.

"Stand beside me, dear, and I will explain what we are doing here." Lady Emmy led her around the table. At first it seemed silly. Emmy took several loops about the table, arm-in-arm with her, walking at a painfully slow pace. She remained quiet, watchful, even though she wanted to ask why they weren't sitting with everyone else.

She realized soon enough.

The riders discussed patrols for each of the dragondoms in their territory. They used the book to write out names, often scratching out one and replacing it with another. Some of the names had been scratched out so many times that the ink was almost unreadable.

When she had the opportunity, she leaned over and took a good look at the large book. It was made up entirely of timetables. Someone had taken on the painstaking task of drawing grids on each sheet of parchment, both front and back. It was in these boxes that names, times, and locations were written.

"Every two weeks, we convene to create patrol schedules," Emmy finally explained. "The riders of Fort Squall's wing leaders and wing seconds are required to oversee this duty. Given that you are soon to be Byron's rider, this will become your responsibility too." They rounded one end of the table and began their walk towards the other end. "We try to plan four weeks in advance, but things often change, especially as of late."

"Is that why they are scratching out and rewriting names?"

"Very good—yes. The book has each wing leader and wing second's name, the names of those assigned to their patrol group, and which patrol locations they oversee. Now, let's see how much of your lessons you remember."

Her stomach fluttered. She needed to get used to thinking on the spot if she wanted to become a fort leader some day. Still, it always made her jittery.

"Give me a thorough explanation of the fort's patrols. How do they work?"

She cleared her throat. "Fort Squall has twelve battle wings, each with a wing leader and two wing seconds. Fort Squall's battle wings are split up into smaller groups called patrol groups, usually six or seven strong, depending on the group. Each group has either a wing leader or a wing second in command. There are some thirty-five patrol groups. They spend approximately two weeks in the field, and two weeks at home. During their time in the wilderness, the groups fly various flight paths that take them past settlements where they check in, carry news, and ensure that the people are safe. While at home, these patrol groups spend time training for aerial combat. The drengr often spend time training for hand-to-hand combat and swordplay, while their riders focus on archery, and other duties, like the one taking place here."

"Very good." Emmy beamed with pride. She exhaled and her shoulders relaxed. "Now, tell me about our territory and how it relates to patrols?"

"Vestur has five dragondoms. At any given time, there are between fifteen and seventeen patrols out in the field, split between Alnore, Arpton, Kadworth, Shaldorna, and Warsile. Pairs are expected to know every flight path through every territory during their training. These flight paths are used by each of the patrols to cover as much ground as possible during their time."

"Excellent." Emmy led her to an empty place at the table. "Today you will merely observe. In the future, you will be an active participant. Sit here and watch the way things are decided. I will leave you for now. When this meeting convenes, you know where to find me."

Emmy bid the table farewell and departed.

She quickly found herself immersed in the task of observation. Assigning patrols was tricky. Certain patrol teams preferred certain flight paths. Other teams preferred new paths. Sometimes this resulted in mature arguments, while other times, the riders' voices rose to unnecessary heights. When the midday meal arrived, she was surprised by how quickly the time had passed.

Byron found her just after she'd finished eating and invited her for a walk. "I know you are supposed to take lessons with my mother this afternoon, but I am sure she will forgive you a few minutes of lateness."

More than happy to accept, she eagerly laced her arm through his. They set out on a path that took them outside the fort and into the field beyond. After some coaxing, she told him about her morning with the other riders. It never got old, having his undivided attention upon her.

"I am glad my mother is exposing you to these rigors early on. I have always trusted her judgment—even if it took me time to realize she was right." A reluctant smile spread across his face.

"She *is* wise." Her grin mirrored his. "But yes, sometimes she can be a bit demanding. Intimidating. Frustrating?"

He chuckled. "To be sure. As is the case with my father. They are both good role models for us. I hope one day I am respected half as much as my father and uncle are."

"Your uncle? As in, Lord Reyr?"

"The very same."

"I've heard stories about him. My heart breaks every time I think of how he lost Gemma."

"Aye. A horrible thing."

They stood in the middle of the field. The long grass nearly reached her knees. Much of it had already turned to shades of gold and brown, results of a long summer. But autumn was here now, and as it progressed, the rain would turn the grass green again.

Byron stopped to face her, his expression serious. She frowned before schooling her features. "There is something I want to talk to you about, Tamara. I am sure you can guess what it is..."

"Us?"

He nodded. "I know you think it unfair of me to keep you waiting like this—I am sure you do. You have every right to think I am being selfish. I know that I am." He took a deep breath and turned his gaze skyward to watch the approach of a small covey returning from a patrol. "I wanted to be sure I made the right decision."

"And have you? Made a decision, that is..."

"I have." He looked back down at her, his expression one of apprehension, made all the more obvious by his long pause.

"And?"

"I would like us to wait for four more weeks. That is all I ask. With war and uncertainty upon us, my peers would have me think that mating is something to be rushed, but I refuse to allow them to make my decisions."

"Maybe your peers see the bigger picture, Byron. Four weeks... four weeks feels like an eternity." A deep frustration took root in the depths of her chest. Four weeks versus tomorrow, or the next day, or the day after...

Was she missing something?

"How will four weeks make any difference?"

"I told you I was being selfish."

She snorted. Her composure evaporated. "Selfish?! Is that what you call it? Byron, I am ready. I have already told you that I am. Why must you keep this from me? Why must it be four weeks? Selfish hardly explains *that*..."

His face changed. He almost looked pained. For a moment, she felt horrid for lashing out at him. Was she overreacting? Was this worth causing him obvious upset?

"The reason it is four weeks, and not two, or tomorrow, is because I would like to get to know you better."

"Get to know me bet—"

"When I make love to you for the first time, Tamara, I prefer we both harbor a passionate love for each other. Duty is one thing—love is another."

She opened her mouth, but her words froze on her tongue. She tried to make sense of what he was saying. She already loved him, what more did he want? Her face must have mirrored her internal remonstration.

"Gods!" He threw up his hands. "I feel as if I am explaining this horribly. Look, I love you Tamara, with all my heart! You are my mate, in that my heart has no choice, nor does my mind, or my body. But when I make love to you, I don't want our bond to be the only deep connection we share. Does that make sense?"

She could do little more than nod quickly. Especially with all this talk of making love. What was she supposed to say? Was passion really that important? Did she want to mate with him for the wrong reasons? "I...I guess."

"You do not need to say anything." He moved forward and swept her into his arms, holding her tightly. At first, she stiffened. They didn't usually resort to physical contact like this. He'd never held her before.

After several deep breaths, her body began to relax. She sank into him. When he finally released her, she felt a great deal calmer.

"Will you honor my wishes in this?" he asked. "Will you afford me the four weeks I request?"

Was there even a choice? Taking a deep breath, she said, "Four weeks, then, but no longer."

He smiled. "Thank you, my lady." A moment later, he swept her into his arms again. This time, the longer he held her, the more she enjoyed how it felt. Maybe this was what he wanted—to physically create a bond with her before the true bonding took place. Perhaps if they often touched like this, waiting wouldn't be so bad. He did know more about these things than she did. Perhaps it was best if she trusted him on the matter.

"I have something else to tell you," he said after setting her back on her feet. "Even though we will not be mated for four weeks, we have been given clearance to begin our training early."

Her hands flew to her stomach as it lurched. "Truly? You—you mean it? Right now if I wish it?"

"Right now. If you wish it."

She laughed, suddenly overcome. All of her frustration disappeared. "I..." She looked up at the sky. Thought of flying. Of training. A thrill shot through her, straight to her bones. "I'm ready."

CHAPTER 37

DINING WITH THE KING

Kastali Dun

Claire's frustration nipped at her heels, following her well into the next day.

"You're brooding," Desaree said, giving her a gentle shove between the shoulder blades. "Still upset over King Talon?"

"Yes," she scoffed.

"It does not do to dwell."

"You're right. I just can't help it. Why is it so hard for him to say 'I'm sorry'?"

"We all have our weaknesses. Even the king isn't perfect. How many mistakes have *you* made in your life?"

"Me? Never!" She placed a teasing hand over heart.

Their eyes met in the mirror's reflection and Desaree gave her hair a reproachful tug. "Well, *I* have made plenty myself. I would guess the king has made just as many, if not more. Perhaps if you got to know him better, you might be more forgiving."

"I'm not like you, Des. You have such a kind heart and a level head when it comes to things like that. I like holding grudges, at least where King Talon is concerned."

Desaree barked a laugh. "As we each have our weaknesses, so

too do we have our strengths. I may be level headed and kind hearted, but I'm not brave like you, or courageous. I could never have gone before the king like you did during your trial. No, I…" Desaree shuddered. "I could not have done that."

"I can promise you, it was all bravado. I was terrified. I'm not really that brave. Mostly, I just do things without thinking, which makes me stupid, if anything. Careless. Reckless."

"We will have to agree to disagree. I mean, look at you. You came from another world. You were an outsider—one who was lucky to have survived the laws of our land. Now you're royal. A transition like that…it's impressive."

"It doesn't come without a price. I mean, we both know what I have to do in the end." Her voice dropped to a whisper. The thought of her promise made her chest tighten. The promise's way of reminding her that she had a job to do.

"A heavy burden indeed," Desaree agreed. "All the more reason to forgive King Talon and move on, whether he apologizes or not. You owe it to yourself." Desaree's voice dropped low, urgent. "Do not be like me. Someone who spent too much time holding a grudge against Caterina. I may never heal."

Claire gnawed on her lower lip, contemplating. Hating the king was exhausting. She exhaled. "Maybe you're right. Maybe I should at least try to get to know him."

"It's better than nothing. If you try half as well as you do other things, I am confident the results will be favorable. Public figures get very little privacy. There is plenty of knowledge out there ripe for the taking. Or, *gasp*, what if you actually made more of a point to talk to him."

"Oh, stop."

"I'm serious. How much do you really know about him?"

"Reyr told me a little about his younger years."

"You mean the time when he was handsome?"

She snorted. "Is that how his life is split? Between the days he was handsome and the days that he became scarred?"

Desaree's cheeks washed with color. She didn't look up from her busy hands. "I suppose. I never really thought about it." Claire made a humming noise. "I once saw a picture of him, you know, a painting from when he was young. It was hidden away in storage. Gods, he was handsome."

"He still is, if you can see past his scars. It's hard for me to picture what he must have looked like younger, before the battle..." She took a deep breath, hesitating. "Do you think the painting is still there? I would like to see it."

"I am sure it is. Would you like me to take you there?"

"I would." She fidgeted with a jeweled hair ornament, turning it in her fingers. The jewels sparkled in the light.

"There was once a time when every woman in the kingdom dreamed of being King Talon's mate. Long, *long* before I was born, of course. This is all hearsay now."

Claire snorted, rolling her eyes. "I don't suppose that surprises me. A handsome young prince? Who *wouldn't* want to marry him?"

"He was a bit of a womanizer, you know."

"Yeah, Reyr told me. He also told me about his parents, about how he got his scars, and about how he stopped pursuing women once he, you know..."

"Yes. He became a recluse."

She sighed. It was hard to hate him, knowing his past. But, no matter what he'd been through, no matter how unfortunate his circumstances were, it was no excuse to act the way he had—

A loud knock echoed through her chambers.

"Coming!" Desaree called. She rushed over and opened the door.

"A message for Lady Claire," came a female voice.

"Thank you, Anya. I will deliver it straight away."

A few more hushed sentences were spoken before the door closed with a quiet click. Desaree turned to face Claire, her eyes sparkling with excitement. "It has King Talon's seal!"

Claire felt the color drain from her face. Desaree handed her the folded parchment. She slit the seal and unfurled the message, quickly skimming the contents with pursed lips.

"Well?!" Desaree said, impatient.

Her heart began to pound. "He...he requests my company for

today's midday meal. He asks that I dine with him privately in his accommodations."

"The midday...oh, gods! That's in an hour."

"So? Who says I'm going to go?"

"Won't you?"

"I... Yes, I suppose I must."

Desaree smiled. "Good, then give me just a moment to send your formal reply. Anya is waiting outside the door." She rushed to Claire's writing desk and opened a bottle of ink. It barely had time to dry before she was handing it off.

Today was meant to be a rest day. They'd gotten a late start that morning—a very late start. That was mostly due to her lack of sleep over her frustration.

"I'm going to make you look perfect," Desaree decided. "Your burgundy gown, and your hair net—the one that I got you. I'll need to give you some kohl for your eyes, perhaps some rouge to pinken your cheeks." She mostly chatted with herself, coaching herself through the process of preparing Claire for the king's company.

Claire hardly heard a word of it, too caught up on the note she held. She read its contents repeatedly, trying to determine any hidden messages.

"Well, you might as well read it aloud while you sit there," Desaree said, fastening her hair net into place.

She exhaled. "Dear Lady Claire—"

"Oh, he is so *formal.*"

"He's a king. Of course he is."

"Very well, continue."

"I admit that this is short notice. I would very much appreciate the honor of your company for today's midday meal—"

"The honor? Gods above!"

"—if it is favorable. Please join me in my tower promptly at noon. Yours truly, King Talon."

Desaree sighed, literal hearts in her eyes. "Yours truly. What a gentlemen. What do you think it means?"

She snorted. "Probably not what you're obviously thinking. Maybe it means his ears were ringing. He probably sensed us talking about him and wants to put things straight, specifically the womanizing part."

The color drained from Desaree's face. "You don't think...?"

"Gods, no! I was only kidding." She chewed on her bottom lip, trying to calm the butterflies in her stomach. This was like yesterday all over again, when he'd requested her company for a walk with absolutely no context. What did he have up his sleeve this time? Another scolding?

CLAIRE PRESENTED herself to the king's guards at his tower. Her stomach tightened into a knot, a sense of dread settling over her. She should have declined his invitation. What was she even doing here?

She exhaled, her nostrils flaring. Trying. She was trying, because she'd agreed to. Her hand slipped inside her pocket, fingers wrapping around the leather pouch hiding there.

"Good Afternoon, Lady Claire. The king is expecting you." The king's guards opened the door for her, ushering her inside. Everything was immaculate. There wasn't a single mote of dust or trinket out of place. Someone had been thorough after the attack.

King Talon strode into the room. "Lady Claire, welcome." He offered a small bow of his head.

"Thank you, Your Majesty." She curtsied, keeping her lips pressed together. Dragonwall's formalities took some getting used to.

"I appreciate your coming on such short notice. No doubt you would prefer to be elsewhere. This way, please." He motioned for her to precede him into the formal dining room. She blinked, collecting herself, then spurred herself into motion. A long table was set with only two place settings. She considered strutting to the head of the table, but deviated to the setting at its right.

She pulled out the chair. King Talon appeared behind her to push it in before taking his own. She frowned, unable to make sense of him.

Give him a chance to show kindness, Cyrus chided. She inwardly rolled her eyes.

The mood in the room felt awkward. She tucked her hands in her lap and took a moment to study her surroundings. The dining table seated ten. Aside from their two place settings, it was otherwise empty. No food had been brought forth as of yet.

The room itself was a bit too closed off for her tastes, but that was the way of castles. It wasn't entirely dreary. Two large windows along the far wall let in some daylight, giving stunning views of the sea beyond.

The rest of the room was lit with wall sconces and an overhead chandelier. Her eyes traveled upward. The chandelier was magnificent, its multiple tiers filled with candles twinkling down at her.

King Talon cleared his throat and she caught him staring at her, his expression unreadable as usual.

"It's a beautiful piece," she offered by way of explanation.

"Indeed. A work of art."

"Did you have it commissioned yourself?"

"No. It's been here a long time."

"Like yourself," she muttered under her breath.

"I must seem quite old to you, no doubt."

"I—" She cleared her throat. Heat flooded her face. "I forgot that drengr have superb hearing. Please, forgive me."

His nostrils flared. "It is forgiven."

Gods, this was already going terribly. Her place setting had been furnished with a goblet of water. She reached for it and sipped, giving herself something to do.

"As you have probably noticed, I have been largely unavailable lately. Recent events have taken every spare moment of my time. Once you became my ward, I had hoped to check on you more often. I have failed rather miserably, as of late—"

Her sip of water went down wrong and she coughed, interrupting his final words. She managed to clear her throat and say, "Your duties are time consuming, Your Majesty. You need not worry on my account. I am used to taking care of myself."

"I am certain you are. Tell me, how are your lessons progressing?"

"Not as well as I had hoped." She stole a glance at him and immediately regretted it. His intense gaze was too heavy to bear.

"How so?" There was genuine curiosity in his voice.

"Well..." She hesitated. Being honest with him, admitting her weaknesses, scared her. She inhaled and said, "I'm struggling, even with simple cantrips."

He frowned, a rare occurrence. "Is it the language? The words?"

She shook her head, then told him about how she felt each time she used magic. How it drained her. How it felt wrong. He listened patiently, which made it easier to open up to him, but also clashed with what she thought about him. "Reyr said I just need more time to get used to it, but..."

"But your instincts say otherwise," he finished for her. She exhaled, feeling surprisingly lighter. "It can take new mages months to get used to magic, but you shouldn't discount your instincts. I owe Marcel a visit. Would you mind if I discussed this with him?"

Huh. Interesting. "I...I suppose it wouldn't hurt."

"Good. Besides magic, all else is well? Your tutors are to your liking?"

"All of them except Mage Targa," she scoffed.

The corner of his mouth twitched, so subtle, she almost missed it. "His personality leaves something to be desired, yes." Her lips parted in surprise. King Talon lifted a shoulder. "I'm allowed to have opinions."

"Right, but..."

"You were honest with me about your magic. You deserve my honesty in return. Even if it's about a certain mage whose company is...difficult."

She choked back a laugh. "I doubt he'd be difficult if I were anyone else. I've got Lady Caterina to thank for that." The king stared at her. "The two of them play off one another to undermine me. I'm pretty sure they do it on purpose."

"I see. Yes, Lady Caterina can be..."

She snorted. "You're trying to find something politically correct to say right now, aren't you?"

"Is it that obvious?" He lifted a dark brow in challenge. She could only stare at him. Already in the span of a few minutes he'd shown more emotion than she'd ever seen.

"I won't tell anyone if you want to admit she's awful." A smile threatened to break free. "Your secret is safe with me."

He huffed, but his next words were serious. "If she gives you any further trouble, come to me directly. I do not want your education jeopardized in any way."

"I..." She exhaled. "I think I can handle myself. But...thanks."

He nodded. "I guessed as much."

She chewed on her lower lip. "She said something—Caterina, I mean."

"*Lady* Caterina."

"Lady Caterina," she parroted. "After my first lesson, she told me to stay away from you. That you were hers." The king leaned back and pinched the bridge of his nose. It was the first time she'd seen him exasperated. She couldn't help but stare, transfixed. "I take it the rumors aren't true, then?"

"What rumors?" he barked.

"The ones about how she's going to marry you and become your queen."

"Gods above," he muttered. "Of course they're not true. I would absolutely never marry that woman."

"Then what started them in the first place?"

He exhaled. "My lower council. They wanted a royal marriage, despite tradition, despite the fact that I am a drengr. I might have let slip that I would consider their advice, if only to shut them up."

"And Lady Caterina?"

"Was one of the proposed candidates. That was before everything with her father, obviously."

"Right." The door to the dining room opened and she nearly jumped from her seat.

Servants entered, arms laden with silver platters of food. Everything was meticulously arranged before they stepped backward to line themselves against the wall, standing motionless like statues. She turned her gaze from them to study what was before her. Perhaps the king had gone above and beyond, given the feast he'd ordered.

He cleared his throat and said, "Before we eat, I have something for you." She frowned at him. "Stay here a moment, please."

He disappeared from the room. Her imagination went wild. He returned with a flat, black box. "I wanted...I think..." He pressed his lips together and thrust the box at her unceremoniously.

Her brows pulled together but she took it from him. "What have I done to warrant a gift?"

He resumed his seat, his posture rigid. "Please forgive me, Lady Claire. This...this is rather difficult for me."

Oh. My. Gods, she couldn't help but think. It was finally happening. That's why he'd summoned her here. "You've never apologized to a woman before, have you?"

"Not once."

Instead of relief, she felt amusement. She bit her lower lip to keep from smiling. "I think the key is, don't build it up so much. Once the words are out, you will find it much easier than you realized."

He rubbed the back of his neck. "I should have apologized to you long before this. You were right yesterday, in the garden." She nodded, solemnly. "I have built it up so greatly, that the idea of confronting you..." He took a deep breath. "My treatment of you since your arrival has been deplorable. For that, I can never forgive myself. I wish to say that I acted out of grief, but there is no excuse I can give to warrant what I did. So...I am sorry."

She blinked at him, her chest pounding. When his gaze lifted to meet hers, she couldn't breathe. There was so much in the depths of his eyes. Grief, regret, even...hope. She inhaled, and felt the tethers that had been cliched tightly around her heart loosen, then fall away. "That's the best apology anyone has ever given me." He sagged in his chair, then nodded. "Thank you."

"I grow tired of fighting with you, Claire. It affects me, deeply. I hope that we might come to a truce now, you and I. That is the reason for my gift." He motioned to the box in her hand. "It is a symbol, if you will, that from now on, I vow to treat you as you ought to be treated, nothing less."

She opened and closed her mouth, unable to form a response.

He cleared his throat. "Anyway, I do not deserve your forgiveness, yet I ask it all the same. No! I beg for it. I understand that it will take time, but I dearly hope to earn it. Is...is what I seek possible?"

"Talon..." His eyes locked onto hers, hungry, as if he desperately needed what she was about to say. She swallowed, resisting the urge to reach for her goblet of water. Her voice was a hoarse whisper as she said, "I... Yes, I will try. It might take some time, but I promise that I will try."

He rubbed a hand down his face. "Thank you. Now, open your gift."

Suddenly giddy, she jiggled the box. It gave a soft clunk, confirming her suspicions. Tugging the ribbon loose, she lifted the lid, then gasped. It was far beyond what she could have possibly imagined.

CHAPTER 38

AN ESCAPE

Kastali Dun

Claire's eyes widened at the sight of King Talon's truce gift. "It belonged to my mother, Queen Ahlessa." His voice sounded very far away. "I want you to have it now."

His...mother?

It was a diamond and sapphire necklace, tucked within folds of black silk. Each sapphire was the size of a coin, perfectly cut facets that glistened dark blue. There were six sapphires in total, held in place with a pave of diamonds.

She gaped at it. Something like this in her world would cost hundreds of thousands, perhaps more. She couldn't quantify it, it was so out of her league. She opened her mouth. "I..." It was on the tip of her tongue to refuse it. But when her eyes darted upward, when she saw the way the king was looking at her, she pressed her lips together.

His body was rigid with nerves, barely contained suspense. "Do you...like it?"

"Yes! Yes, of course. I hardly know what to say. I..." She swallowed, glancing down at the necklace. "I can't imagine what it was like to lose your mother. I know she meant a great deal to you. Thank you for such a meaningful gift. I will cherish it."

He nodded, exhaling. "Good...good. That's good." A pause, and then, "I thought it would complement your blue gown. You were not wearing any jewels yesterday, and a gown like that ought to have...something. That, in particular." He glanced at the necklace before lifting his gaze to hers.

She blew out a breath, trying to untangle her emotions. "That's incredibly thoughtful. You... I'm impressed. You could have gone to a jeweler and purchased a mere trinket. Instead, you picked something that holds great meaning to you."

He stared at her, eyes darting between hers.

She licked her lips and added, "So...you really weren't angry about the color of my dress? We do not share blood..."

He huffed. "I have taken you under my protection. You are my ward. You may wear whatever you like. But I do admit, I took great pleasure in seeing you wear *that* color in particular."

Oh? *Oh*! A small smile pulled at her lips. "Then you would not mind me wearing more of it?"

"Not at all." This time, when his lips twitched, she caught an upward tug at the corners. Almost a smile. Her belly flopped over. She had *almost* made the king smile!

"Now, we ought to eat before the food gets cold. I have already taken up enough of your time as it is."

Just like that, he was King Talon again—formal and unreadable.

He poured them each a goblet of wine then stood and began to carve the large, roasted bird before them. He placed a chunk of meat on her plate and then set about getting some for himself. She began dishing up several items including sweet potatoes, mushrooms in cream sauce, caramelized carrots, and golden buns. It felt like Thanksgiving dinner.

Her chest squeezed as she thought about her parents. Were they worried about her? Did they miss her the way she missed them?

She took a bite and sighed, delighted. The wine was equally as good, though not as strong as what she was used to, which probably made it more dangerous.

"It occurred to me while I was in Lincastle," King Talon said, making conversation, "that you would have liked their market."

She glanced up sharply, relieved. "Oh?"

"It is a coastal city, you see, much like ours. Their market is just as eclectic."

"I'm sure I would have loved it," she said, and she meant it.

The meal was exceptional. She wasn't even too nervous to enjoy it. The wine helped with that.

King Talon went on to tell her about his time in Lincastle and the progress he'd made with the goblin raids. She was surprised by his openness, by how *talkative* he was. She didn't let it show, listening intently to confidential matters spilling from his lips. For weeks, she'd been desperate for news. Now, he was handing it to her on a silver platter. A flicker of a smile threatened to break free.

"Pavv's initial campaign was exceptionally thorough," he explained. "Every one of our villages along the Eastern Barrier Range suffered massive losses. I organized additional troops and relief, but I fear it's not enough."

"What do you mean?" Her brow furrowed.

"There will be more attacks. They will keep coming."

"Oh. But, now you'll be expecting it, right?"

"That still doesn't make it easy. It was a difficult effort, knowing I could either spread my troops thin protecting every village, or concentrate them in hopes of anticipating their next target." He set his fork down and leaned back. "What would you have done?"

"Uhm...me?" He nodded. "Well...are the attacks randomized? Or is there a pattern to them?"

"Random."

"Hmm. Then I suppose it depends on the numbers. How many goblins are you up against? If you take a risk fortifying every village, you will take some of the guesswork out. Your odds will be better if a village is defended with a small force, rather than no force at all. When you look at it that way, it simply becomes a statistics problem."

He stared at her long enough to make her squirm. "You're not wrong," he said at last. Warmth rushed through her and she relaxed at the compliment. "Even a handful of soldiers is more than they had during the initial strike."

"What about the drengr? Can't they do more to help?"

"Yes." He ran a hand through his hair. He wasn't wearing his crown. It made him more...approachable. "Fort Lin is a two-day flight across the desert. For the villages farther north, perhaps three, which means they must be stationed there permanently, to make any difference. Like with our infantry, it's a balancing act. Even still, it doesn't guarantee success."

"But the drengr breathe fire! How many are really needed to kill a horde of goblins?"

He huffed. "More than you would think. Goblins have tough skin and don't burn easily. Plus, they're like ants. They just keep coming and coming." She opened her mouth, then closed it. "Anyway, that's hardly the worst of it."

"The worst of it?"

"They found a way to get ice metal." A scowl formed on his features. She stared at it in fascination, then realized she was staring at his lips.

Ice metal was used in the drengr's sveraks. It was mined by the dwargs and purchased at a steep price. Dwargs, like the sprites, governed themselves. If the goblins had access to ice metal, did that mean the dwargs were helping?

"What about Kane? Is he working with the dwargs?"

Anger flared in his eyes at the mention of the sorcerer's name. "I admire your passion about this. It is unexpected."

"I have always had a passion for politics."

His brows lifted and he blinked. "I see. That explains it." A brief silence fell, then, "You need not worry overmuch about the dwargs. Kane is not working with them." She stared at him and he shrugged. "I have enough spies to know for certain."

She exhaled. "That's good. But still, it's another thing to worry about."

"Add it to my list," he said.

"I suppose your list has grown quite long."

"Quite."

The tension had all but disappeared from her shoulders. Talking to him about kingdom matters was surprisingly...*easy*. He seemed just as relaxed. Or, perhaps that was the wine, working its magic between them. She was on her second goblet now, or was it her third?

Their food was long since abandoned. Forgotten, for the sake of conversation. If this was what getting to know him entailed, it wouldn't be so bad after all. *Look at me, trying,* she wanted to tell Desaree. A bit of pride flared hot in her chest.

"So," she said, swirling her wine in her goblet. "You're back from Fort Lin for good then, now that you've done what you needed to do?"

"It would seem so, much to Lord Donovan's relief—he's the fort leader."

"Oh. Right. Wait...does he not like you?" She leaned forward slightly.

King Talon scoffed. Or was that a snort? "That doesn't surprise you, does it?"

"I mean..." She faltered. No way was she falling into his trap.

"Donovan and I don't get along, never have. He's overly fond of grudges."

"For what?"

King Talon rubbed the back of his neck. Was that ruefulness? "I might not have been entirely honorable towards him in my younger years."

"Do tell." Why was she suddenly so desperately curious?

He chuckled. *Actually chuckled!* "Donovan and I were rivals, you see, and I was overly fond of pranks. I can't count the times my father all but flayed my hide for it."

"Rivals?"

"We competed against each other at tournaments, usually in

the same bracket, purposefully. Donovan wanted to prove that being a prince wasn't the be-all-end-all of things, specifically, by being better than me. I couldn't let that stand, now could I?"

"...No?"

"Plus, we were descended from rival clans, the forest clan and the desert clan. Anyway, one summer there was a tournament at Fort Edge. We were scheduled to fight each other the next day. That night, I snuck into Donovan's tent and stole his sverak, replacing it with a near perfect replica made from a vastly inferior metal and fake gems. Then I got him blazing drunk so he'd be too hungover to recognize my tampering come the morning."

"You're joking! I never pictured you for a prankster."

He pressed his lips together, regarding her. "There is much you do not know about me."

She was coming to see that. Desaree had been right. "So? What happened?"

"As you'd expect. Donovan and I faced each other, me with my sverak and he with a fake sword." His eyes took on a faraway look. "We fought without helms, if I recall correctly. I convinced him that it wasn't necessary. Mostly, I wanted to see his face when he discovered my treachery."

She shook her head, incredulous.

"I got my wish. When our swords struck, I angled my blade just so. His shattered before his very eyes. You should have seen the look on his face."

Her jaw dropped. Their gazes held, then they both burst into laughter. Real, genuine laughter. Talon roared with it, his shoulders shaking. Tears leaked from her eyes. "Oh. My. Gods!" she wheezed, pawing at her face. "No wonder he holds a grudge."

"Yes," he managed, mirth transforming his scarred face into something boyish and...beautiful. "I deserve it. I really do."

She'd never seen him like this. Never seen him so relaxed and unfettered. So...open.

Time flowed by the hour, but neither of them appeared to care. At some point, the servants had cleared their plates. One moment they were there and the next they were gone, and Talon was opening a fresh bottle of wine, refilling their goblets.

"Do you ever get time off?" she asked. "From being king, I mean."

"Time off?" He blinked at her, then set the bottle on the table. "What's time off? Is that something kings do?" he teased.

"That's sad," she said, only partly teasing.

"That's...life." He cleared his throat and lifted his goblet. "To your health, Lady Claire."

"And to yours," she said, clinking hers to his.

She shifted in her seat and that's when she felt it, when she was reminded of it, the looming necessity bulging in her pocket. Her relaxed mood evaporated.

"What's the matter?" The king's brows pulled together.

"Why would something be the matter?" she lied.

"Because you suddenly look as though someone murdered your favorite horse."

"My favorite..." A high pitched laugh burst from her lips. "That bad, huh?" She reached into her pocket and set the pouch on the table.

"Ah. Bedelth informed me that you still had them."

"Why didn't you ask for them back?"

"I had planned to, yesterday, but—"

"Our argument?" she guessed.

"Our argument," he confirmed. This time his expression was easy to read. "I was certain you'd bite my head off so I let the matter go. I...dislike upsetting you."

"You're quite good at it, you know."

The smile that broke over his lips was slow. Slow, but brilliant, and even a little rueful. "It seems to happen without my trying."

"Yes." She exhaled. "Anyway, I thought we could discuss what comes next—for the stones. I can't carry them with me any longer, so I'll give them back on one condition."

His mouth twitched. "Another handmaiden, perhaps?"

"Very funny. No. I want you to return the stones to the sprites for safe keeping."

"Not going to happen."

She blinked. "Excuse me?"

"I said, that is not going to happen."

"But, it's the best place for them!" Her skin heated. She hadn't expected his immediate pushback. He hadn't even considered her request.

"I am aware. However, I do not think the queen will be amenable to it. Shall I show you her last letter?"

"I believe you, but my mind is made up. A lot has happened since you last demanded their return. Surely Jade will understand and take them—"

"Lady Claire, this is not up for debate and I do not wish to argue over the matter. I will take care of the stones." He swiped them off the table, slipping them into his pocket. "My shields and I have already devised a plan."

She balked. "Forgive me if I mistrust your supposed *plan*, since your last one landed us in this mess in the first place." It was the wrong thing to say.

His jaw tightened, eyes darkening. "This discussion is over. I hope you enjoyed your meal. I have other matters to attend to." He surged to his feet, looking ready to flee.

She copied the motion, shaking with anger. "So, that's it? You're just going to shut me down even though you know I'm right."

"You being right is subjective." Her jaw dropped. "I've been making decisions for my people for centuries. I know what I'm doing. Forgive me if I don't follow the orders of some female outsider who knows absolutely nothing about ruling my kingdom."

"Are you serious?!" A derisive laugh fell from her lips. "It's a good thing you never found your mate. I can't imagine *any* woman would enjoy you with an attitude like that."

He flinched. Then his expression wiped completely clean. She realized her mistake, but it was too late.

The king's lack of a mate was hardly his fault. It had nothing to do with him. To watch all the other drengr find happy-ever-afters while never finding his must have hurt terribly. More than she could ever imagine.

Her anger evaporated. "Oh, my gods. I...I... I shouldn't have—" It had been a cruel thing to say. Using his misfortune against him. Slapping him would have been kinder. Her eyes darted around the room, looking for an escape. "I'm sorry. Please excuse me, Your Majesty."

She fled, racing through the keep. She passed the door to her chambers and kept on going. She didn't want to see Desaree, to tell her how things had gone. She didn't want to see anyone.

How could she have been so thoughtless?! It didn't matter what he'd said to spur the words. That was no excuse. Yet, in those moments, she'd wanted to hurt him, to cut him deeply. Well, she'd done exactly that.

Desperate for an escape, she found herself facing the postern door hidden within the keep's herb garden. It was the only unguarded door into or out of the castle. She glanced around. Not a soul was in sight. Before she had time to consider her actions, she brushed the ivy aside and stepped through, right out into the city.

CHAPTER 39

AN OPPORTUNE MOMENT

Kastali Dun

Eagle watched the crowded street from his shadowed position. City inhabitants went to and fro on business. Some engaged in jovial chit chat while others took to their errands with bowed heads or intent expressions. No one spared him a moment's notice. He stood against a shadowy wall, beneath the eaves of a wealthy city townhome. His wide-brimmed hat was pulled low to hide his face, while his arms were crossed with bored impatience. He often spent time here. It was a good lookout to watch those entering and exiting the castle. It was one of two streets leading to the main portcullis.

Today had been uneventful, mostly spent making note of anything that might help him gain access to his quarry. He was about to abandon his watch for other business, when he blinked into the crowd. He blinked again, then sucked in a gasp.

She was dressed in burgundy, her hair twisted elegantly in a chignon, making her way hastily down the lane and away from the keep. It couldn't be! He couldn't be so lucky. Except, it was. Lady Claire walked right past him, none the wiser.

He pushed off the wall and melted into the crowd. Something didn't add up. Where was her entourage? Her guards? Her ladies?

There wasn't enough time to question it. He trailed after her, keeping close.

She wandered with no particular direction in mind, slipping down one street, then another. The set of her jaw and tension in her shoulders told him she was agitated. His frown deepened.

Unprotected and alone, wandering through the city. It could be a trap. And yet...

Since arriving in Kastali Dun, he had gained entry into the keep more than once, usually under various disguises. Even within the castle's confines, Lady Claire was difficult to obtain. She was the second most protected person in the keep. Unbeknownst to her, King Talon had many guards keeping an eye on her movements throughout the fortress.

Here she was, suspiciously alone.

The longer he tailed her, the more certain he was. His excitement heightened. Silently, he urged her onward, deeper into the city, farther from the keep.

They rounded a corner. She glanced over her shoulder, faltered, then dodged down another street. He kept walking, then circled back. The streets had grown mostly empty in this part of the city. All the better for him.

She made her way down a narrow lane that was fully deserted. The tall buildings around it, some leaning, left it partially shadowed. Here she stopped again, her back to him. His heart quickened. This was it. He might never get another chance like this.

Keeping to the shadows, he knelt and gathered a stray rock.

His quarry continued down the narrow lane, this time more rushed. Did she sense him? Was she afraid?

Excitement set his heart racing. He crept forward, following her down another street. It was obvious she was lost in the maze of side streets that made up most of Kastali Dun's underbelly. Within seconds, he was behind her. She gasped and whirled, but it was too late. Rock in hand, he rendered her unconscious. She dropped. He caught her up, lifting her gently into his arms. It wasn't his wish to hurt her—not more than he had to.

After a brief glance in each direction, he rushed away. Keeping to the deserted streets, he managed to stay hidden from sight. His hideout was a large cellar beneath the *King's Crown*—a rundown tavern in the Pauper's District a few blocks away.

Ten minutes felt like a massive burden to carry a lady in a heavy gown. He'd half a mind to strip her of it and leave it behind. But, he allowed her her dignity and carried on.

He entered The King's Crown through the back, slipping down the cellar stairs before any of the tavern wenches noticed. He'd already worked out a deal with the owner. The man had received a fair number of gold dragons in exchange for his silence. In return, he was given use of the large cellar with a *no questions asked* policy.

He emerged into the dimly lit space. There were no windows, only candle light. Men sat around a makeshift table, gambling. They looked up in mild surprise.

A chair clattered. "Gods above! Is that...?" Monroe, like the others, was a recent hire.

"Yes, yes, it's her!" he barked, shifting Lady Claire's weight as he surveyed the men. He felt a drop of perspiration slide down his temple.

"Well, ain't she a *pretty* little thing," Tark said, looking up from his game. All the men working for him were paid well, but that did not make them gentlemen.

"You'll keep your hands off her, Tark, you hear me?" He lifted his brows in warning. "And while you're at it, go and fetch Collier. It looks like we will need his services earlier than anticipated."

The others remained seated around the wooden table dominating the center of the room. Tark looked as though he might protest, then he nodded and scampered away.

"How did you get her so quickly—and by yourself, no less?" Monroe kept his voice low. "I thought the plan was to wait for Collier—"

"Plans change,," he said, trying to suppress his impatience. Lady Claire was growing heavier by the second. He glanced about the cellar, trying to find an adequate place to deposit her. His hired hands returned to their game, casting their cards into a pile, no offer to help whatsoever. There was a stack of coins accumulating before them, and the stink of drink permeated the damp air.

"Here, put her here." Monroe moved to the side of the room and spread a moth-eaten blanket over a pile of straw. He, at least, had some sense.

Eagle laid Lady Claire down and checked her head. There was a trickle of blood from where he'd struck her, but not much. She would recover.

"What do we do now?" Monroe asked, whispering.

"Stick to the plan. I won't breathe easily until Collier gets here. If she wakes up before that—we are all dead. As soon as the merchant contract goes through, we will depart north."

In the days prior, he'd spent a fair bit of time and effort working out how to keep Claire's magic at bay, and how to successfully transport her away from the capital. Her magic was the hardest part of his undertaking, but if Collier arrived in time, it wouldn't be a problem. The transport would be a little trickier. All wagons and wains were subject to guard searches at the city gates. The only way to get excused from the examination was with a specialized merchant license.

Certain merchants coming and going from the city were given top priority. They were permitted entry and exit via a separate express lane. Their belongings were not searched because they often carried so many goods that the task was too tedious.

He'd been working to acquire the document and was assured by one of the senior merchants—he had paid the man well for his silence—that the deal would be granted in two days' time. It cost him a fair bit of gold too, but there was a great deal of gold to come if he succeeded.

With all of this in mind, he had constructed an elaborate plan to capture Lady Claire. But, plans changed. Now it was a matter of keeping her quiet for the next few days until he had his permit. "Collier had better hurry," he muttered, glancing at the woman with growing unease.

"What if someone notices her absence?" Monroe asked.

"They might." He shrugged. "Looked to me like she was already running away. She had no guards—no protection. Let's hope they assume the same—that she simply ran away. If they know she's been kidnapped, there'll be a man hunt. Right now we lie low and hope for the best."

Monroe inclined his head. "You're the boss."

"Find a gag," he said, glancing at one of the others playing cards. "I don't want her screaming when she wakes up." Several men jumped into action. He eyed Lady Claire's pretty face and moved a strand of hair that had fallen over her eyes. Yes, this one would scream bloody murder when she awoke, and he couldn't have that, could he?

CHAPTER 40

THE SEARCH FOR CLAIRE

Kastali Dun

Reyr was early. The other shields had not yet arrived. He took a seat opposite Talon, who, as usual, was brooding. Darkness had already fallen and the evening meal had long since passed, though he'd missed it. A fire crackled in the fireplace, casting shadows about the sitting room. "How was your midday meal?" he dared to ask.

"My midday meal?" Talon blinked at the flames.

"Yes, your midday meal—with Claire."

"Oh."

"Did you both behave yourselves? Did my coaching work? Did you apologize?"

There was a long exhale, then, "It could have gone better."

"That explains your mood." He leaned forward, bracing his forearms on his knees. "What happened, exactly?"

"We had an argument. Surprise surprise."

"All right." He could tell the king wasn't going to make this easy. "But, did she like your gift?"

"She did, or at least, I thought she did." When he continued staring, talon added, "She left it behind, so I cannot be sure."

"I see. And this argument, did you say something to upset her?" He knew the answer, of course, but he had to ask anyway.

"I did my best! Everything was going well after I fumbled my way through an apology. An apology she thanked me for, mind you." A brief flare of pride filled Talon's voice.

"Well, that's good."

Talon's features moved through several emotions before settling into a frown. "She insulted me—my ability to rule. It triggered me. Words were exchanged. Then she insulted me again, regretted it, and stormed out."

Reyr's lips twitched. He pressed them into a firm line to keep from smiling. "Insulted you, hmm?"

"It wasn't funny—at the time."

"Oh, I'm sure it wasn't." His smile broke free.

"What is this?" Talon demanded, noticing his expression. "You think I deserved it?"

"Forgive me, Your Majesty. Surely it wasn't that bad. What did she say?"

Talon's head thumped back against the arm chair. He shut his eyes. "She said it was a good thing I never found my mate. That no woman would enjoy my attitude."

Reyr was equal parts amused and appalled. On the one hand, Claire was right in that most women wouldn't enjoy the king's attitude. On the other hand, a comment like that, a strike against his misfortune finding his mate, was hurtful. Cruel, even.

Talon had long since found peace knowing he would remain alone. Despite that, his failure still needled him. Claire's comment no doubt struck a blow. Hence, his brooding.

"I am certain that she did not mean it—"

The door opened. Bedelth, Jovari, Koldis, and Verath strode into the room. Reyr looked up to find Talon in the same position, his expression wiped clean, as if the conversation had never happened. The others took their seats. Talon said nothing, keeping his head back and eyes closed like a petulant child.

"Well then," Reyr said. "Shall we get started?"

"Don't see why not," Koldis answered, his eyes darting towards the king in question. "Unless this isn't a good time—?"

The tower door burst open, slamming against the wall. Silence fell. Talon's head jerked upward, eyes flying open.

Desaree rushed into the room, her face pale, eyes wide. Guards followed, their expressions grim. Verath jumped to his feet, going to her. "What is the matter?" he asked, his voice low.

Reyr's brows furrowed, studying the tender way Verath took Desaree's hand. Interesting.

"Where is she?!" Desaree demanded, eyes darting around the room.

"Who?" Verath tucked a strand of her hair behind her ear, trying to calm her.

"Claire! I thought she would be here!"

Reyr surged to his feet, his heart taking off in a frantic gallop. The others stood as well.

"Is she unaccounted for?" Talon asked, striding across the room. "Has she not been with you today?"

"Not since this morning. She left to come here and never returned. I can't find her anywhere."

"I do not recall seeing her at dinner," Jovari mused.

"And you checked the library? The mages' wing? The training yard?" Talon's expression was hard, but his eyes flashed with worry.

"Of course. Do you think I am frantic for nothing?"

"Peace, Desaree," Verath murmured. "No one is accusing you of negligence." His whispers were like gentle caresses.

A piece of information clicked into place.

To Verath, Reyr said, *"You never told me you were fond of Desaree."*

"I did not tell you because it is my business," Verath snapped.

"Fair enough." He pushed the thoughts from his mind. There were more important matters at hand.

"Well, she can't have left the keep," Koldis said with more certainty than Reyr felt. "The guards would never permit it."

"Not to mention," King Talon added, "she is well aware of my rules on the matter. She knows not to disobey me."

"I'm not certain she takes your rules as seriously as she ought." Reyr was beginning to panic. *"Claire!"* he called, hoping her mental block would let him through. There was no answer.

The king took charge of the situation. "Jovari, Bedelth, have the keep searched at once."

"Wait!" Desaree cried. Everyone froze. "The postern door—the door in the garden. Claire knows about it."

"The...*what?*" Talon blinked, taken aback.

"The door that Tess uses to sneak out to the market," Desaree explained. "Claire saw Tess use it once when we were working in the garden. She knows about it. The door is not guarded. Claire might have..." Desaree's eyes widened. "Gods above!" she gasped. "What if Claire is wandering around the city at this very moment?!"

"You are certain that Claire would do something so reckless?" Koldis asked.

Reyr's stomach hardened. Yes, Claire would definitely do something reckless if her mood warranted it. She was impulsive in that way.

"I think we ought to trust Desaree," Verath said. "She knows Claire better than the rest of us."

"Claire is impulsive," Reyr found himself saying to Talon. "If the two of you had an argument and she was upset, she might have done it."

"Damn her!" Talon cried. He had gone quite pale at the idea of Claire leaving the keep. He ran a hand through his untamed hair. Reyr had only seen him like this once. The day Claire risked her life by jumping from the king's tower balcony to protect the dragonstones. Bedelth's news had reached them in Lincastle, leaving Talon frantic and powerless. This time, however, Talon was not powerless.

"Change of plans," he said. "Jovari, Koldis, put out a castle-wide search. Speak with everyone if necessary. Find out if anyone has seen

Claire since this afternoon. Make sure the Castle's guards are on full alert. Bedelth, Verath, go to the city guard. Alert them of the situation. Organize a search of the city's streets. Reyr, you're with me. We will fly to the fort immediately. Desaree, thank you for your information."

Everyone jumped into action until Reyr and Talon were left alone in the room. They went to the tower's balcony where they could transform and take flight. The two of them launched into the sky simultaneously, flying the short distance to the fort.

Fort Kastali's leaders, Karanth and Eva, were more than accommodating. They organized search teams for the wilderness beyond the city just in case Claire had somehow slipped out of the city gates. When Karanth first suggested the possibility of it, Reyr did not miss Talon's groan of despair. The thought of Claire getting as far as the wilderness terrified them all.

"This is my fault for keeping her against her will," Talon muttered. "I knew this would happen sooner or later. She hates me. She would jump at any opportunity to get away from me, from here, and return home."

"I do not think so," Reyr said. "Perhaps once, but not now."

As Karanth divvied out orders, Eva made sure Talon's wineglass remained full. After the delegation finished, Reyr and Talon departed to search the city.

They flew low over each district, often doubling back to be sure they'd checked thoroughly. The streets were a hive of activity. Bedelth and Verath had roused the city guards, now searching with torches held aloft. Onlookers spilled out of buildings, curious.

They circled for hours. Regular updates flowed in, but none of it was good. Claire was nowhere to be found.

"*Order the guards to search everything,*" Talon growled, growing more frantic. "*Homes, inns, shops, storage facilities. Search the ships at anchor, the warehouses at the docks. We must find her.*"

"*We do not have a warrant for that,*" Reyr reminded him, even though he was just as desperate.

"*I don't care!*"

"*My king, be reasonable.*" They made a wide circuit above the city. "*You cannot disregard the political system and its laws. Without reliable proof, there can be no warrant. Without a warrant, there can be no legal search."*

"What good is my title if I cannot use it?!" Talon demanded.

"You may be king but you are not above the law. I want her found as badly as you, but we both know what it will do to your reputation if you break your own laws."

"TO HELL WITH THE LAWS!" Talon's voice was a painful blast in his mind. *"I will not have her injured, or worse. I will not have it!"*

"Reyr is right," Verath said. Always the voice of reason. He swooped in, joining them in the air over the city with his red, glittering scales. *"I do not think she has left the city, Your Majesty. The guards have been informed—no one is to exit the gates without a thorough search. We will find her."*

They continued searching into the wee hours of the morning, double and triple checking. When at last dawn began to peep from the horizon, Reyr insisted that they return to the keep to regroup, and discuss an alternative plan of action. *"Let us not forget,"* he said, *"that Saffra has the ability to scry. We will see if she can find Claire's location."*

"She'd better!" was all Talon had to say to that.

The other shields escorted King Talon to the keep, while he completed several checks with the various search parties. The updates remained the same. There was no sign of Claire. As if she had vanished without a trace.

No matter how many times he called her telepathically, she gave no response. He had never missed her voice like he did now. She'd never been quiet for this long. She was alive, he knew that much. If he pushed, he felt her presence like a faint whisper, but that was it.

~

SUNLIGHT WAS SPILLING over the city. Reyr returned to the keep. His stomach tied itself in knots over what he had to do next.

Bedelth, Jovari, Koldis, and Verath were posted up outside the tower's door. The guards had been dismissed. Reyr headed straight for the door.

"The king wishes to be alone," Koldis said by way of explanation.

Reyr paused, bristling. "Why do you sound amused by that?"

The others huffed.

"Because the reason is…amusing?" Koldis grinned suggestively.

"Just tell him," Jovari said, "before he explodes in a rage."

"Lady Caterina dropped by," Verath said, ever the voice of reason. It was the last thing he'd expected to hear. "She insisted upon comforting her king in his time of need."

Reyr's irritation disappeared. "I bet he loved that," he muttered. "I assume she is gone now?"

"Oh yes." Koldis's smile widened. "She scurried away as quickly as she came. Talon nearly burned her to a crisp. Don't think I have ever seen him in such a rage."

"I can hardly blame him." Reyr blew out a breath and reached for the doorknob.

"You sure you want to risk it?" Koldis asked.

"I'll take my chances."

The others shrugged but otherwise offered no further warning.

He found the king on his terraced balcony. Talon's back was to him, but his body was curled inward. Reyr stood motionless for almost a minute, watching him. When Talon's body heaved with a silent sigh, he strode forward without thinking. "The entire city is out searching, Talon. We will find her. We will."

Talon whirled, his face full of emotion. "This is all my fault!" he spat.

Reyr staggered back a step. There were tears in Talon's eyes. He had to blink to make sure he was seeing clearly.

"I've never felt fear like this. Never. It's ripping me apart."

"How can you blame yourself?" Reyr demanded. "You did not send her through that door."

"I should have gone after her. I allowed her to leave. I was so…" Talon dragged a hand over his face. "I was upset by her insult and I let her go. I should have run after her. But I let her go…"

"Anyone would have done the same."

"But I am the king!" he cried. Reyr sighed. What could he say? Talon would blame himself no matter what. "How could I have let this happen? Am I really so terrible? I continue to fail again and again!"

"You need to stop talking like this."

"If she is dead…"

"If she is dead, then what?" Reyr demanded, growing impatient.

"Then…" Talon glanced about. "Then I may as well jump from this balcony."

He refrained from rolling his eyes. "And what? Sprout wings? Fly away? You are no coward, Talon. You are our king."

"Sometimes I wish I *were* a coward. Dragonwall deserves better."

Reyr closed the distance and grasped Talon's shoulders, giving him a rough shake. "She is *not* dead. Dragonwall deserves *you*! Now, enough of this."

"I don't want to feel this way," Talon said, his voice turning into an anguished whisper. "Why does it hurt so much?"

"It hurts because the woman you love is missing and you blame yourself."

Talon blinked, recoiling. "I…I do not love her."

"Then you are lying to yourself."

The moment he said it, he realized his words were meant for both of them. His heart dropped. How could he have let this happen? How could he have allowed himself to fall in love with the first woman his king had ever loved? He should have seen it coming.

He collected himself and said, "There is something I need to tell you."

"Can it not wait?"

"No. It cannot."

"Then what?"

"I've been keeping something from you—a secret. Claire's secret."

Talon's eyes narrowed. "Explain."

Shame pressed heavy on his chest. "Claire has telepathic abilities. She can hear and communicate with the drengr. All of them."

"What?!" Talon rasped, his expression morphing from anguish to disbelief.

"I promised that I would not reveal her secret."

Now, he had broken that promise. She might never trust him again. But, when it came to his king, his oath, there was never a question.

"She...she can hear everything we say?"

"Yes."

"And she hid this from me?"

"That surprises you?" His brow furrowed.

"Why didn't she tell me?"

"Because she was terrified of what you might do if you found out. You don't exactly have the best track record."

"I apologized to her for that!" Talon roared.

"I know. I know." Reyr held up his hands, placating.

"All this time...she...she's heard everything? From all of us? Everyone?"

"Yes. Everything. Everyone. She's gotten better at blocking the voices when they become too much, but for the most part, her abilities are involuntary. Until recently, she had no control over them. That was the reason for her headaches."

Talon's expression hardened. "I assume you have already tried to use this telepathic ability to find her?"

He nodded, swallowing down his shame. "When Desaree first came to us, I tried to call out to her. I had hoped she would answer. So far...nothing."

"Because she's dead?"

"She's alive."

Talon ran a hand through his hair. "All this time and you never told me? You put her above your oath to me?"

"I..." He hung his head.

"Oh, gods." Talon's face paled, his scars going white. "I have said so many things about her. No wonder she thinks I am a monster."

"There is no excuse I can give for my breach of oath. I should have told you sooner." The king's eyes flashed. "I allowed her to come before my duty. My feelings for her clouded my judgment. I justified it by telling myself that if you ever asked, I would tell you the truth. Hiding secrets is no better. Please, forgive me."

"It was badly done," Talon agreed, his voice barely leashed. "You love her then?"

"I will never love her more than I love you. You are my king, my brother in all but blood—"

"*Yet* you love her."

"Something fierce." He deflated, his body hollowing out. "But... I can fix it. I'll suppress everything I feel for her. It was stupid and reckless. I allowed it to happen before realizing it. Allowed it to come between us, my oath..."

"Easier said than done."

"I can do it. I just need...time and space. I've already made the arrangements."

"What arrangements?"

"My brother needs me. Once we find Claire, I'll go north to assist with war preparations. Distance will be the best thing for me."

The king was silent for a moment. "I am not sure I like the idea. My need for you is just as great, if not greater."

Reyr's heart squeezed. "I will beg you if I must. I can no longer hide what I feel for her. I love her, just as you do. I must go." The last of his words came out strangled.

Talon exhaled. "I have always trusted your judgment, Reyr, more than anyone's. If you must do this, then I won't stop you."

His muscles loosened. "Thank you."

The king hesitated. "I must return the dragonstones to Esterpine. Claire has demanded it of me."

"Okay?" That was news.

"We will depart together, once Claire is found. We can share the sky for a day or two. Then I'll go north and you can go to your brother. Will that be agreeable?"

"Yes, thank you, my king."

Talon nodded, then turned and walked over to the balcony parapet, staring out over the sea.

"Talon..." he hesitated. Talon glanced over his shoulder. "Please know that I am truly sorry for what I have done. I hope that someday you will forgive me, perhaps when this is all over."

"Already forgiven."

He frowned. He did not deserve Talon's quick forgiveness and was surprised to receive it. Still, his heart wept to see Talon's disappointment in him. His king's sorrowful gaze returned to the sea.

He stepped beside him, quiet for several painfully long moments. At last he said, "We will find her, Talon. I swear to you that we will."

"I know..." came Talon's response. "And once we do, I will gain her and lose you. It is an outcome I am struggling to accept."

He exhaled. "You will not lose me forever," he murmured.

"I should hope not."

It took everything he possessed to hold himself together. He stood with clenched muscles, trying not to let his body gasp with grief. It was too much. The truth was out. He had done what he'd come to do. He could no longer bear Talon's emotions. With a final apologetic look, he took his leave.

CHAPTER 41
PARALLEL COINCIDENCE

Kastali Dun

Saffra struggled to find sleep, tossing and turning. Her dreams followed the face of an adolescent girl. She knew the face...from somewhere. Every time she awoke, she opened her eyes to gaze at the darkened canopy above her bed, but the memory of that face swam in and out of view.

She drifted off to sleep again, and her dreams changed...

Isabella wept in a man's embrace. Her frantic cries were muffled against him. "My daughter...my only daughter...Irelia..." The man was equally distressed, though he controlled his emotions well. He wore a crown. It was King Eymar, the first king of the drengr monarchy.

Saffra blinked, trying to make sense of what she saw. It was the story of a new kingdom and a dead princess. Princess Irelia had been the first child born into the monarchy and she had never lived to womanhood.

King Eymar made soothing sounds, petting his mate's golden hair. "We will find her," he said. "Surely she is only missing. Perhaps lost in the city streets."

They stood within the king's tower. It looked different from what she was used to. Its original state, long before new trends required changes to the furnishings.

Something about Queen Isabella looked different, too. She appeared run down, almost frail, especially compared to how she had looked in Saffra's earlier visions. Her face, though riddled with grief, was tired.

A door slammed, echoing through the chamber. King Eymar and Queen Isabella looked up—so did Saffra. A man entered. He was obviously a drengr, by the looks of him. "My king," he said, his voice deep and rich, with the hint of a strange accent. His movements were hesitant and even a little stilted, as if he wasn't comfortable with his humanity. "Guards have been summoned to search for the princess. Every street is alight with torchlight. Our own have taken to the skies. They will search beyond the walls of the city. We will not stop until she is found."

A hopeless gasp escaped Queen Isabella. Once more she buried her face and wept. "I fear she is gone forever."

"You fear she has been kidnapped, my lady?" A look of alarm passed over the drengr's face.

"Worse. What if she...?" The queen could not finish her statement.

"Gods above, my love. She has not died. I can feel it in my heart."

"If she has been kidnapped, Your Majesties, we will make her captors suffer. They will feel my wrath," said the drengr. The king nodded before turning back to comfort his queen.

"Irelia...Irelia. Oh, gods! I want her back!"

A familiar face swam into Saffra's mind. She finally placed it. The girl from the painting in the castle. Princess Irelia.

Queen Isabella's sobs echoed in her mind. They morphed into something more coherent. Loud pounding and a voice—

SAFFRA OPENED HER EYES. The pounding continued. Someone was calling her name. For a moment, she heard only the sobs of Queen Isabella, until that morphed into Desaree's frantic voice.

"Give me a moment!" she cried, jumping from her bed.

"*Irelia...Irelia...*" The cries echoed. Her bare feet scrambled across the floor.

She threw open her door. "Gods above, Desaree! What could

possibly warrant such a racket?" The moment the words were out, she gasped. There were tears streaming down her face. "What... what happened?"

"She's gone!"

"Who? Irelia?" Saffra felt as if she were still dreaming.

"Irelia? No, Claire! She's missing!"

"Claire? But I do not..." She rubbed her forehead, trying to wake up.

Desaree grabbed hold of her hand and pulled into the hallway. "Come with me."

Two guards rushed past them, shouting, "Make sure you check the upper floors."

Heads popped out of doors wearing confused expressions.

Saffra blinked, letting Desaree drag her down the corridor to the window at the end. "There, look out over the city."

Her gaze fell upon the city. The hairs on her arms prickled to attention. Words from her memory came floating back to her. "Every street in the city is alight with torchlight," she whispered. Except, it wasn't Irelia who was missing, it was Claire.

"You see?" Desaree said. "They are searching for her."

"How...how did this happen?" She turned to Desaree. "Tell me everything."

Guilt pooled in the pit of her stomach. She'd been gone for so long, tending to Daxton.

They retreated to her room where Desaree explained everything. Claire had been invited to King Talon's tower to dine with him. It was a last-minute invitation, but she had accepted. "I helped her get ready and saw her off, but she never returned." Fresh tears rolled down the handmaiden's cheeks. "I thought she was with the king the whole time. How could I be so stupid? Claire detests him." She covered her face with her hands and let out another sob. "I should have gone looking for her earlier!"

"Take a deep breath. You cannot shoulder the blame for this. Are you sure she did not vanish into the secret passages?"

"I...I think so. I can feel it in my heart. She took the door—the postern door in the garden. Even the guards inspected it after I told the king. There were fresh footprints in the dirt smaller than Tess's feet. We both know Claire has small feet."

Saffra frowned, uncertain. Something did not feel right. "Unless we search the passages, we cannot be certain. Let King Talon and his Shields conduct their search, but we will conduct one of our own."

At last, Desaree nodded. She followed Saffra out into the corridor. They went to Claire's chambers. There they could safely open the door without being seen.

Saffra used her magic to get them into the depths of the keep. They plunged deep into the castle, going lower than they had ever gone before. Desaree carried a torch while Saffra created little orbs of light that followed along with them. Every so often they called for her, but no answer ever came.

They wandered at random, abandoning caution.

"She might have gotten lost down one of these," Saffra pointed out. "We haven't been down any of them yet." They took staircases they had never used, and narrow corridors that were completely uncharted. They went on until they could hear the sounds of trickling water and smell the damp sea air. Down here, the walls were more cave like. They no longer looked as if they belonged to the castle.

"She couldn't possibly be down this far, could she?" Desaree's voice was a high squeak.

"We cannot know for sure unless we check," Saffra said. "We owe it to everyone to be certain." As she spoke, the passage they followed opened up. They faltered. The orb lights continued on a short distance, flooding the way ahead. Both of them gasped.

Stretched out before them was the largest cave Saffra had ever seen—the only cave she had seen, for that matter. She was stunned into silence. Desaree, too.

It was impossible to tell how vast it was. Their light was not powerful enough to illuminate everything. Out of instinct, Saffra pushed her hand forward, motioning for the orbs to go further. They zoomed away, out into the center of the cave.

"What...?! How...?" Saffra took a step forward, her gaze intent on the cave. It wasn't empty. Despite the dim light, two distinct features stood out among the frightening shadows of stalactites and stalagmites. An edifice made of bulky stones and a pair of broken onyx pillars.

"Is that...a *temple*?" Desaree asked.

"I...I don't..." She took off across the cave, careful with her footing in the dim light.

"Wait!" Desaree called. "Where are you going?"

"Stay there if you wish, but I intend to find out what this is."

A few moments later, she heard Desaree following behind her, muttering something about danger. Yes, this was potentially dangerous, but she needed to know. They dodged little pools of water that had accumulated in various dips in the rocky floor. When she reached the stairs, she climbed to the top of the rock feature. "I knew it!" she whispered when she saw what stood before her. "I knew it!" she said again, this time louder.

"Knew what? What is this?" Desaree came up beside her, panting from the climb.

"Well, it *was* a gate, I think..."

"As in, one of the portals Claire used?" Desaree's face was pale, even in the glow of her torch.

"It would seem so." Saffra noticed the way Desaree regarded the gate, as if a monster might step through at any moment and attack them. "I do not think you need to worry. It seems to be destroyed."

Saffra had seen gates before. The kengr gate in her vision, and the one from her childhood. These pillars, which should have towered over her, had been broken. Most of the large pieces lay in chunks, scattered about the rocky platform. Only two stubs jutted up from the rock now, no taller than a small child, just barely visible at a distance.

"I thought there were only four gates," Desaree mused. "This does not make sense. One in each territory as the stories said. But this suggests a fifth."

Saffra shook her head. "Why is it destroyed? How is it that no one knows about this?"

So many questions. Unable to answer any of them, she turned and gazed down at the small temple building. It looked smaller from her elevated vantage point.

"Well, one thing is certain," Desaree said. "Claire is not down here. I think we had better leave this for later."

Saffra froze, remembering their purpose. She wanted to uncover this mystery, especially after her dream of Queen Isabella and Princess Irelia. She had a feeling—she couldn't have explained how—that Princess Irelia's disappearance was linked to this gate. The idea was like a nagging fly, pesky, but just out of reach.

She felt a warm hand in hers. Desaree had come up beside her. "Come on. Let's leave it for later. I am too worried to focus on anything else. I don't even know if we can find our way back."

Saffra gave the temple one final look before nodding. She squeezed Desaree's hand in return. "You're right. We can come back later. Besides, we should have her with us when we explore this. Wait until she sees it! She is going to be beside herself with surprise."

They made their way back the way they'd come. Fortunately, it did not take long to retrace their steps without getting lost. They were able to follow their dusty footprints, and unlike last time, the footprints did not steer them wrong.

When they finally returned, the first hint of dawn glowed on the horizon. They both looked a little bedraggled. Desaree even had a smudge of dirt on her cheek.

They flopped down on the sofa with loud sighs. "Well," Desaree said, "now that we know she is not in the passages, what do we do?"

"I...I am not sure." Saffra chewed on the skin of her lower lip. "I wish I had an answer for you, but I believe you now. Claire must have gone through the postern door. Perhaps I can scry her."

Desaree groaned. "Who knows how long that will take. What if something happened to her? What if she is lost in the city? What if she is in danger at this very moment?!"

Saffra's heart sank. "You're right. Even with Cyrus it took time to finally see him. I have *hardly* mastered the art."

"King Talon and his Shields will find her, won't they?" Desaree's voice cracked.

"I'm sure they will. I just wish there was something more we could do…" Saffra trailed off. She leaned her head back against the sofa and shut her eyes. Her mind was packed full, racing over all that had happened. "What a mess," she said at last. "First my dream. Then a secret cave. And now Claire is missing. It is all too coincidental." She opened her eyes and frowned, trying to put together pieces of a puzzle she was certain existed.

"Wait…your dream?" Desaree's head tilted to the side. "What dream?"

"Just before you came, I had the strangest dream. Now I fear that it was not a coincidence." She told Desaree about what she had seen. "I always believed Irelia simply died," she said. "The stories say so, but in my dream, she was missing. Even the king said he could feel it—that she was alive, I mean."

"I always heard the same," Desaree said. "I heard that Irelia simply died but no one ever knew—"

"Wait a moment!" Saffra's heart began to race. "What if she was pronounced dead simply because they never found her?"

"A possibility I suppose," Desaree scowled. "There is no way to know the truth. Either way, I pray that Claire's fate is not Irelia's…"

"Something tells me it won't be," Saffra said. "Listen, the gods must be using these two events to show that Claire and Irelia are linked. I have long wondered why Queen Isabella and Claire look nearly identical. Have you ever noticed that?"

Desaree began nodding, her eyes wide.

"Irelia must be the link that bridges them together. Do you think?" Her mind was already speeding rapidly over possibilities. Her thoughts went to the cave beneath the castle—to the broken gate. "Desaree! What if—"

Her chamber door burst open. Jocelyn stood in the doorway, breathless. "There you are!" she cried, clutching her side. "I have been looking everywhere for you. You must come at once!"

Both girls jumped up immediately.

"Is it Claire?" Desaree asked.

"No!"

"Dax!" Saffra cried, realizing it at once. She had sent Jocelyn to sit in with him while she got some sleep. Jocelyn must have come by earlier while she was in the passages.

"He is awake," her handmaiden said.

"We must go at once. Desaree?"

"I'll come with you."

"There is something—"

"Please, Jocelyn, we haven't a moment to spare. We can discuss it on the way." Saffra had not intended to sound so snappy, but she could not afford to linger. He was awake. Claire was missing. The world was chaotic. She needed Daxton's love and support now more than ever. The three of them rushed away.

"How did he look?" Saffra asked as they sped through the keep. "What did he say? Did he ask for me?"

"I...well...that is..." Jocelyn struggled.

"Surely he asked for me?"

"Forgive me, my lady, but I must warn you. Dax is not himself."

"What do you mean? What happened? Is it his injury? Is he in pain?"

"No, it is something worse. Daxton did not ask for you because he does not know you."

Saffra came to an abrupt halt. Desaree and Jocelyn did the same.

"He...he does not know me? But..."

"He remembers nothing. He woke and did not know me, did not know Marcel. He did not know where he was. Everything we asked him—he could not remember."

"But...why wasn't I summoned immediately?" Anger manifested as heat in Saffra's face.

"Forgive me, my lady. We were in such shock. I looked for you in your quarters and you were gone. I searched the keep before trying your quarters again."

"Of...of course," Saffra said, feeling ashamed for her accusations. "You are not to blame, Jocelyn. You have done well."

"Surely he is okay," Desaree whispered, squeezing Saffra's hand in reassurance.

"I will be the judge of that," Saffra said.

The three of them rushed off. When they reached Marcel's quarters, they raced inside without knocking. They found Marcel with Daxton, a quill in hand, taking notes on various things Daxton said. Upon their entry, Daxton turned to them. "Hello," he said. His voice was soft and his gaze questioning. "This man claims the strangest things. He claims I was attacked by the vodar." Dax chuckled. "Are those not creatures of myth?"

Saffra rushed to him, throwing her arms around his neck and kissing his forehead, his cheeks, his nose. "Thank the gods," she whispered. When her lips landed on his, he stiffened. He didn't kiss her back. She pulled away to look at him, running her fingers over his furrowed brow.

"I do not understand," he said. There was obvious confusion in his voice. "I do not mean to be rude, but do I know you? Is this normal?"

Saffra felt the blood drain from her face. She pulled her hands away and sat down beside him. "But, of course you know me, my love." Her eyes searched his, begging for a sliver of recognition. His dark gaze met hers, but there was no remembrance within. "How can you not know me? We are to be married soon. You are to be my husband."

Daxton's eyebrows pulled together. "I do not think so. I think I would know if I was to be married. Especially to a pretty woman like you."

"But...but you are. We are. I am yours, remember?"

"Forgive me, my lady. How can I remember when I do not even know your name?"

Saffra's eyes widened. It felt as if she had been punched in the gut. "My name...my name is Saffra," she whispered. "You know me. I...I'm Saffra." She panicked, looking from Dax to Marcel, hoping to find answers within Marcel's face. "What is happening to him?"

Marcel appeared troubled. "An after effect of the poison."

"Impossible! Claire was poisoned and her memories remained intact."

"Claire is not entirely human. She has magical blood, remember?"

Saffra's breath began coming in gasps. How could this be happening? It felt as if her world—everything she knew—was shattering around her. Was this the price to pay for loving a human? She looked once more upon her beloved. As she gazed at him, she saw only blankness in his face. There was nothing there that hinted of his affection for her, nothing that showed he cared.

He must have sensed her distress. "I am sorry, my lady. Please forgive me. I cannot...I do not remember..." He sat back against the pillows and his face turned away from her to gaze upon the wall beyond. It was as if he had never known her.

"I cannot..." Saffra stood and backed away from Dax. "I cannot bear it." A sob escaped her chest. She felt as if her body was splitting apart. Another sob escaped. She looked from Desaree, to Jocelyn. There was pity in their faces. No, she could not take another moment of it. Taking one final look at the man she loved, at the blank face he wore, she turned and fled.

CHAPTER 42

INSIDE THE CELLAR

Kastali Dun

Claire's awareness wavered for hours, accompanied by a mishmash of bizarre dreams. She helped her mom feed the chickens, except the chickens breathed fire and looked more like miniature dragons. She went to the Indianapolis County Fair with her grandfather, who had died a long time ago. She threw a baseball back and forth with her dad, but she was holding a shield instead of a glove, which made it impossible to catch the ball.

She found herself in the forest, surrounded by lush foliage and glowing lights. Her bare feet delighted in the softness of the mossy ground. It felt like home and she never wanted to leave.

She made her way through the blueish mists, inhaling deeply, taking in every smell, every sound. Damp earth mixed with florals and wood. She reached out to touch a nearby tree. Energy thrived within it. The tree was happy, just like her.

"This is your home now." A musical voice startled her.

She whirled. "Queen Jade."

"We have been waiting for you, Claire..." The spriten queen opened her arms.

"You...you have?"

"Of course. You bear the mark of our people. You are one of us."

"Then, I can stay?"

"Forever, if you wish. This is your home. Your place is here."

Warm tingles spread to her extremities. It was on the tip of her tongue to accept. She wanted to live within the roots of the trees, to dwell among the unicorns and flowers, to drink up the knowledge offered by such an ancient people. Except—

"I cannot stay," she said. "I must return. My place is in Kastali Dun."

She could not leave her friends behind. She glanced around the forest. Speaking of friends... How had she come to be here?

"Well, that's too bad. I am afraid I cannot let you leave, my dear." Queen Jade's voice changed. It grew harsh and hostile. The queen's face changed, melting away and turning ugly. "You see? You can never leave. You will be mine forever."

She gasped.

Kane stood before her, red eyes glowing an awful shade of blood. Fear rooted her in place. She tried to lift her feet, to run, but she was too heavy.

Was he real? No, she was dreaming. He was in her dreams. But, how?

"I managed to collect some of your...essence. You so wisely left behind your blood. You don't remember? That night the vodar injured you on your journey?"

Her leg gave a painful twinge where she had been wounded, but the dream continued.

"My magic allows me to use your blood to haunt your dreams, if I so desire. Come to me..."

"No!" she hissed. "I will never be yours." She turned to run, but vice-like fingers closed around her forearm, holding her in place. She battled, screaming and pulling against the sorcerer.

. . .

Her eyes flew open. She thrashed against a firm grip holding her arm. It wasn't Kane.

"Calm down, lassie, calm down!" It was a gruff, unrecognizable voice. A foul-smelling cloth pressed over her nose and mouth. It made her suddenly dizzy. "Yes, I know. Rather horrid, isn't it?"

"Eh, Collier! Quit trying to woo the lass. It's your turn, or you gonna forfeit yer hand?"

"I'll do as I like, Tark. Mind your own. And yes, you might as well toss my cards. I must be away." Collier looked over his shoulder at a man standing in the corner and said, "My work here is done, Eagle. I trust you'll uphold your end. You got all you need from me for now." He returned his attention to Claire. "There now, that's a good lass. Sit back and relax..."

She blinked and did as suggested, unable to think clearly.

He walked away, tossing the rag upon the card table.

She stared up at the wooden beams on the ceiling. Her back was pressed to a wall. Everything was spinning, like she'd had too much to drink. Her mind throbbed and her stomach churned. She swallowed the excess saliva pooling in her mouth.

There were men in the room, all strangers. The only light came from candles and a few wall sconces. The floor was dirt. She took a deep breath, trying to clear the putrid smell from her nostrils. The scent of damp earth flooded her senses. They were underground.

Underground?!

Her heart took off in a gallop. She lifted her hands and found them restrained, her ankles, too. A gag filled her mouth with an awful taste, clenched between her teeth.

Oh, gods! Panic set in.

"What's going on? Where am I?" she cried. "Help! Someone help me!" The words came out garbled and unrecognizable. The men did little more than glance her way before disregarding her.

Her breaths came faster and faster. Fragments of her memory returned. Her argument with the king, the postern door, her agitated trek through the city...

She'd been kidnapped, and it was all her fault! She was the world's biggest idiot.

Talon's face swam into her mind and she groaned. He was going to be so, *so* angry with her. She'd never be allowed outside the keep again, if she even made it back.

She glanced towards the stairs, then back at the men playing cards. Quietly, she began scooting across the floor. With her ankles bound, she couldn't walk. But if she could get out of this room—

"Where do you think you're going, lassie?" One of the men stood, walked over, and dragged her back into place. "Stay! And don't try that again."

She cursed obscenities at him.

He merely laughed and said, "No point in complaining. Scream all you like. No one's going to hear you down here, not with that gag in place."

Her shoulders slumped. This was hopeless. No matter how loudly she shouted, she was stuck.

Except...

Her thoughts sharpened. She clawed at the barrier in her mind, ripping it free, and did the only thing that felt right. *"Talon?! Can you hear me?! Please! I need your help!"*

She wasn't sure why she called to Talon over Reyr. Perhaps it was because Talon was the most powerful person in the kingdom. Or perhaps it was because she knew that he would do whatever necessary to help her.

"Claire?"

She sagged against the wall. *"Oh, gods. You're there. You can hear me."*

"I can hear you." There was no mistaking the relief in his voice.

"Talon, I...it's all my fault."

"What happened?" he demanded. *"Where are you?"*

"I..." She glanced around. *"I was kidnapped. I don't know where I am, somewhere in the city. Underground I think. A cellar? I...I'm scared."* The last was barely a whisper in her mind.

"Are you alone?"

"No. there are...there are others, six other men, preoccupied at the moment."

"Did they hurt you?"

Disoriented, she took stock of her body. Her mind was nearly paralyzed, as if it knew what was happening but couldn't do anything about it. The rest of her appeared in order. *"No...not badly. I'm okay, I think."*

"Good. That's good. If they lay so much as a finger on you..." There was no mistaking the simmering rage in his words. Nor the promise.

The rest of her defiance towards him crumbled. Their past no longer mattered. The hatred she had once harbored towards him evaporated. She was left with nothing but guilt for her reckless actions.

"Talon, I'm so sorry. I never should have disobeyed you. I was so distraught when I left the keep. And...and...I never told you about my ability when I should have. You must be furious with me." Her skin flushed hot.

"Claire..." His voice was so soft. Not a hint of anger. *"All that matters is your safety."*

In that moment, she realized their conversation wasn't private. She wasn't alone. She felt each shield's presence, soothing, reassuring. Reyr was there, anxious to carry out orders, desperate to find her. Jovari was pacing grooves in the floor. She felt Koldis's anger, his desire to deal justice. Bedelth was the patient one, like a silent giant. And then there was Verath, brooding over the strategy of everything. All of them were with her, a lifeline to her escape.

"Are you restrained?" Talon asked.

"I—yes, my wrists and ankles," she said.

Several angry growls answered, but Talon's was the most distinct. *"Can you use your magic to break free? We've got guards swarming the city and drengr patrolling overhead."*

"I can try." Her confidence flared into life. Why had she been so worried? If she could take on the vodar with her magical green fire, she could certainly take on six criminals.

She focused on her bonds first, attempting to break free. She spoke the magic word for cut, *"Bita."* It came out garbled and nothing happened. She said it again, fighting the enunciation as she worked her tongue around the gag. Still, nothing happened.

Was it because she couldn't pronounce the word perfectly? No, that wasn't right.

Perspiration broke out on her brow. She was sticky and bedraggled. Something was wrong—very wrong. Her body wasn't responding to her magic.

"Claire?"

"I…I don't understand. Why isn't it working? I spoke the words exactly as I've done before." As quickly as it had come, her confidence vanished.

There was a long silence before Reyr said, "Do you think it's possible, Your Majesty? Could it be poison? Dragon's bane, perhaps?

"What's dragon's bane?" Her breaths came quickly, chest rising and falling in renewed panic.

"Claire, did they make you drink anything?" Talon asked. "Eat anything that tasted odd?"

She tried to remember. "I… No… I haven't… I haven't eaten anything. Nothing to drink."

"You're sure?"

"Wait…" Her mind turned over. "Oh, gods. They poisoned me. The rag. A man named Collier. It smelled awful."

"That explains why she sounds rather disoriented." This, from Reyr to Talon.

"Is it… Am I…? Am I going to die?" When she thought of poison, she thought of the vodar. Poison like that required immediate attention.

"I don't think so." Still, Talon sounded furious. "You are not in pain. That alone is a good sign."

"Talon, the city has thousands of cellars," Reyr pointed out. "If she cannot use magic, then we need a new plan."

Her body began to tremble. "So…you're not coming to get me?"

There was a snarl of helpless frustration from Talon. "Not yet. Not until we can narrow down your location. But we will find you."

"Okay…"

"I need you to be strong. Can you do that for me?"

"I—yes."

"Good. I will find you. I promise." Talon's words were followed by silence, but he never really left her, nor did his shields. She could still sense them.

HOURS PASSED and she grew stronger, or, the poison grew weaker. If she could hang on long enough, maybe it would pass through her system. She kept a close eye on her captors, listening for anything that might give away their location.

One of the men stood and came over to her. He smelled of booze and piss—a less pleasant alternative to Collier. Her nose stung and she crinkled it. Without warning, he shoved the same disgusting rag over her face. "Collier says every couple of hours, so take a big whiff, lassie. Oh, holding your breath, are you? Well, I'm a patient man. Aren't I, Ben? Aren't I patient?"

"Aye, Tark." Ben said. The men in the room chuckled. "But, don't toy with her, eh?"

She held her breath until her lungs were screaming. At last, she was forced to inhale. She took a deep, gasping breath.

"There now. Not so hard, eh?" Tark gazed down at her, eyes gleaming with something that made her gut churn.

Poison spread through her. The world tipped on its side and her stomach twisted. She nearly blacked out.

"Leave her be, Tark." A voice sounded from the corner of the room. She was only vaguely aware of it.

"*Talon...*" she whimpered. "*Talon...*"

"*I'm here.*" There was so much rage in his voice.

"*They...they did it again. They drugged me...I'm...I'm scared. My heart is...it's racing.*"

"*Shut your eyes. Take deep breaths.*" She did, letting him coach her through each inhale and exhale. "*How does that feel? Better?*"

"*Yes, a little.*" It was a weak whisper of a thought.

"*Good, a little is better than nothing. Now, think of something happy, something to take your mind off your fear. Can you do that?*"

"*I...*"

"*Tell me about your home.*"

"*My...my home?*"

"*Yes, your home—where you came from.*"

"*I...you've never asked me that before.*" Something of her old personality fought its way through. She smiled. "*You really want to know?*"

"*I do. Yes. Tell me about it.*"

She kept her eyes shut, allowing her mind to float away until she was soaring over corn fields. "*I live on a little farm in a place called Indiana. Every year we plant corn as far as the eye can see. The fields smell like damp earth and the dirt is always squishy beneath your toes. When I was little, I liked running barefoot through the fields.*" She fell silent for a moment. "*When the tassels on the corn are tall enough, and the sun sets over the field, everything glows golden. You can look out from the porch swing and see all the gold along the horizon, and the pinks and oranges in the sky...*"

"*It sounds beautiful.*"

"*It is.*" She smiled again. Her heart felt lighter. Whatever Talon was doing—it was working. "*Every Saturday morning, Mom makes the most delicious pancakes.*"

"*Pancakes?*"

"*I always douse them with butter and syrup. God, they're so good. You would love them. And coffee. You people need to invent coffee already.*"

Talon's chuckle was audible in her mind.

"*Whenever I need to get away, I hide out in my room. It's the best room in the house. It's like a library. The walls are covered with shelves of books. So many books I've lost count.*"

"*Is that so? You like to read, then?*"

"*More than most things, yes.*" She missed her books. She missed her parents, her home, her world, everything. Despite that, thinking about home helped. She continued to recount little snippets—whatever came to mind—and Talon continued to listen. The more she recounted, the better she felt. The poison's potency remained, but her mind no longer panicked.

She opened her eyes and took stock of her surroundings, still intent on finding something that might reveal her location. There wasn't much in the room to make it identifiable. Several columns of crates were stacked against one wall, unmarked. Big oak barrels were stacked against another. She frowned.

Oak barrels...

"There are...I think there are barrels of alcohol here! Lots of them." She counted as she spoke. *"Twenty, at least."*

"A tavern?" Reyr was in her mind. He had never really left.

"We visited every tavern and inn last night," Koldis said.

"Yes, but we did not search their cellars," Reyr reminded him. *"She could be hidden in one."*

"Is there anything else, Claire?" Talon asked.

She exhaled. *"There's nothing else distinguishable. A table in the middle of the room. Nothing is labeled. I can't be sure."* She felt hollowed out inside. There had to be hundreds of drinking establishments in the city, hundreds of underground storage rooms.

"We will obtain warrants for all of them, if we must," Verath said.

Talon's shields kept her company as they obtained warrant after warrant and began searching establishments throughout the city. Every so often, Talon asked her more questions about her home—likely to keep her occupied.

The card game at the table had ended. The men stood, stretching and giving each other a hard time. One of them, their leader by the looks of him, began moving about the room. He collected things in a satchel. "Morgan and I have business in the city," he said. "Keep an eye on her. We will be back soon."

They ascended the stairs.

She saw the opportunity and seized it. *"Talon, two of the men are leaving. I think one of them is the leader."* She described their appearance and clothing, which was plain at best, and then returned her attention to the commotion in the room.

"Might as well have another round." The four remaining men returned to their game, taking swigs from a bottle. Soon, their curses and jeers flowed loudly.

Tark was by far the nastiest. "I need to piss!" he roared, then stood up and made for the stairs. His gaze fell on her as he passed. A cruel smile spread across his face, slow and deliberate. "What are you lookin' at, lassie?" She shuddered and looked away. "Like what ya see, eh? Well don't worry, I'll be back in a mo' and you can have a piece of this."

She saw his crude gesture out of the corner of her eye. The men at the table catcalled in response. Bile rose in her throat and she swallowed it down.

Tark returned as promised, towering over her. She shrank away as his slimy gaze deliberately raked over her body. Her fingers trembled. She pressed them into the folds of her gown, sandwiching them between her legs.

"What do you think, fellas?" Tark drawled. "Think we got enough time before Eagle returns?"

Her gaze swam, filling with angry, fearful tears, making the small pieces of straw on the floor blur.

"I think we got plenty o' time," one of them said. Two of them stood up, filling the small chamber with their formidable height. The other stayed seated and watched with lazy amusement.

"*Claire?*" Talon's voice turned from calm to agitated.

She didn't answer—she couldn't answer. She was too senseless over what was happening, or about to happen.

"What do you think, Ben? You hold her and I'll take her? We can take turns too, if you like."

Her round eyes finally darted up to find Tark's nasty smile. "*You'd* like that wouldn't you, lassie? One final hurrah before we take you up north? And don't worry, if you like it, you'll have plenty o' time with us during the journey."

Bile churned in her stomach. She tried to keep her breaths steady but they came too quickly. Fast enough that little pricks of light burst in her eyes.

"I'll hold 'er steady for ya, long as I get my turn." Ben walked over.

"No," she cried. She shrank in on herself as Tark unfastened his belt. A whimper escaped her lips. Tears began falling down her cheeks. Ben reached down to grab her. She cowered away from him, crying out. His fingers latched around her arms, pulling her up—

There was a loud thud and the cellar filled with commotion. Thundering footsteps echoed down the stairs. She felt a flare of hope that Talon had finally found her.

"Ben! Tark!"

Both men froze. Ben quickly released her, stepping away as if he'd been burned. She gave a sob, equal parts relief and despair, and backed up against the wall, as far away as she could get from them.

Eagle appeared at the foot of the stairs. "What in the gods' hell do you think you're doing, eh?"

"Just havin' a little fun, sir," Ben called, as if they'd meant nothing by it. "We weren't actually goin' ta touch 'er." They retreated to the table, taking their seats.

"Clarie?! What's happening?" Talon's cries, which she'd tuned out, came roaring back. Her mind stumbled and tripped over reality. *"Talk to me. Are you okay? Did they hurt you?"*

"I...they tried...they were going to..." She couldn't say it.

When the king next spoke, his words were a roar directed at Reyr. *"I'm done playing by the rules. The people's privacy be damned. I do not have all day to wait for signatures on scraps of parchment."*

"Talon...I'm okay." She tried to calm him down.

"Did they touch you?" he said at length.

"I...they tried. Their leader came back."

Eagle walked up with a cup of water and a plate of food, bringing her conversation to a halt. He set the cup and plate down in front of her. The sight of it made her want to vomit. "Listen, lassie, if you promise to be silent, I will remove your gag so you can eat."

She couldn't stomach food, but she nodded anyway, eager to get the damn thing out of her mouth.

Eagle removed the gag before giving her a look of warning. She turned her eyes away from him and sat with the plate on her lap, massaging her jaw.

After gulping down some water, she looked at her food. Cheese that looked more mold than anything. A roach peeped out from beneath the hunk of bread and her stomach heaved. She turned away and squeezed her eyes shut.

"The lady is too *high and mighty* to enjoy our kind of food," Tark baited. "Too used to eating at the king's table." He came over and snatched up the untouched food, but forgot to reattach her gag. She threw him a look of intense loathing, which only made him chuckle with pleasure.

The moment his back turned, she reached out with her mind for every single blip of consciousness in the vicinity and said, *"Help me!"* Then, she filled her lungs and screamed bloody murder.

It was immediately followed by the roar of a drengr, then another, and another. She almost didn't register the fist that struck her flesh. Pain erupted on her face, stars bursting into her vision. Her lip split open, filling her mouth with the taste of blood. Defiant, she lifted her face to gaze up at Tark. "You're going to pay for that."

She was vaguely aware of multiple drengr voices bombarding her mind.

Tark's face contorted, splotchy with rage. "We told you to behave!"

"You never should have removed my gag." She gave him a wicked grin.

He roared, lunging for a fistful of her gown, ready to land another blow.

Eagle appeared and closed his hand around Tark's wrist. "That's enough, Tark," he said. "Our instructions were explicit. We are not to harm her. Now, we're out of time. We need to split. Wagon's upstairs. Get to packing. You've got five minutes."

The others had already jumped into motion. Eagle turned to her. She licked the blood off her lip just in time. He shoved the gag back into her mouth and secured it in place. Not that it mattered anymore. They were kidding themselves if they believed the drengr hadn't already pinpointed her scream.

Tark gave her one final look of loathing before relinquishing his hold on her.

She ignored him. *"Did it work?"*

"It did, you brave girl." Talon's voice oozed with pride.

The poison laced rag came out of nowhere. She sputtered as it was pressed against her face. Her stomach churned and everything began spinning. She gasped, struggling to breathe. The edges of her vision blackened. *"Talon..."*

"Hold on, Claire," he called, but his voice was already fading. *"We're coming for you!"*

The last thing she saw was a strange, detached image from the eyes of a drengr. It launched from the balcony of the king's tower, high into the sky. There was another beside it, with scales the color of gold.

Everything disappeared and she sank into blissful darkness.

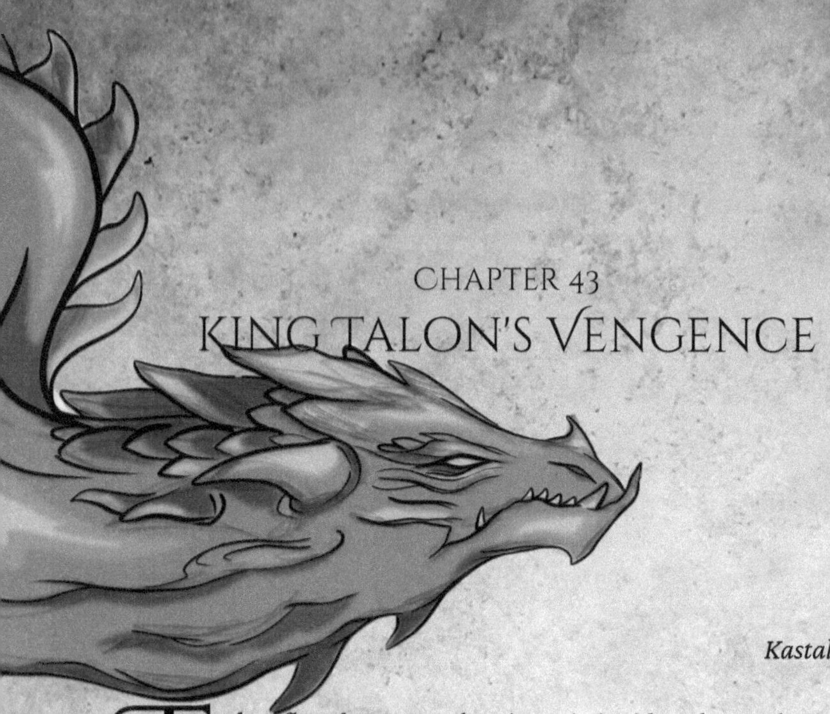

CHAPTER 43
KING TALON'S VENGENCE

Talon flew low over the city. His insides churned with hot dragon fire, desperate to break free. He'd done his best to hide his emotions from Claire, to keep his voice calm for her.

His chest expanded. He was so damn proud of her and her quick thinking. The moment her captors had removed her gag, she'd known exactly what to do. Her scream was the perfect way to pinpoint her exact location.

He descended, his shields alongside him. They transformed, landing forcefully but gracefully on two feet. The streets were narrow and dirty. It was no surprise she was in the Pauper's District. The lowest of the low.

Dilapidated buildings towered over him, leaning inward, casting everything into deep shadow. Only a sliver of sky could be seen. Only a few stars with it. An old woman spotted them and rushed away.

The city guard was already on its way. In minutes, the street would be swarming. They needed to act quickly. He glanced at his shields, nodding. They fanned out. He scanned the buildings until his eyes stopped on a crumbling facade of plaster and stone. There was a tavern on its lowest level. It's worn sign had a carving of a crown and the words *King's Crown.*

His lip curled in disgust.

"Jovari, Koldis, go left. Verath, Bedelth, guard the front. Reyr, you're with me."

He and Reyr jogged along the street, then slipped down an alley. They stopped at a small door, unsurprised to find it locked. Grunting with satisfaction, he glanced over his shoulder and smiled at Reyr, then he kicked it in. It flew inward, breaking from its hinges with a loud bang.

"Talon?! Is that you?" Claire's voice was in his mind. He faltered at the sound of it, relieved that she was conscious again.

Earlier, when she'd first contacted him, hearing her voice had all but brought him to his knees. Even after a full day of communication, the sound was honey on his tongue. Sweet and thick and deliciously golden. Not that he'd admit that to *anyone.* Just as he wouldn't admit how jealous he was to discover she and Reyr had shared this secret.

"I'm here," he said, sending her his reassurances. *"Everything will be all right."*

Reyr stepped up beside him. *"Shall we?"*

"Let's."

They plunged through the doorway and into a small cookery. The dim light did nothing to disguise the filth of the place. Three tavern wenches cowered in the corner, clutching one another.

"All exits are guarded, Your Majesty." This, from Jovari. *"None will escape."*

"Ladies?!" He growled, flashing them a feral grin. The wenches in the corner yelped. "Point me in the correct direction of the cellar."

The middle one lifted a shaking hand, pointing down the hall.

"Much obliged. This way, Reyr." They thundered down the hallway.

"Talon, be careful." Claire's voice again. *"They know you're coming."*

His steps faltered. Was that concern in her voice? Surely not. In no reality would *she* be concerned about *him*. He was inclined to tell her that six men was nothing. That he could kill every last one with his bare hands. Instead, he said, *"I will be."*

They stopped at the top landing to listen. Agitated voices sounded below. A shiver of eagerness skittered down his spine. Something dark within him stretched its wings and shook itself awake. The beast inside was waking up.

"I want their leader alive for questioning," he told Reyr. *"The others are fair game."*

"As you wish, my king."

"And, Reyr?

"Yes?"

"Take your time. No magic."

"Of course." Reyr's eyes danced with anticipation. *"I would hate to kill them too quickly."*

He plunged down the stairs, Reyr hot on his heels. There was no one he would rather have at his back. The sound of their boots on the wood thundered.

He surged into the cellar. For a moment, time froze. He spotted Claire across the room, curled in on herself, her shoulders hunched. Her face was tear-stained and bruised. Her lip, bloodied. A draconic growl filled the room. It took a moment to realize that it was his. He would kill every last one of them for what they'd done to her.

Her eyes latched onto his. *"You're here,"* she managed, sounding relieved, as if she hadn't wanted to believe it until she saw him. Gods, he loved her voice in his mind.

"I'm here." He felt a sudden need to show her exactly how he planned to punish her captors.

Time settled back onto its axis. The momentum from his descent sent his body plunging into action. The first clang of metal rang out as his sverak struck inferior steel. The men converged upon him. He stepped aside, moving faster than their human bodies. A blur to their lumbering.

The sound of Reyr's sverak rang out, reverberating through the small room. There was hardly anywhere to move. A body flew through the air, crushing the table, giving them more space. The man quickly rose and jumped back into the fight.

He and Reyr split the opponents between them. Six to two was excellent odds. It was a shame, really. It was almost too easy.

A set of dual blades swept towards him he deftly deflected. At least one of them had some training. The blades came again, and again, while the other two brandished knives, hoping to distract him. Only, he was a cat and they were mice, and this was a game that would end with their deaths.

"That's Eagle, their leader," Claire said.

He studied the swordsman's fighting style, ignoring the other two. "I might actually enjoy this," he growled, blocking another series of blows. "If circumstances were different. But you took something that doesn't belong to you, someone I care about, and that is unforgivable."

Eagle only grunted.

"What's the matter?" he taunted. "Nothing to say for yourself?"

Sweeping around, he whirled towards one of the knife bearers. He plunged his blade straight through the man's torso. The point emerged through his back, bloody and covered with gore. He ripped it free. The wound was fatal, and would ensure a slow, painful death.

To his credit, Eagle only blinked, then began again with a new series of swiping blows. The other knife bearer took several steps back. He eyed his comrade bleeding out on the ground, then jumped back into motion.

He caught a brief glance at Claire, watching with wide eyes.

"Which of them struck you?" he demanded, trying not to distract himself with the sight of her.

A long pause and then, *"The one Reyr's fighting. Gray tunic and brown pants. His name is Tark. He...he tried to rape me."*

The world stilled around him. For a split second, he saw red. Then something inside him snapped. He lunged for the other knife bearer and removed the man's head. Then he sent a command to

Reyr. Like a well rehearsed dance, they moved past each other, switching places.

Reyr kept Eagle busy.

Talon found himself face to face with three new opponents. "Good evening, Tark," he said when his blade met Tark's. Whatever Tark saw in his expression made the man's eyes go wide—

White hot pain seared his back. He swore under his breath and spun. Claire let out a surprised cry. His heart skipped.. *"I'm fine,"* he told her. *"It's already healing."*

The pain was sharp enough to make his eyes water, but it faded within seconds, disappearing entirely.

"Are you sure?" The worry in her voice lit a fire in him, renewing his desire to show off. Gods, what was wrong with him?

"Positive." His blade was deliberate as he plunged it into the man's gut, holding it for just a moment before he removed it and whirled back to face Tark.

Tark wielded a pair of knives, but not very well.

He bared his teeth. "I am going to enjoy this very much."

"Please, Your Majesty!" Tark's companion dropped his weapon and stepped away. The stench of piss filled the air. Distracted by the easy target, he lunged and stabbed him in the leg, making it impossible for him to go anywhere. The man sank to his knees, crying out.

He and Tark entered a dance of their own. Across the room, Reyr was still engaged with Eagle, keeping him busy so he couldn't escape. Tark lunged, swiping erratically, grunting with each movement.

Talon dodged with minimal effort. "You're pathetic," he spat. "Drunk and uncoordinated."

He blocked one of Tark's swipes and punched him in the gut. Tark went flying across the room. He held fast to both blades and immediately rose, his movements stilted.

Talon advanced, sverak lifted. "I might have killed you swiftly like the others, but you don't deserve that, do you?"

Tark backed up, his eyes going wide. The blood drained from his face. "Please."

"Did you harm her?"

"Please," he said again, not answering.

"You struck her," Talon roared. "You tried to rape her?!"

This time Tark didn't bother fighting. Talon's blade found its mark on his throat. "I didn't do no such thing!" His face transformed into a painful grimace.

"Do not lie to me!"

"I...I...please!"

"You lot are all the same," he scoffed, disgusted. "You always beg in the end."

Once more, the scent of piss filled the air. He leaned forward and made a show of sniffing. "You stink, Tark. You're nothing but filth."

Tark whimpered.

"Would you like to know something? A little secret?" Tark's wide eyes searched his, desperate for a shred of mercy. "I'm going to make it hurt. I'm going to make you scream until your throat is shredded and your body is spent."

Tark's fear filled his nostrils. Instinct kicked in. Raw hunger filled him, fueled by what he smelled. His muscles coiled. It took every bit of his control to keep from killing Tark here and now. He wanted to mutilate him—to rip him to shreds with his jaws and his claws. His body itched. His skin rippled with glittering black scales—

"*Talon!*" Claire's voice. A warning. He blinked.

He couldn't afford to lose control here. Not now.

"I'm not going to kill you just yet. No. I want you to think about what's waiting." He leaned in, his mouth close to Tark's ear. As he whispered his intentions, the whites of Tark's eyes grew larger. It gave him a great deal of satisfaction. Then, before Tark could process his death sentence, he knocked him unconscious. Tark crumpled to the floor. When he next woke, he'd be in a dungeon cell where he'd have plenty of time to contemplate exactly what was coming.

CHAPTER 44

HANDS OF COMFORT

Kastali Dun

Claire took in the carnage, bodies scattered across the cellar floor. A decapitated head lay mere feet away. It was Ben's face, eyes wide and unseeing. She couldn't bear to look at it. Only Eagle remained standing. Tark was also alive, but he was a crumpled heap on the floor.

A metallic scent filled the air.

She closed her eyes, taking a deep, steadying breath. When she opened them, Eagle and Tark were gone and Reyr was crouched before her. Talon stood at his side. She could feel their eyes cataloging every bruise, every scrape, every injury.

Talon's lingering fury was a potent presence, taking up space in the room. She didn't dare look up at him. Couldn't meet his gaze after everything that had happened between them.

Reyr reached for her, cupping her head in his hands. He planted a kiss atop her hair. Relieved tears blurred her vision. It was over. It was all over.

"No need to cry," he murmured. "You're safe now." His eyes were soft and full of love, but there was something tortured about it, and she knew that something had changed since she'd last seen him. He cut her restraints and removed the gag. She took a gasping breath and wiped her eyes, trying to pull herself together.

"Give us a moment, Reyr." Talon rested his hand on Reyr's shoulder. "See to the others."

Reyr stood. "At once, Your Majesty."

His footsteps receded and silence fell.

She stared at Talon's boots. Her cheeks flushed hot. Despite her addled mind, she recognized the regret pooling inside her. It flowed in like torrents of water, filling her up entirely. The words she'd said before—her cruel comment about not finding a mate—couldn't be taken back. Rivers only flowed in one direction. A person couldn't simply scoop up the water and put it back. Then there was her shame, for being so careless and disobeying him, which had landed her in this situation.

Her chin trembled. The silence stretched. It grew heavier until Talon spoke. "When you were taken, I wanted to burn the city to the ground." His boots had flecks of blood on them. "This entire ordeal... I thought I had lost you."

A flash of movement and he knelt beside her, face level with hers. She closed her eyes, felt his hand hover over her injuries. "*Ender mein,*" he muttered. His magic was hot as it spread over her jaw and mouth. She licked her lips to clear away the blood. They no longer felt swollen and painful.

"Much better," he said. "No more trace of Tark's fist." He took her chin in his fingers, turning her face about, examining it. She kept her eyes closed to avoid his gaze.

"Look at me," he demanded, keeping his voice low.

Their eyes met. She didn't see anger, not even frustration.

He should have been furious. She'd been cruel and reckless. Her emotions felt like a used up rag, rung out. What little strength remained, fractured. Tears dropped down her cheeks and a sob escaped her chest. She put her face into her hands and crumbled.

There was a moment, perhaps two, which passed unaltered, then Talon's hands were on her. He wordlessly swept her into his arms, moving her onto his lap. He tucked her head under his chin and rocked her.

"I'm sorry," she managed. "I'm so sorry..." Her words were muffled and nearly incoherent. His arms tightened around her. He offered comfort even when she didn't feel deserving of it.

They stayed that way, with only the sound of her crying to break the silence. Eventually, her tears slowed and her body calmed. Still, she clung to him.

He carried her out into the fresh air. It was dark. People were gathered in droves, packed tightly into the narrow street. They held torches aloft, bickering and speculating. There were armored guards, some of whom held back the crowd.

She buried her face in Talon's chest, trying to blot out the world. He set off at a rapid pace. A soldier rushed up behind him. "I brought your horse, my king, just in case?"

"Lady Claire is not fit to ride. Return him to the stables."

"At once, Your Majesty."

She pulled back to look at him. "Talon, you don't have to...I mean...I can..." The words died on her lips. His expression was unyielding and it held no room for argument. The remainder of her protests died on her lips.

He set a clipped pace through the city. It was a twenty minute walk. She settled down in his arms. With every step, she felt calmer, more herself. More importantly, she felt safe, as if nothing could touch her.

They passed beneath the portcullis. "Welcome back, Lady Claire," said a guard on duty. They all stood at attention as the king passed.

When they entered the keep, she expected Talon to put her down. He didn't. He strode up the main staircase, then through the large first floor corridor, off to the right, up another flight of steps, through several more corridors, and into the south wing. He didn't slow his pace until they reached the tower.

Still, he did not put her down.

The tower guards greeted them and opened the door. He walked through the main room to the bathing chamber. Only then did he set her on her feet, keeping an arm tightly around her waist. "Can you stand?"

"Yes, I can manage." Her voice was rough and unused.

Talon stepped away. They stood staring at one another. She was not in a fit state to converse, so she studied him, looking first at his face, and then the rest of him. There was a wealth of emotion in his gaze. All of it confusingly clashed together. How could someone look frustrated, concerned, and troubled, all at once? She took in his bloodstained clothes, torn and filthy, and his ridiculous hair. It looked more beastly than ever, tufted and matted all over.

Her mouth twitched.

"I can't stand the smell of that cellar on your skin," he growled, making her thoughts scatter. "Remove your clothes and get into the tub."

Her mouth opened, then immediately snapped shut.

She turned to look at the large tub made entirely of black granite. It was partly sunken into the floor, with a tall lip around the edge. The rest of the bathing room was just as grand, with potted plants, stacks of towels, a giant window looking out over the sea, and candles—a whole sea of candles that someone painstakingly lit.

This was a chamber fit for the kings and queens of Dragonwall.

The sight of the tub made her heart ache with longing. A bath sounded perfect. She wanted to wash away the poison and filth of her experience.

Once more, her gaze landed on the king. She expected to see him scowling and impatient. It was the opposite. He waited, silent. When it was clear he intended to remain, she said, "You want me to undress in front of you?" Her words came out breathy and incredulous.

"You need a bath. I intend to see that it happens. Apparently, I cannot let you out of my sight."

"You need a bath worse than I do," she fired back.

His brows lifted. He looked down at himself, then back at her and shrugged. "I suppose I do. Later, after I see to your needs."

"Surely Desaree can see to my—"

"I am perfectly capable!" His eyes flashed dangerously. "Do you doubt me?"

"I...no...I don't doubt you, Talon."

"You may see your friends later." His voice softened. "They have been sick with worry. For now, your time belongs to me."

A lump rose in her throat and she swallowed it down.

Several moments passed in silence. When he did not move, she shrugged and undid the ties on her gown. It slipped off her body, pooling on the floor in a heap. She removed her chemise, keeping her back to him. Part of her longed to know what he was thinking, but most of her was too frazzled to care.

Naked, she walked over to the tub. Like the others in the castle, it was full of hot water. A small bit of steam lifted. She dipped a hand beneath the surface to test it out. It was perfect—hot, but not scalding. Her nose caught the faint scent of eucalyptus.

She climbed in and submerged herself until only her head remained above the water's surface. The heat eased her muscles. A breathy sigh fell from her lips. The fog cleared from her mind as she sat at the pool's edge, her back still facing the room.

She jumped at the sound of Talon's voice. "There now, stand and turn so I can wash you."

He was beside her, next to the tub. His tunic sleeves were rolled up to the elbow, revealing powerfully corded forearms. Her gaze snagged on a long scar running the length of his right forearm. There were several others scattered about it. His other arm was unmarked.

Her thoughts caught up to his words, sending her heart wild. "I...you..."

He wanted to wash her? That's what this was about? That's what he meant by seeing to her needs?

Taking a deep breath, she stood up to face him. His eyes widened, and his jaw dropped. She blinked, taking in the sight of him, frozen with a sponge in hand. "How?!" he demanded. She frowned. "How is that possible?"

"How is *what* possible?"

But he wasn't staring at her face. He was staring at her torso. She glanced down and froze.

"*Oh*. Right. That."

"Unbelievable." He reached forward. His fingers were gentle, tracing her flesh. The intimate touch sent a shiver down her spine. She erupted into goosebumps.

He dropped his hand and stepped away. "You never told me about this. Does Reyr know?"

She shook her head. "Only Desaree."

"Good." His expression smoothed, becoming unreadable again.

She lowered herself, shielding the majority of her body. "Are you angry with me?"

His silence was unbearable. He dropped her gaze and began lathering the sponge, intently focused on his task. At last he looked up and said, "I'm too relieved for anger." He walked over and held out a hand. "Stand, so I can wash you."

She swallowed, eyeing his hand. Finally, she complied. The water came to her waist. Still, her cheeks flushed to know her breasts were on full display. He didn't even look at them.

She placed her arm into his open palm. His fingers closed around it as he began to gently wash her. She might have protested, but Talon had a look of determination about him. He needed to do this. This was his way of affirming that he was good enough to care for her.

Something in her mind clicked into place. Did he blame himself for what she had done? Did he see her kidnapping as an inability to care for her, to protect her? It wasn't true—far from it. This was all her fault, her mess. And yet...

Talon needs to do this for you, and for himself, Cyrus said, solidifying her theory. She breathed a sigh of relief, glad to have Cyrus with her again. The poison must have worn off.

Talon was silent, washing first her arms, then her neck, chest, and stomach, before moving to her back. The only sound was trickling water from the sponge every time he rinsed it.

Her muscles began to relax. It was soothing, his ministrations. This wasn't simply dirt he was washing away, but the experience of being kidnapped. Only time would heal her trauma, but his careful hands set the process in motion.

She bit her lip to keep quiet. It was on the tip of her tongue to thank him. To thank him for knowing exactly what she had needed even when she hadn't seen it herself.

He stepped over to the opposite side of the tub, to a submerged ledge. "Stand here so that I can get your lower half."

And just like that, her relaxed mood evaporated, replaced by shy embarrassment. Why did she suddenly care that he would see her entirely? He didn't seem bothered by the request. He simply stood, waiting for her to follow orders.

She rose and moved to the shelf. This time, she kept her face trained on the wall. The water was only partway up her calves.

He quickly set about washing her legs. Once he was busy, she allowed herself to glance down at him. Her heart skipped a beat at the sight.

Was it attraction she felt, swelling in her chest? No, she pushed the notion from her mind. She was simply taken aback by the sight of the king—for he was a king in every sense of the word—hunched over, washing her. Dragonwall's outsider.

She pressed her lips between her teeth as he made his way up to the peak of her thighs. Her heart raced as the sponge slipped in between them. The hot bath turned scalding, turning her skin flushed. He didn't look up, thank gods, keeping his gaze focused on the task at hand. Nor did he linger. It would have been awkward if he had.

"Leg up," he instructed, ready to wash her right foot. She lifted it and placed it into his waiting hand, but nearly lost her balance. She had to grab both of his shoulders for support. The sponge tickled the sole of her foot and she let out a giggle. It brought his questioning eyes to hers.

"It tickles," she breathed.

The corner of his mouth twitched. He finished both feet. "There," he said. "All that's left is your hair."

Relieved, she quickly submerged herself again.

He stepped away for a moment and then returned with shampoo. Eagerly, she moved over to the rim of the tub. It was a blessing to have her back to him. He did not see her close her eyes when his fingers began massaging her scalp. Goosebumps pricked her skin. She loved getting her hair washed at the salon, it was one of her favorite ways to pamper herself. Since coming to Dragonwall, there was little pampering to be had.

A moan fell from her lips. His fingers briefly stilled at the sound. She thought she heard a small, satisfied huff fall from his lips, or perhaps she'd imagined it. Then his efforts continued.

A deep calm settled over her. She was disappointed when he finished. "Time to rinse." He lightly pressed her scalp. She scooted forward and dipped beneath the water's surface. His hands stayed in place, working out the shampoo. When she popped back up, he gathered her hair in his fingers and twisted it together, wringing it out.

"There, now you are clean."

It felt like waking up from a confusing dream. There had been nothing sexual about any of this. And yet, the intimacy was screamingly undeniable.

"Would you like to stay in the water for while?" His voice came from the other side of the room.

"Yes, please."

His face was shadowed, but she saw him nod. "Very well. I will see to your dinner and return to collect you."

When she next blinked, he was gone.

"Come. It is time to eat." Talon's voice roused her. She blinked herself awake and realized that she must have dozed off, her head comfortably tilted against the tub's ledge. Her skin was pruned.

"You are hungry, are you not?" He sounded amused.

"Ravenous." On cue, her stomach grumbled.

She rose from the tub and found herself gathered up in a giant towel. She expelled a breath, leaning into the soft material as he wrapped it around her. He proceeded to dry her, rubbing the fabric gently over her skin.

Her hair came next. He folded it into the towel, squeezing out the water. Then, to her shock, he quickly braided it down her back and tied it with a thin strip of leather.

She was gaping by the time he gathered a fluffy bathrobe and slipped it around her.

Talon stepped back to regard her. She bit her lip to keep from smiling. It was difficult to reframe him with the person she thought she knew. She had once believed him a monster, but these weren't the actions of a monster. His touch was too gentle. His gaze, too soft. His efforts, too thoughtful. No, these were the actions of a lover.

Her stomach swooped. Before she could question it further, he said, "Come," and took her by the hand, leading her from the room. His skin was warm, hands callused and firm. She gratefully held on.

They did not go to the large banquet table in the adjacent room. Instead, he led her to a smaller breakfast table beside the living area. A spread of food had been placed there. She stared, taking it in.

Talon dropped her hand and pulled out a chair for her. Once they were seated, he quietly studied her. "Well?" he said. "Are you going to eat?"

She nodded, then hungrily attacked the food. She grabbed whatever she could and heaped it onto her plate before scarfing it down. Talon leaned back with his arms crossed, watching her every move. When her stomach was satisfied, she heaved a sigh.

"Talon, I...I really am sorry for what I said to you about the whole mate thing—"

"Stop apologizing. It isn't necessary."

"But it is!" She threw him a glare, though it lacked her usual venom. "What I said was thoughtless and cruel."

"You want to talk of being cruel?" he scoffed, his voice low. "How about my cruelty, hmm? Shall we talk of all the ways I have been cruel to you? Of how I treated you when you arrived at my keep, under my protection?" His eyes glittered with anger, but it wasn't directed at her. "Your one cruel statement is nothing compared to how I mistreated you." His breaths came faster, chest rising and falling in rapid pants.

"When you were taken," he said, this time with a calmer voice, "my faults replayed in my mind, over and over. All I could think about was how, for one brief moment, I had actually threatened to kill you in the dungeons. For that, I can never forgive myself."

"Talon, you already apologized." Her mind shifted to the necklace he'd given her. She'd stupidly left it behind, as if it were meaningless. It was anything *but* meaningless.

"You think an apology makes everything better? That it fixes my actions?"

"I...no...yes? I don't know? Why do I feel like we are fighting again?"

He exhaled, running a hand through his hair. "I don't want to fight. Thank you for your apology, but please, no more. You owe me nothing. I am responsible for you, and I have no one to blame but myself."

She bit her lip, tempted to protest.

He stood up and went to the mantle. The box was there, containing the necklace he'd given to her. Was it yesterday? Two days ago? Three?

He set it on the table. "I meant what I said before. I do not like arguing with you. It makes me..." He blew out a breath. "It upsets me."

Then he sank into his chair, evidently flustered.

"I'm sorry that I left your special gift behind. I hope my behavior does not translate into dislike. I was just..." She trailed off.

He waved a hand, dismissing the matter. "It's fine."

They fell silent. She glanced at him and said, "I should have told you about my ability to hear the drengr. I shouldn't have made Reyr promise to keep my secret. It was wrong of me to ask him."

Talon huffed. "Love makes people do strange things."

She scowled, taken aback. "No. That...that's not why I did it."

"But you care for him, yes?"

"I... *Oh.*" Talon had often seen them together. Of course he would assume they cared for each other. "I don't like him like that," she blurted. "He's a dear friend, my dearest, in fact. He's the only person who believed in me. But..."

Talon stared at her.

"Reyr told you about my ability, didn't he? That's why you weren't surprised by it." Everything suddenly made more sense. "I expected you to freak out about it."

"Yes, he told me." His jaw flexed with irritation. "He also told me that he loves you."

She reared back, then sputtered, "I'm sure he meant only as a friend."

"No, Claire, he is in love with you."

"Oh, gods." She dropped her head into her hands. She should have anticipated this. The signs were there, but she'd purposefully ignored them.

Was it her fault for being too nice? Had she encouraged his behavior? Perhaps she'd spent too much time with him.

"Do not blame yourself."

She looked up. "Why shouldn't I?"

"Because it's impossible not to love you." He shrugged. "It is no fault of yours. He...he has been alone for a very long time."

"So?!" she scoffed. "So have you!"

He lifted a shoulder—a casual shrug.

"I will only ever love him as a friend. But knowing this, how can we go on as we have?" Her lower lip caught between her teeth. "I don't want to lose his friendship."

Reyr meant too much to her. Fresh tears welled up in her eyes. How could she have been so stupid?!

"I did not mean to upset you." Talon's voice was low and sincere.

"It's—it's fine. I'll deal."

"You should sleep. You have had more than enough. I had my servants make up my bed for you. I never use it anyway." Her lips parted, eyes widening in shock. "You may return to your room in the morning. Until then, I have matters to attend to in my study. If you need anything, you may call on me there."

"Your...your bed?" she sputtered. She glanced in the direction of his sleeping chamber. The door was open and candlelight spilled out.

"Is that an unfavorable request?" He lifted a brow in challenge.

She shook her head. The thought of returning to her room was daunting.

"Very well, then." He stood. There was a brief hesitation, then to her complete surprise, he bent down and kissed her forehead. "Good night, Claire. I am glad you are safe."

CHAPTER 45
CLAWS OF FIRE

Kastali Dun

Talon sat at his desk, staring down at a blank sheet of parchment. He owed Queen Jade both an admission and an apology. Though, he wasn't sure which was harder, admitting to one's wrongs or apologizing for them. He rubbed his temples, sighing.

At least it would be easier than his apology to Claire.

He opened his desk drawer and removed Jade's letter, skimming its contents. She'd called him things like inept, rash, and naive. Removing the stones from their protected location was likely the poorest decision he had ever, or would ever make.

And yet...

His mind selfishly drifted to Claire. How might things be different if Cyrus had never sought the dragonstones? Would Claire be happy at home with her family eating *pancakes* and drinking *coffee*? Would she be safe? Surely that was a better place for her. Even still, he hated the thought of never knowing her.

He shoved the letter away and set to work.

. . .

Queen Jade,

I made a mistake removing the stones from your protection. It was a rash decision, one made out of fear, and I am sorry. From one ruler to another, I humbly seek your forgiveness.

I have come to my senses. The forest is the best place for them, both for their safety and the future of our kingdom. I have a few matters requiring my attention, after which, I will depart Kastali Dun for Esterpine, where I might seek your forgiveness in person.

Sincerely,

King Talon

THERE. Short and to the point, even if it sounded a little sniveling. Purposefully done, of course, to stroke her ego.

He reached into his pocket and removed the dragonstone pouch, spilling them onto his palm. One black, the other gold. This wasn't the first time he'd interacted with them and it probably wouldn't be his last. He felt their power, seeping into him, warming his hand before spreading.

Clenching his jaw, he tucked them away. He folded and sealed his letter, then set it aside to be sent in the morning. Several hours had passed since Claire had gone to bed. He went to check on her.

The sliding doors were closed. Quietly, he cracked one open. A thin sliver of light shot into the room. Claire lay asleep in his bed, her golden hair fanned out around her. Behind her eyelids, her eyes darted rapidly. She twitched, then stilled.

He frowned.

An ugly feeling took hold of him, fresh rage welling up at the thought of what those men had done to her. Their actions would haunt her dreams for weeks, perhaps even months. It would not do.

The dark thing that lived inside him stirred.

"Bedelth, are you busy?"

He doubted that any of his shields would be sleeping tonight.

"Never too busy for you, Your Majesty. Have you need of me?"

"Aye. Come at once."

He was working the ties on the sleeves of his doublet when Bedelth entered. His shield strode across the room, pulling the laces into place.

"Have you been down to the dungeons this evening?" Talon asked, keeping his voice low.

"No. Koldis is there now, keeping watch. He is impatient to begin."

"I am impressed by his eagerness."

"Aye." Bedelth looked thoughtful. "I believe Claire's kidnapping was harder on him than he cares to admit."

"Perhaps she is growing on him," he said.

Bedelth's chuckle was a deep, draconic rumble. "I think she is growing on all of us, Your Majesty, but not in the way you are thinking. We merely care for her." That was more than he could say for himself, but he dared not admit just how much he felt for her. "Shall we go down to the dungeons together?"

"I need you to remain here." Bedelth frowned. "I told Claire that I would be available should she have need of me. I cannot…I do not wish to leave her alone."

The matter of Claire's captors *could* wait, but he had too much pent-up anger.

"Wait, is she…?" Bedelth looked over at the closed doors and his eyes widened. "She's here?!"

"I dare say she is." He sighed. "I wanted to make sure she slept. She would have stayed up all night, chatting, no doubt, had I allowed her to return to Desaree and Saffra. She needs rest."

"As do you, my king. You look too weary."

He shut his eyes, exhaling. Yes, he *was* weary. But his weariness was bone deep, a result of years upon years of burdens. "I try so hard to please them, you know I do. Sometimes I feel as if I'm stretched in a hundred directions. All while my failures nip at my heels. I think I shall never be good enough."

"I beg to differ. You are twice the king your father was, and your father was a great king."

He inhaled and squared his shoulders. "I will recover."

"Good, I shall wait here until she wakes."

"Thank you. Hopefully I will return before then, but if not, see to any needs she may have. When she is ready to leave, escort her to her chambers."

"As you wish," Bedelth said. He began to walk away. "Your sverak, my king. You will want it with you."

"Ah. Thank you."

Bedelth retrieved it and handed it over. Their eyes locked. Things that went unspoken—but were deeply understood—passed between them. Bedelth was a brother he was lucky to have beside him.

He found Reyr in his room.

"Is everything all right?"

"I am heading down to the dungeons. Thought you might like to accompany me. Koldis is already there."

"I would like nothing more." Reyr stepped out and shut his door. "And Verath?"

"He does not wish to be disturbed this night."

"Perhaps he is with Desaree. Although…I suppose it is none of my business, as he informed me."

He lifted a brow, looking his shield over. "Why do I get the impression you feel snubbed?"

Reyr blew out a breath. "I shouldn't be."

"Verath is entitled to his privacy. It is not your business, but it is mine, as his king."

"So, you know then?"

"Yes, I know. He came to me anxious and guilt ridden, asking for advice."

"When was that?"

"On the eve of our trip to Fort Lin. Gods, it feels like an age ago."

They rounded a corner and several early-risers passed by. He fell silent for a moment until they were out of hearing range. "At first I was surprised by it—that he should seek me out. I told him much the same as I would have told you, had you come to me early. I cannot deprive a person of love, no matter what that person has promised me. My only requirement for Verath is that he exercise caution when walking the fine line drawn around his oath. As of yet, he has not miss-stepped."

"Nor will he ever." They both knew enough about Verath to know that much. "He is a finer drengr than many of us will ever be."

"Aye. I think you are right."

Verath was the oldest of his shields, and by far the wisest. When he was young, he had only just taken his oath for King Tallek when King Tallek was called north to fight the Kalds. He was the only shield in history to serve two kings. Most served one king long enough to take up a quiet life afterward, like Lord Avreaen.

"He is older than both of us," Reyr said. "I should hope he would be wiser."

They both chuckled.

The cells beneath the keep were dark and ominous. They strode through the darkness to the screamers, where Eagle and Tark were being held. Koldis sat in vigil outside their cells with a single torch for a light. He rose from his chair to greet them. "Your Grace, I was hoping you would be along soon."

Talon nodded then glanced at the closed door. "No problems, I trust?"

Koldis shrugged. "Tark has been moaning something terrible. I've had to bang on the door several times to shut him up. Eagle has been silent."

"Shall we start with Tark then?"

"Very well, shall we?" Talon led the way. Koldis held the torch, but even with it, there was little light in the room, making their shadows appear monstrous. Reyr went about the chamber, muttering under his breath as he lit several wall sconces.

"Hello, Tark," he said, placing himself before the man. Tark's arms were above his head, tied to one of the many steel bars along the low ceiling. His feet were free to move, not that they would or could go far. Tark spat onto the dirt.

"That is no way to greet your king, *scum*." Koldis slammed the blunt end of his torch into the side of Tark's face. "And that was for Claire, by the way." He looked pleased with himself.

"For Claire's sake, you'll be receiving much more than that tonight." Talon felt the sadistic grin as it spread across his face.

"You won't hear me screamin'."

"No?" he baited. "Singing a new tune, I see. Do you know why we call these rooms the screamers? You will scream. I can promise you that."

"Ain't gunna give you the satisfaction, *King*. Not even if you beat me for it."

Talon's laugh was inhuman. "We shall see about that. But no need to fret just yet. Since it is only your first time, and I long to get better acquainted, we will start easy. I'll save the fun for later. Another time, perhaps."

Reyr brought Talon the first object. Without removing his eyes from Tark, he took it. He did not need to see what he held. He already knew what it was.

"Are you familiar with the Claws of Fire?" Tark's eyes flashed, but he said nothing. "I thought not. It was invented here, in the keep. In this very room. Perhaps you are curious about how it got its name?"

"You gunna talk me to death, Dragon? Get on with it." Again, Tark spat on the dirt at Talon's feet.

"The Claws of Fire is similar to a common flogging whip with one brutal difference. At the end of each tail there is a thin, dragon's talon—from the pinky, just here." He held up his pinky finger. "When the talons strike the human body, they rip the flesh apart until your skin feels as though it is on fire." It was satisfying to see Tark's eyes bulge. "There now, have I got your attention?"

"Do your worst."

"Oh, I will. Shall we begin?" He did not wait for an answer. Koldis made quick work of Tark's tunic, ripping it down the back and exposing his flesh. A few moments later, the screamers came alive.

CHAPTER 46

TORTURE

Kastali Dun

Eagle heard a scream, drawn-out and piercing, cutting through him like shards of glass. His skin crawled. He knew who it belonged to, though he cared little for the man. He cared more for what would come next.

He was surrounded by torture devices. They lined the walls, set up along the perimeter of the room. He could not see them now, not in the pitch blackness, but he'd spotted them when the king's shields brought him in.

And then there was the stench. Mildew, earth, and old blood. It was enough to drive anyone mad with fear.

He pulled at the ropes binding his wrists. There was little hope of untying them, but he had to try. The sounds of Tark's screams made him desperate. Tightening his abdomen, he kicked his legs up, folding in half. He wrapped his ankles around the ropes just above his hands. For a few painful seconds, he writhed and struggled against them, but it was no use. He cursed and let his legs fall back to the ground.

They'd removed his weapons, taking everything that could be

367

used as a means for escape. Perhaps this was the end. Yet, he refused to believe it.

Scream after scream, he listened to Tark's pain. Whatever they were doing to the man—and he did not want to consider what— was agonizing. It could be heard in the raw quality of Tark's voice.

Eventually, the screaming stopped. That was when true fear manifested itself. He knew he'd be next.

Tiny beads of sweat rolled down his back. His fisted hands were clenched so tightly, he could feel the drawn blood trickling down his wrists. His breath wheezed in his lungs. They felt tight and constricted, making him fight for each draw. By the time the door burst open, there were little stars swimming in his vision.

Three drengr males entered. His vision swam in and out of focus. They set about their business. One was lighting wall sconces, another was out of view fussing with instruments, while the third stood before him, motionless.

His skin crawled as his gaze sharpened. Feral eyes raked over him. Dragonwall's king. "You put up quite a fight earlier."

Eagle bowed his head. There was no telling if his cooperation would reduce his sentence, but if there was any hope of doing so, he was more than willing to try. To hell with his contractor at this point.

"Based on your expression, I imagine you know what follows."

He swallowed. "Not that I care overmuch, but is he dead?"

"Tark? No. Though he very nearly was when we finished. Koldis has healed him. Tomorrow, he will face much worse." A low chuckle rose from the king's throat. "I promised him a painful death. I always keep my promises."

Eagle shuddered. "I take it you dragons eat humans?"

"We eat scum, if the need arises." This from the drengr in the corner. "The rack is ready, Your Majesty."

The king nodded and then stepped back into the shadows. There wasn't time to wince. The other two were upon him, untying his bonds and dragging him to the back of the room. The king watched on.

"Wait," Eagle cried, looking over his shoulder. His feet dragged.

The drengr holding him paused. "Aren't...aren't you going to question me? Give me a chance to be truthful? I will tell you anything you wish to know."

The king motioned with a dismissive flick of his hand. Eagle was placed in front of the rack. The sheer size of the rollers and ratchet mechanisms made his stomach churn. He'd be pulled apart entirely. He began to tremble and his bladder lost its control.

They hoisted him onto it.

"No, no, no, no," he began to mutter, shaking his head. They did not hear him, or more likely, they did not care. His hands and feet were positioned.

"Please," he cried, straining to look at the king. Real men didn't beg. He couldn't recall ever doing so. That no longer mattered. "Please, Your Majesty. *Please*. I'll tell you whatever you wish to know! I swear it!"

The bindings on his wrists and ankles chafed.

The king's face appeared in his peripherals. "I know, Eagle. I know," he cooed, leaning in close. "You will tell me now, or you will tell me later. It makes no difference when. If you think spilling your secrets will result in any kind of happy ending, you are poorly mistaken."

"But..."

"Ah. Perhaps you are thinking that you might try to use your information as leverage. Trust me when I say, you'll be screaming for reprieve, for any chance to divulge what you know. In fact, I suspect it will come *clawing* its way to the surface long before I ever ask for it."

The king moved away.

His mouth opened and closed but nothing came out. For a moment all was still—all was silent. Every inch of him was shaking. His breathing came as shallow gulps while his lungs constricted in dread.

"You may begin." Like an axe on a chopping block.

The ratchet mechanism began to click. One, two, three, four, five...he tried to count. Each brought him closer to pain.

It started as a dull ache. The ropes around his ankles and wrists were so tight, they hurt more than the rest of him. Slowly, gradually, he could feel the pressure on his body, stretching, pulling. Soon, he was clenching his jaw in pain, willing himself not to scream—it wasn't bad enough—not yet.

Click. Click. Click.

The ratchet turned and true agony surfaced. His legs felt the worst of it, especially his knees, as the excruciating pain took hold, latching on, then spreading throughout his body. He heard screams, raw and guttural. They were *his*. He was hardly aware of his mouth as the sound wrenched free. He fought to hold himself together, as if tightening his muscles would keep his body from being torn in two.

Blackness engulfed him. He saw nothing of his surroundings. Every sense was overcome by what he was feeling.

Something snapped. He felt, rather than heard the pop. Severe agony radiated out from the point in his knee. His eyes were wide, so wide, that they hurt.

Another pop, followed by a pain so extreme in his shoulder, that his world fell away. He was hardly aware of the other snaps that followed. Then the ratchet clicking stopped. For a moment he was suspended in time.

Then the pressure lessened. The ratchet clicks reversed, easing the tension. All he knew was that the pain had decreased. There were still pools of it, radiating out from his knees, shoulders, and wrists—the places where his body was the weakest.

Someone stood over him. Warmth began spreading through him. He'd never felt anything so joyful. The pain dissipated. Even more sluggishly, his senses returned. His mind was still frantic, but he could think a little more clearly.

"Not bad for a warm-up," he heard someone comment when the ratchet stopped.

"Shall we begin again?"

Oh, gods. Oh, gods, no!

His breath sputtered. He blinked, panic welling up. The ratchet began turning once more. This time, he cried out in fear. In hopelessness. In desperation. "Please! I beg of you!" He found the words tumbling from his lips. "I had no idea the mess I was getting into. I never planned to harm the girl! I was only meant to bring her to my contractor. Please! Please..."

He was sobbing now.

Click, click, click...

The familiar agony of being pulled in two directions mounted.

"My contractor offered me unimaginable riches. More gold than I have ever seen! You must understand..."

His muscles burned as the ratchet turned, stretching him further, until there was no more for his body to give.

"PLEASE!" he screamed.

"Stop." The command was spoken quietly. He only heard it because it meant the pain would cease, at least for the moment.

The king loomed into view. His face swam in and out of focus. Eagle's own eyes were full of watery tears, tears of misery.

"Your contractor—tell me about him."

"He...he..." He could hardly think for all the pain he was in. His vision was cycling from light to dark, intermittently.

"Koldis, reverse the ratchet several clicks. I am interested to hear his answer."

The pain reduced. His muscles were so tense, so tight from holding his body together, that they were bulging.

"Must I wait?"

"S-sorry. My-my contractor never...he never gave his name. But...he was... There was something abnormal about him. He couldn't have been fully human."

"What makes you say that?"

"His eyes—his eyes. Oh, dear gods above... I can't... His eyes were red. I caught—I caught a brief glimpse of them."

He wanted to say more—to stall—anything to prolong the impending agony of his torture. His mouth opened to speak. His mind attempted to form a coherent statement as the world around him slowly faded from view. His vision went black, welcoming him into oblivion.

CHAPTER 47
END OF A VOYAGE

Dragonfire Sea/Kastali Dun

Captain Bennett looked out over the sea's dark blue waters towards the horizon. If one crossed the Dragonfire Sea, they would find Oshea. It was far enough west that the two countries rarely interacted. He himself was from Oshea, though he believed few in these parts could claim such.

His parents had taken him away at the dawn of an Oshean civil war, one of many in Oshea's bloody history, or so he'd been told. He'd never known his parents. They'd died during their journey to settle in a new country.

The sea had always fascinated him, especially knowing where he'd come from. It was part of why he'd become a sailor, to see Oshea with his own eyes. Now, he was a ship's captain.

He'd come a long way.

He blinked, shifting his gaze towards the landmass on his left. They were less than a day away from Kastali Dun. Their journey had not been without excitement—not at first, anyway.

With drengr escorts, the *Lady Faith* was untouchable.

Two days after departing from Fort Squall, they'd spotted pirate ships in pursuit. His crew's first reaction was one of fear,

372

memories of their previous battle still fresh in their minds. But then the drengr had taken flight, jumping from the deck and transforming into giant beasts. Their riders had watched alongside the crew. Seeing dragons in the sky turned fear to confidence.

He had watched the whole confrontation through his spyglass. The drengr used their strength to rip apart entire masts before unleashing their dragonfire. It took less than an hour before all four ships were burned wreckage. Nothing spreads faster than dragon fire. He'd always heard the saying, but now he knew it to be true.

The drengr had demonstrated their worth ten-fold.

"Port ho!" came a cry from the crow's nest.

He retrieved his spyglass and got sight of Kastali Dun's peninsula. Beyond that, its ports. Home at last. The tension knotting his shoulders fled.

The sun was quickly falling from the sky. Soon, the darkness would swallow them up, bringing with it a lively evening in the city. A shiver of excitement raced down his spine.

Beaky took flight and circled the ship. The deck was a mess of bodies as the crew worked to prepare for mooring. *Lady Faith* sped along, steadily approaching the Bay of Bandu.

Night fell upon them as they entered the bay. He stood motionless, looking ahead. Something was wrong. He'd seen the city from afar countless times, but he'd never seen it in this state, its streets crawling with torches.

He walked over to Keenan, one of the drengr escorts. Beaky chose that moment to land on his shoulder. "Looks like something's going on in the Pauper's District," he said. He'd grown up there, in one of its many orphanages, until he was ten. Until he'd taken a job on a ship as a cabin boy.

Keenan was silent, his eyes open but unseeing. "A lady is missing—a royal lady—King Talon's ward."

"Lady Claire?" His brow furrowed. From what Lord Davi had told him, she'd become something of a local celebrity here, especially for those of lower birth. An outsider taking up a prominent position in the keep? It gave them something to hope for.

"Yes. The very same."

"*Lady Claire. Lady Claire,*" Beaky squawked.

"That is surprising. How could she have gone missing?"

A long silence, like he was communicating with others of his kind, and then, "No one knows what happened. The king has mounted a city-wide search."

Bennett shook his head in disbelief.

"Drop anchor!" Jonah shouted behind him. They were safely in the bay now. Until they were given permission by the dockmaster to dock, Lady Faith would remain here.

Beaky squawked and flapped her wings. As she jumped, the pressure on his shoulder increased, then disappeared. "*Drop anchor, sea dogs! Drop anchor.*" Her squawking rang about the ship's deck.

"I think, Captain Bennett, that it would be best if you and your crew remained aboard the Lady Faith tonight." Keenan gave him an intense look.

"You're sure? We were greatly looking forward to land tonight."

"Aye, I am positive. With guards on every street, it would be safest to avoid the city."

His cew weren't criminals, but he caught Keenan's meaning. Men at sea were often rowdy when greeted by land. His were no different. They got themselves into plenty of trouble. With guards occupying every empty space of the city's streets, they might become a liability. He didn't need any of them locked in irons tonight.

"Very well. What of you and yours?" Bennett worried for the safety of his cargo. Without the drengr there to protect it, who knew what might befall them?

"Durstan and Sable will remain while the rest of us go ashore to assist the king."

"Very well." He held out his arm in common drengr fashion, bidding Keenan farewell. "May the wind be at your sails, or rather —" He cleared his throat. "—beneath your wings."

Keenan chuckled. "And may it carry you into calm seas."

Keenan then released his forearm and departed shortly thereafter with his rider and eight others. Durstan and Sable watched from nearby on the deck.

Disheartened, for he was truly looking forward to good food and strong rum—the grog aboard was losing its potency—he headed below.

~

KEENAN and his rider Krista returned the following morning. The crew gathered around to hear his announcement. "Lady Claire has not yet been found," he said, his voice solemn. "Everyone must remain aboard the *Lady Faith*."

His words were met with several groans.

"Quiet, you lot!" Bennett snapped, stepping in to mitigate his crew's bad manners. He understood their frustration. After so long at sea, they were all desperate to go ashore. That was no excuse to voice their complaints in front of a drengr.

Keenan did not appear offended. "Believe me," he said, "it is for your safety. I doubt any of you wish to run into a testy drengr." He turned to Bennett and said, "You alone may venture to the docks to meet with Master Arden."

Bennett nodded, then glanced at his men, noticing the dismay on their faces. They would recover soon enough. "Very well. I will depart at once."

It took several hours to track down the dockmaster and get him alone.

"You'll not believe the trouble set upon me with the searches goin' on!" he said in a huff. He was a direct opposite to his usual jovial self. They retreated to his warehouse office where they might enjoy some of his fine wine. "Men all over the place," he continued, going on about the searches as he moved about his desk. "They're swarming the docks, wakin' me up from my sleep. Bad business, that lady going missing. *Bad* business."

To Master Arden, everything was *bad business*, but Bennett nodded all the same.

When he finished complaining, he said, "Your cargo is going straight to the king's forges. But with all this,"—he waved a hand in annoyance—"there ain't no drengr available to handle the cargo. You'll have to wait it out."

"What about docking?"

Arden shook his head. "Best not to risk it—knowing what's aboard..."

He agreed. Too much temptation. If pirates wanted what he carried, others would too. Ice metal was thrice more valuable than gold.

"And my crew? Are they free to go ashore now? They crave a good time and they've earned it. I can split them into three groups, give them turns guarding the cargo."

"Aye. They been cooped up, I know." The dockmaster shrugged. "I see no problem with it." He paused for a moment as if to think better of his words. "Just be careful. Tell 'em ta be on good behavior, if you catch my drift?"

"I understand." He bid Master Arden farewell and rushed back to the ship. The moods of his men improved after they were given permission to disembark, provided they be on their best behavior as the dockmaster had said. They laughed and agreed, but he saw the real truth in their eyes. Straws were drawn and a select group was permitted to disembark first. Two-thirds remained on board as guards. He was lucky enough to draw a straw that sent him ashore.

He went straight to Seafarer's Row. He and Jonah enjoyed themselves a little too much, and by the end of the night, they found themselves in the Sea Dog. It was home to one of his favorites.

"How about I get you another drink, my dear *captain*?" He smiled at the sound of Colleen's voice. He always paid her a visit or two when he returned to the capital. "How your body must *ache* for the good stuff."

She was a saucy woman.

"Aye, my little wench." He pulled her onto his lap and stroked her hair before saying, "Give me some of your best."

"*Some of your best. Some of your best,*" Beaky squawked. She'd taken up roost in the rafters just overhead, using it as an opportunity to gaze down and irritate him at every possible moment, especially now.

"That bird of yours hasn't stopped talking, I see." Colleen gave him a wink before rising from his lap. He gave Beaky a warning glare, then followed the tavern wench with his gaze.

Despite the constant commotion from the city-wide search, the Sea Dog was bristling with happy patrons as pockets emptied and bellies filled. No sound from beyond its doors could be heard through the loud, crude talk, and music from the hornpipes.

"Will you be stayin' here tonight?" Colleen was back with his drink. She handed him a stein of the Sea Dog's finest beer and held her hand out for payment.

He passed her a silver. "I suppose I'll be staying as long as it's yer bed I'll be sleepin' in."

She feigned surprise, scolding him before waltzing away to serve a few patrons who had just entered.

Jonah joined him moments later, a bonny lass at his side. They both sat and ordered drinks.

"And what's yerrr name?" he growled, looking at Jonah's wench. He was already fairly fuzzy, having demolished several steins in the Mad Dragon a few hours prior. Kastali Dun boasted more taverns than any other city in the kingdom. Seafarer's Row had the best of them. Everything a seafaring man could desire along the street overlooking the docks. Every window gave a good view and every establishment offered plenty to drink.

The young woman smiled sweetly, blushing. "My name's Jenny, if it pleases you, sir."

Jonah butted in. "Jenny here was just telling me how she rents a room over yonder at Kohlmann's Inn." Jonah gave him a sly look. Kohlmann's Inn was a brothel.

He wondered if Jonah would be paying for her, or if she was servicing his good looks. His first mate was handsome, after all.

The Sea Dog grew louder and more rambunctious. All the

while, speculation circulated about why a royal like Lady Claire had disappeared.

"She's been taken by pirates and dragged out to sea," one man claimed.

"She's run from the king's scars," said another.

He kept an eye on Colleen, hoping she would take him up on his offer. He was a sea captain, after all, and his position had its perks.

It was well past midnight when someone stumbled in, drunk by the looks of him. "She's been found!" The shout drew a sudden silence from the Sea Dog's patrons. "Lady Claire's been found, bless her! Rescued by the king, no less!"

The alehouse erupted into roaring cheers. Those who were losing steam were suddenly alert again. "Hip-hip-hooray!" some called. Others toasted to her health and the energy in the room returned.

"Shall we go upstairs, my mighty captain?" Colleen found her way to his lap. "I can pretend to be Lady Claire and you can rescue me." Her warm hands were on his shoulders as she whispered in his ear.

"Aye, my sweet girl, we shall!" A girl she was not, but he still enjoyed the implication of youth given by the title. She had never revealed her *true* age to him, but he was certain she was in her mid-thirties.

She took his hand and pulled him from the table. With one swift movement, he lifted his stein and drained it before slamming it back down with a thud.

Some of his men spotted his retreat. They gave victory whoops and cheers as he passed, hand in hand with Colleen. Beaky took flight from the rafters to follow after. The cheers chased them all the way to the stairwell and beyond.

~

THE MORNING DAWNED humid and gray. He groaned and gripped his head, bracing himself for the splitting headache that came pounding its way to his consciousness. Why did he always get so drunk?

Beside him came a soft snore. Colleen was naked, tangled in blankets. Without waking her, he rose from the moth-eaten bed, donning his trousers and shirt. He managed to slip from the room with the woman none the wiser. If everything went well, he might visit her again tonight.

His day consisted of a significant amount of waiting around. First, he waited on Jonah. They visited Master Arden together. Then they both waited on the dockmaster to work out the details of the offloading of their cargo. Once those matters were settled, he waited on the few men aboard the Lady Faith to get her to the docks. By the time she was safely secured, the day was done and night had fallen.

Luckily the king, who's charge was now safely tucked behind castle walls, was more willing to attend to the matter of his cargo. The king sent a convoy, including two of his own shields by the name of Bedelth and Reyr, to oversee the procurement of the palettes. Bennett offered Reyr an especially warm greeting. He gave him news of his twin brother and told him of his visit to Fort Squall.

They saw to the matter of offloading.

"Best to fly it in and deposit it in the keep before transporting it to the forge," Keenan warned as they moved the heavy stuff from the hull.

By the time it was finished, he was sure his chances for a night-time rendezvous with Colleen would be gone. A cheeky woman like her wouldn't last long in the Sea Dog. Any number of men were probably waiting to snatch her up.

Nonetheless, with the ship docked and their business complete, he and Jonah trudged their way from the docks to Seafarer's Row.

Jonah grinned all the while, likely anticipating the evening to come. "Glad that's over," he said at one point.

"I, too. Thank the gods."

Their cargo was deposited and secure, his pockets were bursting with gold dragons, and a celebration for a journey well-done was in order. So, like any sea man, he let the night take him where its currents flowed, and as it so happened, into Colleen's bed once more.

CHAPTER 48
TRUST FALLS

Fort Squall

Tamara took a deep breath—the deepest she had ever taken. She needed a lot of air for what she was about to do. She also needed courage.

"A trust fall is always frightening the first time." Byron had tried to comfort her before they had agreed upon it. The truth was, nothing short of, "Never mind. You don't need to do this," would erase her fears. Besides, she *had* to do this! If she wanted to begin her training, she could not progress without completing the first set of drills.

She looked down and swallowed. Beneath her, she could see nothing more than green and brown blurs. The color was endless, kissing the sky in all directions. Their altitude was spectacular and terrifying all at once, and it made it impossible to discern anything beyond the landscape's color. In a way, that was good. If she saw the ground—truly saw it, like individual details for trees and animals—things would be different. She certainly wouldn't do what she was about to.

She crouched in the dip where Byron's neck met his wing joints. The warmth of his scales radiated through the soles of her feet. As instructed, she kept her body scrunched tightly in a ball. Her hands held nothing more than a single neck spike. The downward strokes of Byron's enormous wings kept them fairly stationary—an accomplishment that should have been impossible.

"Remember to wait until my wings reach their highest point before you jump."

"Okay..."

"Are you ready?"

Her heart flapped wildly. *"I think?"*

This was it. Time to act! She watched Byron's wings complete their downward stroke before returning to *high point*.

Her thoughts sharpened.

She sprang from his back, as if jumping from a cliff into water. Byron's mind disappeared, their contact severed. Her body sailed outwards into nothing. A floating feeling took hold of her. Then she was falling. She saw the land again and panicked. Without Byron's mind, terror made her muscles lock up.

All she had now was trust...

Trust falls were the first drills required of pairs before they began training. It was a crutial item, and if she didn't do it successfully, they couldn't move on to aerial maneuvers. To her absolute dismay, there were a series of them to be completed.

This drill was meant to reenact a worst case scenario. Occasionally a rider's harness might break, or a rider might be trying an epic maneuver in the sky and somehow fall. Thus, both rider and drengr needed to be comfortable with the occurrence.

Depending on the rider's orientation, the drengr might be forced to snatch them safely in their claws. Or, if the rider was positioned just right, a drengr might swoop up beneath them. Trained riders accomplished every scenario with ease, regaining their position on their drengr's back.

For this particular drill, she would pass so long as she completed the fall without fear. Getting over her fear was a big milestone. After that, she could focus on the types of falls and remounts required.

She opened her eyes. The ground was still far below. The wind screamed past her ears. It felt so isolating, falling through the sky unhindered.

She caught a flash of blue. A gasp left her lips. Byron was falling beside her. With the ground forgotten, she began to giggle. They were falling *together*. It was odd to see him like this.

Her fear disappeared. What was the point of being afraid when he was right beside her? He'd never allow her to come to harm.

They continued to plummet head-first towards the land below. Byron's next move was to sweep up underneath her and catch her on his back. She would have to grab ahold of him quickly to get herself into position. She glanced over at him falling beside her, his wings tightly tucked to his body. Time moved slowly.

When she was ready, she opened her arms and legs, changing her position. If she were truly diving from a cliff into water, she would have belly-flopped. The change immediately slowed her fall. Byron shot past her. When she next blinked, he was spreading his wings to slow his fall. He came up beneath her. She kept her gaze on the spot where she wanted to land, his harness. She reached as she collided with him. The impact was jarring, painful even, but she was fully focused. She groped for the harness, but all she found was empty air. She began to slip, trying to get into position. For an instant, she made skin to scale contact. Byron's mind was there, infinitely reassuring.

A single blink, and he was gone.

Everything happened so fast after that. She toppled off him. There was sharp pain on the back of her head. The world around her went black.

***

She opened her eyes, struggling to comprehend where she was, let alone what had happened. Gavin and Tella's faces swam into view just behind Byron's. He supported her head in his lap.

"Where...?" She sat up and looked around. They were in the middle of a field. "Was...was that a dream? Did I fall? I..." She patted herself and then pinched herself. Was she still alive?

"Gods, Tamara, I am so sorry." Byron sounded horrified.

She whirled around to face him. "Why? I'm the one who messed up. I lost my hold."

"I'm talking about my wing. I struck you in the head as I slowed my descent. My wing came down just as you slipped off. You lost consciousness."

"So I really did fall?"

"He caught you, dear girl, with little effort I might add." Gavin's face was full of patience. "He snatched you up in his claws and brought you to the ground gently, healed your head wound, and here we are. Now, shall we try again? The day is coming to a close, and we ought to return to the fort soon."

"Let's call it a day, Gavin." Byron began lifting her to her feet. "I think Tamara has—"

"No." She staggered upright. "I want to try once more. I should be allowed a second chance at the least. If I wait until tomorrow, I will be awake all night...again."

"You're sure?" Byron's face showed obvious concern.

"Absolutely certain."

Gavin and Tella nodded then moved away, transforming and taking to the sky before she had the chance to process that she just volunteered to do this whole falling thing again. This time, she was determined to do better.

Byron moved away and transformed. She vaulted onto his back with ease. That was the first thing he'd made her practice. Now she could complete the action like a seasoned rider. They launched into the sky, flying up to where they had been before.

Once more, the ground was far below. Gavin and Tella kept their distance, hovering in the air the same way Byron did, watching her progress. This time, she got into position more quickly, using the strength of her arms to spring onto Byron's back. She balanced on the balls of her feet, keeping herself steady enough to crouch. She held firm to one of his neck spikes.

"You will get it this time, now that you know what to expect." Byron's words were calm and confident.

Taking a deep breath, she released her grip and sprang away from him. This time, she kept her eyes open the whole time and even smiled as she plummeted through the air. It did not matter how poorly she performed because Byron would catch her no matter what. All she needed to do was focus on the sky and the next steps.

He caught up to her and then dove past her as she slowed her descent. She watched him carefully as he opened his wings and swept up beneath her. This time she reached out sooner, taking a firm grasp of his harness just as her body collided with his. Her teeth clenched at the jarring contact. They continued falling together before he pulled them out of the dive. With all the strength she could muster, she pulled herself forward and upright.

"Well done!" Byron cried, taking off into the sky again.

A wide grin spread across her face. *"I did it! I really did it! And it was not half as bad as I thought it would be!"*

She felt Byron's amusement before he spoke. *"Things are always easier once they have been accomplished. Now that you have done it, it will never seem as frightening as before."*

Gavin's voice sounded in Byron's mind—a sensation that still felt strange. *"Well done, Tamara. You and Byron should be proud."*

He was right. Completing a trust fall was hard enough but made harder without a bond in place. As far as she knew, she and Byron were the only ones at the fort to complete one under such unique circumstances.

"Thank you, Gavin." Byron's voice radiated pride.

They returned to the fort at nightfall. It came as no surprise when they found the dining hall crowded with bodies and decorated with banners the color of Byron's ice-blue scales. Completing a trust fall was considered a rite of passage among the drengr community. It was always a cause for celebration.

The room erupted into cheers when they walked in. Music began to play. Davi and Emmy approached and offered warm hugs. Others clapped them on the back, congratulating them as they made their way to a table near the front of the room. It was a feast to be remembered, just like the accomplishment it celebrated.

Her friend Sophie found her, offering a huge smile. "I'm so proud of you! I knew you would do it!"

Her cheeks flushed under the excessive praise. She loved Sophie. The two of them found some time to steal away so that she could tell her all about the experience. Byron found them sometime later and swept her away to celebrate by themselves.

There were several places along the battlements of Fort Squall where they often walked, famous for privacy. It was in one of these places that he swept her into his arms, twirling her in a circle. "They looked at me like I was crazy when I told them we could do it." He set her back on her feet and took her face in his hands. "Falling without our minds linked...it's almost like falling blind." He planted a chaste kiss on her lips before dropping his hands. Then he took her hand and placed it around his arm. They continued their walk, well aware that they had succeeded at something everyone doubted was possible. They had done a blind trust fall successfully, and she had survived to live another day.

CHAPTER 49

A NEW BEGINNING

Kastlai Dun

Claire sat obediently while Desaree pinned her hair in place. Queen Ahlessa's sapphire necklace sat on the vanity, sparkling up at them. She grabbed the lid and covered it.

"Oh no!" Des swatted her hand away. "You're wearing it."

"It's just so...*excessive*. Besides, why do I even have to go?"

"Because I said so."

"Since when do handmaidens dictate their lady's schedules?"

Desaree offered her a stern look. "You've locked yourself in here for four days. I understand that you need time to heal, but you cannot hide forever."

"Yes I can." Her voice came out petulant.

"You *especially* cannot hide from King Talon."

She shot Desaree a *what's-the-big-deal?* glare.

Desaree huffed. "*How* many times has King Talon knocked at your door?!"

"Three," she grumbled. "Three times."

"And *how* many times have I turned him away?"

She mumbled something incoherent under her breath.

"Gods above!" Desaree tsked. "You've got me turning away Dragonwall's king, of all people! What would my mother say?"

"I assure you, he'll live."

"He's worried about you, Claire. Don't crinkle your nose at me! You should have seen how he looked the last time I refused him."

"Oh?" She lifted a brow. "And how did he look?"

"Like he might gobble me up!"

She laughed. "I think he prefers livestock."

They both laughed. Desaree calmed down and said, "The least you can do is walk with him. That is all he requested."

A heavy sigh fell from her chest. "I suppose you're right. It is just a walk."

"There now. *See*?" Desaree smiled. "That wasn't so hard."

"Yes it was!"

"Because you have feelings for him?"

She groaned, as if that would change matters. She'd already told Desaree everything. "It's probably just rescue romance syndrome," she decided. "I mean, it's too cliché to be anything else, right? I'm not the only one to fall for their rescuer. It happens all the time in books and whatnot. It'll fade. In time."

Desaree snorted. "Reyr rescued you too. How do you feel about him?"

She tutted. "Fine. Point taken."

She frowned at her reflection. It hardly made any sense. She'd gone from hating his guts to...well...*liking* him. There'd never been any in between. Shouldn't there have been an in between?

Des finished her hair and attached the heavy sapphire necklace around her neck. "There. You're ready."

"I look...wow." She studied her reflection. The combination of her royal blue gown with the sapphire necklace was astonishing. She traced the gems. "He has good taste, doesn't he?"

"To be sure!" Desaree stepped back, hands on her hips.

She looked ready to step foot on the red carpet at the Academy Awards. All for a simple walk?! Her stomach dropped with apprehension. She didn't want to do this. What she *did* want, was to melt into the shadows and go unnoticed by anyone, especially him.

"Wouldn't...wouldn't my beige brocade be better than *this*?"

"I know you doubt me." Desaree bent over and affectionately rested her chin on her shoulder.

She sighed. "I'll just have to trust your judgment, then."

There was a knock. Her heart leapt into her throat. Oh, gods!

Desaree strode for the door while she rushed to stage herself in her living area. After formally greeting *His Majesty*, Desaree melted into the shadows.

Talon spotted her immediately. His gaze roved her from head to toe, lingering longer than necessary on her necklace. "Lady Claire, it appears you do *not* have the plague after all."

"I...it..." She snapped her mouth shut and internally cringed.

Talon's lips twitched and he said, "No need to fret. Your time away from court has treated you well." She managed a nod. He took a step towards her. "Are you...are you doing all right?"

She pressed her lips between her teeth then said, "I'm getting there. I still feel...I don't know. It's hard to explain."

"I see. Will you let me know if there is anything I can do?" His eyes were heavy with concern.

She thought she heard Desaree quietly swoon in the corner, but she ignored it. "Yes, of course. Thank you."

The king cleared his throat. Once more, his gaze fell to her chest. "I did not expect to see you in that."

She exhaled. An unexpected smile tugged at her lips. "Someone once told me that this dress needed a necklace—*this* necklace."

"That must be the first advice you have taken from me." His face stayed neutral, but his eyes glittered with smugness.

She suppressed a chuckle. "Funny, Your Majesty. Very funny."

"It's a beautiful day out. Shall we walk?" He offered her his arm.

They emerged into the corridor. There were three people waiting for them. Bedelth, and two castle guards. When Talon saw her studying them, he said, "You'll get used to it."

His meaning was clear. She was about to see a lot more guards in the future. "And what about Bedelth?" she asked, flashing the shield a grin over her shoulder. No hard feelings—she didn't mind having him around.

"There is often a shield by my side, Lady Claire. Why do you think they are called *king's* shields?" His eyes sparkled with mischief.

"Yeah, yeah, yeah," she grumbled back, offering him a teasing eye roll before turning away. He chuckled.

They were under intense scrutiny as they moved through the keep. It came as no surprise. At first, she was on edge. It was exactly what she'd expected—silent judgment from everyone. As if every single person living and working in the keep had come to gawk, and even laugh at her stupidity.

Until—

"It's a blessing to have you back, Lady Claire! We were all very worried." The castle's baker had stepped into view. He removed his cap and bowed deeply.

She released Talon's arm and curtsied. "Thomas! Thank you." A big smile spread over her face. "You know, I look forward to your spiced bread every morning at breakfast. It is always a delicious treat."

Thomas's face turned a deep shade of red. "Thank you, my lady. Oh, bless you!" He glanced nervously about. His eyes did not land on King Talon a single time.

"How is your dancing these days?" She fondly recalled the old man's spryness on the dance floor. The night of Verekblot had left her with many happy memories.

His face lit up. "Better than ever, Lady Claire, better than ever! Say, we all miss you at our little parties. I do hope you might consider coming to one. I'd be glad to have you back as a partner."

"I..." She bit her lower lip and glanced up at Talon. He looked on, a small smile tugging at the corners of his mouth. Otherwise, he said nothing.

"You will always have a place in our hall," Thomas added, "if that's what you're worried about."

"Thank you. I...that means a lot to me."

Thomas bowed again, mumbled his thanks, then strode away. They continued their walk through the keep. Talon's eyes danced more than ever.

The unexpected occurrence didn't stop with Thomas. Other servants—particularly those who knew her personally—offered her words of comfort. They bowed and said things like, "The gods smile upon you, Lady Claire." And, "Anything you need, my lady, don't hesitate to ask."

It was overwhelming.

"Dragonwall's people admire you," Talon observed, looking thoughtful, which only made her skin flush.

They reached the keep's royal garden. Talon led her in, taking them along the perimeter path. It passed flowerbeds, then shrubberies, and finally a copse of exotic trees. Other paths veered away from it, leading towards the central portions of the garden, but they didn't take those.

It was a stunning day, crisper than usual, not a single cloud in the sky. A cool sea breeze toyed with the loose strands of her hair, tickling her skin. The sun was hot on her back, warming her through, but not unbearably so.

She inhaled, shutting her eyes. Talon was a solid presence by her side. She leaned on his arm, using it for balance. Slowly, her muscles began to relax. "Perhaps Desaree was on to something," she mused, smiling up at the sun, letting it heat her face. "I shouldn't have hidden away for so long. It's beautiful out here."

"Was it the court you were hiding from? Or me?"

She licked her lips. His eyes snagged on the motion. Something hot dropped into her belly. "Both, I suppose."

"I see." He fell quiet.

"I was worried what they'd think of me. What they'd say. That I was careless. That I overreacted. That an entire city was forced into high alert because I let my emotions get the better of me. That I'm not setting a good example. That someone in my position should behave better. That..." She exhaled. "Well, you get the point."

"I do." He hesitated. "And me? Why were you hiding from me?"

Her heart skipped a beat. "I... There was a time when I absolutely despised you."

He winced. "And now?"

"Now? I respect and admire you." She stole a glance, pleased to see his mouth turning up into a pleased smile. Her gaze lingered over his scars. He was sensitive about his appearance. She didn't want to make him uncomfortable by staring.

"I am honored you feel that way. Respect and admiration are admirable qualities to have earned, especially from you." Their eyes met. His irises were the color of brushed aluminum in the sun's light, with little golden flecks scattered throughout. She was the first to drop her gaze, focusing on the garden's path instead.

"So, if you hold me in such high regard, why have you been avoiding me?"

She let out a heavy breath. "Because I am ashamed."

"Claire." His voice was low. The way he said her name...

Oh, gods.

"I told you before to stop apologizing for what happened—"

"No! I mean—it's not that." They rounded a corner, walking past a bed of exotic plants.

"What, then?"

"I misjudged you, from very early on." Her gaze slid over a cluster of purple, unfamiliar flowers before finding Talon's face. "That's what I'm ashamed about."

"It was warranted. Deserved, even. There's no shame in that."

"Perhaps." She fell quiet. A pair of hummingbirds caught her eye. She gazed at them, following their quick movements. "Nature has a way of lifting one's mood, doesn't it?"

"It certainly does."

"I guess you should know, being a creature of the sky and all."

He made a sound of assent in the back of his throat. All grumbly and low. It sent an eager shiver down her spine.

"Does it ever get to be too much?" she wondered. "Being the king? Ruling? On display all the time? I suppose you can't do what I did—simply disappear for days at a time."

Talon chuckled, and she found her attention riveted on his face.

"I do occasionally hide away, but it's rare. Usually, Reyr drags me back into the public eye. And yes, it frequently becomes too much."

"It must drive you mad," she mused. His eyes gleamed, a spark of something primal in them. She huffed. "Yes, I suppose it does make you a bit mad, doesn't it?"

"Indeed. I will always be a bit mad. But, I do the best that I can. When it becomes too much, I seek refuge in the only thing that has ever been mine."

She stopped and turned to him. "And what's that?"

"Can you not guess?" He lifted his brows, studying her face.

"Oh!" Her heart expanded in her chest. "Flying! You go flying."

"You enjoyed it too, didn't you?" His voice was pitched low. They were close, too close, leaning towards each other, the distance between them all but gone. When had *that* happened?

"I... Yes." Her voice was barely a whisper.

She shook herself and the moment fractured into a thousand pieces. Grabbing his arm, she pulled him along. A comfortable silence fell as they moved through the copse of trees. A few passers by greeted them respectfully.

She cleared her throat. "I have something to ask you."

"Oh?"

"After what happened, I don't ever want to feel powerless like that again. I want to expand my training."

"But there was nothing more you could have done. The poison—"

"No. I'm not talking about my magic. I'm talking about self defense."

He grunted. "Women do not generally engage in weaponry or combat. Saffra is a unique exception, given that she is not a rider. But..." She held her breath. It didn't matter—his answer. She'd do it regardless. But, she really, really wanted him to give his blessing. "If this is what you want, I will see it done."

"Thank you." She felt light and airy, like she might float away. "Also, I'd like to keep Cyrus's sword."

There was a long hesitation. "I am reluctant to part with it, but it makes sense that you should have it. Very well. It is yours."

"Thank you," she said again. She tried and failed to hide her smile. "You know what?"

"What?" His eyes danced with curiosity.

"We just agreed without arguing." A bark of laughter escaped her lips. "That almost never happens, does it? Shall I continue asking for things?"

He laughed. The sound sent birds into flight. Her stomach flopped and she began to laugh too. "Do not push your luck *too* far," he warned.

"Oh, all right." She feigned disappointment. They fell into another comfortable silence before she said, "How come you haven't asked me about my mark?"

She'd half expected it to be the first thing out of his mouth.

"I was waiting for you to come to me about it."

"Oh."

"I didn't want to push you into it after...everything."

"Thank you." She swallowed. The silence stretched out before them. "Am...am I a sprite?"

"A sprite?!" He sounded alarmed.

She stopped, forcing him to face her. "Why else would I have one of their markings on my body?!"

He inhaled, then exhaled. "I suppose it's a possibility."

"A *possibility*?" She balked. "Talon, people don't randomly acquire sprite markings for doing magic, do they?"

"Not that I know of."

"Okay...so?"

"We cannot make assumptions based on that alone. This requires the attention of someone more knowledgeable than me."

"So...you really don't know?"

"Not with certainty, no." He reclaimed her arm, intent on continuing their walk.

"I think I'm a sprite," she decided. "I must be. There's no other explanation. I think I've known for a long time, even before my mark appeared. Seeing it only made the realization more frightening."

"What makes you think that?" He sounded genuinely curious.

"You really want to hear my theories? I can share them, if you're interested."

"Does this mean I've earned your trust?" He looked eager, almost boyishly so.

"Yes, so long as you behave yourself." It felt so easy to talk to him, so natural. Why hadn't it always been this way? But she knew why. Still, she was glad things had changed between them.

"I shall try my best," he said, placing a hand over his heart.

He listened as she explained her reasons. She told him about the moment she set foot in the Gable Forest, how something inside her had clicked. She explained her strong connection with all living things in the forest's depths. How she'd found Esterpine when all other outsiders had failed. How she'd recognized the wood in the throne room by scent alone. "But more than all that, my magic has been wrong."

He frowned. "You told me it hasn't felt right for you."

"Exactly. That practically confirms my theory. Plus, obviously, the mark."

"It's convincing, I admit, but I believe you've overlooked one important detail."

"Oh?"

"Sprites don't leave their forest. They simply don't. Isabella was an exception, so far as I know. How could their blood have made it into your world, into *you*?"

She chewed on her bottom lip. "I think I have a theory for that, too."

"I should have known." He pinned her with a stare. "Let's have it then."

"Irelia. Irelia is the key."

"Irelia? The dead princess?"

"Yes. You're probably going to think this is completely insane. Saffra did."

"Saffra already knows?"

She winced. "I talked to Desaree and Saffra about it when Saffra told me about her dream and—"

"Saffra had a dream?"

"A prophetic dream, yes. The night I was kidnapped—the night Dax woke up. It wasn't exactly about the future, but the past."

"Hmm." He appeared thoughtful.

She told him everything about it, careful to include all the details. They had walked two circuits around the garden by the time she'd finished. She was growing more and more convinced with each passing minute. The parallels were too coincidental. "It's like the gods were trying to show us something. I think they were trying to show us that I'm related to Irelia. She's the reason I have sprite blood. She traveled into my world through one of the gates."

"Claire." Talon sighed. "Irelia vanished over fifty thousand years ago. If you are related to her, that would make you a very distant relative." He shook his head. "Forgive me, but it seems far-fetched."

"Who says time moves the same here?" She frowned, and that frown deepened the longer she studied his expression. "You don't believe me, do you?"

"It isn't that. I'm just...this is a lot." His expression changed to one of determination. "I will speak to Jade about it. She will have answers."

She stopped abruptly, turning to face him. "You're going to see her? To see Jade?"

"Yes. I leave in two days. I am doing as you asked—returning the stones."

"Oh..." Her stomach dropped. It was exactly what she'd wanted. No, what she'd *demanded*. So why did she feel so...disappointed? "Should you really leave with...with so much stuff going on? The last time you left, the vodar attacked the keep."

"This needs to happen. We both know it."

Her shoulders dropped. "You're right."

"I dare say you will not miss me at all. You'll be too busy with your new training schedule."

Excitement coursed through her, making her forget her disappointment. The idea of learning to defend herself was fortifying. She hated feeling vulnerable. This was her opportunity to do something for herself.

They'd reached the garden's entrance. He dropped her arm and turned to face her. The afternoon sun shone brightly on his black hair and crown.

"There now," he said, smiling down at her. A smile just for *her*. "An entire conversation and not a single argument. I like this new truce between us." He glanced down at his mother's necklace—a symbol of their new beginning—before finding her eyes again.

"We should consider this a new beginning—for both of us," she said.

"I would like that." His throat bobbed. "You know, this is the happiest I have seen you all afternoon. Am I to understand that you are now well enough to return to the public's eye?"

"I suppose. I cannot hide forever, can I?"

"No indeed. I will see you at dinner."

She groaned. "I forgot about dinner."

"I'll understand if you wish to decline, but your presence in my hall would bring me pleasure."

"I'll go," she blurted, before she could stop herself. She internally cringed. Since when did she cave so easily?

"Thank you." He stepped back and bowed. "And thank you for gracing me with your company this afternoon. My guards will escort you back to your chambers. When you arrive, you will find two more waiting in the corridor outside your door. It is time you get used to them."

It was on the tip of her tongue to protest, but she stopped herself. His eyes darted over her face, expecting her to. When she said nothing, his chest fell with obvious relief. "I am glad you understand. Thank you. See you tonight."

With that, he strode away. Bedelth winked at her, then followed. She was left to watch their retreat in the presence of her new official entourage.

CHAPTER 50

THE KING'S NOTES

Kastali Dun

Claire returned to her chambers. Desaree and Saffra were waiting in her sitting area. Warmth radiated through her chest. It was nice having friends to greet her.

Des jumped up to fuss over her. "There you are. Look at you, all flushed and smiley. It looks like your walk did you good." There was no mistaking her smugness. "Oh, and did you see the guards in the corridor?"

"I did see them. Hopefully they won't be too much of a bother, seeing as King Talon gave me no choice."

Desaree fetched a pitcher of water and poured her a cup.

"I, for one, am glad," Desaree said.

"Me too," she admitted.

Desaree's eyes widened. She clutched her chest with exaggeration. "Gods above! You mean to say that you did not argue with him over it?"

"Oh, stop!"

"So, tell us about your walk," Saffra demanded.

She took a seat beside her and said, "You know, it went surprisingly well."

398

Desaree snorted. "That's it? Surprisingly well?"

A stray thread was coming undone on the sofa's upholstery. She began picking at it. "Talon and I have turned over a new leaf. We've agreed to a fresh start."

"Oh, suddenly it's *Talon* now," Desaree said, sharing a knowing look with Saffra. "Fresh start means first name basis, apparently."

Claire held up her hands and laughed. She knew they wouldn't stop pestering her, so she relayed every detail of their conversation, from her desire to begin training, to requesting Cyrus's sverak, to her spriten mark. "You obviously have sprite blood," Saffra said. "I'm surprised he's so hesitant to believe it. The signs are all there."

"It's a difficult truth to handle," Desaree said in defense of the king.

"What else?" Saffra asked. "Besides what you talked about, how did he act?"

"He was..." She trailed off. A soft smile came to her lips. "He was kind and attentive. He listened patiently. He seemed intent on touching me, like, every time I dropped his arm, he'd grab mine again." Desaree and Saffra squealed. "And he smiled! A lot! I even got him to laugh."

It felt like a monumental accomplishment every time that happened.

"But, enough about me," she said, hardly eager to pick apart every detail of Talon's behavior. "How is Dax? Any progress?"

Saffra's demeanor changed instantly, the light going out of her golden-brown eyes. "No. I've tried everything," she whispered. "He still doesn't remember anything."

"What if you took him around to the places he used to frequent? Like, to the training grounds and all that?" she asked. "Would it trigger his memory?"

"Marcel wants to keep him isolated." Saffra didn't sound pleased about it.

"But...why?"

"We do not trust him—Marcel, specifically."

"Is he that bad?" She felt her heart break a little.

Saffra hesitated. "Marcel looked through past records to see if this is normal. Apparently, poison can do this to a person if it's bad enough. But, more than that, Dax is showing similar symptoms to the nasks,"—there was a sharp intake of breath from Claire and Desaree—"after Kane infiltrated their minds."

"Oh, gods!" Claire felt the blood drain out of her face. After Kane used Stefan Rosen and Euen Doyle, he'd left them empty husks of themselves. Was that going to happen to Daxton?

"He can't have been a nask," she found herself saying, because she refused to believe it. "Cyrus would have known." But she had no proof. "Look, vodar poison is dark enough. I would know. It's probably just that."

She reached for leg, for her scar. Beneath the fabric of her gown, all that remained was a thin line the length of the old wound. It was a black pinstripe, the poison isolated from plaguing her ever again, thanks to the sprites.

"Dax almost died," Saffra said. "Humans do not come back from something like that unharmed."

"Exactly."

Desaree leaned forward. "What can we do to help? Surely there is something. What if we go to him every day and help him understand who he is?"

"Yes, surely we can do something!" Claire agreed. "Whatever you need."

Saffra's eyes filled with tears. "I don't think..." She stifled a sob with her hand. "You both speak of telling him who to be and winning back his heart. You cannot tell a person who they must be. They must feel it themselves. I fear I will never be lucky enough to win his love a second time."

"But you can!" Claire cried.

"She's right," Desaree said. "Why not try?"

Saffra exhaled. "I suppose it is worth a try," she admitted. "I cannot give up on him entirely. I will not."

"We'll do whatever it takes to help you, you know that." Claire leaned in and gave her a hug.

～

It was nearly dinner time when a knock sounded at the door. They were so intent on coming up with ideas to help Dax, that all three jumped at the sound. One of the guards popped his head in. "Delivery for Lady Claire."

Claire's jaw dropped. "Thank the gods we weren't dressing or something!"

"Forgive me, my lady," he said, a blush rising on his cheeks. "I'll wait, next time."

"Thank you."

"I'll get it," Desaree said, rushing over. She took the large box and her eyes grew wide. "It's so *heavy*."

"It must be Cyrus's sword," Saffra said, showing clear excitement over the idea. "The king obviously wasted no time delivering it."

"There is also a message." The guard's head was still in the doorway. "Lady Claire."

She went straight to him and took the letter. He bowed then retreated, shutting the door behind him. She looked from the folded parchment to the suspiciously large box.

"Open the letter first," Desaree said, failing to disguise her excitement. "It must be from King Talon."

"It is." She broke the seal, quickly reading the contents. It was brief, but by the end, she was smiling.

"Oh, it must be good," Desaree whispered.

Dear Lady Claire,

As I write this, I find my mood greatly improved from our walk. True to my word, I have sent along Cyrus's sverak. Care for it well.

Regarding your training, I admire your perseverance and determination. I may not have said that earlier. Ink and parchment make a person bolder. I would hate to be the warrior opposite your blade.

I relayed your request to my shields. Unsurprising, they are eager to assist. Jovari and Koldis have claimed the right to your education—something about knowing you better. They were adamant. I hope you believe me when I say, you are in capable hands. You begin at dawn tomorrow, and please attend your regular lessons afterward. I do not have the patience to deal with a certain mage's complaints in lieu of your absence (you know who).

That is all for now. Please keep your word regarding dinner tonight. I am looking forward to your presence in my hall.

Yours truly,

King Talon

GIVEN HER ABILITY, Talon could have relayed this information telepathically. Instead, he'd written her a letter. It was flattering and made a whole lot of sense.

She folded the note and tucked it into her skirt.

"Well? What did it say?" Desaree and Saffra gazed at her.

She grinned. "I'm to begin my training tomorrow morning. I need to be at the practice field at dawn." A giddy shiver raced through her. She glanced at her entry table where the large box sat.

Saffra stood beside it and ran her hand over it. "Shall we open it?"

"I..." Claire shook her head. "I don't think we should. Not yet." The truth was, she simply wasn't ready.

Their faces fell, but they accepted her decision.

They walked down to dinner together. Quite casually, Desaree said, "Verath and I have decided to open an investigation against Lady Caterina tomorrow."

Claire nearly tripped, whirling to face her handmaiden. "What?!"

Desaree's eyes darted towards the guards following.

"What do you mean by *investigation*?" she pressed. "And why didn't you say something earlier?"

"The two of you have so much going on—important matters of your own. I did not wish to intrude."

"You are as much a part of this group as any of us. Saffra and I do not deserve more attention than you. Des, what's going on?"

"Verath wishes for me to reclaim my title of lady. You both

know the story of how my mother died. Verath swears that it is suspicious—"

"It is suspicious," Claire and Saffra said in unison before sharing a look and then a giggle.

"To prove that the Rosens stole my title, an investigation must be conducted. In order for that to happen, I must petition the king."

"What does that entail?" She knew nothing about petitions.

"It means," Saffra said, "that she will have to go before the court and make a request."

They resumed their walk and continued the discussion. By the time they reached the dining hall, it was decided that she would stand beside Desaree in court. As Desaree was her handmaiden, she felt responsible for her. Saffra would be there too, but not beside them. She would sit on the council.

"And it's imperative that you do this *tomorrow*?" Claire asked, surprised by how last minute it was. "Don't you need more time to prepare?"

"I am as prepared as I will ever be. The king is leaving in two days. I must do this tomorrow, or we will have to wait. Verath wishes to begin the investigation while the king is away."

"Well, I'm not letting you do it alone, that's for sure."

They took their usual seats in the dining hall. She glanced up at the head table. Reyr was caught up in conversation with Bedelth, and try as she might, she failed to catch his eye. Almost as if he was purposefully not looking at her.

Her stomach sank. Come to think of it, he hadn't stopped by once since her kidnapping. His avoidance hurt more than she cared to admit.

Her eyes locked with Talon's. She gave him a small smile. He bowed his head in her direction before returning to his conversation with Verath. She reached into her pocket and felt his note.

Dinner was an odd affair. The patrons at her table—after awkwardly bringing up her kidnapping—were harshly scolded by Desaree, who was beginning to show signs of nervousness. No one could blame her. After all, who wanted to go before the king in his hall under *any* circumstances?

Saffra, on the other hand, was quiet. She seemed only half-present. No doubt, running through scenarios of what might happen if Dax never got his memory back.

After dinner, she bid the others goodnight, hugging them fiercely. She also had an early morning, but instead of going to bed, she went to her desk. She sat for a few minutes, preparing her writing supplies, silently gathering her thoughts.

She rolled her quill between her fingers, adjusting it awkwardly several times, and dipped it into the ink pot. It had taken some getting used to, but she had greatly improved her penmanship. It was nowhere near as pretty as Talon's.

Dear King Talon,

Thank you for your letter. I have not opened Cyrus's sverak yet. I think I lack the courage for it (at the moment).

I admit, I am eager for my lesson tomorrow. I'll be sure to arrive promptly at dawn. Desaree isn't happy about that, by the way. She says it's a grand task getting me out of bed in the morning.

I know you told me to attend my lessons as usual, tomorrow. I would like to inform you that I have decided to miss a portion of them—just in the morning. No fear in that respect, of a certain instructor coming after you. I hope you will not be upset with me, but there is something impor-tant I must do. My honor depends on it. That is something you can understand, yes?

Sincerely,

Claire

p.s. You do not need to bother with the title of lady when you write me letters.

She smirked, recalling the time Talon had scolded her for using his name without his proper title. It had made her furious at the time. Now, she simply didn't care.

The ink dried. She used a stick of wax to seal the letter, holding it over the flame, then dripping it onto the parchment. Her seal was nearly the same as Talon's, with an outline of his dragonhead sigil around her initials.

She passed it off to one of her guards.

Now, the waiting began.

She turned in for the night, lying awake in bed. Whenever she closed her eyes, she was back in the cellar, bound and gagged. Eventually, she lit a candle and got up. The fire was dying, so she threw a log on and took a seat with a goblet of wine.

Minutes passed.

"Micah?" She opened her chamber door, addressing one of the guards. "Have any notes arrived from the king?"

"None, my lady. Have you need of him? I can send for him?"

"No! No, of course not." She hesitated. "If a message arrives, please slip it under my door."

"Of course, my lady."

She returned to the sofa and her goblet of wine. Less than an hour later, a note slid under her door.

Her heart skipped. "About damn time," she muttered, much happier than her complaint made her sound. She snatched the letter and got comfortable at her desk.

Dear Claire,

Thank you for returning my letter. It was a pleasant surprise. Pardon the delay in my response. I just received word of a pirate attack in the Scattered Islands. It altogether spoiled my evening. I wanted to settle my nerves before writing to you.

Regarding Cyrus's sverak—courage will come, in time. Have patience. You do not need to practice with it tomorrow. Your trainers would never allow it.

That reminds me, if waking you up is as challenging as Desaree claims, perhaps you ought to be abed? Your sleep is important.

As to your final matter, how could I be angry? Do not abandon your honor. I would not have that from you. However, I can see that you are hiding something from me. Will you not tell me? You told me today that I had your confidence. Now I am especially curious.

Yours truly,

Talon

p.s. You may also send all future letters addressed without my title. Goodnight.

SHE WAS GRINNING. She didn't realize how silly she was being until she took up a fresh sheet of parchment and her quill. Only then did she blink and take a deep breath. "Just one more," she decided.

It took nearly half an hour to compose.

DEAR TALON,

I am shocked by your news. A pirate attack?! Can you tell me more? I would love to be included in more of Dragonwall's war efforts.

Anyway, I am sorry that your evening is spoiled.

Regarding my important deed, thank you for your approval. I wish I could tell you more. This is not my secret to reveal. I daresay you will know soon enough.

And you are right, I ought to go to bed. I will as soon as I send this. I am up late because it has been difficult to sleep. In my dreams, I often relive my darkest moments in the cellar. It leaves me terrified of sleep. There! That is a secret between you and me.

In any case, I will give tonight's sleep an honest effort—I promise.

Sincerely,

Claire

p.s. Goodnight back.

SHE FINISHED her letter and passed it along to her guards. She was surprisingly giddy about passing letters. They were the most common form of communication in Dragonwall; she felt silly for not thinking of it sooner. Taking a small box from her desk, she tucked away the two that Talon had already given her. Then, but only because she'd promised, she went to bed.

She lay awake for a long time, thinking of the possibilities the future might hold. She and Talon were finally on the same page—they were working together. It was a massive win, but was it enough? She needed him on her side, but his support would only get her so far.

Sprite blood flowed through her veins. Part of her knew that mastering her sprite magic was imperative. But, it would require training she couldn't get here in the capital.

Eventually, she drifted off.

Her dreams were scattered and incomprehensible. They shifted from comforting to terrifying. Tark's face swam in and out of view. Talon was there, saving her. Queen Jade encouraged her to come home to the forest. Kane grinned back at her with malice, assuring her she would fail. The stones begged her to come for them.

THE SHARP PEAKS of the Northern Barrier Range stretched below her. Wrath flapped his mighty red wings. Each downward stroke took her further from familiarity and closer to the unknown. Darknest appeared, nestled in the mountains. A thrill shot through her. She longed to explore its secrets.

Her eyes slid over the deserted stronghold. Its ramparts were in ruins. She had considered this place for its potential before settling on Shadowkeep. Now, it would serve a new purpose. She hated to part with her final stone, but it would be safe here.

Wrath landed. She slid from his back and retreated into the fortress. Its crumbling corridors were large enough to fit dragons. She set off to explore its depths. Like most dark places, nature had greedily laid its claim. Somewhere within, an animal yowled. Leaves on overgrown vines rustled in greeting as she walked past. Little critters screeched and fled from her light as she appeared. They felt her power—her disturbance. They knew what she carried.

Darknest opened its heart to her, willingly spilling its secrets. She found a home for her dragonstone deep in its bowels. There she set about the necessary enchantments to keep it safe.

As she finished her final incantation, her vision detached and she was expelled, as if leaving her own body. She blinked. Kane appeared before her, standing over the glowing orb of protection placed about a red dragontone. Fear shot through her. She needed to leave—to escape.

Kane's last words hung in the air like a heavy mist. He turned to her. His eyes widened. "Oh, it is only you," he said. "How did you get here?"

"I—"

He clicked his tongue. "You have behaved very badly, Claire. I am afraid I cannot let you leave. Not now." He reached for her.

She jumped out of reach—

HER EYES FLEW OPEN. She was sitting upright, panting. She scrambled from her bed and lit a candle. Every shadow felt ominous, as if Kane lurked within them. Her gaze darted back and forth, searching. But...no. She was safe.

Her thoughts settled, and the details about her dream receded. A few minutes later, her breathing returned to normal. No matter how frightening, Kane couldn't touch her, not here.

She padded barefoot across her sleeping chamber. The stone wall was cold against her palm. When she closed her eyes, she could almost feel the hum of the castle's magic—sprite magic, she realized. She wasn't sure how it might help her, but she said a little prayer, begging the magic to help her, to keep her safe. It seemed silly, but what did she have to lose?

Then she crawled back under her blankets. Perhaps the magic *did* hear her. This time, she drifted off into a peaceful sleep filled with blue mists, sentient trees, and ethereal beings. Kane would not show himself again—at least, not tonight.

CHAPTER 51

PREPARATIONS

Kastali Dun

Desaree awoke to the sound of Claire's guards, delivering her wakeup call. "Two hours before dawn," a muffled voice announced. Silence fell. Her stomach was already in knots by the time she left the comfort of her bed. She envied Verath, who groaned and turned over before going back to sleep. Lucky for him—he did not have to display himself before the kingdom requesting an investigation.

She rushed to get ready. When she applied the final touches to her hair and gown, she permitted herself another glance at her bed. Verath was sleeping soundly, tangled beneath the covers. They had not yet made love, but she hadn't the strength to deny his company. Especially last night, with her growing her nerves. Her cheeks warmed as she recalled his comforting arms.

She sighed, giving her appearance a final check. Time was of the essence. Getting Claire to her first training session would be a nightmare.

Grabbing her beaded purse, she leaned over and gave Verath a kiss on his forehead. His hand shot from beneath the covers, pulling her down onto the bed. She squealed in surprise. He wrapped her in his arms and gave her a proper kiss before helping her to her feet.

"You look especially lovely today, Desaree." His eyes flared with heat. She loved him like this, his hair sticking up on one side, messy with sleep, his voice gravely and unused. An ache formed in her belly.

"I will see you in the throne room later this morning," he added. And just like that, the ache was gone, replaced with anxiety. "Remember what we discussed."

"I will," she managed.

She gave him a tender glance before departing.

Gods, it would've been so much easier to barricade her door and stay locked inside with him all day. Instead, she crossed the hall. The guards let her in and shut the door behind her. She went through the tedious task of illuminating the large interior of Claire's quarters. She found a note on the floor of the entryway. When she saw the king's seal, she rushed to Claire's sleeping chamber.

Waking her charge was another task altogether. It was dark outside, so opening the curtains would be no help. She shook Claire until she was coherent.

"Okay...okay. I'm up," Claire managed to slur.

Her hair was a mess, and there were dark circles beneath her eyes. "You look as if you hardly slept."

"I hardly did."

"Bad dreams again?"

"Yes," Claire sighed, flopping backwards, about to go back to sleep.

"Do not even think about it," she said. "Look, the king has sent you a letter."

"Why didn't you start with that?!" Claire vaulted from the bed and snatched the note from her, disappearing with it.

She sprang after her, screeching, "No! Come back. We haven't the time!"

"Come on, Des," Claire groaned. "It's going to drive me crazy if I don't read it now."

Desaree chased her around her quarters, panting. Her patience snapped. "Claire Evans! Stop this right now. Set it down and go have your bath." She placed her hands on her hips.

Claire feigned a pout, but she set the note down and sulked off.

Bath completed, Desaree helped her into her clothes. A light blue tunic and leggings, with a wide belt to hold everything together. "This is the most comfortable thing I've worn since coming here," Claire sighed. "Why can't I wear stuff like this every day?"

"Because you're a lady," she snapped, still hanging by a thread. "We've been over this already. Ladies have appearances to maintain."

Gods, she sounded so snappy.

"Okay. Okay!" Claire held up her hands.

Her impending public appearance was suffocating. She swallowed and felt her palms grow sweaty. Would Caterina be present in the throne room? What was she thinking, accepting Verath's request? Was her title really worth the anxiety?

There came a gentle tap on Claire's door. "Enter," she called.

Micah popped his head in. "Breakfast delivery, Miss Desaree," he said before letting Sarah through the door.

"You can leave it there, thank you."

Sarah deposited the tray on the dining table, offering her a warm greeting. After she left, Desaree took one look at it and her stomach soured. There was no possible way she could eat.

Claire dropped into a chair and began piling food onto her platter. Desaree's mind snapped back into action. "No time for eating," she said. "Grab whatever you can take with you. We must get you to the second level of the keep. Look outside. You are about to be late."

Claire glanced outside, then sighed. "Yes, I suppose so..." Her eyes darted towards the entry. "Talon said I did not need to bring Cyrus's sword. I suppose Koldis will make me practice with a wooden sword anyway. No doubt he'll enjoy laughing at me too, when I make mistakes..."

She left Claire to her rambling and went to collect a few things.

When she had everything Claire might need—a cloak for warmth, her coin purse, and a pair of gloves—she shooed Claire from the room.

They arrived at the practice grounds late—what a surprise. Jovari and Koldis were waiting, arms crossed, wearing looks of bemusement. There were already many others practicing.

"Good morning, Claire, Desaree. Shall we get started?" Jovari stepped forward, ushering Claire away.

She watched from a distance as they moved to the side of the practice grounds. There was a weapons rack, from which Claire selected a wooden practice sword. Jovari and Koldis verbally coached her, going through the basics.

She found a grassy vantage point to watch Claire's progress. It was impossible to keep her thoughts in check. What information might an investigation dig up? Did she really want to know the truth of how her mother had died? Was she safe from Caterina's wrath? Or, would this make her a direct target?

Bodies danced across the practice grounds.

She looked over to find Claire engaged in a round of sparring against Jovari, both with wooden practice swords. Koldis offered critiques in a stream of constant gestures and shouting. Claire was obviously frustrated. Every so often, she shouted an exasperated comment back at Koldis.

With just a few moves, Jovari disarmed Claire. He did it again and again. Claire grew more determined, trying to land a lucky blow. Jovari held his own. Claire was so focused she did not complain.

Desaree chuckled. Her lady was no match against the king's shields.

Or...was she?

Desaree blinked. She blinked again.

Claire's stance and demeanor had changed, as if something had come over her. She blocked Jovari's blows and began imparting blows of her own. Jovari frowned, confused. By the time Claire had him flat on his back, wooden sword positioned at his throat, Koldis was keeled over in laughter.

Desaree stifled a giggle. Cyrus must have shown himself at the opportune moment, lending his combat skills to Claire's pathetic ones. Too bad for Jovari!

Practice ended.

She assessed her charge, frowning. Claire's hair had come undone from its tight plait, and—

"You're covered in dirt! Gods above! You might as well have rolled around with the pigs. I cannot take you to court looking like *this*." She'd require another bath.

"Oh, come on, Des." Claire's voice was breathless. "It's not that bad."

"Not that bad," she muttered under her breath, scoffing.

"Gods, that was so fun! Did you see what Cyrus did?"

"I did," she said, a soft smile spreading across her lips. "Quite impressive."

"Let me put this away and we can get going," Claire said, grinning from ear to ear. She raced to the weapons rack, then the two of them set off for her chambers.

"I'm going to be so sore tomorrow," Claire groaned. "I feel like jelly. How much time have I got for Talon's letter? I want to answer it before court."

"No time *whatsoever*. You are going straight back into the bath. Then we must get you ready for court. I think your silver and gray gown today. It will complement mine quite well."

"I've never been to court as a lady." Claire's steps faltered. The idea seemed to make her anxious.

"You'll do just fine."

～

BY THE TIME Desaree was finished, Claire looked regal enough to be queen. With Claire beside her, the king was sure to grant whatever she asked for. Right?

"You have nothing to worry about," Claire said, grabbing her hands. "You have every right to demand an investigation. He'll approve your request."

Desaree nodded, forcing down the lump in her throat. "I'm so grateful to have you with me."

"I'll be with you every step of the way."

"It must have been frightening—facing the king alone in the throne room during your trial."

Claire hesitated. "It was one of the hardest things I've ever done. I wouldn't wish it on anyone—that feeling of intimidation and fear, but, well, he's not so bad." She sighed. "Anyway, I'm happy to stand with you, Des. I think you're doing the right thing."

"Thank you. That means a lot."

Claire's eyes darted towards her desk. "I wonder if the king suspects what's coming? Did you tell Verath I'd be with you this morning?"

"Verath does not know. He believes you will be in your lessons, which he says are extremely important. I..." Desaree caught her lower lip between her teeth. "I kind of wanted to keep your appearance a surprise."

"I'm your secret weapon," Claire said, eyes gleaming.

"Something like that."

"Do you know what to say? Should I say anything?"

"Um...I..." Desaree frowned. "I suppose we should work you into Verath's original plan, since he doesn't know you will be with me."

Several ideas tumbled into her anxious mind. She formulated them, telling Claire everything she and Verath had discussed. A bell began to toll. "Come, we mustn't be late."

Court began at the ninth hour daily, except for rest days. Nine strikes of the bell signified its start.

They raced through the keep. Claire's guards trailed behind them. Along the way, Saffra fell into step beside them. "Lovely cloaks," she said, studying them with anxious eyes. "As you know, I must sit with the lower council. That will only work to your benefit, if a vote is called for."

"I think that's wise," Claire said.

They reached the hallway leading to the throne room. Saffra's eyes twinkled. She took each of their hands and kissed them both on the cheek before rushing off. They watched as she disappeared through a guarded side door entrance into the throne room.

Desaree took a deep breath. Claire's hand found hers and squeezed tightly. She looked over at her dear friend. "I suppose we cannot put it off any longer," she said. "I am ready." With that, they pulled their hoods up and joined the crowd at the throne room's entrance, heading inside.

CHAPTER 52

PETITIONING THE KING

Kastali Dun

Claire stood with Desaree as the doors to the throne room swung open. They went unnoticed—for now. A surge of patrons swept forward. They hung back, allowing others to push their way through. Apparently, members of the court often fought over positions to get the best vantage points. Whole arguments broke out, leading to unprofessional behavior. Naturally, those of higher birth usually won.

Court was an important part of Dragonwall's society. It was a time for those of nobility to gather for news, airing of grievances, witnessing of important cases, involvement in rulings, and the like. It was also an opportunity to flaunt wealth. Attendees wore their most expensive clothing and jewels. It gave the appearance of power, and people in Dragonwall's court always wanted to look powerful.

She glanced down at herself. Beneath her velvet cloak was a silver gown. It looked astonishing on her, with long sleeves and a rigid bodice made of silver satin. The skirt was a darker shade, but it was still just as beautiful. The gown's neckline was a deep scoop, leaving her chest heavily exposed. Ties in the back pulled everything tight, accentuating her breasts.

The crowd had thinned as she and Desaree moved forward. They linked arms, sneaking in, keeping to the back. They found a place close to the throne, but well hidden within the many bodies. With so many voices, it was impossible to be heard, so they did little more than exchange scarce whispers.

The sound of a staff striking flagstones announced the king's entry. The hall fell silent. Everyone went down on one knee, heads bowed in respect. She lifted her eyes to look at him. A thrill of excitement sent fire racing through her veins. She could see him easily, but he couldn't see her.

"Rise," he called, bringing them to their feet.

The steward began with announcements, reading from a massive scroll, unfurled in his hands. Updates on taxes and expenditures, new construction taking place near the warehouse district, allocations for land grants, more guards for the city, et cetera. The list seemed never-ending.

Eyes began glazing over. Yawns sounded. Her attention started to wander.

"Lastly," the steward said, glancing down, "that brings us to the fall tournament."

The mood changed instantly. Kastali Dun played host to a yearly tournament in the middle of the fall season. People came from all over the kingdom, some to compete, others to sell their unique wares, most to simply enjoy the festivities.

"It will last a full week, and because it's a fifth-year, the Champion's Ball will occur on the final evening. Attendance for the ball is by *invitation only*. Invitations will be sent out tomorrow."

Excited chatter spread through the hall like dragonfire.

"That is all." The steward rolled up his scroll.

Those closest to her began discussing plans for the tournament and the ball to follow. She and Desaree kept their heads down, listening with quiet interest. Giddiness raced through her. She'd always wanted to attend a ball; it reminded her of something out of a storybook.

The steward's staff called them to attention. "There are no new cases or rulings scheduled for today. We will move straight to grievances." He unfurled a new scroll. The chronicler sitting at his desk leaned forward, scribbling notes on a fresh sheet of parchment. His quill could be heard scratching in the silence.

Requests to air grievances were generally submitted in advance.

"Sir Robert Thatch," the steward called, reading the first name. "You may now step forward and air your grievance."

Like everyone else, they stood on their tiptoes to see who this Robert person was. He appeared to be a middle-aged man, financially stable because his clothes looked more expensive than the average courtier. Not to mention he carried the title of sir, which counted for a lot here.

A person did not have to be wealthy to submit a grievance. Even the poorest could petition the king's time. However, it was often harder for the poor, so mostly middle and upper class citizens were found to utilize the resource.

Robert reached the king's dais. The steward stepped forward to offer a few hushed instructions. Robert nodded, then he bowed deeply and addressed the king. "Your Majesty, I am here to bring a matter to your attention. I understand your time is valuable, so I will be brief. I have been cheated and wish to seek compensation." His gaze flicked over at someone on the side of the room, pinning his angry eyes on another courtier.

"You may continue," King Talon said,

She watched with interest. It wasn't so much Robert's plight that held her attention, but rather, the king's reaction and solution. She enjoyed watching from within the audience. It allowed her to see a different side of him, one wrapped in politics and court.

It gave her a thrill to know he had no idea she was here.

She smirked, thinking back over how badly he'd wanted to know her secret deed. Would he be surprised when she appeared? Would he treat her differently in a public space?

After Sir Robert Thatch, others came forward with their own grievances. Each was given a brief amount of the king's time. The attention of the courtiers began to wane. She, too, began to struggle, shifting her weight from one foot to the other.

Gods, what a tedious job! How did he stand it, sitting on that throne, listening to complaints for hours on end? Her respect for him grew.

She glanced over at Desaree. Her handmaiden hadn't lost her nerve. She wore a determined expression.

"Are you okay?" she mouthed. Desaree gave her a curt nod, even though she looked a little ill.

A small group of people had made their way to stand before the king's dais. They looked like farmers, from their shabby attire and unkempt appearance. As she studied them, she realized something wasn't right. Their faces were wide-eyed and their movements jerky.

"Good Morning, Your Majesty. Thank you for seeing us. I am the mayor of Swinston."

"Where's Swinston?" she whispered to Desaree.

"It is north of here, part of Celenore."

While Swinston was unfamiliar, Celenore was familiar. She had spent a great deal of time on her geography lessons with Mage Joren. Celenore was one of four dragondoms belonging to the territory of Eigaden. The other three dragondoms were Iassila, Galadhal, and Eryas. Eigaden had the fewest Dragondoms, while Kengr had the most, at seven.

She turned her attention back to the dais. "We wish to bring a frightening matter to your attention, my king."

"What might that be?" King Talon asked.

"We are experiencing an epidemic of death."

Several people began to whisper. Was it the plague? A murderer?

She ignored them and kept her eyes on the group.

"Our children were targeted first, Your Majesty, and then our women…"

"You suspect foul play?" King Talon sat erect on this throne.

"I suspect something far worse, Your Majesty. I suspect demons."

A heavy silence fell.

"What evidence have you?"

"Blackened bodies, Your Majesty." The mayor motioned behind him. Two men stepped forward carrying a shrouded body. The shroud was removed. Claire gasped, but her voice was drowned out by the crowd. Several people screamed.

"It's poison!" she whispered. It was a child's body. The skin looked identical to Cyrus's. Every inch was blackened.

The steward called for silence.

"There is a single wound, here—" The mayor of Swinston peeled back the child's tunic to reveal a stab wound, or what was assumed to be one. It was hard to see with the caked-on blood and blackened skin.

"It must be the vodar," she whispered. Why would they do such a thing? Obviously this was Kane's doing.

Her stomach churned at the thought. Taking a kingdom was one thing. Targeting its women and children was just sick.

"Kane is growing bolder," Reyr said to Talon.

Talon's eyes flashed with suppressed fury. *"I will leave you to handle this, Reyr. Get them away from the public's eye. Give them comfortable lodging and arrange for a private meeting. This is too gruesome for court."*

Almost at once, Reyr stood and spoke with the group. His words were hushed, and the whispers in the hall made it impossible to hear what he said. He ushered them from the hall, taking the dead body with him.

Two more grievances were brought forth. She was surprised but also relieved that court wasn't canceled. She chewed on her bottom lip. This was taking forever. Had Verath failed to get Desaree's name on the list—?

"Desaree Kendall, you may now step forward."

She blinked. Desaree elbowed her.

"Desaree Kendall?" Desaree's name was called a second time.

Right. It was time. They removed their hoods.

Cries of surprise erupted around them. Realization swept through the hall. Those closest began to bow and curtsy, stepping back to give her space. Her face burned as hundreds of eyes fell upon them.

They moved forward. The crowd parted. They emerged before the throne.

Her gaze instantly met Talon's. They curtsied. Her mind flashed back to the last time she'd been here. At that time, she'd held his gaze out of hatred. Now, there was only respect. His scars did not frighten her. His strength did not frighten her. His inner monster did not frighten her.

An amused grin settled on the king's lips. His visage had been stony the entire morning. It was the first show of emotion, and it was entirely for her.

Flutters erupted in her belly.

"So, this was your secret all along?" The richness of his voice made her heart skip.

"Yes, Your Majesty. Are you surprised to see me?"

"Quite. But also pleased."

The steward shuffled over and whispered a few instructions, which seemed to go in one ear and out the other. She glanced at Talon's shields. Verath's intense gaze was locked on Desaree. The others looked just as amused as Talon, though they hid it better. Koldis was the only one with a wide smile on his lips.

"Greetings, Your Majesty." Desaree's voice rang with confidence. "I stand before you because I have been wronged. When I was a girl, my birthright was stolen from me, my inheritance stolen, my life—stolen. I wish to seek retribution for the wrongs I have suffered."

This was the part the king would either invite her to continue, or turn her away. It was rare to be dismissed, but it happened occasionally.

"Verath?" Talon asked. *"Did you know about this?"*

"Aye, my king." Verath's gaze didn't leave Desaree as he spoke. *"It was my idea."*

"*I see. Then you both have my full attention.*" The king looked down at Desaree. "Your words disturb me, Desaree Kendall. Please continue."

"Thank you, Your Majesty. I wish to reclaim my title, if it is within my means. By right I should be Lady Desaree Kendall. Furthermore, I wish to bring the thief to justice."

Hushed whispers broke out.

Claire kept her face forward, careful not to look at Desaree or anyone else. She was certain that Caterina was somewhere in the audience. If only she could see her face at this very moment.

"If your parents were Lord and Lady Kendall, then such titles should pass to you by right. Why, then, is there a problem?"

"My parents are both dead, Your Majesty. My mother remarried after my father died. Her husband, my stepfather, inherited her title. Shortly thereafter, he disowned me."

"I see. I assume someone of his line is still living and in possession of the title you claim is yours?"

"Yes, Your Majesty."

"Very well. Have you proof of foul play?"

"I do not yet have proof," she said, her shoulders straight, her chin lifted. "I request that a full investigation be carried out."

"I see. It is within my means to grant such an investigation, but before I can, you must present the name of the accused. Who then do you wish to investigate?"

"Lady Caterina Rosen."

Desaree's words brought chaos. The entire hall erupted into fierce speculation. One voice could be heard above them, shouting, "She is full of lies! Lies, I tell you!" In response to Caterina's cries, a hush fell upon the audience. "Permission to speak for myself, Your Majesty?" Caterina said, emerging from the crowd.

"She shows herself at last," Claire muttered, finally glancing over at Caterina, who had just placed herself in direct view.

"You may speak for yourself, Lady Caterina," the king said.

Caterina stepped forward, just out of arm's reach. "Do not listen to these baseless accusations. She lies—I can prove my innocence."

"She does not lie," Claire said, raising her voice. "I can vouch for her innocence."

Talon gave her a nearly imperceptible nod.

"You?" Caterina barked. "Since when does an *outsider* hold more credibility than me? I have a solid reputation to back up my name. What do you have?"

"Silence!" Talon's quiet command seemed to echo from the walls. "If what you say is true, Lady Caterina, then you have nothing to fear from a formal investigation." Caterina's skin paled. Talon turned his attention back to Desaree. "You are familiar with the necessary requirements to carry out an investigation? You will require a liaison and a witness, as will the accused."

"Yes, Your Majesty. I understand the process."

Claire smiled.

"I wish to stand as Desaree's liaison." Verath stood, walked away from his position at the base of the dais, and took his place beside Desaree.

"I should have known..." Talon's smug remark was addressed to Verath. "Very well," he said aloud. "Am I correct in guessing that Lady Claire will stand as your witness?"

"Yes," Claire said. "I wish to act as her witness in this investigation."

His eyes glittered down at her, and she saw pride shining in them. "Very well, Lady Claire. Lady Caterina, who do you name as your liaison and witness?"

"I will support Lady Caterina as her liaison." Mage Targa stepped forward.

Claire shuddered.

Caterina's friend, Renna, appeared too, offering to stand as witness.

"Well, this will be fun," Claire muttered.

"Good." King Talon nodded. "It is settled, then. No need for a vote as there are willing people in each party. As Dragonwall's king, I give my permission." He turned to the chronicler. "Let it be known that an investigation will be carried out with Desaree Kendall as the accuser and Lady Caterina Rosen as the accused. We will reconvene for the trial in approximately six weeks, on a date agreed upon by all parties involved."

She breathed a sigh of relief. It appeared as if Desaree did the same. It was done. All that was left to do was bring Caterina to justice, and she knew that few things in life would give her greater pleasure than that.

CHAPTER 53

A BALLGOWN

Kastali Dun

Claire sat at her writing desk, fidgeting with King Talon's letter. She'd waited all day, but now that it was within her means, she hesitated. Part of her was still reeling from the events of the day. After an exciting morning at court, she'd attended the remainder of her lessons with Mage Sepia, and then with Mage Targa. Everything carried on normally, as it usually did. No one brought up her kidnapping, nor her presence at court. Only Caterina's dangerously flashing eyes and Targa's larger than usual sneer were evidence that something had happened.

She glanced over her shoulder. Desaree was still sitting at the sofa with a book in hand.

With clumsy movements, she broke the seal on the letter.

Dear Claire,

My blood boils when I think of your captors. I would kill them all over again, if it banished your nightmares. I would make it hurt, too.

Nightmares or not, you need sleep. I hope you have kept your prom-

ise, that you are resting, that your sleep is dreamless. Assuming you have, then good morning, and good luck in your lessons today.

Know that I am waiting in suspense, because you will not tell me your secret. I am an excellent secret keeper, by the way. Perhaps you will consider me worthy in the future. I will not disappoint you.

Regarding the pirate attack. I will happily arrange for a briefing. I think the details are better relayed in person. Notes can be dangerous. Shall we meet?

I look forward to hearing from you.

Yours truly,

Talon

OH, gods. She read the letter three times before setting it aside. Then she gathered a blank sheet of parchment, prepared her writing supplies, and got to work.

DEAR TALON,

I have only just read your note. Desaree runs a tight ship. By now you know of my secret deed. Was my presence in your court a surprise? Did I do the right thing?

As for your offer to meet, I agree. Seeing as you depart tomorrow, I am available to meet at your earliest convenience.

Sincerely,

Claire

THERE WAS ONCE a time she wouldn't dare ask for Talon's advice on *anything*. Now she was eager to know his thoughts. Eager still, to meet with him.

Her muscles were practically humming with anticipation.

She sent her letter on its way and took a seat beside Desaree, who looked up from her reading. "Gods above! Look at you!"

"What about me?" She feigned innocence. "Okay, okay. I think I might be meeting Talon this evening. He promised me some information."

"It must be *spectacular* information."

Her gaze narrowed. "Look, I told you already, what I'm going through is probably just some temporary rescue romance syndrome thing."

Desaree snorted. "Right. I'm sure it will all just fizzle out. In a few days, you'll be back to hating his guts."

"Exactly!" She knew it was a lie, but she crossed her arms anyway.

Desaree clicked her tongue. "You really do have genuine feelings for him, don't you?"

"*Feelings*!?" she all but hissed. "I don't know what you're talking about."

"It wouldn't be wise, Claire. He is a drengr. The king, no less."

"*Oh*, and your feelings for Verath? Are those wise?"

"Hardly! But Verath is not Dragonwall's king." Desaree chewed on her bottom lip, then shrugged. "There is nothing to be done now. Feelings are feelings."

"Des, I think you are jumping to conclusions here. I don't..." She trailed off, because Desaree was right. She didn't want to admit it, but the truth was staring her in the face. "Okay. Fine. Maybe I feel something. I just don't know what it is. It's..." She sighed and slumped against the sofa. "I suppose I find him intriguing. Before now, I hated him too much to look deeper. Now that I have, he's one of the most complicated people I've ever met."

"And his scars?"

She shot Desaree a glare. "I'm not shallow. I mean...they are hard to look upon, but not in the way you think. I don't see him as ugly. It's just, when I see his scars, I'm reminded of what he went through to get them."

Desaree exhaled. "Well, I cannot judge you. There is something exhilarating about forbidden romance, is there not?"

"You should know! And besides, Talon isn't interested in romance. He swore off women a long time ago, remember?"

"Perhaps, but you did not see him when you were kidnapped. I did. He cares for you more than you—"

A loud knock interrupted them.

"That must be Talon's answer." Claire sprang from the sofa just as the guard popped his head in. She went to retrieve Talon's letter before shooing him away.

"What does it say?" Desaree asked.

She broke the seal.

Dear Claire,

You asked for my advice on your behavior in the throne room this morning. That is also something better left said in person. If you insist upon catering to my availability, how about dinner in my tower tonight, just the two of us? If you agree, please send your response and meet me at nightfall.

Yours truly,
Talon

Claire read the note twice before looking up at Desaree. Her voice shook as she said, "King Talon requests my company for dinner."

Desaree pressed her lips between her teeth to keep from smiling. "Very well, we had better get you ready, but after—"

Another knock sounded at the door.

"Good gods, are we to have no peace?" Desaree demanded.

"Perhaps another letter from the king? Or Saffra?"

"Probably not. I was about to say that I arranged to have Madame Rosanne stop by before the evening meal."

"Madame Ros—?"

"Pardon the intrusion ladies, but Madame Rosanne is here to meet with you." Her guard, again.

Madame Rosanne swept into the room, followed by several young apprentices. They looked as if they would soon collapse beneath the weight of fabric bolts, piled so high, their faces were hidden. They seemed to sway beneath the weight.

She planted her hands on her hips. "I was under the impression that Madame Rosanne did not make house calls."

Desaree looked a little guilty. "I might have persuaded her. After all, you want a ball gown, don't you? And yours is sure to be the best in all the kingdom."

"A—?"

"Ah, Lady Claire!" Rosanne rushed over, giving her a warm hug and motherly kiss upon the forehead. "It is wonderful to see you, my darling. Shoo, shoo, over there, dears." She turned to direct her apprentices. One of them rushed forward carrying a small book, handing it to Rosanne.

Claire huffed, taking in the scene before her. Her room was transformed by bolts of tulle and silk brocade. A servant entered with afternoon tea. There was no point in fighting it now. "Well," she said. "It looks like my afternoon is accounted for, but I had better get an answer to Talon before I forget."

She scribbled a quick note and sent it along. Then she devoted her full attention to the task at hand.

They sat down at her breakfast table, pouring tea and adding little finger foods to their small plates. Rosanne took a few sips before saying, "In this book, I have drawn several ideas for your ball gown. Yours must look the best—no question about that. I plan to make you something the kingdom will *never* forget."

Her words sent a thrill straight down Claire's spine.

"Now, take a look at these..."

The three of them flipped through the pages of Rosanne's book. Like her others, the drawings came to life as each page was turned. After flipping through a few, she noticed a theme. "Rosanne, these gowns are beautiful—all of them. But why are they all black?"

Come to think of it—

She looked up. Everything the apprentices had brought in was black.

There was a long silence and then, "Lady Claire, I thought that would be obvious."

Desaree cleared her throat. "She thought you were going with

King Talon. That would mean wearing black—his dragon scales, of course."

"But—" she sputtered. "Talon and I—we aren't—that is to say —we aren't going together." A long silence, and then, "Are we?"

"You are King Talon's ward and a grown woman. After your rescue...well, I am not the only one who made the assumption." Rosanne shot Desaree a pointed look.

Desaree shrugged. "We all just assumed as the king and lady of the castle, you'd lead the ball."

Her jaw dropped. "You're joking, right?"

"Not at all." Desaree shifted, showing signs of discomfort.

Claire took a deep, steadying breath. "I suppose I shouldn't be surprised. And what about King Talon? Does he know about this?"

"I cannot be sure," Rosanne said.

"I see. Will you both excuse me for a moment?" She scooted her chair out and walked off.

Desaree and Rosanne were taken aback. Before they could say anything, she left her chambers. Her guards were surprised. Two of the four followed her down the hallway. She stopped before King Talon's tower guards.

"Is he in there?" she asked, quite unceremoniously.

"Aye, my lady. Packing." They stepped aside and opened the door. She strode into his tower and found him wandering about, packing, just as the guard had said. Several of his servants followed him as they gathered items he wished to take.

"Lady Claire!" He stopped dead in his tracks. "I did not expect to see you so soon. Is there something I can help with?"

"Did you know about the ball thing?"

"The ball *thing*?"

She exhaled. "Madame Rosanne dropped by. She's in my room at this moment with bolts of *black* fabric. She's under the impression we are going to the ball *together*. Yet, this is the first I have heard of it."

"I cannot understand why she would make such an assumption."

A frown tugged at her lips. "But, can't you? *Apparently* everyone expects it. You're the king. Surely you know about all the gossip circulating. Is it true? Do people expect it?"

"They do, but I never assumed you and I would be going together."

"Oh…" Her chest deflated.

Talon emptied his arms and walked closer. "Lady Claire, you look disappointed. Am I to understand that you like the idea of us going to the ball together?"

"I…well…" She twisted her fingers together, fidgeting.

"Would you like to accompany me to the ball? It would be an honor to parade you about on my arm."

She schooled her features. "Yes, we ought to go together. I would like that."

"Then you are fine with a ballgown of my color?"

"I am, Your Majesty."

Talon's eyes flared, as if her use of his title shattered the familiar moment that had surrounded him moments before. He took a step backwards. "Very well. Then we shall go together. And dinner tonight? You will still come at nightfall?"

"I will." She turned and rushed away. On her way out, she felt his eyes glued to her back, but she dared not look. She was afraid of what she might see.

She returned to her chambers. Desaree and Madame Rosanne were still flipping through the book of Rosanne's drawings. "It is decided," she announced. "King Talon and I will attend the ball together. A black ballgown it is."

Desaree's face was especially smug.

She spent the remainder of the afternoon working with Rosanne on designs. In the end, she insisted on adding a great deal of modern flair to hers. Women did not usually expose their arms, but she insisted on a strapless sweetheart neckline and long gloves. The fabric was to be a mix of silks, lace, and little iridescent beads, so that the dress shimmered like Talon's scales. The thought heated her skin. She was actually looking forward to attending the ball with him. Perhaps Desaree was right, things between them had certainly changed.

CHAPTER 54

DINNER WITH TALON

Kastali Dun

Claire made her way to the king's tower for the second time that day. Desaree had insisted on an evening gown, a blue silk brocade with golden embroidery that buckled like a robe, covering most of her chest and shoulders. The embellishments along the trim made it sparkle.

"Good evening." Talon was waiting in the large entryway. He bowed as she entered. She returned the greeting then glanced around. Unlike earlier, his packing was complete; his main chamber was tidy. "I finished packing just before you arrived," he said, by way of explanation.

"I'll have no one to send letters to when you're gone," she realized. The words were out before she could stop them. She pressed her lips together, hoping he didn't notice the hot flush that crept over her cheeks.

Talon chuckled, the sound a low rumble in his chest. "You may still send me letters. I believe the sprites are familiar with parchment and ink."

"That isn't what I meant, and you know it."

His eyes danced, but he said nothing more.

They sat down to a quiet meal. The last time she'd been in this dining room, she'd made a mess of things. She planned to be on her best behavior. The king's servants waited on them before fading into the background.

"I was proud of you today." Talon was the first to break the silence. "That is the second time you've held your ground in my throne room."

Her chest swelled with warmth. "Desaree is my handmaiden. She's my responsibility."

"Even so, most ladies wouldn't support a handmaiden's decision to go against a court lady, let alone stand beside her."

Her heart was suddenly made of thousands of wings, fluttering and flapping. "Thank you," she breathed.

They ate for a few minutes in silence before he said, "Do you still wish to know more about the pirate attack?"

She sat up straighter in her seat. "Yes, I was hoping to."

"Good." He leaned back in his chair. "Pirate raids are not abnormal for our coastlines. But over the past five years, we've seen a drastic increase. Pirates are usually solitary operators, looting for their own benefit. These have been coordinated, as if they're working together."

"How bad are they?" she dared ask.

"Some are mild, stolen goods and destroyed dwellings," he explained. "Others have caused death and devastation."

"That's horrible!"

"Early on, I thought it was a response to the increased cost of merchandise transport." He shook his head. "It's been difficult to predict their movements. I know now that they are working together, but I don't know where they will strike next. Their latest target was an island village, relatively isolated, in the Scattered Islands. They abducted a majority of women and children for the slave trade."

"Slave trade?" she cried.

"Both Pavv and Oshea support slavery. Pirates are not usually so bold as to take people, but they grow bolder."

Her stomach churned. She set her fork down, abandoning her

food. "Maybe they know war is coming. They will grow bolder because of it."

"Agreed. I must do everything I can to protect my people, especially now." He sighed, scrubbing a hand over his face. "I fear I am failing already, rather badly."

"Do you think the pirates are working for Kane?"

"It is possible."

They both fell quiet. When she next looked up, he was playing with his food, pushing his mashed potatoes around with his fork. "It wouldn't be surprising," she said, "if Kane is behind everything."

He grunted in agreement.

She thought back to the events of that morning. To the frightened farmers, and the dead child. "Your Majesty—"

"Call me Talon, please." She stared at him. "Really, I prefer it. You already forget my title half the time, anyway."

He hadn't *always* preferred it, but she let it go. "*Talon*, then, what happened to the farmers at court today? I think the vodar are behind whatever happened to that little boy."

"Yes, I believe you're right. I examined the child's body. The blackened skin was identical to Cyrus's."

Her throat thickened until it was almost impossible to swallow. "What was the Child's name?"

"Calen."

"Calen..." she whispered. It felt right to say his name. "It's barbaric—what Kane's doing. All those women and children dying at the hands of the vodar. If he's behind the pirate attacks, too, making those monsters steal people for the slave trade..."

"Claire..." Talon reached out, clasping her forearm through her sleeve. He gave a gentle squeeze. "You must not worry yourself overmuch. This is my burden to bear, not yours."

"But...what if this is my fault?" The thought made her sick. She swallowed down the acid rising in her throat. "Kane must have told his demons to attack these people because of me."

"What?! *Why* would you think that?" Talon's eyes darkened.

"When I killed some of his wraiths, when I stopped them, I upset him."

"Claire you cannot—"

"Then you defeated Eagle, and I slipped through his fingers *again*. He's getting back at us, Talon. We've—no, *I've*—made him angry."

"Stop it," he snapped. "This is bigger than you, Claire. You cannot take responsibility for these deaths simply because you have thwarted him."

She was breathing hard. She wanted to agree with him, really, she did. But...she couldn't. "Have you pried any information out of Eagle?"

His expression darkened. "Everything I needed."

"And...Tark?"

A muscle in his jaw began to tick. "Tark had nothing to offer me." His voice was low and controlled. "I did what I promised. I tortured him, then I took him outside and...well, never mind the details."

The blood drained from her face. "What did you do to him?"

"Please, do not ask me."

She blew out a breath. "What about Eagle? Is he dead, too?"

She wasn't sure why she wanted to know. Eagle had orchestrated everything, but to him, it had only seemed like business. She never sensed anything personal about his behavior, unlike Tark and the others.

"Eagle is in the dungeons."

"Is he still...*sane*?"

"He is whole, but sane? Who can say? I will schedule a public execution when I am ready." Talon finally took a bite of his food, then looked up at her. "Do my actions displease you? I can tell something is bothering you."

She shrugged.

"Say whatever it is that's on your mind."

"Shouldn't you...that is to say...why not just leave Eagle in the darkest dungeon and let him grow old, all alone? That seems like a harsher punishment than putting him out of his misery." For some reason, the idea of executing him publicly didn't sit well with her.

Talon sighed but said nothing.

She chewed on the inside of her cheek. "He's a good fighter, too."

"There are thousands of good fighters in the world, Claire. That is no reason to spare him."

"Have any of those thousand worked for Kane? Have any of them *met* Kane? Do they know what he's like?"

His lips pressed into a thin line. "Point taken. Very well. I will surrender his fate to you."

Her mouth snapped shut, surprised by Talon's release of control. An ironic thought came to mind. "You know, not so long ago, it was my fate he controlled."

"Then his life belongs to you, anyway."

She nodded. "Thank you."

"I will refrain from an execution and keep him in the dungeons. In return, you will decide what is to be done with him. He cannot remain there forever, taxing our resources. Are these fair terms?"

She considered his offer. "Yes. I accept." It wasn't necessarily the *correct* thing to do, but it felt right. Either way, she didn't want to beat the topic to death. She cleared her throat. "Tell me about your upcoming trip to the forest."

"Can't say there is much to tell." He lifted his goblet and took a sip of wine, gazing into the cup's depths. "What would you like to know?"

"I don't know. The details, I suppose."

"It will take a little over three days to reach the forest, assuming we make haste. I plan to. I plan to travel with some of the drengr-rider pairs from Fort Kastali for protection. I am taking a gamble, assuming that Kane's vodar will remain tied up in Celenore."

"We don't know how many he has."

"Exactly. Anyway..." He paused. "Emissaries will meet us at the forest's edge. They will guide us to Esterpine. You know, now that I think of it, if we had *you* with us, I suppose we would do things differently. Hmm? I'm sure you could find the city as quickly as the queen's own."

Excitement made her fingertips tingle. "I should go with you!"

"You cannot. Your lessons, remember? Besides, you will be safer here."

And just like that, her excitement fled. She slumped in her chair. Who was to say she'd be safer *anywhere*. But, he was probably right. She did have her lessons, and she'd only just started training with Jovari and Koldis.

"I get the feeling you really aren't looking forward to this journey."

"We both know I would avoid it if I could." His eyes closed. He rubbed them.

"You know, if you just apologize to Jade, admit you were wrong, she will probably forgive you right away."

He snorted. "You, of all people, know I am terrible at that sort of thing. Besides, I already did. I wrote her a letter."

"Well, that's a start, at least. Though, I'm sure she'll expect more groveling upon your arrival."

He groaned, sliding low in his chair like a petulant child. The behavior was so unlike him, that she grinned.

The remainder of their dinner flew by. He refilled their wine goblets a few times. A large platter of cheeses, fruits, and sweet caramel dip was set before them. Her appetite returned and she quickly attacked the spread.

She felt his gaze like a hot brand against her skin. He watched her pick out the yummiest fruits. She dipped them in caramel before devouring them. "Mmm. They're so sweet."

His low chuckle made shivers race down her spine. When she looked up, it was to find his eyes dark and intent, fixed on her mouth. "I instructed the cooks to select the ripest fruits from harvest."

"Perks of being a king..." she teased.

"Something like that," he said, his voice low.

"I like good food, but I'm not sure it's worth the sacrifice of being a ruler. Not after standing through an entire morning court session."

He took a sip of wine, his expression sobering up. "You get used to it. Every day is busy, from sunup to sundown, with hardly a moment to think. It takes focus and an immense amount of devotion to run a kingdom."

"And unlike everyone before you, you've done it all alone." She couldn't help but stare at him as she said this. It was admirable. He was truly something.

His eyes darted between hers, trying to read her. "Are you... *impressed* with me, Lady Claire?"

"I am," she decided, smiling at him before returning her attention to the platter. She picked out several cubes of cheese and paired them with blackberries.

"I should go," she said at last. "Desaree has imposed a strict curfew on me."

Talon's eyes danced. "She really does run a tight ship, doesn't she?"

"The tightest."

They shared a smile that made her belly flutter.

Talon sighed. "I suppose it is for the best. My shields will be arriving soon. Your company has been a treat, Lady Claire. Thank you."

"Likewise." There was no mistaking the happiness in her voice.

He escorted her to the entryway. She leaned on his arm in a friendly manner and glanced up at him. "I suppose we will not see each other again until your return?"

"Correct. You will behave, I hope?" He released her hand from the crook of his arm and turned to face her.

An evil grin spread across her face. "Behave? Me? Hmm. You must have me confused with your other ward."

He huffed.

"All right, fine. I will do my best to follow your rules without complaint."

"Good." His shoulders relaxed. He flashed her a brilliant set of white teeth. "Perhaps I shall bring you back a gift, then." His eyes held hers, making her breaths falter. The moment stretched out before them. She wished it would last forever. All too soon, he bowed and bid her goodnight, sending her on her way.

Kastali Dun

Reyr was the last to leave the king's tower after their meeting that night. During the span of the evening he had packed, eaten dinner, tied up loose ends, and attended to his king. There was only one thing that remained. A single, daunting task.

He stopped outside of Claire's door, standing quietly. Her guards did not question him. They stood silently aside. Laughter from within drifted through the door. The sort of happy laughter that rubbed off on him and made him smile.

He turned to the guards. "I assume she is with Desaree and Saffra?"

"Yes, my lord."

He hesitated, second guessing himself. What if he just left? It'd be easier that way, easier than facing her. But...no. She might eventually forgive him for leaving, but she would *never* forgive him for leaving without saying goodbye.

He fortified his nerves and knocked. The noise from within ceased. Desaree's face appeared, though she wasn't surprised to see him. She ushered him inside.

"Good evening, ladies." He greeted them, bowing deeply. They were arranged in the sitting area, sharing a bottle of wine. He cleared his throat. "I'd like to speak with Lady Claire alone, if you wouldn't mind?"

"I was just about to head to bed," Saffra said, rising. She said her goodbyes and vanished.

"I suppose I'll do the same," Desaree said, disappearing a few moments later.

He tried to appear relaxed, taking a seat across from Claire. He had not been alone with her since her kidnapping. An awkwardness filled the air. It was a foreign thing, something that didn't usually happen between them.

"How are you feeling?" he asked.

"Okay, I suppose." She eyed him warily. "It took a couple of days to calm down, after everything happened. I've had trouble sleeping. Lots of nightmares, and more of Kane's dreams."

"Hiding more dragonstones, I take it?"

"Yes, he just hid the last one."

"I see." He fell into deep thought. Perhaps it would be prudent to use her knowledge to hunt down the remaining stones. But that was a task for another day.

"You look recovered," he observed.

"Life's returning to normal, I suppose. As normal as can be expected, I mean. You heard about what happened at court today, I'm sure."

"I did. And I'm sorry I wasn't there to see it. That was a very brave thing you did. We all admire you for it."

"Thank you." Her smile didn't reach her eyes. She picked at a stray thread on her sleeve, fidgeting. "Reyr, why haven't you been to visit me? It's been five days since—"

"I... Forgive me. Talon keeps me busy."

Gods, this was too much. It was too hard to lie to her. He loved her too much.

"You've been avoiding me, haven't you?"

He didn't answer. Silence fell between them. Nothing like the comfortable silences they were used to. Everything was different now. It left his heart aching.

"Gods, Reyr! Seriously?!" His gaze snapped up to find hers flashing with anger. "So what? So you love me. That doesn't suddenly change things between us."

"But it does! Surely you can see that."

She barked a laugh. "So that's it, then?"

Helpless frustration made his chest feel heavy. What did she expect from him? He had already given her his heart. Did she fail to understand his misery?

"You're going to avoid me from now on, aren't you? You think it's easier to forget that I exist, than to confront your inner demons."

He laughed bitterly. "I could never forget that you exist, Claire. Not even if I wanted to. You are always somewhere in my mind, a dominant, permanently fixed presence."

Just like Gemma had been.

"Oh..." She hesitated. "If you aren't going to ignore me, then why—"

"I am going away." His words were abrupt. "I am leaving the capital."

"You're—*what*?" Her eyes widened, frantically darting between his. "But you will be back, won't you?"

He exhaled. "I cannot say. I will stay away for as long as it takes."

"As long as—as long as what takes?"

Irritation made him scrub a hand over his face. She already knew why he needed to leave. Why did she need him to say it?

He hated himself for it, for betraying the memory of Gemma by loving another, and saying it would only deepen that hate.

"I will stay away for as long as it takes to stop loving you." His words sounded icy. Gods, he wanted to hate her for being so lovable, for being the reason he had to leave.

A single tear rolled down her cheek.

"No." He clenched his jaw. "Don't you dare."

"I can do whatever I want," she said. "You're the one leaving me. I have every right to cry." She swiped at her cheeks. "How can you do it? How can you leave? I thought...I thought..."

"You thought what, exactly?"

"I thought you would always be on my side. You've always had my back. Please don't leave. Coming to Dragonwall was the most difficult thing I have ever done. Now you're just... going to leave me here in the capital?"

"Gods woman!" he roared. "Are you blind? Why do you think I've had your back all this time?"

"No, don't you dare! Don't you dare say it!"

"Everything I have ever done has been because of how I feel for you. All the way back to the beginning."

"You hardly knew me then!"

"But I cared for you more than I should have," he said bitterly, "to my own detriment."

"Please, Reyr." More tears slid down her cheeks. She was beautiful even when she was crying.

"Damn you!" He surged to his feet, attempting to escape his thoughts. He retreated to the other side of the room like a wounded animal.

It didn't matter. She followed him. "Please, Reyr..."

"Do not ask this of me again. It has already been decided. I leave at dawn with the king."

"Tomorrow morning?" She looked betrayed.

"Last I checked, that is what dawn means."

She flinched. "You don't need to be an ass!"

His skin was on fire. He bit his tongue to keep from apologizing.

"Wait just a minute." She scowled. "Did the king put you up to this? He did, didn't he? He's making you leave."

"Why would he do such a thing?" he demanded.

"I don't know. Because you hid my secret from him?"

"The king has nothing to do with this. I am leaving because I need to. Talon agreed that it is for the best."

"Then...can't you...can't you change your mind and stay?" Her voice cracked. "We can fix this. I'm sure of it. We can see less of each other, or whatever you need. Whatever it takes. You can't just—"

"Stop it!" he hissed. "Stop being so greedy, Claire! Gods, how selfish are you?! How dare you ask this of me?"

"How is it selfish?" she cried. "You're my friend. I didn't ask you to fall in love with me! You betrayed me by doing so, but I'm not holding it against you, and I won't…if you stay."

"Tell me then. Do you love me? Tell me that you love me, and I will stay." He shouldn't have asked. It was wrong of him. The tormented human side living deep within wanted to hear her say it, even though she wouldn't. He knew this.

"Of…of course, I love you—"

"No! Not in *that* way." He couldn't seem to breathe. "Tell me you're *in* love with me."

"I…" Her fists were clenched at her sides. Deep down, he begged her to say the words he so desperately wanted to hear. "You're not playing fair, Reyr. You're not."

"None of this is fair."

She sank to the floor and wrapped herself in a ball, crying into her arms. He wanted so badly to drop down beside her and take her into his arms. Instead, he stared at her, fortifying his resolve. He needed to leave. Every second he spent here, watching her like this, was a second too much. "I hope that someday when I return, we can meet as friends, and that you will forgive me. Until then, I must go." He bowed to her, though she hadn't looked up at him, then turned and walked from the room.

As the door closed, he caught a glimpse of her still on the floor, weeping. His breath fled. He turned and did the same, racing down the hall.

He returned to his chambers, slamming the door harder than he should have. Turning in frustration, he roared. The bellow slammed against the stone walls. In the dim light of his entry chamber, he took his frustration out on the nearest wall. He rammed his fist into the stone. The wall shook. Shards of rock and mortar flew everywhere.

A mere human would have broken every bone, but his

crunched and then quickly healed. It felt good to vent. The pain in his fist was a welcome distraction. He hit the wall again, and again in the same place, hacking away at the stone until there was a deep rut in the rocky surface.

"Reyr?"

"What?!" he yelled back at Talon.

"Do you need me?"

"I told her. She did not like it."

"I assumed as much. Would you like some company?"

"I...no."

"Well, too bad. I am coming over anyway."

Not but two moments later, there was a quiet knock on his door. When he said nothing, it opened slowly. Talon entered, carrying one of his vintage bottles of Baylin brandy. The year was nearly impossible to come by, but nothing was impossible for King Talon.

True to their friendship, Talon said nothing. He silently went to the wine cabinet and removed two small cups, into which he poured generous amounts. "Last one before the road, old friend?" Talon handed over one of the glasses.

They were departing together at dawn with the company of Bedelth, and a slew of Fort Kastali's Drengr. He alone would split off and go to Fort Squall. His stomach tightened.

"How is it?" Talon asked.

"The brandy? It's good, quite good. Thank you for dropping by, despite my mood."

He was grateful for Talon's intrusion and the distraction it posed. After they finished their first, they went for another, until they soon found themselves drinking deeply for old time's sake. Hours seemed to pass quickly. They joked over stories and all the stupid things they'd done growing up together. Both of them had gotten into plenty of trouble.

Eventually, they fell silent, lost in their own thoughts. Just before he left for the night, Talon said, "It will not be forever, Reyr. You will heal." Their brandy bottle was nearly empty now.

"I hope you are right."

And he did. Truly.

CHAPTER 56
HOPE

The Skies over Eigaden

Reyr extended his wings, stretching them until his muscles strained. It felt good to fly, to *really* fly. He welcomed journeys like these. Talon's hulking black shape and Bedelth's glittering orange one soared in and out of the cool clouds scattered across the sky. He would miss them once they parted ways.

Accompanying them were twenty-four of Fort Kastali's pairs. Every one of them had been hand selected by Talon. It was more of their kind than had ever been seen in the forest. Gods! How the Sprites would love that. He almost wished he could be there to see it.

He beat his wings against the air currents and took his golden form higher and higher, breaking formation with everyone. He allowed the distance between them to build until he was circling high above like an eagle. The bodies of the drengr and their riders shrank into small specks. The air was emptier up here. Breathing was harder. The silence was deeper. He growled with excitement and took himself through several aerial drills, performing a coordinated dance with imagined foes. His true foe was the air, which gave him very little the higher he went.

After he'd had his fill, pushing his muscles to the limit, he descended. His breaths came in great gasps. It felt good to get his blood pumping.

His chest tightened. He was alone here in the sky. Very alone. There was no rider upon his back. Claire was far behind him now. Nearly three days—three *painful* days—had passed since saying goodbye to Kastali Dun. To *her*.

With Bedelth and Talon as travel companions, and a large entourage to accompany, they had departed the capital, flying north through the wilderness. They'd covered ground at a rapid rate, sleeping little, and often flying well into the night. He ached for what he'd left behind, but he also rejoiced for what was to come. The choice hadn't been easy, but it had been right.

Still, he felt like a fleeing coward.

"We will be at the forest by nightfall." Talon's reminder sharpened his focus. He reentered the flight formation. *"The sooner we arrive, the better. Carrying these stones puts me on edge."*

"We know..." Bedelth snorted, sending smoke pouring from his nostrils. The air swallowed it up.

Everyone had felt the side-effects of Talon's burden, not just Bedelth. The king's mood had gone from tolerable to dismal. He was prone to snapping at them when his patience tired. Everyone learned to keep a safe distance, especially the entourage from Fort Kastali.

The stones put Talon on edge, but leaving Claire even more so. The king's fondness for Dragonwall's outsider was growing, which was obvious to most, including Reyr. Perhaps part of why Talon rushed to reach the forest wasn't simply to reach the safety of the sprites, but to hurry their journey along. The sooner the king completed his quest, the sooner he could return to Claire.

The Flat River snaked along the countryside below, traveling all the way to the sea. The forest, which lay directly north of them, had already manifested upon the horizon. Very soon, Reyr would break away and fly northwest to Fort Squall. While he hated to leave his king, he knew that Talon would be well protected. Assuming she found Talon's letter agreeable, Queen Jade would have a group of envoys ready to escort him to Esterpine, where he'd stay for a week.

This meeting was important. It was also the first to occur since King Tallek's time. Talon had never met Queen Jade in person, he had only heard about her from his father. If he was successful, an alliance against Kane might be struck. But for that to happen, Talon needed to regain favor.

"Just pretend you like their food," Reyr had said a few days ago.

"I can pretend to," Talon had replied, "if that is what it takes." That would be the funniest part of it all. Talon was too proud to behave any other way.

"Oh, believe you me, you will be crying for meat before the end."

Their conversation still made him chuckle. Talon was going to have an uncomfortable time winning over the sprites while secretly despising their food.

Their last day in the sky together passed quickly. When it was time to break away, the party landed on a wide stretch of prairie. Bedelth, Reyr, and Talon transformed to say their farewells in human form. It would be some time before they would see each other again, and the idea of being separated was difficult. Who knew how long it would be before he returned to the capital?

He said goodbye to Bedelth first, giving him a warm embrace, then he turned to Talon. "Take as long as you need," Talon said, gripping his forearm before pulling him in for a hug. "I want you happy, healthy, and whole when you return. That's an order."

"I will see it done, my king." Their eyes met, and he could see Talon's concern.

"Make sure you use your time wisely, Reyr. Fort Squall must not fall."

"I will do everything in my power to keep that from happening." They both knew what would happen if Fort Squall fell to Kane. The North and South would be largely cut off from each other. The forest created a strategic barrier between the two halves of Dragonwall, making Fort Squall the most enticing stronghold in the kingdom.

"See that you do. Take care of yourself, brother. Farewell." With that, Talon and Bedelth transformed and jumped into the air. Seconds later, the twenty-four pairs took to the skies to follow. They assembled into formation and continued their flight north.

"Farewell, my king," He sent the thought just as the party disappeared on the horizon. When he was very much alone, a hollow feeling settled in the pit of his stomach. Never before had he felt so small. All around him, the land stretched on for leagues and leagues. As he stood, gazing as far as he could see, a refreshing breeze picked up, drying the thin layer of perspiration on his forehead. With the breeze he felt something else, something new. He felt change; it was coming whether he wanted it or not.

Riding on the currents of change was something dark. It waited just beyond his foresight. The next time he saw Talon, things would be very different, and not in a good way. Sighing, forlorn, he transformed and jumped into the air, flying northwest.

The land beneath him sailed by. He recalled the last time he had been over these parts. It seemed like an age had passed since he'd first escorted Claire to the capital. Now she stayed while he fled. How strange this twist of events was, but his efforts were not in vain. Fort Squall needed him more than the south did, more than Claire did.

How long did they have until Kane delivered the inevitable hammer blow? How much opportunity for preparation was there? Would there be warning? When dragons swept from the mountains and made their way south, burning and torturing villages along the way, would Fort Squall have enough time to present an adequate counter-attack?

These fears played through his mind over and again as he neared his destination. He had a new purpose now, and a great fate tied to it. The pressure was immense, but also necessary. It was exactly what he needed to keep his dark thoughts occupied.

When the sea materialized on the horizon, followed a while later by the city of Squall's End, a calm sense of reassurance settled over him. The small city began to grow. As it did, something else swelled within him. That something was hope. Fort Squall was special. It would always be special. Seeing the city stretched out before him, and beside it, Fort Squall, left him smiling. It wasn't the kind of smile humans wore. It was a dragon's smile, feral teeth and all.

What he saw before him made things suddenly clear. He wasn't running away from Claire, nor from his love for her. Not at all. He was coming home. Coming home meant healing, and that was exactly what he intended to do.

~+~+~+~+~+

The Dragonwall Series continues in book 3: Verath the Red which can be found here: Verath the Red

If you enjoyed this book, please consider supporting me by leaving a review or rating on Amazon and Goodreads. These help get my book noticed which is important for indie authors like me.

If you would like to stay up to date with book news, new releases, spoilers, and bonus content, sign up for my newsletter mailing list at https://www.authormelissamitchell.com/newsletter signup

ABOUT THE AUTHOR

Melissa Mitchell is a fantasy romance author and creator of the seven-book *Dragonwall* series. Her love of fantasy began with *The Dragonriders of Pern*, and she now writes stories full of dragons, magic, hidden royalty, and slow-burn romance. She holds a PhD in physics and lives in Atlanta, Georgia with her husband, a husky, and four very spoiled bunnies. When she's not writing, she enjoys baking cookies, bullet journaling, and figure skating—usually while plotting her next book.

Visit her online at: authormelissamitchell.com

Also by Melissa Mitchell

The Arcane Artifacts

Bound by the Blood Ruby

The Dragonwall Series

Talon the Black

Reyr the Gold

Verath the Red

Koldis the Green

Bedelth the Orange

Jovari the Blue

Dallin the Violet

The Lady Witch Series

Wielder's Prize

Wielder's Bond

Wielder's Might

Witch's Ruin

Witch's Heart

Witch's Crown

Royals of Dragonwall Series

For the Crown

Stand Alone Titles

Blood and Ballet